HOUSE OF STRIKING OATHS

OLIVIA WILDENSTEIN

HOUSE OF STRIKING OATHS

BOOK 3 OF *The Kingdom of Crows series*

For information contact:

OLIVIA WILDENSTEIN

http://oliviawildenstein.com

Cover design by *Olivia Wildenstein*

Art underneath the cover by *Lauren Richelieu*

Fallon and Lore paintings by *@crimson.spine*

Map art by *Chaim Holtjer @stardustbookservices*

Editing by *Laetitia Treseng at Little Tweaks*

Proofreading by *Rachel Theus Cass*

Lucin Glossary

Altezza – Your Highness
basta – it just is
bibbina(o) – baby
buondia – good day / good morning
buonotte – goodnight
buonsera – good evening
Caldrone – Cauldron
carina – sweetie
castagnole – fried dough rolled in sugar
corvo – crow
cuggo – cousin
cuori – heart
dolcca – honey
dolto/a – fool
furia – fury
generali – general
Goccolina – Raindrop
grazi – thank you
-ina/o – affectionate ending to first names
Maezza – Your Majesty
mamma – mom
mare – sea
mareserpens – sea serpent

merda – shit
micaro/a – my dear
mi cuori – my heart
moyo/a – husband/wife
nipota – granddaughter
nonna – grandma
nonno – grandpa
pappa – dad
pefavare – please
perdone – sorry
picolino/a – little one
piccolo – little
princci/sa – prince / princess
santo/a – holy
scazzo/a – street urchin
scusa – sorry
sergente – sergeant
serpens – serpent
strega – witch
soldato/i – soldier/s
tare – land
tiuamo – I love you
tiudevo – I owe you
zia – aunt

Crow Glossary

ab'waile (oh-wahleea) – home
adh (aw) – sky
ah'khar (uh-kawr) – beloved
ag – and
álo – hello
annos dòfain (awnos duffen) – anus dejection
bahdéach (bahdock) – beautiful
bántata – potatoes
beinnfrhal (benfrol) – mountain berry
behach (bey-ock) – little
bilbh (beehlb) – dumb
bìdh (bye) – food
chréach (kreyock) – crow
cúoco (coowocko) – coconut
dachrich (dockreh) – incredible
Dádhi (daji) – Dad
dalich (daleh) – sorry
dréasich (dreesseh) – dress
dihna (deena) – don't
éan (een) – bird
fallon – raindrop
fás – not yet
fihladh (feelaw) – leave

fin (fion) – wine

fios – know

focá – fuck

guhlaèr (guhlair) – okay

ha – I

ha'rovh béhya an ha théach'thu, ha'raì béih (haroff beya an ha thock too, haray beh) – I wasn't living until I met you, merely alive.

ha'khrá thu (hakraw too) – I love you

Ionnh (yon) – Miss

ínon (eenon) – daughter

khrá (kraw) – love

khroí (kree) – heart

leath'cinn (lehken) – half-Crow

Mádhi (maji) – Mom

mars'adh (marsaw) – please

mo bahdéach moannan (mo badock meanan) – my beautiful mate

moannan (monan) – mate

Mórrgaht (mawr-got) – Your Majesty

mo – my

moath (mof) – north

murgadh (murrgaw) – market

né (neh) – no

o ach thati – oh but you do

ríkhda gos m'hádr og matáeich lé – much longer and I may kill him.

rí (ree) – king

rahnach (rawnock) – kingdom

rih bi'adh (reebyaw) – King of the Sky

sí (see) – she

siorkahd (shuhrkaw) – circle

siér (siuhr) – sister

sífair (sea fair) – serpent

sé'bhédha (shehveha) – you're welcome

tà (taw) – yes

tàin (tawhhn) – ass

tach (tock) – the

Tach ahd a'feithahm thu, mo Chréach (tok add a faytham thoo, mo kreyock) – The sky awaits you, my Crows.

tapath (tapoff) – thank you

thábhain (hawben) – tavern

thu (too) – you

thu leámsa (too leh-awmsa) – you are mine

thu thòrt mo focèn ánach (too thurt mo focken anock) – you take my fucking breath away

tuiladh (twilaw) – more

uhlbheist (ulbeeheist) – monster

Historical Timeline

MAGNABELLUM

Great War waged 522 years ago between the Kingdom of Luce and the Queendom of Shabbe.

Costa Regio wins the war and becomes the first Fae King of Luce.

PRIMANIVI

Battle waged 22 years ago between the Crows and the Fae.

Costa's son, Andrea, who has ruled over Luce for the last century, is killed. Although his death is attributed to the Crows, he was murdered by his own son, Marco.

Marco threatens to kill humans to force Lore to surrender, thus winning the battle.

He is crowned King of Luce.

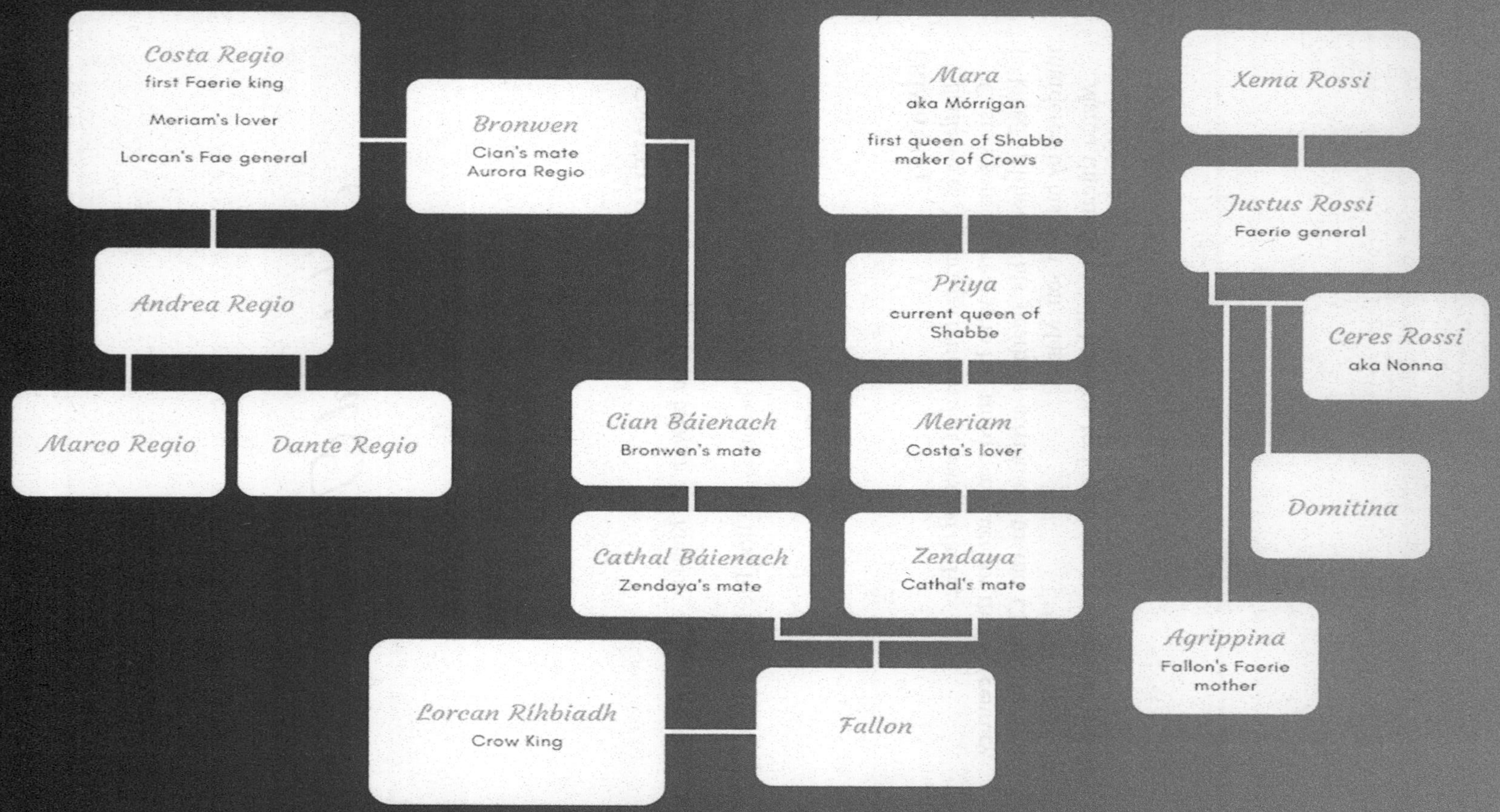

Costa Regio
first Faerie king
Meriam's lover
Lorcan's Fae general
Bronwen
Cian's mate
Aurora Regio
Andrea Regio
Marco Regio
Dante Regio
Cian Báienach
Bronwen's mate
Cathal Báienach
Zendaya's mate
Lorcan Ríhbiadh
Crow King
Fallon
Mara
aka Mórrigan
first queen of Shabbe
maker of Crows
Priya
current queen of Shabbe
Meriam
Costa's lover
Zendaya
Cathal's mate
Xema Rossi
Justus Rossi
Faerie general
Ceres Rossi
aka Nonna
Domitina
Agrippina
Fallon's Faerie mother

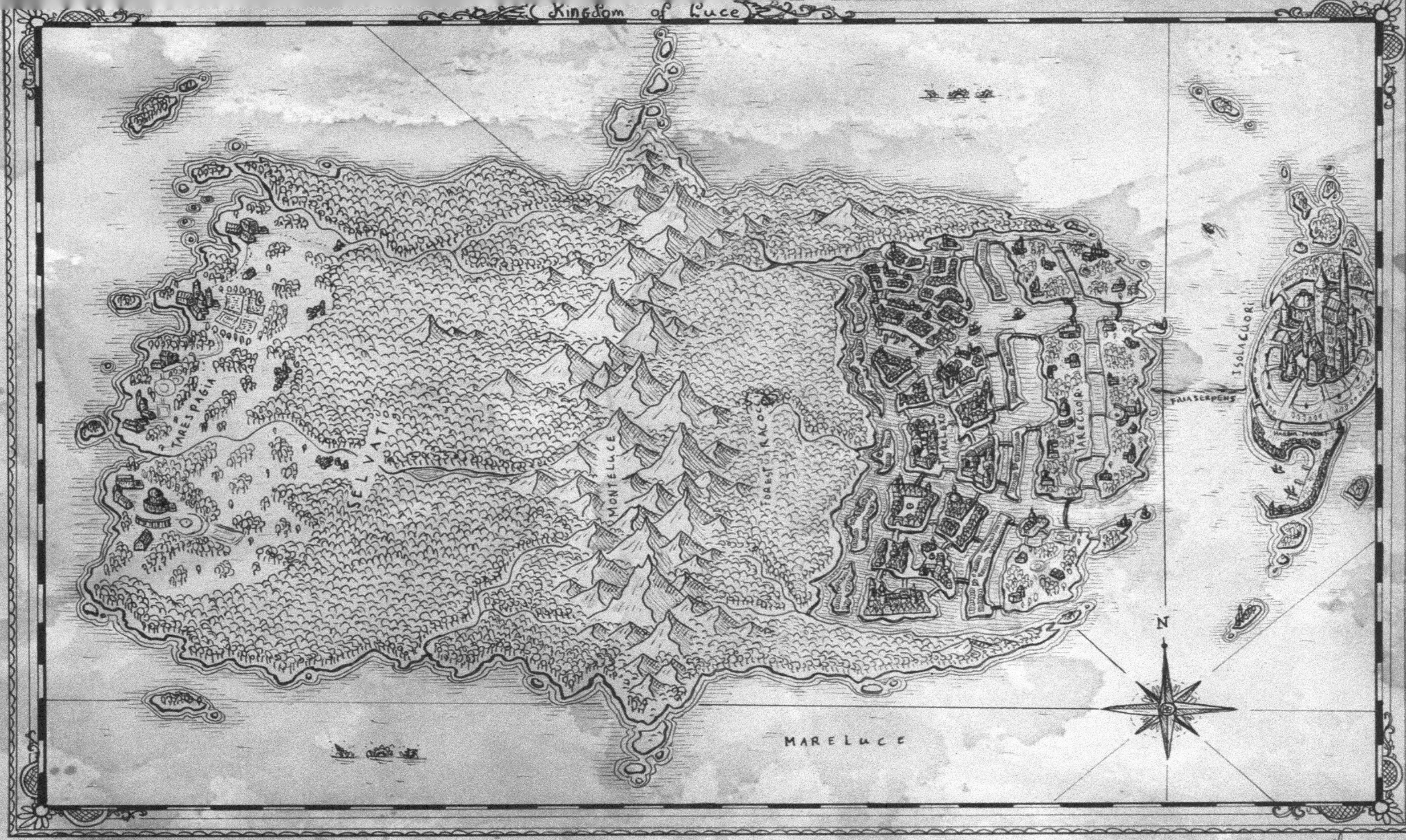

Kingdom of Luce
TARESPAGIA
SELVATI
MONTELUCE
FOREST RACOC
TARECUORI
FILIASERPENS
ISOLACUORI
N
MARELUCE
Chaim 2022

Earn your
crown.

PROLOGUE

LORE

Cathal lobs a glass vial atop the ochre map of Luce unrolled on my desk. “Mattia found it amidst the wreckage.”

I pinch the leather cord laced around the jar that is no larger than my thumb and lift it. It swings in the gray light of the second dawn without my mate.

“There isn’t much blood inside, but perhaps enough for Bronwen to draw a sigil?” Cathal spears his fingers through his snarled black hair.

“A sigil? Cathal, she cannot manipulate blood magic.”

The whites of my general’s eyes are crimson, giving the huge man a demonic stare to go along with his attitude. “What can it hurt to fucking try?” I may have lost my mate, but he’s lost both his mate and daughter.

No. Not lost.

I tear that word to shreds.

We’ve been fleeced of our women.

Forced to exist without them.

I raise my gaze from the vial. “You’re right. It cannot hurt to try. Do you recall the shape of that sigil Daya used to penetrate walls?”

His jaw tenses, and in spite of his nascent beard, I don’t miss how sharp the square bone becomes at the mention of his mate. “No, but Bronwen might. Meriam did teach her once upon a time.”

To think that Bronwen once looked upon the Shabbin sorceress like a mother.

"Has she had anymore"—I stare so hard at the map that the ink blurs—"visions?"

"Not that she's shared with me." Cathal squeezes the bridge of his nose and shuts his eyes. "If Dante hasn't turned Aoife into a forever-Crow, I will."

It was Connor who suggested that Fallon must have been airlifted into the valley, because she'd left the tavern sometime after lunch, and it would've taken her far longer than a couple hours to travel down the mountain by horseback. We figured it was Aoife because all the other Crows had been accounted for—save for Imogen.

Although Cian is convinced that Aoife flew Fallon into the valley on my mate's request, Cathal believes Aoife acted out of selfishness. I still haven't made up my mind about her true intent. Aoife is attached to her sister and could've been attempting to retrieve her, but she's also loyal to a fault and a true friend to Fallon.

And Fallon, for all the love I have for her, is impetuous and passionate, guided first and foremost by her heart.

I can imagine her beseeching Aoife to take her to Dante.

My grip tightens around the vial's leather cord. Before I can hurl it at the wall and spoil one of our only chances at breaching the obsidian tunnels, I set it down. "Is Gabriele still denying having told Fallon where to find Regio?"

Cathal nods.

"Up his intake of salt. I don't care if he chokes on the condiment; I want the fucking truth!"

To think I allowed the Faerie inside my kingdom's walls . . . Bronwen may have seen him dying at the hands of Tavo, but I expect I will be the one to murder him.

Before I disintegrate into shadows to pay Dante's imprisoned friend a visit, I walk to the window that overlooks Shabbe, hands linked behind my skull. "What of Lazarus?"

"He swears he didn't slip Fallon obsidian powder."

"Search his rooms."

"We have."

"Again. Search them again!" I glance over my shoulder and lock eyes with Cathal. "You and I both know that is the only way to hush a bond."

"There are books in her room, Lore. Are you certain that the use of obsidian powder isn't mentioned in one of them?"

I wheel around, and although Cathal, out of everyone, doesn't deserve my rage, he's on the receiving end. "And where, do tell, would she have procured herself obsidian powder?"

His nostrils flare at the snap of my voice. "Perhaps when you allowed her to wander around the Fae lands!"

Our spat blisters the air . . . blisters our moods. I'm about to yell at him to interrogate every Crow within my walls when a shadow takes shape beside us—Cian.

The male looks more ragged than Cathal and me, even though his mate is tucked safely between our walls.

"Lore?" His dark eyes are downcast, fixed on his mud-speckled boots that he keeps shuffling from side to side.

"What paltry news do you bring, Cian?" When his lids close, my skin begins to crawl.

"Bronwen needs to speak with you."

"She's seen something?" his brother asks.

Cian palms his nape and gnaws his lip. When he still cannot meet my stare, frost radiates to my farthest extremities.

"Great Mórrígan, it was her," Cathal murmurs. "She's the one who gave my daughter the obsidian powder."

"I'm sorry, Lore," he croaks. "I only just found out."

I burst into smoke and tear through the darkened hallways of my castle toward the rooms he shares with a woman I am about to erase from the bloody face of the earth. I find her sitting by a crackling fire, rocking in the chair that Cian strapped to his back to lug out of that derelict cottage in the woods she called home for five centuries.

Even though Bronwen is slight, the wood creaks as she sways. "Before you tear into me, Mórrgaht, you'll want to hear me out."

I loathe when she calls me Highness because it pitches me back to a time and place when her father was my general and she and I weren't yet friends. Although, *are* we even friends? A friend wouldn't poison my mate and lead her to my enemy.

Heart feeling like a lump of pyrite struck with flint, I rumble, "Talk."

She turns her white eyes in the direction of where I stand with my arms folded against the blood-soaked breastplate I haven't removed since the carnage in the valley. Then again, I haven't had the need to pitch it off for I've not slept, not showered, not eaten, not even fucking sat down. All I've done is prowl my stone floors and soar through my thunder-stricken air.

The bedroom door swings open. "Lore—please." The feathers are still melting off Cian's limbs as he stalks toward his mate to protect her from my looming wrath.

Although every Crow can morph into smoke, none, save for me, can hold the form for very long.

Cathal strides in after his brother, expression stamped with the same fury that swells my veins. "How dare you go behind our backs, Bronwen!"

"Do you remember when I told you that the Shabbins were 'looking,' Lore?" Her fingers fall to her lap, to a square package wrapped in cloth nestled in the folds of her red dress. As she rocks in her chair, she begins to unwrap it. "The day Antoni and his friends left the Sky Castle."

"I forget nothing," I say through gritted teeth.

Cian grips her shoulder. Is he giving it a squeeze to urge her to go on, or to remind her that he is present? What am I going on about? Unlike the two of us poor sods, their mind link isn't broken.

"I told Fallon I could not feel who was using my eyes."

Cian's lids slip shut and their corners crinkle—out of shame or concern, I cannot tell.

"Who?" My word is as vaporous as smog yet singes the brisk air like lightning.

She plucks aside one flap of cloth, then another. "Meriam."

My gaze jerks to her face at the sound of that reviled name.

Silence. It buzzes, swarms, festers.

"She's been looking for a while now. Ever since Fallon was a babe, she's been using my eyes. Watching her grow. I grew wary and worried of her attention, even though I knew she was incarcerated in the Regio dungeon. Especially after Zendaya . . ." Her eyes glisten like the ice that frosts Monteluce in the dead of winter. "After Daya stopped looking."

She untucks more eaves of cloth, pulling my tapered stare back to her lap. What the bloody underworld is in there?

"I called upon the Cauldron many times during those years to ask whether Meriam would become a hindrance to Fallon's destiny, but Fallon's fate never changed, and though I stayed wary, I stopped tormenting myself with a future in which the Crows didn't reconquer Luce."

My lungs ache from how hard I clutch each breath before releasing it. "The Cauldron isn't always right!"

"Perhaps not about the journey, but it is *always* right about the destination. It would be a mistake to stop listening to its guidance."

"Are you saying the Cauldron told you to drop my child into Dante's lap?" Cathal's hands are fisted at his sides, his knuckles pale from how hard he flexes his fingers.

"No, Cathal." The cloth finally falls away to reveal a chunk of gray stone that seems to have been cleaved from my mountain. "That was Meriam."

Cathal's eyes grow so large that his irises become mere specks in the pinkened pools of white.

"Meriam needed Fallon." Bronwen's brown fingers skim down the ruffled edges of the timeworn rock with such reverence that I begin to wonder if the Cauldron's done away with her damn mind. "And Fallon needed her."

CHAPTER I

I'm no bird—not yet, anyway—and yet Dante has locked me in a bloody cage.

I cling to the golden bars of my newest lodging—a wine cellar taller than my two-story house in Tarelexo—and scream obscenities at the top of my aching lungs. I'm surprisingly fluent in lewd language. To think Sybille and Phoebus consider me the prim one. My best friends' mandibles would unhinge at the amount of filth I've tossed at my jailers upon awakening from my magic-induced slumber.

And Lore . . . how he'd growl at my use of foul language.

What I wouldn't give to hear him complain.

What I wouldn't give to hear him breathe.

I press my hand against my chest and knead the aching muscle within. The pain between my ribs is so acute that it drowns out the dull throb at the back of my scalp where my head hit rock, then bone.

Once I've transformed my grief into anger, I curl my fingers around the bars of my prison and go back to raging, my shouts echoing against the glass bottoms of dusty vintages spiraling up the sides of this obsidian cellar.

I try to remember how long I've been locked up for, but all that comes to mind is the memory of Dante shoving me down the darkened tunnel toward another obsidian wall, and Justus waiting there for us—soldiers and Aoife nowhere to be seen.

I remember sinking my teeth into the meaty part of Dante's hand, which had elicited a satisfying growl from his throat, but which, unluckily, had made his grip tighten around my neck.

I remember Justus swiping his thumb across my lids, smearing the scent of copper in the darkened air. My stomach had heaved when my crumbling vision had caught the scarlet streak of blood on the pad of the Faerie general's finger.

Just before my consciousness had faded, I remember wondering how it was possible that a Faerie, and a man at that, could perform blood magic, a power reserved to Shabbin females.

"Hey, Faeries," I yell at the soldiers standing like stone figureheads against the walls of my prison. "Where, do tell, has the cockered gopher and his trusty mole gone? Are they digging up some more little tunnels to hide from the Crows?"

The four uniformed wallflowers continue pretending to be one with the stone at their back.

Yes, four. Apparently, even though I'm under lock and key and suspended in midair, I necessitate that many pure-blooded males to keep me from escaping. I suppose I should be flattered but I'm not; I'm incensed. Especially since hours have passed—days, even—and neither Justus nor Dante have deigned to pay me a visit.

I crane my neck to study the sturdy chain holding up my cage. I wonder whether it's long enough for me to swing myself into the wall and crack the stone. Can metal shatter obsidian?

At the very least, it would get someone's attention. Perhaps the impact would even pop open the gated entrance to my suspended cell.

Since trying will only cost me energy, and I possess an excess of that, I bend my knees and funnel all my weight into my feet. The chain groans as the cage begins to swing. I straighten my legs, then crouch, repeating the motion until my gold pen sways like the pendulum of a cuckoo clock.

The thin cot and wool blanket—the only items in my cage—glide across the floor, bumping into my ankles before retreating like a wave and jouncing off the opposite wall. If I close my eyes, I can almost pretend I'm sitting on one of the wooden swings roped around the massive oak branches in Scola Cuori's gardens. But I don't close my eyes. I keep them wide and trained on the soldiers below. All four of them are looking up. Actually, make that three.

One must've gone to alert a higher-up to my erratic behavior.

By the time the cage finally clips stone, sweat has gathered at my nape, gluing the high collar of my shirt to my skin. The ding propels vibrations into my legs, which I bend and straighten with added fervor.

"Stop this madness immediately, scazza!" an amber-eyed soldier barks, fiery palms at the ready.

"By all means"—I grunt—"melt my cage!"

When the cellar wall rushes at me a little faster than anticipated and the metal floor shatters an entire row of wine bottles, I turn my head and squeeze my lids to avoid glass projectiles. The only thing I get splashed with, though, is wine.

"Lastra, rope down the cage!" the same Faerie hollers at a green-eyed soldier.

I spring my lids wide just as the cage bowls down another row of surely valuable drink. Metal groans as the bars warp, angering the hinges. I suspect that with a few more hits, I may just succeed in cracking this damn thing open.

An emerald vine streams out of the soldier's palm and wraps around the bars. The pureling must not have anticipated the momentum of my cage because, suddenly, he's airborne, too. Had I not felt so full of wrath, I may have grinned.

His shocked yelp rends the air in the dungeon, but it's swiftly snuffed out when the fool crashes into the wall, unshelving more old bottles. For a few heartbeats, his limp, wine-soaked body sways from his magic vine like the black-teethed savages who accosted me in the wilds of Tarespagia. But then, his loss of consciousness snuffs out his magic, and he drops to the floor, his creeper sparkling out of existence.

While the amber-eyed soldier rushes to his side, an air-Fae blasts my cage with wind. Instead of halting the mad rocking I've achieved, the gusts of his magic spin my cage. My stomach jerks into my throat at the maddening whirl, then plummets when the ceiling begins to groan.

Strangling the bars with my fingers, I jerk my attention upward.

Although my hair swirls around my face and whips my wide eyes, it doesn't hide the cracks webbing the ceiling.

My cage is about to fall.

Since my magic is bound, and my ears, round, dropping from this high up may just kill me. In the words of Lore, *focá*.

Another deeper crack slashes the ceiling, sprinkling my upturned face with stone pellets. I want to yell at the air-Fae to stop shoving air at my twirling cage, but at the same time, if the ceiling caves, then perhaps so will the ground above it. Unless the tunnels have been excavated kilometers deep . . . Here's to hoping the Fae got lazy during their great dig.

I twist around and, back pinned to the bars, survey the cot. When it brushes against my boots, I fling myself onto it. Its reediness is a double-edged sword, because it both knocks the breath from my lungs and allows me to roll myself into it.

Cocooned like a silk worm, I suck in lungfuls of air as I await the imminent collapse. When it comes, I release my frenzied breaths with a squeak.

The cage sinks so fast that my mattress-clad body rises like a petal caught on a breeze before shooting downward. I clench my lids, tucking all I can tuck of myself inside my downy shell.

Yelling erupts around me. The din transports me back to the night in the cave. If only I'd tried harder to find Lorcan before rushing out of his highland fortress. If only I'd read Bronwen's ill intent inside her white eyes. If only I'd run Dante through with my sword instead of Dargento.

But I didn't because I was a trusting fool.

The cage crashes into the ground, yet somehow . . . somehow, I don't. I float as though some winged being has caught me.

Lore? I croak down the bond.

When no honeyed voice or caw sounds around me, I'm forced to accept the fact that my savior is no Crow but an air-Fae worried about banging up the king's precious prisoner.

I shut my lids for long seconds and breathe through my heartache. *I hate you, Bronwen. I hate you so godsdamned much. I hope Lore found out what you did, and I hope he separated you from your mate like you separated us.*

"What the bloody Cauldron is happening in here?"

Ah, just the man I wanted to see. And kill.

The sound of Dante's voice sharpens my listless pulse and mood. "Set her down, Cato!"

Cato?

My heart starts and stops, starts and stops as I drift toward solid ground.

My Cato. Well, not mine—*Nonna's*?

Shock slackens my grip on the mattress, which flops open like a poorly tied scroll, and I sit up so fast that the blood roars between my temples. There, before the dinged bars of my cage, long white hair bound into a plait, stands the man I'd pictured at Nonna's side.

But Cato Brambilla didn't choose her side; he picked the Regios'.

CHAPTER 2

I stare at the white-garbed sergeant, and he stares back. The foolish romantic in me was under the impression that the day Marco fell, Cato had headed to Shabbe to find my grandmother. Evidently, Cato cared more about his station than his heart since he remained in the service of the Faerie Crown.

Political ambition brings out the very worst in people. It brought out the worst in me when I hunted down iron birds for a crumb of Dante's affection and regard. Although I regret the manner in which I went about collecting Lore's crows, I don't regret the end result, because a life without Lore wouldn't have been worth living.

I glance up at the stone ceiling, at the spiderweb fissures that have appeared around the metal fixture from which dangled my cage. Are the cracks wide enough to let my words through?

Lore? I whisper to the sky that he rules over.

Had I not been surrounded by soldiers, I might have attempted to project myself toward my mate, but I don't dare leave my body. Besides, if my voice cannot slip out of this underground prison, then my consciousness surely cannot squeeze through either.

"Sprites, check the ceiling." Dante's voice flicks my gaze back to his face. "Plug any hole with obsidian mortar." His expression is as cold and hard as the gold armor he wears. Gone is the jewel-eyed, gentle boy who gave me my first kiss in a Tarelexian alleyway. "Were you out of your bloody mind? You could've died!"

Like you care, Dante Regio. Actually, the Faerie King probably does care since he wants to marry me to ally himself with Shabbe. "You really should've considered my mortality when you stuck me in a fucking cage, Dante."

His blue eyes narrow on my violet ones; I can tell he hates what he sees, the same way I loathe who he's become.

"Unlock her door," he snaps.

"Immediately, Maezza," his minions respond, approaching my prison.

As they begin to fondle the warped bars of my cage, I'm cast back to the day Phoebus unlocked his family's vault. Little had we known that what lay behind the armored door would change our lives forever.

"I'm being freed?" I roll my fingers around the edges of the cot I still sit on.

Dante trails the dance of his soldiers' fingers. "Your magic is; you're not."

My heart holds still before stampeding like a herd of warhorses, drowning out the loud click of my cage door.

My magic?

That means . . .

That means that I'm about to meet Zendaya, the woman who made me. The woman who would've birthed me had Marco not ambushed her.

Oh my Gods, I'm about to meet my mother!

The hinges screech like my wild pulse. Even though I still rue the night Bronwen cast me on Dante's lap, I'm excited. Really damn excited.

"Get up," Dante snaps.

I level my gaze on the Faerie King who fills the doorframe of my golden cage like an oil portrait.

"Will you require assistance?" Dante asks.

I narrow my eyes, spilling what I think of his offer into my expression. If he so much as touches me again, I will bite him—*again*.

The memory of my teeth sinking into his flesh ferries my attention to his hand. I don't expect there to be any wound—after all, the man is a pureling and purelings heal rapidly—and yet, gauze adorns his flesh. Either less time has frittered by than I assumed, or Dante Regio is healing slowly.

"How long have I been your prisoner?" I ask as I finally get to my feet.

Dante's eyes blaze like the candles oozing pale wax along the sconces carved into the obsidian walls. "Meriam must perform the spell while the moon is full." He turns on his boot and stomps toward a narrow opening in the black rock. "Come."

"Meriam will unbind my magic?" I'm ready to meet my mother; I'm wholly unprepared to meet the witch who doomed my mate, my parents, and me.

On the threshold of the tunnel, Dante peers over his shoulder. "Did you expect me to do it?"

"Obviously not, but I—" I lick my lips. "I thought my mother would be the one to unbind it, since she was the one to bind it."

"Fal, your mother is dead. She died shortly after Meriam ripped you from her loins and stuck you in that Faerie carrier."

That Faerie carrier has a name, I want to growl, but my tongue has become rooted to my palate and all I manage to push out is a hushed, "What?"

"Zendaya. Is. Dead. Meriam bled her dry before casting her desiccated corpse into Mareluce."

My body lists back from the force of Dante's revelation. I fling out my arm, clasping the nearest bar to keep myself upright. "That's impossible."

My father felt her, didn't he? Cauldron . . . I can't remember.

"Did you believe Shabbins to be invincible, Fal? All creatures can perish, though some are trickier to kill than others."

"No. But—but . . ." A shudder rolls up my spine, spreading until all of me trembles. But I also believed my mother to be alive.

As I try to make sense of all that Dante's lobbed at me, he steps into the tunnel. "Let's go. I don't want to risk waiting another moon cycle for you to come into your power."

Even if I wanted to follow, I cannot, for I'm frozen in shock.

My mother is dead. My heart cracks for my father. Oh, Dádhi.

Lore said mates don't do well without each other. Will Cathal Báeinach choose to go on with his life, or will he choose to become a forever-Crow? I selfishly pray he chooses life, because I yearn for him to be part of mine. I'm suddenly glad for the obsidian walls because they'll keep this horrific secret from entering Lorcan's mind a while longer.

Cato steps into my cage. "Fallon?" He doesn't tack on anything else. Doesn't ask if I'm all right or if I desire help, but there's a hard glimmer to his gray eyes that makes me think he might care. It's probably my imagination. Even if the sergeant's heart isn't as sharp as his ears, he still chose the Regios.

He's not your friend, I remind myself before I can latch onto yet another male undeserving of my trust.

"You don't want your magic? Fine." Dante does not sound fine about it. "We'll just stay holed up underground for another month. Here I thought you'd be glad not to sleep in a cage."

My eyes sting. I blink, but it does nothing to whisk away the moisture slickening them. "Gods, you've just told me that my mother is dead. Give a girl a minute, you unsympathetic codpiece."

"What did you just call me?" His voice is low yet reaches me just fine.

I don't bother repeating what I said, not because I worry about retribution, but because I'm certain he heard me just fine. After all, he *is* a pureling.

"I'll let your slight slide. I'll even help you retrieve her body from Filiaserpens"—Dante makes a vague gesture with his wounded hand, as though motioning toward the trench that runs from Isolacuori to Tarecuori—"and allow you to give her a proper burial if you follow me now."

The memory of Gabriele's speculation the day he escorted me to Isolacuori for my luncheon with Dante hits me square in the heart. He'd mentioned my mother laid in Filiaserpens. To think it was no theory.

I fasten my heated eyes to Dante's form. "How magnanimous of you, Maezza."

Although steeped in shadows, I don't miss the tick of his jaw.

"Fallon," Cato says softly, and I think he's about to chastise me, but I'm wrong. He crooks his elbow and tips his head to his proffered arm.

I'm done leaning on men. Perhaps I'm being rash to discard Cato.

He truly might possess an excellent reason for aiding the Regio cause, but I currently don't have the mental wherewithal to figure out where his allegiance lies. Especially not when we're surrounded by so many soldiers.

I shuffle past him and then past the rest of the prison guards. "There's something I don't understand."

The Faerie King watches me approach, his expression inscrutable. "And what is that?"

"Why in the world do you deem freeing my magic a sound idea? You must realize that, the second it's unbound, I will paint a death spell over your heart."

A haughty smile coils his lips.

I cross my arms. "It's not an empty threat, Dante."

His gaudy boots jangle as he takes a step in my direction. I wonder how sharp his metal spurs are. Sharp enough to slice through skin? Granted they aren't made of iron, but surely if wedged inside his throat, they'd cause some damage.

"I've no doubt that'll be the first sigil you'll ask Meriam to teach you, but you see, Fallon, my grandfather was not only a formidable king but also a prescient man."

"All Costa Regio was is scum. Just like the rest of his bloodline."

Dante presses his palm to his gold plastron, over the spot where a heart should've beat. "You wound me, Fal."

"Stop using my nickname."

"Fine. Moya it'll be then. I realize we aren't lawfully wed yet, but it's only a matter of hours. You're welcome to call me Moyo."

"I will never call you Husband," I say between clenched teeth. "And don't you fucking dare call me Wife." My abrasive tone finally flattens his simper.

Dante's gaze tapers. "You're fearless, aren't you? I used to find that trait admirable, but now I see it for what it makes you —childish."

The knot of my arms tightens at his slight. "And yet you still wish to marry me . . . I was aware you'd lost your moral compass the day you stuck a bloodied crown on your brow, but I hadn't realized you'd shed your mind along with it. I may accept to be unbound, but I will never accept to marry you."

The bones in Dante's face seem to realign beneath his skin, sharpening his features. "You will accept."

"Did Bronwen feed you some prophecy that I would say yes? Because if that's the case, I've another prophecy for you. One that doesn't end well for you, but ends superbly for me."

"Prophecies are for fools."

Such an ingrate. Why the Cauldron am I still expecting appreciation? Especially since I've every intention of taking back the sunray crown. "A prophecy got you on the throne."

"Lore's weakness for his little 'curse-breaker' got me on the throne. He would've remained a shadow king had I run you through with my blade in Xema Rossi's grove."

"So that was your plan?"

He works his jaw from side to side as though chewing on something—probably the answer to my question. He must sense I'm one millisecond away from plucking the sword from his scabbard and going to town on his neck because he takes a step back.

"I imagined you and he would've gotten married the day Marco fell, but Ríhbiadh is a master manipulator, isn't he?"

"Don't change the subject."

"Striking an alliance with King Vladimir of Glace with the pretense that he'd marry his daughter Alyona so that the day he finally made his move on you, you'd be none the wiser of his intent."

I fold my arms even tighter. "His intent?"

"To marry you for your magic." Dante releases a snort. "Crows are such crafty creatures."

The only thing I retain from all Dante has just spewed is that Bronwen has failed to inform her nephew that Lore is my mate. Otherwise, Dante would know that the Crow King isn't after my magic.

How interesting that you kept that to yourself, Bronwen.

In a syrupy tone, I make a suggestion that is evidently not one at all. "Or perhaps Lore has enough magic of his own that he doesn't feel the need to exploit mine?"

My attempt to incinerate Dante's ego backfires when the Faerie King smiles. Fucking *smiles*. "Here I thought you acted naïve to trick people, but it's not an act, is it?"

I scowl. "What is that supposed to mean?"

"It means the Crimson Crow kept you in the dark." Dante runs the tip of his tongue over his teeth as though savoring the moment.

I bet he is. "How about you enlighten me, Maezza?"

"It'll be my pleasure, Fal."

I want to yell at him to stop using my nickname but keep quiet to hear his grand admission.

"Spouses—be they human or other—can manipulate their Shabbin wives' blood magic."

CHAPTER 3

S*pouses can manipulate their Shabbin wives' blood magic?*

Dante's words roll through my mind like small rocks on a shore, jagged edges scraping my skull, leaving gashes behind. I trust Lore. Dante's reveal doesn't change that. Nevertheless, I'm a little upset and a lot hurt that I had to learn this great secret from the Faerie King.

Why, Lore? Why wouldn't you share this with me?

Come to think of it, wouldn't my father have told me? He has to know, right? After all, even if he and Daya lived only a handful of months together, surely they discussed this, right? Could the Crows not be aware of this connection?

Unless . . . unless it isn't true! "Was Meriam the one to supply you with this information?"

Dante's eyes narrow. "I'd heard it from other mouths before Rossi made me aware of it."

"Rossi?"

"Justus Rossi. Your grandfather."

I roll my eyes. How dippy does he think his slumber spell made me? "That man is not my grandfather."

"Interesting."

"What is?"

"That you'd consider Ceres and Agrippina kin, but not Justus."

"I don't see how that's interesting. Or relevant. Or even new information."

Back in the day, back when Dante and I were friends, back before he'd sailed off to Glace, he and I had had many conversations. Have they slipped his mind or did they just never register? I cast these thoughts away because what do they matter?

"So how did Justus come by this information? He wasn't alive when Meriam raised the wards, so he mustn't have learned it from Shabbins."

Dante watches me, waiting for me to connect the dots.

Justus used blood magic to get us into these tunnels.

Which means . . . I gasp. "Nonna is Shabbin?"

An air of smugness drapes over Dante's face. "Not the nonna you're thinking of."

I blink so many times and so fast that my lashes wallop my cheekbones. "Justus is married to Meriam?"

When Dante nods, all the blood deserts my extremities and I shudder.

"After he swam back to Isolacuori and transported Meriam out of the dungeon to—" He stops talking so abruptly that it jostles my pulse.

"To . . .?" I prompt him, hoping he'll let slide where in Luce we are. Beneath Lore's mountain? Beneath Tarecuori?

Dante dips his chin. "Come to think of it, his marriage to Meriam makes him even more of a grandfather now."

Even though I'm aware he's skirting my question, I cannot help but growl, "That man will *never* be my grandfather; the same way I will never consider that malign witch family."

The same way I will never call you Husband. I don't utter this out loud because my molars have wedged themselves together, but I must transmit the sentiment loudly and clearly because Dante's easygoing air morphs into a hardened mien.

He turns and starts back down the tunnel, the jewels in his long brown braids clinking like his spurs.

Where the room we left behind rose to incredible heights, the ceiling here is so low that it just about grazes the top of Dante's head and presses against my skin and airway, thinning the oxygen around me. However fast and hard I breathe, I cannot seem to get enough air into my lungs.

"Dante, wait!"

He doesn't.

"I've a bargain for you!" I call from where I stand stubbornly still, Faerie soldiers breathing down my neck.

He snorts. "Bargains don't adhere to your skin."

Merda. I forgot he knew that.

He finally stops his mad dash, though, and turns. "Nevertheless, I'll gladly strike one with you once your magic—"

"A witch's power dies when she does!" My rapidly pounding heart makes me sound out of breath.

"Planning on ending your life, moya?"

My head rears back, because no. The only life I'm planning on ending is his. And Meriam's, which is the reason I piped up in the first place. At least Dante's ridiculous comment serves to take my mind off my cramped surroundings, easing the constricting feeling in my chest.

"Since Meriam apparently bound my magic, if she dies, it'll release her hold on me. No need for spells or full moons."

"If she perishes, so do the wards, and so does her spell on the Regio bloodline. Not happening."

My tongue vibrates with my pulse. "What s-spell?"

"Right. You interrupted me before I could explain my grandfather's brilliance." He accompanies his declaration with a smug smile.

The words *go on* burn the tip of my tongue, but I know he will go on with or without prompting because Dante relishes my ignorance.

"Nonno Costa convinced Meriam to make Regio blood impervious to Shabbin spells. Which is the reason why I don't fear your magic's release."

Death by spurs or iron blade it will be, then. "Won't activating my magic pitch my body beyond the Shabbin wards?"

"You're of Meriam's bloodline, so you're immune to her wards."

What? My jaw falls, its hinges all but squeaking from the sudden collapse. "But my mother— My mother couldn't penetrate them until they weakened two decades ago. And my great-grandmother, the Queen, she cannot sail past them." Unless . . . "Can she?"

"No. But if they'd been on this side of Meriam's wards at the time of their creation, they could've stayed."

After a solid minute of silent gawping, I finally click my jaw back into place, but another question scratches at my mind. "If I'm immune to the wards, does that mean I'm immune to Meriam's magic?"

"No. Only the Regios. *Me.*"

"And Bronwen," I point out. "Let's not forget Luce's rightful queen"—*and traitorous wench*—"right?"

"She forfeited her claim to the throne for a meeting with her stepmother."

"Excuse me?"

"Her stepmother. *Meriam.*" After a beat, he says, "How strange that we share an uncle and aunt . . ."

Although tempted to hiss out that he can keep Bronwen all to himself, I ask, "How long have you known that she was your aunt?"

"Meriam informed me of Bronwen's identity when she and I met after my coronation." He runs his thumb over the bandage on his palm as though to soothe the wound beneath. "The witch has proved a prodigious weapon in my arsenal."

"Too bad Justus got to her first. Come to think of it, why don't you have their sham union annulled so you can marry her?"

"Only death can annul a blood-bind."

"That's an easy fix. Kill Justus."

He tips his head. "Wouldn't that make your day."

"More than my day. My whole year. My whole lifetime. I'd be forever grateful."

"Except your grandfather is not expendable, and I've no need for your gratitude."

"You've need for my approval. You cannot marry me without it." Right?

"Like Bronwen said, we'll have plenty of time for long chats later. After all, we must wait until the rest of Lore's crows fall to return—"

"The—rest?" My voice is thready and barely noisier than my ratcheting breaths.

He tilts his head to the side. "Did I fail to mention one of his five crows is presently a block of iron?"

Numb.

I go numb.

Blood rushes into my eardrums, heightening the sound of my distressed breathing.

Iron, my mind yells. If Lore transformed into iron, then he's not a forever-Crow. "Did your soldier forget to baste his blade?" I croak.

Dante stares at me, his eyes twin pools of muck. "It wasn't my soldier who drove his obsidian blade into the Crimson Crow. It was my commander."

My body teeters. "Your—" I whip out one hand, flattening my palm against the cold stone wall. "Dargento survived?"

"Dargento?" Dante sounds genuinely surprised. "No. That male didn't survive your wrath."

"Then . . ." My heart misses a beat.

He cannot be saying what I think he's saying.

He cannot mean—

CHAPTER 4

"Did you really believe Gabriele took refuge in the Sky Kingdom, Fal? That he'd double-cross me, his dearest friend? His king?"

My mouth goes so slack that I choke on my next inhale.

"Unlike you, my friends don't betray me." Dante ambles back toward me, his gait downright leisurely. "Such a good friend that Catriona was, huh?"

I can hardly focus on his condemnation of the poor courtesan who got caught in the crosshairs of Dargento's vendetta, too busy reeling from the fact that I misread Gabriele. That I brought this upon Lore when I begged him to give the Faerie a chance.

Horror weakens my knees and I list. As the ground rushes to meet my bloodless face, I squeeze my lids shut. Instead of obsidian, air pillows my body, breaking my fall, and then hands wind around my biceps and gently pull me back upright.

When I crack my lids open, Cato stands before me, a slash of white against the darkness. Even his eyes appear uncharacteristically pale, reminding me of eyes I loathe, eyes that landed me here, in this Underworld with the Devil himself.

"Make sure my betrothed makes it to Meriam's chamber unscathed. And before fucking daybreak!" Dante's voice splinters the deep silence, yanking me out of my stupor.

Cato releases one of my arms but keeps ahold of the other. I want to shrug him off, but I've not the energy to fight him. Besides, if I'm held up by anyone, I prefer it to be him.

"How did he do it?" I ask Dante, seeking holes in his story. "There's no way Gabriele could've smuggled in obsidian without the Crows noticing."

"You overestimate your little vultures." Dante's voice is so near that I crane my neck. Slowly his brown skin and mahogany tresses replace Cato's lighter coloring.

Instead of grating, his pettiness settles my nerves, because I've discovered that people are only petty when they're insecure. "How?" I repeat.

"You really want to know?"

"No. I'm just asking to make small talk," I deadpan.

His jaw sharpens. "He ingested the obsidian weapon and shat it out."

I stare at Dante, waiting to spot a tell that he's lying, but the man has schooled his expression into an unreadable mask.

"Gabriele will go down in history as a great hero."

Not if the Crows win. And they will. Bronwen saw it.

"You forget that the history books are written by the victors, Dante Regio." The words Lore once told me groove Dante's brow. "Tell me, did he also ingest a sealed vial of Meriam's blood to shit out and slather on his little weapon?"

"That would've been rather pointless since the Sky Kingdom blocks any form of magic other than the shifters', right?"

Thank the great Cauldron and whoever enchanted Lore's realm. My relief is so intense that, after deserting me, blood gushes back into my organs, fortifying both my limbs and morale.

"His mission was to weaken Ríhbiadh, and he succeeded." Dante's gruff tone chafes my mood. "There are four more crows to stake and vials of Meriam's blood circulating through Luce, freely given to soldiers and civilians alike."

His threat should irk me, but I'm too busy rejoicing that my mate hasn't lost his humanity to give a serpent's ass.

"By the time we emerge from our stronghold, the shifters will be an extinct race of supernaturals."

He says I overestimate the Crows. Well, he evidently underestimates them. "I never imagined you'd be the type of man to send your best friend to slaughter."

A nerve flutters his temple. "Gabriele volunteered for this mission."

Keeping my tone placid, I say, "You didn't stop him, Dante, which makes you responsible for his death."

"They've yet to kill him."

"Do you expect him to walk out of the Sky Kingdom alive?" I ask just as Bronwen's prophecy zips through my mind like a thieving sprite: *You will not die at our hands, Gabriele; you will die at the hands of your Faerie general.* I shut out her voice. She may see the future and attempt to influence it but she cannot possibly control it.

"Knowing those savages, no."

"Then his death is on you."

His bandaged hand shoots up and cinches my neck, his grip as bruising as the night he dragged me into this obsidian pit. "Tart is not a good look on you, Fal."

A crazed smile digs into my unwashed cheeks. Gods, I must be an appalling sight. A shame Faeries cannot die of fright.

"I'll make sure—to cultivate it," I wheeze out.

His fingers tighten.

"Planning on—murdering me—next?"

He lifts me, his thumb digging into my carotid. "I did not. Murder. Gabriele."

"Maezza, please. We've no healer down here." Cato's tone is fraught with worry. Could he actually be concerned about my well-being, or is he trying to remind Dante to go easy on the female whose blood he plans on exploiting?

Dante's fingers spring open and air races down my bruised throat, burning like fire. I clutch my neck and massage the abused skin, my eyes so full of spite that Dante falls back a step. Unless he falls back because he doesn't trust himself not to squeeze the life out of me.

"You're lucky that I've use for you," he spits out.

He and I evidently have a very different definition of luck.

"Now, pick up the pace!" He whirls around and pounds into the darkness.

Several minutes trickle by and we're still marching like ants down the narrow tunnel. Between the airless darkness, the nearness of the walls, and my aching throat, my lungs spasm.

As I rub my chest, attempting to ease the discomfort, I murmur, "I thought you'd be in Shabbe."

Cato's gaze journeys over my profile, lingering on the reddened marks stamped around my throat. "I swore an oath to the Lucin crown."

By oath, does he mean he struck a bargain? And if so, was it with Justus or with Dante? Are these men holding him captive down here?

"It's a great honor to serve the king. It'll be an even greater honor to serve his queen." Although low, his voice seems to resonate between the dark walls.

"Eponine of Nebba is rather lovely." And crafty . . . I suppose I deserved her deceptive answer. After all, I did corner her into confessing Meriam's whereabouts. Had I been her, I would've led me astray as well.

"I meant you, Fallon," he replies softly.

I stop kneading my sore chest. "Is there something that's escaping me about modern marriage rites? Don't both parties have a say?"

"They do."

As we turn down another bend, I ask, "Then why the Cauldron is everyone so convinced I'd ever agree to marry a spineless king?"

Dante halts right in front of me, and even though he's broad—made broader by his armor—I don't miss the sprawl of the room behind him.

"Because that spineless king"—Dante's pupils are tight with loathing—"will feed your little halfling friend a steel blade if you turn him down."

Dante steps sideways, revealing a sight that stops my heart.

CHAPTER 5

Antoni sits gagged in the middle of another lofty obsidian room, blue eyes wild behind clumped locks of light-brown hair. When his gaze lands on mine, my pulse detonates. I rip my arm out of Cato's grip, then reach down for the sword in his baldric. Before I can yank it out and behead the Faerie King, Cato shackles my wrist, urging me to calm down with whispers that don't reach my thundering eardrums.

Glaring at the sergeant, I snatch my hand back, then spin around and slap Dante. "You bastard! You fucking bastard!"

"Fallon, stop!" Cato's yell reaches me at the same time as the vines from an earth-Fae's palms.

They slink around my arms, my abdomen, and my collarbone until I'm as trussed up as the boars Marcello roasts on spits. I thrash but that only tautens my bindings. When the vines reach my ankles, I teeter into Dante's chest, my cheek smacking the gold breastplate.

Fucking Faerie magic.

One of Dante's hands settles on the small of my back, holding me up; the other grips my hair and levers back my head. "You will regret slapping me, moya."

"The only thing I'll ever regret is our afternoon on Barrack Island." Since my mouth has yet to be gagged, I launch a wad of spit into his face. With immense satisfaction, it slithers down the bridge of his aquiline nose.

The burn of his gaze is forbidding, and yet it doesn't frighten me. "Remove the sailor's nails!"

"What?" I choke. "No!" I twist my head toward Antoni, leaving many strands clutched in Dante's fist. "NO! Antoni's for naught." Oh Gods, oh Gods, oh Gods . . . what have I done? "Remove my nails! Take mine!"

"A queen has need for nails; a prisoner does not." Dante watches the two soldiers close in on Antoni, whose eyes shine with dread.

"The only use I'll have for them will be to scratch your face, so you best take them, Dante."

He slides me a bored look.

"Please don't hurt him." I hate that he's reducing me to begging. "Dante, please."

His eyes meet mine. They're so cold, they spread ice through my veins.

A tear trips over my lash line. "Please, command them to stop."

He doesn't.

As Antoni's wounded grunts turn into feral cries, heated tears bleed from my eyes.

I weep for him.

I weep with him.

The torture feels as though it lasts an eternity. When his keening abates, I dare a look in my friend's direction.

Antoni lies on his side, hair splayed around his sweat-soaked face, lids clamped shut, fingertips crimson. A slick puddle blooms beneath his bound hands. I shift my gaze to his chest and survey it until I catch the shallow rise and fall of his rib cage.

Alive. He's alive. Knowing this does little to drive away the horror and guilt battering my own chest. I'll avenge you, Antoni. I swear it.

I turn the full force of my glare back on Dante. "What made you so cruel?"

"You, Fallon. You made me like this. Before you awakened the shifters, I didn't thirst to dethrone my brother."

"You crossed Filiaserpens!"

"So what?"

"So it's a rite of passage for Lucin kings! Which means you thirsted for that throne before I gifted it to you, so don't you fucking dare blame me for the heartless man you've become."

He snorts. "If I'm heartless, what does that make your little buzzard king? Do you know how many dead bodies he's left to rot on my soil?"

I'm fully aware that my mate is lethal and has spilled blood. The same way I'm aware Lore considers himself a monster, but no one is as monstrous as the male whose hands are still holding me clamped against his body.

"At least Lore protects his friends. Will you have any left at the end of your vendetta against the Crows?"

Dante's mouth firms into an unyielding line. "This is not a vendetta; it's a fucking war. One you brought about."

Under my breath, I mutter, "What a man you are. Forever blaming others."

"What was that?" His eyes are black with indignation because, of course he heard me. After all, our faces are so close that his rank breath pelts my damp cheeks. "You best stop insulting me or I'll take it out on your little sailor."

I squash my lips tight because I don't want additional harm to befall Antoni.

After I've kept mute for a full minute, he says, "That's better."

Again, I'm clipped by his foul breath. I pop my lips open to ease the assault on my nose. Did the inside of his mouth always smell like stale seaweed and decaying gums or is it a side effect of the Nebban chemical he's been ingesting?

I decide not asking is safer for Antoni.

"Must I keep you bound or will you start behaving?"

"I'll behave," I grumble, because who in their right mind would advise their tormentor to keep them cuffed?

At the same time as Dante releases my hair, the vines recede from my legs. My skin prickles as blood gushes back into the strangled sections of flesh.

"Justus, open the vault!"

Of course the general is here. I'm almost surprised he wasn't part of the procession of soldiers who marched me over.

Also . . . "Why are we going inside a vault?"

Dante's palm finally comes away from my back, but it's only to land on my upper arm and curl there. "Because that's where I keep my newest treasure."

Does he mean Meriam?

He drags me out of the entryway and into another windowless room. Although obsidian covers most of the surfaces, one wall is a solid gold panel tiled with faceted onyx in the shape of a giant 'R' full of swoops and whorls.

Dante jerks me toward where Justus stands with his back to us. I really don't appreciate being manhandled, but a glance at Antoni's motionless form has me biting the complaint off my tongue.

As I stare at my friend, my mind wanders to Imogen and that human rebel leader, Vance, who went after Antoni and both vanished as a result. Are they here? Or are Aoife's qualms about her sister having been turned into a forever-Crow justified? I don't ask in case Dante isn't aware that they tried penetrating the tunnels.

Like my cage, like the Acolti vault, the armored gold wall is being unlocked with magic. Justus streams water from his palms at the faceted stones. I note that he doesn't project his magic on all of them. He spurts water in fits and starts, hitting a low stone before aiming for a higher one.

I don't even try to memorize the sequence because I've neither water magic nor access to a pole I could use to press on the stones—if that could even work. At some point, the metal groans and a seam appears from ceiling to floor.

Justus directs his liquid magic at the vein, widening it until it can accommodate a full-grown body. Only then does he turn and level his blue stare on me—a stare I, once upon a time, thought I'd inherited from him. "Meriam, our granddaughter has arrived."

I recoil at the term. I may share blood with the woman, but she's by no means my grandmother, just like Justus is absolutely not my grandfather.

Justus studies the hand clamped around my bicep. "Meriam will need to see her alone."

"Out of the question, Rossi."

"If she unbinds Fallon's magic while you're touching her, she risks endangering you, Maezza."

"Fine. I will not touch her, but where Fallon goes, I go. You may trust the witch, Justus, but I don't."

A nerve feathers Justus's jaw. "Very well." Justus nods to the slender passage he's coaxed into existence with his magic and gestures for me to enter. "Your magic awaits, Fallon."

I barely register his words, much too transfixed by the sight of two inked circles on his palm. Lucins don't do tattoos but the general of the Lucin army does? Also, why have I never noticed it before? Sure, his hand is forever fastened to the pommel of his sword, and sure, I've met him only twice, but still . . . those circles are so large and dark, one would need to be blind to miss them.

Dante's grip slackens on my arm before falling away completely. "Let's go."

My heart batters my ribs as I stand stock-still.

"Now, Fallon. While the moon is still full."

I swallow a great many times, my eardrums buzzing with my revving pulse. Mixed into my dread is a dash of excitement.

I'm about to possess magic. And from the accounts I've heard, incredible magic.

My fingers tremble and prickle as though my blood is ready to burst from my flesh. I roll them into my palms, my stomach seesawing as I take the first step toward the woman who will forever change my life.

For the better, I decide, because apparently, I haven't become a complete pessimist. I may not be able to use my magic against Dante because of Meriam's ancient spell, but I will be able to use it against the rest of the world.

I glance up at Justus as I approach. Though the planes of his face are taut, the corners of his mouth keep dipping, and his throat, bobbing. Could the great Lucin general be nervous? I want to think that he is, that he senses that my second order of business will be to kill him. Unless he, too, made himself Shabbin-proof?

I wouldn't put it past the plotting male, who's a most cunning man—a phoenix risen from a watery grave. No, a phoenix is too grand for the brute who mutilated his own daughter. Justus Rossi is a plague, an infectious disease that rots everything he touches.

My eyes are drawn back to his palm, and I suddenly wonder if the two interlocked rings of ink could be some sort of Shabbin sigil—a shield of sorts. If I were Justus, I would've stocked up on magical shields, what with being in the company of a very vengeful woman about to have power at her fingertips.

CHAPTER 6

When I reach the opening of the vault, I stop. Yes, Dante insisted on entering the giant safe with me, but what if it's a trap? What if Meriam doesn't plan on unbinding my powers? What if she plans on killing me? After all, with my mother gone, I'm the only Shabbin left in Luce. The only person with the ability to awaken the Crows.

I squint into the obscurity, spotting the gleam of eyes. I back up a step, smacking into a large body. I twist my neck to find Dante looming over me, gaze riveted on the sight beyond me.

"I—I . . ." I lick my lips. "I don't like tight spaces." I try to back up, but Dante blocks my backpedaling.

"The vault is tremendously roomy, I assure you." Justus sounds as though he's speaking from the other end of the tunnel we've just traveled. "My mother has been stockpiling her riches from a very young age and separates from nothing, neither for profit nor for charity."

My attention leaps to Justus, who's staring into the rectangular room, and I freeze for a whole other reason now. "Your mother?"

"Xema Rossi."

Xema Rossi lives in Tarespagia, which means—

Which means—

Oh. My. Gods! Eponine didn't mislead me. Lore was wrong. She didn't lie!

My epiphany is so momentous that it ratchets up my pulse. The general's gaze travels back to my face. Settles. Does he see that I just connected the dots thanks to his slipup? Does he care?

"Why can't we meet out here?" I gesture around what appears to be a dungeon.

"Because my wife sits inside and cannot come to you."

His wife . . . My pulse stutters at the title. In truth, Justus and Meriam are incredibly well-suited for one another, both of them crafty and ill-intentioned. "How in the world did you get her to marry you?"

Justus smiles, but it's an ugly smile. "Simple. I proposed marriage or death. She preferred marriage."

No shit, you psychopath. "How romantic. Is that how you got Nonna to marry your crazy ass?" My eyes widen as I realize I've just called one of my jailers an ass, and a crazy one at that. Granted, he is, but *merda* . . . What if he, too, takes out his bruised ego on Antoni?

I scramble to think of something that could placate his temper before it can erupt, but I come up short.

"Blood of my blood, fruit of my daughter's womb . . ." The eerie dulcet pitch shears through the stifling tension, snapping my eyes back to the vault. "Come forth so I may finally lay eyes upon you."

Meriam is real. She's really real.

"What did the witch say, Justus?" Dante's rough timbre smacks the rounded shell of my ear.

I frown, because not only did she *not* whisper her unnerving summons, but also, Justus is standing just as far away as we are. Is the Nebban compound affecting more than Dante's stomach juices?

"I've yet to master Shabbin, Maezza, but I believe she said something about blood."

Fucking . . . *what*?! Goosebumps scatter over every millimeter of my body, surely giving my skin the aspect of serpent scales.

"Speak in Lucin, strega!" Dante inflects the word witch with great disgust.

A heartbeat later, the voice rises again from the pit of darkness. "Very well. Child of Shabbe and of the Sky Kingdom, grandson of

Costa Regio, come forth so I may bind your bloods and break Fallon's curse."

When I don't move, Dante shoves me, sending me stumbling forward. Under normal circumstances, I would've snarled at him, but the present circumstances are not normal.

I fucking speak Shabbin!

Well, I understand it, at least. I don't think I speak it. Unless I do? Sybille and Phoebus have told me I mutter many unintelligible things in slumber. What if I sleep-talk Shabbin? What if I dream in Shabbin?

Understanding a foreign tongue feels like a supernatural prowess. To think Meriam has yet to unleash the true magic in my blood.

"Fallon, darling, come to me."

I should probably be irked that the imprisoned sorceress has called me darling, but what arrests me is her phonation of my first name. The double 'L's roll off her tongue like a bolt of silk, overshadowing the last syllable, which she pronounces *an* instead of *on*.

"Is Abi the royal family's surname, Rossi?" Dante's gruff murmur slaps my thrumming eardrums.

Abi? When did she— Oh, is that one of the words she uttered? Oddly enough, it doesn't automatically translate into my mind when Dante says it. Perhaps because of his accent? Unless I only understand Shabbin when Meriam speaks it?

I suppose that would be peculiar, but any more peculiar than people who can transform into birds? That's a resounding no.

"In Shabbe, children wear the names of their mothers after their own, so Fallon would be Fallon amZendaya." The rope of Justus's burnt-orange hair sticks to the navy velvet that espouses the strong lines of his four-century-old body. "Abi means darling."

My heartbeats coil around my ribs and lash my skin like a serpent caught in a fisherman's net.

"Are you not eager to taste your true potential, Little Queen?" Meriam whispers from the darkness.

I'm about to tell her that I will not be going through with the marriage Dante has planned for us, but I'm thankfully stopped from planting my foot in my gullet by Justus's grumbled, "What did Dante say about speaking in Shabbin, Meriam?"

He sounds like ancient Headmistress Alice when Sybille and I would return from playtime, clothes splashed with grass stains in the spring and mud in the winter.

I lick my lips. "What did she say?" I pray the rising color in my cheeks doesn't give away the fact that I understood her just fine.

Is she aware? She must be if she insists on using the foreign tongue. Will she tell the others or will she keep it our secret? What am I going on about? Why in the world would this woman want to share a secret with me?

Silence laps at the room. "Forgive me, Maezza. I forget Costa had all the Shabbin books burned the day he tossed me inside his dungeon instead of his bed."

Meriam's admission makes me loathe the first Lucin king a whole lot more, and not because of the dungeon part—that was entirely deserved—but because he destroyed a foreign culture to rewrite history the way he saw fit.

"We should proceed to the wedding and unbinding ceremonies while the moon is at its brightest." Justus flicks his ponytail over his shoulder.

How do they all know how bright the moon is? Is there a window somewhere in this dungeon? Wouldn't that be counterintuitive?

"Light the vault!" Justus commands a fire-Fae.

An amber-eyed male approaches almost reticently, his Adam's apple rolling in his throat as he gloves his hand in fire. Without penetrating any farther, he streams his flames toward the far wall, igniting a recessed arc. The flames catch and spread, scampering up dozens of channels, forming lines of varied length that drench the solid black vault in light. I'm so blinded by the glowing Lucin sun crest that it takes my eyes a moment to adjust.

And when they do . . .

Although the room sparkles with hoarded riches, the only thing I see is the woman seated in a gold throne, one hand resting on her lap, the other, on her armrest. Justus mentioned our family likeness, but I'm not prepared for how much she resembles the mother I will never meet.

The cruelest sorceress to have ever lived not only studies me right back, but her bow-shaped mouth curves into a smile that seems cut into her unlined face with a dagger. "Hello, Fallon, darling."

CHAPTER 7

I stand frozen at the entrance of the vault. Even the air in my lungs feels like it's turned solid.

"Inside. Now." Dante's hand connects with my spine, jolting me out of my stupor and propelling me through the narrow entrance.

The man really needs to stop bossing me around. Unwilling to look away from Meriam, I don't ferry a glare his way, but oh, do I grit my teeth and plot how I will push him around once armed with magical blood.

Meriam's pink gaze strokes over my hair that's the same deep auburn as hers, even though mine hits just below my shoulders and hers spills down to her waist like my mother's. "She will need to come nearer, Maezza."

I plant my feet wide. "Are you so lazy that you cannot even stand to greet your darling granddaughter, Meriam?"

My snide remark is met with a quiet, "They've not told you of my predicament?"

I frown.

Dante leers at the seated woman. "Your grandmother is trapped to the throne she desired so dearly."

"What do you mean, *trapped?*" Though smaller than Marco's in Isolacuori, her throne is a perfect replica to the sunray throne.

"She's become one with it." Justus flattens his palm on the small of my back. "Careful what you ask the Cauldron for, little Fallon, for the Cauldron grants every wish, and sometimes in the most terrible ways."

I'm in such shock, that when Justus applies pressure to the base of my spine, I skate right across the buffed obsidian, almost ending up in Meriam's lap. The second his hand falls from my body, I lurch back, but I don't get far because the general has anticipated my retreat and planted himself behind me.

"She will not harm you," he murmurs.

"Not harm me?" I snort. "That woman killed her own daughter. What's stopping her from ending *my* life?"

Meriam dips her chin, which is as pointed as my own. Why must we resemble each other so? Why couldn't I have taken more after my Crow father? "Why would I harm my curse-breaker?"

"*Your* curse-breaker?"

"Yes. Mine." She tilts her head, and the auburn mass shifts, revealing her right arm. When she sees me glance at it, she hooks her hair with her opposite hand and presses her cascade of curls farther back to offer me an unobstructed view of her misfortune. "Who else has been cursed by the Cauldron?"

The Crows. I smother the answer. Frankly, it's best that no one makes the connection or they may reconsider keeping me alive.

Dante pulses out an impatient breath. "She cannot harm you, Fal, because your lives are bound."

My heartbeats become suspended, and a dull buzzing nips at my eardrums. "What do you mean by bound?"

"My cunning daughter's last spell was binding our two lives so that if you suffer, I suffer. If you die, I die. Did you not feel how the earth shuddered when you were shot with a poisoned arrow, because Justus felt it, didn't you, husband?"

"I—I . . ." I try to remember, but the night became fuzzy after Lore sliced off the wildling's hands. "If Zendaya's dead, why are we still connected?" I draw my gaze over the golden folds of her dress that drape across her motionless form as though cast from actual metal.

"Because Zendaya used *your* blood to bind us. Technically, you magicked me."

"I was still inside her womb. Or was I already inside Mamm—

Agrippina's womb?" Whatever. "The point is, I was a blob afloat in a sack of fluid inside someone's abdomen. How the underworld did she manage to coax blood from my veins?"

"When babes are connected to our bodies, our bloods are mixed. Zendaya sliced her finger and drew the sigil over her stomach before she exiled you from her loins . . . before I could null the magic in both your veins."

Not only do the fine hairs along my arms rise but my eyes also fill with rage, because I can picture the altercation that ended my mother's life in too-vivid detail. "Is that why you murdered your own daughter? Because she tied our lives together?"

"People have killed for less." The fingers of the hand not soldered to her lap curl around her armrest. "Why so surprised?"

How much rot lies beneath this woman's skin? Instead of turning her into gold, the Cauldron should've turned her into refuse. It should've decayed her skin and gangrened her organs.

I almost wish the poison which had coursed through my body had stopped my heart so it could've stopped hers in turn. I suck in a breath as the realization that I possess the power to bring down the wards unfurls through my soul. The Crows would be saved. The Shabbins would be free. What's one life when so many are at stake?

I swallow as Lore's face brightens the backs of my lids, then swallow again as I remember him telling me that he'd rather live a thousand years without a throne than a day without me. The memory defuses my desire to end the Shabbins' and Crows' plight. If I cannot find another way, then perhaps I'll entertain the idea anew, but I'm too selfish to terminate my life.

Dante blows air out the corner of his mouth. "Bloody cut her magic loose, strega, and pronounce us man and wife."

My nostrils flare. "I'm not getting—"

"Chop off the sailor's tongue, and do it with an iron blade!" Dante yells.

"NO!" Perspiration beads along my upper lip. I lick it away. "Don't touch him. I'll cooperate."

He shoves me toward Meriam. "Unbind her."

"First, the betrothal spell, Maezza, for the unbinding will rid me of much blood and energy."

"Don't you have to unbind me while the moon is full?" I say this so quickly that the words blur into each other. "Best to start with that one."

Meriam observes me with those odd-hued eyes of hers before shifting them to Justus. Even though she does not speak to him out loud, I sense they're communicating silently. Can they? Santo Caldrone, what if I end up with Dante's voice in my mind? What if it replaces Lore's?

"I strongly suggest we begin with the blood-binding, Maezza. It'll take but a minute."

"Will it even work if her magic hasn't been triggered?" Dante regards Meriam from under sloped eyebrows.

"Her blood is still Shabbin, Your Majesty."

"Fine. Let's get it out of the way."

She nods. "You'll have to step nearer as well, for I will need to draw the spell on both your hands."

Dante's stance stiffens. For all his desire to make me his, he seems mighty chary of getting too close to the sorceress.

As he stares at Meriam's thin fingers that will soon redden with magic, I rack my brain for a way out of this undesirable marriage. The only one I can think of is to faint. Not ideal, but I remember Phoebus going down like a sack of potatoes the first time Sybille had her monthlies and it had stained the back of her dress. He thought she was on the verge of expiring from some iron-inflicted wound to her nether regions. His eyes had rolled skyward and his body had gone as limp as an overcooked noodle.

Though I'm not looking forward to a concussion, I go through with it, adding a breathy, "I'm feeling unwell."

After I hit the ground, I play dead.

"Get up, Fal."

Nope. Never. When the noxious scent of rotted teeth fans across my face, I play extra dead.

"Can Meriam perform the rites if Fallon is unconscious?"

Anger jolts through me, jamming my molars and driving an angry flush across my collarbone.

"Yes," Meriam says.

Well, screw a shrew. Not only will I be married off to a psychopath with a crown fetish and halitosis, but my new lump on my banged-up head was for naught.

Hands creep beneath my shoulders but are replaced by another set—ones with shorter, callused fingers. "I'll hold her up, Maezza. You will need your hands unencumbered." Of course Justus Rossi is the one to come to my rescue. After all, he's so very excited to marry me off to his king.

I'm tempted to keep the ragdoll act up a while longer, if only to save my eyes the pain of staring at Dante as he steals another precious liberty from me, but my lids slam up.

"Ah. Feeling better, moya?"

"No," I bite out.

Leering like the barmy fool he's become, he asks, "Ready to become mine, Serpent-charmer?"

I tilt my head, and although Nonna taught me not to provoke purelings, I cannot help but hiss, "I'll never be yours."

"Let me rephrase myself." Dante's blue eyes flash with hostility. "Are you ready for your *blood* to become mine?"

"My blood's useless, so whatever floats your gondola."

A nerve agitates the skin beside his temple as he turns his attention back toward Meriam. "Proceed, *strega*."

"Slash your palm and Fallon's, then join hands so blood can meet blood."

Dante makes quick work of cutting the inside of his hand before bringing the bloodied blade toward me. I ball my fingers into fists and stick them behind my back.

"Your palm."

I shake my head.

Dante seizes my arm and all but pops my shoulder out of its socket as he pulls my hand toward him. "Don't make me break your fingers. Or Antoni's."

A weak gasp springs up my throat, and I uncurl my fingers. His blade races across my skin. Like the wake behind a ship, my flesh splits apart and oozes a line of blood no wider than the seam of winter tights.

Just before Dante shoves his sword back into its scabbard, Meriam nods to her index finger. "Please prick my skin, Your Majesty."

The Faerie scrutinizes her extended finger as though he expects her to trick him.

I pray that she will.

CHAPTER 8

Dante lifts his sword point toward her, his knuckles straining over the hilt of his weapon as though to keep her from seizing it. But Meriam doesn't attempt to steal his sword. She merely presses her finger to the sharp tip until blood bubbles.

The tears pooling behind my lids trip out. *I hate you, Bronwen. I hate you so fucking much. I hope Lore eviscerates you.*

"Now join hands and step nearer." Meriam tilts her head toward the hand resting on her throne's armrest, and her auburn mane swishes over her jagged shoulder. In spite of its length, the Shabbin resembles a human beggar in dire need of a wash and fattening fare.

"This is a trick!" I sputter as Dante takes my hand.

A groove forms between his brows. "Rossi?"

"It's no trick, sire. I'd swear a bargain, but it wouldn't be of much use."

In some corner of my distressed mind, I ponder what he's just said. What does he mean, it wouldn't be of much use?

"Lastra, feed the general salt," Dante commands.

"I can feed myself salt." Justus roots around his jacket pocket for the gold snuffbox he'd tendered my way the day I was brought to Isolacuori for my hearing. The rubies embedded on the lid sparkle as he thumbs it open and pinches out a few flakes.

Once Justus has swallowed them, Dante asks, "Is this a trick, Rossi?"

I stare at Dante's hardened face—a face I know all at once too well and not at all. So many questions blister my tongue, the first being: *How long have you been plotting to use me?*

"This is no trick, Maezza. You will walk out of this vault bound to my granddaughter like I am bound to Meriam."

I start shouting bloody murder, praying my voice will carry through the stone and reach a Good Samaritan's ear. Perhaps one of the Rossi servants . . .

The general sidles against my back and clamps his palm against my mouth. "Don't interrupt, Fallon."

As he shoves me toward Meriam, I yell, "Doodoo it!" I pray she understands I'm trying to say *don't*. Oh Gods, what if she thinks I'm encouraging her? I try to yank my hand away from Dante's, but though my skin is clammy and slick with blood, I'm no match to his strength. "Aw bug you, Meeyam, doont go froo—"

"For fuck's sake, Rossi," Dante growls. "Control your granddaughter."

Goosebumps erupt all over my skin and sink straight into my marrow when Meriam brings her bleeding fingertip to the edge of my pinky.

"Pleeef," I croak against Justus's palm. "No."

The jolt of power that radiates from me shocks my lungs, and I suck in a bladed breath that makes my chest ache.

Chanting Shabbin words about unity and power, she draws her finger over the hills and valleys of my knuckles before curving it around Dante's hands.

I shake. With horror. With despair. With rage.

I think of Lore, of how all I'm feeling will surely pale in comparison to what he'll feel once he learns his mate was married to another male. He'll rip out Dante's heart.

Justus bands his free arm around my waist, keeping me upright and steady, forcing me to endure the unpleasant tingle of his new wife's life essence on my skin and the sharp burn of where my gash connects to Dante's.

Meriam keeps murmuring her incantation, keeps ribboning blood around both our hands. I try one last, desperate time to pull away, but between my grandfather's restraint and Dante's unwavering grip, my attempt is futile.

I don't understand why she's going through with this. Will it somehow release her from her throne?

She swirls her pointer finger through the lines she's drawn, linking them all, and although I've never seen this spell performed, I know when it's done. And not because her blood sinks into my pores and vanishes, but because I feel this . . . this . . . tingle race across my palm, sealing my fate.

My lungs compress, like I'm holding my breath underwater when what I'm holding in is a scream. With a frantic tug, I finally break free of Dante.

The Faerie King lifts his hand and twirls it in front of his face, eyes wide with awe while mine are wide with shock, and then with despair at the sight of the interlocked rings tattooed beneath the smear of our mixed bloods. I flip my hand over, and sure enough, the same dark circles blemish my skin.

Anger slickens my lash line, hotter than my new brand, wetter than the salted dribbles of my tears. A ring, I could've gotten rid of, but a tattoo . . . Until I murder Dante, I will have the reminder of our connection inscribed on my skin.

On the upside—because yes, I always thrive to find upsides—I now understand the meaning of Justus's tattoo, and it's not a shield. That man cannot fathom the pain he's in for. I will tear him to ribbons with my magic and then stomp on them.

"Is it done?" Dante breathes out.

"Yes." Meriam's voice jolts me out of my disturbing thoughts. "Now step back so I may attempt to unbind my granddaughter."

"Attempt?" Dante lowers his marked hand.

"We've already discussed this, Maezza. Without Lorcan present, if her Shabbin side is too tangled with her Crow side, there are chances I will not manage to pick apart my spell."

"And I've already told you that including Ríhbiadh is not a possibility."

Meriam suggested working with Lorcan to unravel my magic? Doesn't she realize he'd kill her before she could even slit her finger?

Oh, Gods. I need to warn him that he cannot kill her, because killing her will kill me.

CHAPTER 9

As Dante backs up, I try to regulate my breathing, but it's no use. My heart pounds too fast, contracting my every muscle.

"Untie the lace at your neck." Meriam's voice draws my gaze back to hers. "I need to have access to your heart."

Chills rake down my spine, pinning my boots to the vault's obsidian floor. I want magic, but I also want to live. Giving the witch access to my heart feels dangerous.

What if she stops it?

What if her spiel about our lives being bound is all one great lie?

What if—

A hand grips the ties at my neck and yanks. I track the brown fingers to the white sleeve of the jacket Dante wears beneath the gold armor, then farther up, to the rigid jaw and frigid eyes.

"Don't touch me," I snarl.

Dante flings me a glare. "Then fucking react, moya."

I grind my molars.

Meriam holds her fingers up and waits for me to willingly take the single step that'll, once again, put me within her reach. "I know you fear me, Fallon, but you need to trust me."

I snort.

"This'll be my last warning, *strega*. You speak once more in Shabbin, and I will cut off your tongue."

Merda. I go as quiet as a temple mouse, praying that Dante didn't catch the sound I made. The one that screams: *The Serpent-charmer is fluent in Shabbin*! I rub at my collarbone and glance at Dante, who's wholly focused on Meriam.

My relief at his obliviousness wanes when I roll my eyes as far to the side as they can go and catch the general hiking up one of his tawny eyebrows. Cheeks flaring, I whip my attention back to Meriam.

"Forgive me." She holds her palm aloft, and only then do I notice that she, too, sports the horrid tattoo. "I get mixed up between Lucin and Shabbin. Both tongues sound the same inside my head." She fans out her raised fingers as though to stretch them.

The blazing Lucin crest at her back ricochets across their tips that gleam as though coated in oil. I assume she's spread her blood across all five of her fingers, but a squint reveals the shiny patches are blisters. Probably the result of years of pricking. Is that what awaits me? New calluses? Here I was, so very thrilled to have shed my old ones.

"I was explaining to Fallon why I need access to her heart."

I peer around me this time, waiting for Dante's reaction, waiting to ascertain the language in which she spoke.

"Take off your blouse, moya." He nods to the fabric crusted in dirt and maroon droplets.

I bare my teeth, loathing the new title he's forced upon me almost as much as I loathe him.

When I don't attempt to pull it off my head, he heaves out his black sword, snags the keyhole neckline, and draws his blade down, ripping open my shirt, and gashing the brassiere beneath. Thankfully, it doesn't tear off, but that does little to dull the new wave of wrath spiking my pulse.

"What the underworld is wrong with you?" I hiss, fisting the frayed edges of my shirt to keep it from revealing all.

Meriam crooks her finger toward me.

When I don't go to her, Justus hefts me so that my feet no longer touch the ground and moves my body nearer to his wife who gently tugs on the eaves of my shredded blouse.

"The spell must be spoken in Shabbin. No one should interrupt me once I begin chanting or they will taint the magic." Meriam looks at Dante as she says this, clearly meaning him.

He works his jaw from side to side, and it clicks like an anchor chain. "Fine. Proceed. Justus, try to keep track of all she says."

"Fallon, I know you despise me but the blood-bind was necessary. I swear I will explain all, but first let me give you the gift I've kept from you for twenty-two years."

I glower at her.

"You will need your magic to break out of here."

My reluctance to trust her is so potent it jostles the rhythm of my heart.

"Don't you want to see your mate again?"

I want that more than I want my magic.

"Trust me, my darling."

Trust the witch who just bound me to a demented Faerie? I resist the urge to say *I think not* out loud, fearing it may come out in Shabbin. Nevertheless, I'm aware that to escape . . . to survive, I will need magic since I've stopped believing in miracles many moons ago. So I finally let go of my shirt, offering Meriam's bloodied fingertips access to my heart.

She better not stop it.

The instant the tip of her index finger meets my flesh, a jolt a thousand times stronger than the one I felt during the blood-bind hits my heart, which seizes and hardens.

And hardens.

No beat vibrates my skin.

As the gold surrounding me dulls and the glow of Faerie fire darkens, a thought whispers across my skull: she may not have tricked Dante, but she tricked me.

You dumb, dumb girl.

My mate's face brightens my lids, and even though he cannot hear me, I murmur into the void stretching between us, ***Forgive me, my love.***

CHAPTER 10

The muscle in my chest holds so still that I think, *this is it, my very last moment on this godsforsaken earth.*

I hate that Meriam is the last face I'll see.

I hate that Justus is the last man I'll feel.

I hate that Dante will bear witness to my death.

At least he won't have my magic. Oh, the irony that even on my death bed, I manage to locate a silver lining. Me and my fucking optimism. Perhaps if I'd been acutely pessimistic, I would've survived longer.

In my next life—if there is such a thing as reincarnation—I will be cynical and negative to a fault. And I will not fucking trust anyone. And I will say *fuck* a lot.

I can hear my mate *tsk*. He so hates when I swear.

Oh, Lore. Since I've yet to lose consciousness, I speak to him some more through our inexistent bond. I tell him not to go and play hero. I'm not worth avenging. ***However, make sure to murder Bronwen and Meriam.*** **And** ***Justus. Just don't murder Dante in case there's some truth to Bronwen's prophecy.***

There probably isn't.

She probably just said all she said so Lore didn't risk his skin while she devised a ploy to send me down into the bowels of the earth for my slaughtering.

You got your wish, you old crone. Now die.

I wait to see my life flash before my eyes, but the only thing that flashes is the pink in Meriam's irises as her pupils tighten before distending like the tide. How is the sight of her eyes still so crisp? I frown because, although my mind is a dark place—pitch-black, really—the vault is all golden again. And twinkling.

Bu-bump.

I drop my chin into my neck and stare at the palpitating skin Meriam uses as her canvas. When did my heart resume beating?

Under her breath, she begins to hum, then adds soft words to her hum. I think it's part of the spell until she murmurs, "Fallon, listen to me. Listen, but do not react to anything I share with you so the others aren't aware that what I spill into your ears is no spell."

I blink.

Her lashes are so low that they fan across her high cheekbones, black and thick like crow wings. "I will free your Shabbin magic, but we'll pretend that I failed. Swallow once if you understand."

My *not*-deadened pulse strikes my neck with such force that it takes me precious seconds to get my throat to dip.

"I've much to tell and will start with your mother. She isn't dead. I saved her, but it's of the utmost importance that everyone around us keeps believing that she's gone."

My heart holds still, before firing bangs as loud as the cannons Marco used on Lore that fateful day in the south.

"Understood?"

I swallow.

"Although I never married the man with whom I created your mother, I was married once before. To the first Faerie King. I cannot speak his name or the others may catch on, so I will refer to him as C."

I feel her sketch loops of blood across my collarbone.

"My mother was furious, but your mate"—when she reaches the point of my shoulder, she slashes her finger through the coils, spearing them onto a straight line—"he was glad for me."

The bloodied curlicues must penetrate, because the skin beneath them burns as though she's painting with fire. But the rest of me . . . the rest of me is ice.

"In case you weren't aware, he and C. were close. Your mate considered C. family, an uncle of sorts."

Not that I ever considered Lore an open book, but Meriam is making me realize that the man I'm magically bound to is a complete tomb, one I will need to pry open once I return to him. The thought that I may be able to go home to him this very night spikes my already frenzied pulse.

Before the sun rises, I'll possess magic.

Magic I can use to slip out of this prison.

"I imagine he's told you that I helped C. with his coup?" Meriam's satin-smooth voice snaps my mind back to the here and now. "But the only hand I had in overthrowing the shifters was letting the effect of obsidian slip."

"Like you let slip the use of Shabbin blood *on* obsidian?" The dig slips out before I even realize that I've produced sound.

Her eyes go wide; mine, wider.

Merda.

Without turning my head, I shift my eyeballs to the left, finding Dante's blue gaze cemented to the scarlet drips on my chest. A relieved exhale balloons my lungs but snags on its way out because Justus's grip on me has grown snugger. Dante may have missed my question, but Justus hasn't. *Focá.*

"What did I say about speaking, Fallon? You mustn't. Unless you don't care to receive your magic and hear the end of my tale?"

I press my lips together, adequately chastised by her rhetorical question.

"I should never have told C. of their obsidian curse, but I was young and blinded by love; drunk on the dulcet falsehoods he poured into my ears. I didn't see that he was using me for my blood. I didn't understand that his love was tainted by greed. My mother did, though. She threatened to come to Luce to sever my union. C. suggested that I create the wards to keep her from interfering with our lives, and, silly girl that I was, I heeded his suggestion, painting a barrier between my homeland and Luce."

Meriam studies her motionless thighs cloaked in gold, her punishment for betraying her people.

"After C. passed, J.'s father became my jailer. He was a cruel man, much like his wife. It was only after he left this world that J.'s mother had me carried from this vault to the dungeon in Isolacuori. She wanted me gone. A. appointed J. as my keeper. He'd bring me food and drink, though my cursed body required none. One particularly harsh winter, he brought me a wool blanket."

Her eyes soften as they set on the male at my back. She cannot possibly like the man, can she?

"Don't get me wrong, the man loathed me and all I represented, but he feared Shabbins and worried that if I perished from a common cold, my wards would perish along with me." She sighs. "For decades, we coexisted, both mistrusting of the other. Once, A. sought me out to have a spell cast. I pretended that my curse had rid me of magic. J. saw through my lie, but he didn't call me out on it. Thankfully, A. had had such a terrible relationship with his father that he'd never learned to shape our symbols or he may have forced my hand. Or tried his own hand."

She adds another swirl, another line. Her blood dribbles into my brassiere, staining the silken fabric. Perhaps because I'm in too much shock, or perhaps because my body recognizes her blood for what it is—magic instead of gore—my stomach doesn't lurch.

"Many times, I attempted to end my life, but living was my punishment. I began to think that only once my entire body had turned to gold would the Cauldron allow me to pass on to the next realm, so I willed my transformation to be swifter. That night, I dreamed of the Great Cauldron. I dreamed it was telling me that as long as a Regio lived, my curse would endure.

"The following day, Fate dropped M. into my lap. Or rather, into my dungeon. The boy asked many questions, most about his grandfather, whom he'd adulated, as opposed to his father, whom he found lacking. Though he didn't outright speak about unseating him, I understood that he desperately wanted the throne. So I gave it to him by revealing the location of the ward stone. I told him that whoever possessed that stone possessed all the power."

Though her irises don't whiten, they glaze over like Bronwen's when the Shabbins take ahold of her sight. In Meriam's case, I believe she's wandered into the past, reliving this memory.

"Desperate as he was, he accepted my bargain and had me carried to the lowest level of Isolacuori. Though it bore no markings, I found the stone. How could I forget the second greatest mistake I ever made? I instructed him to pry it from the wall, and hungry as he was for power, he did. He carved it right out, and the earth shook. The tremor was so strong that the stone slipped from his hands and broke. How I rejoiced, Fallon. I thought my wards were finally gone."

Her eyes take on a faraway gleam, as though she was back in the bedrock of Isolacuori with Marco Regio.

"M. tried to annul our bargain, claiming that the stone broke. But he'd dropped it, so I had no problem calling it in. Anyways, my demand that he murder his father aligned with his ambition, so it suited him just fine."

I suck in a harsh breath that suctions Justus's still-clamped palm to my lips.

"M. abandoned me in the dank substratum of Isolacuori. Since I was stuck in my throne, he worried not about me escaping. I was near enough to a wall that I painted a sigil that allowed me to hear all that was happening in the castle. I found out that my daughter had come and freed your mate, and drawn a sigil to enclose Luce. I found out about her pregnancy and then I found out that A. had fallen." Her elegant throat bobs with a swallow. "I imagined the gold melting and pooling at my feet now that the last Regio was gone."

My brow puckers in confusion, because Marco was a Regio.

"I imagined myself rising from this loathed throne and treading freely over stone and water. Sailing to Shabbe and groveling to the Cauldron and to my people, earning their forgiveness. Being pardoned." Emotion thickens her voice until it's no more than a quiet rasp I must strain to decipher. "What delusions I had, Fallon."

No fucking kidding, you crazy witch. I try to step back, but Justus keeps me rooted to the spot.

"I only found out that A. had a blood-heir after M. returned to fetch me, crown glittering on his head and a brash smile gleaming between his lips."

When her gaze settles on the prince I made king, who in turn made me his prisoner, my eyebrows knit. Is she saying that M. was not A.'s true son?

"We do not have all night, Meriam." Justus's voice jerks her gaze back our way.

After holding his stare a beat too long, she lowers her eyes back to the whorls of blood she's painted on my chest. "Please release her and step back, Generali, or you'll hamper the course of my magic." She must read my intent to run because, the second Justus frees me, she says, "If you move out of my reach, Fallon darling, not only will you not get your magic, but you won't learn about your mother. Don't you want to know what became of her?"

What a low blow, Meriam. Of course I want to know what befell Zendaya.

"I heard my guards babble about the unrest in Luce, about your mate's crows falling left and right. I knew that my daughter would seek refuge in Shabbe, but to do so, she had to return to the Holy Temple to remove her ward rune. I struck a new bargain, this time with J."

She dots blood across my collarbone, and I cannot help but wonder if she's doodling or if the sigil is that intricate.

"I revealed where he'd find your mother in exchange for carrying me to the Holy Temple and sitting me amongst those golden idols the Fae revere."

My skin crawls with goosebumps. Here I thought Justus and Dante were evil, but in comparison to Meriam, the two Faeries are choir boys.

"My intent was not to trap my daughter but to help her."

I scoff. Is she truly expecting me to believe that load of serpent shit? The gold must've breached her brain.

"I understand if you don't believe me. After all, I isolated my people, abandoned my daughter, gave magic that wasn't mine to give, and let slip secrets that ended a great king's reign and instigated an ignoble one's."

Her bright-pink eyes, the hue a perfect replica of Minimus's sunlit scales, firm with a resolve that I find more unsettling than heartening.

"I may have been punished for all of it, but so was the rest of the world, and though I deserved my curse, your mate, your mother, your father, the Shabbins—none of them deserved the misery I brought about."

Her speech is so impassioned that it draws a frown to Dante's face.

"Twenty-three years ago, I failed to make everything right. I failed to give my daughter the chance to end me. I'm done failing, Fallon darling, but to succeed, I need you."

Is she asking me to . . . is she asking me to *kill her*? Is there some loophole where if I end her life with magic, it doesn't end mine? Is this why she's freeing my magic? So that I can use it to snuff out her life? I mean, I'm all for her death. It would solve many things.

I hear Dante mutter something to Justus about the time it's taking. I take advantage that his attention is on the general to murmur, "Wouldn't killing you kill me?"

"It would." She smiles, and the curve of her lips is filled with such melancholy, that my heart trips. Did I misinterpret her demands?

Will she kill *me* now?

She drags her thumb across my mouth, painting my lips crimson. "That day in the Holy Temple, the day I'd planned to have my daughter end my life, she took one look at me and cast that spell that tied our lives together. Our *three* lives. So if you kill me, you'll also kill her."

CHAPTER II

My stomach churns and churns until it's as knotted as the ruby design on my thudding chest. Yes, Meriam said my mother was alive, but now I've proof she lives.

I'm so shocked and relieved that I gasp. Or attempt to. My lips don't part. Oh my Gods, did she magick them closed? The godsdamn witch paralyzed me! I bet she's about to start cackling; I'd deserve to be cackled at. After all, I walked right into her web of blood.

But Meriam doesn't cackle; she sighs. "Forgive me, darling, but I'm not done with my tale or with your unbinding."

My lids lift a fraction higher. Goodie. I've not lost control of my entire body.

"My grandmother used to say, *When immortals make plans, the Cauldron laughs*. I finally grasped the meaning of that saying that night in the Temple when your mother bound us. When she realized her mistake, when she realized I wasn't her enemy, it was too late to alter the spell because she'd propelled you into her friend's womb, and your blood was now tied to your Faerie carrier. My stepdaughter now knows the truth. My new husband explained what he could when they met to negotiate the terms of your capture."

Is Meriam saying that Justus is in on . . . on *everything*? My eyeballs strain toward the male, who watches Meriam's finger glide across my skin like a ship on water, before rolling back toward her.

"Everyone in that temple was so certain that your mother had lost her child for her abdomen had flattened and she'd bled profusely. No one but me noticed that she'd slipped you into another's womb."

She closes her eyes, and a tear—an *actual* tear—skips down her pale cheek.

"We were locked up in separate cells. Your mother went mad in that dungeon. Her cries would echo against the stone walls day and night. It was agonizing. I begged J. to allow me to sedate her, but he still didn't entirely trust me and refused to lodge us in the same room. I heard from the other guards that he would hook healing crystals into her ears and change them once their magic wore off. It was a small kindness, but one I never forgot. Just like that woolen throw. Like most Faeries, J. was misguided and misinformed, but deep down, in his heart of hearts, he was a good man."

I snort, and it sounds like I'm gagging on air.

"He stayed loyal to the Faerie Crown because he was worried about being replaced by someone who would terrorize those who weren't pure-blooded and murder them on land instead of tossing them into Mareluce."

Drowning is not a better fate, Meriam.

She smiles. "Your grandfather—"

Not my grandfather.

"—made people walk the plank to give them a chance at a better life in Shabbe."

I cock an eyebrow, and yes, the arc of brown hair over my eye is plenty able to wiggle, unlike my useless lips.

"I may have disclosed that serpents swam every Faerie victim to our shores."

I cannot reconcile the man she's describing with the intimidating general I grew up with. Are we even speaking of the same person?

"That man is the reason your mother survived. The day you were born, Z. sensed it and clawed at her shackles until she'd ripped off her nails, and then she screamed bloody murder until her pleas finally carried over M.'s Yuletide revel to J.'s ears. She'd exhausted herself so deeply that he carried her limp body into my cell."

As though to commit its shape to memory, she traces the sharp outline of my jaw. Though her finger is covered in blood, I'm . . . I'm not disgusted.

"That night, I did the only thing I could think of to end my daughter's suffering." Another tear courses down her cheek. It trips off her chin and beads on her solid gold lap. "To set her free."

What did you do? The question whooshes up my tight throat but is reduced to cinders before it can even smack into my sealed lips. As it glides back down, I choke on the words, and then I choke on my scorching breaths. My chest burns with a fire that leaps from my skin into my veins before penetrating into my lungs, saturating them with what feels like flaming oil.

"Breathe, my darling. The burn will subside. Breathe. They cannot know that it's working." Voice ethereal like the fog that lifts off Mareluce in the winter, she adds, "Breathe, my girl."

Tears pool in the corners of my eyes. I try to tilt my head up, but my neck is locked in place. Like a steel blade fed to a forge, fire ravages my spine, scorching each one of my vertebrae as though to liquefy them for the hammer of pain about to come down. I grit my teeth, forcing back the screech threatening to tear up my throat.

"Steady." Meriam lifts her fingers to my lips and drenches their seam in more blood just as the blow of her power comes. Or is it my power?

Whoever it belongs to, it's vicious and unrelenting, striking my spine from tailbone to skull, propelling a scream up my throat, which bangs noiselessly against the backs of my gritted teeth.

"I can feel it. It's almost done." She dances her bloodied fingertips across my cheeks, smearing the tracks of my agony. "Almost done."

I try to clench my fists but she must've cast a spell over more than my lips because my phalanxes do not bend. When the pyre billowing beneath my skin gloves my heart, more tears spill from my eyes.

I want to plunge into the gulfs of the Glacin sea.

I want to drive a dagger into my skin to release the blistering pressure.

I want to peel away my flesh before Meriam's spell reduces my insides to ash.

I want . . .

The pain stops.

The fire withdraws.

The burn becomes a subtle tingle that galvanizes my blood. I peek down at my bared chest festooned with as many markings as a wildling, expecting my skin to shine, but beneath the eddies of Meriam's blood, I'm wheat-colored, as usual.

How strange to feel so altered yet look so ordinary.

"I will release you from your paralysis now." Her speech slows. "Remember to act . . . as though my unbinding spell . . . has failed." No wonder Meriam is spent. Most of her blood is currently out of her body. "And, Fallon, darling . . . remember to keep loathing me."

Acting magicless should be a cinch. After all, I don't know the first thing about sketching sigils. Acting like I loathe the woman who was used by a vicious man and misunderstood by all others . . . now that will be a feat.

The devil on my shoulder tiptoes nearer to my ear and susurrates: *What if all she fed you were lies? It wouldn't be the first time the gullible girl that you are fell for untruths.*

Though I mentally flick the devil off my shoulder and smother him beneath my boot for good measure, his words linger . . . fester. I will not rush into pinning Meriam to my family tree, but doesn't my fellow convict deserve the benefit of the doubt? After all, wouldn't forging me into a weapon be illogical if she wanted me weak?

A tiny whisper gusts from beneath the sole of my shoe: *What if she's forged you into* her *weapon?*

Instead of flattening my boot some more, I shift on it, allowing the devil to rise back to my shoulder, for I prefer to be guided by the devil I know than the ones surrounding me.

CHAPTER 12

Meriam scrapes her cool thumb across my lips before slashing it through the intricate pattern on my chest. With a shake of her head, she looses an exasperated growl.

"What?" Dante's posture hardens until his shoulders are so square, they jut out at harsh angles from the gold plastron. "What happened?"

Meriam flattens her lips. "We forgot to factor in that it was still summer and that dawn rises early." She lifts a trembling hand to her head and knuckles her perspiration-glossed forehead. "Next month, I will need to start the unraveling the very minute the moon illumines the sky."

As she speaks, the invisible bindings of her magic peel away from my skin. Though she's given me no wings to spread, I feel as though I'm emerging from a cocoon, equipped to soar.

"*We*?" Dante's eyes bulge. "Do not place the blame on me, strega! If we're confined underground an extra fortnight, it's because *you* failed." Like a child throwing a tantrum, Dante wallops her gold throne with his sword. The only thing he achieves, besides displaying his high temper, is fracturing his obsidian blade.

A smile worms itself across my mouth, but I banish it before anyone can see it and drop my gaze to the ground. On its way, it hits the crimson whorls, and I shudder. Using the remains of my tattered shirt, I wipe at the gory mess until the fabric is as reddened as the band binding my breasts. My stomach rolls again, and this time, I retch. Nothing but bile bastes my palate, and Gods does it burn.

Another wave of nausea surges through me, and I hinge at the waist, splashing the vault's floor with the measly contents of my stomach. "Can someone—wash away—the blood?"

Although not the only water-Fae in attendance, Justus Rossi is the one to oblige me. He circles my body, glittering palms already held aloft. As he hoses me down, his gaze scrolls over every millimeter of my face. Is he friend or foe? Meriam didn't actually say.

Not that you can trust her, murmurs my trusty devil. I do wonder whether he's aware that the blood he washes off me stoked my magic. As he raises the spray to my face, I shut my eyes and seal my lips, feeling the lingering heat of Meriam's spell stream off me in rivulets.

"Rossi, have the smith who made this ridiculous sword tossed into Filiaserpens and command Tavo to find one capable of fashioning weapons worthy of the fucking Lucin Crown." Dante tosses his crumbled sword at a white marble bust, clipping off the point of the model's ear.

My heart twinges, because the ruined whorl makes me think of Mamma's ear, the one Justus chopped off with an iron blade to punish her for having me out of wedlock. Does he regret it now that he knows that I do not belong to Agrippina Rossi?

"Serpent-charmer, back in your cage!"

My gaze vaults off the broken bust and lands on Dante. If anyone deserves to be locked in a cage, it's him.

"No cage. I'll behave. I s—" I almost speak an oath before remembering that, now that I am unbound, it will adhere to the bargainee's skin.

Dante lets out an ugly laugh. "You? Behave?"

"Maezza, if I may make a suggestion?" Justus's query stops Dante at the vault's door.

Is it foolish of me to pray that Justus will back me up? If he did, though, that would answer the question of his allegiance. How wild would it be if Justus Rossi were working with us instead of against us? Of course, that would beg the question of why, and since when?

"Let the smith live."

So much for hoping Justus Rossi had a conscience . . .

"He's working on a foolproof design that interlocks the obsidian into the iron—"

"Are you calling me a fool, Rossi?" Dante's soft delivery spears the air.

Oh, how the nerves at Justus's temples jump. "Of course not, Maezza."

Dante may have grown unpredictable, but his desire is clear—he wants Luce to himself. What does Justus Rossi long for?

A man whose agenda is unclear makes for a frightening nemesis. My only hope is that Meriam, cunning woman that she clearly is, knows what he's after.

Gods . . . Meriam might be on our side. Who the Cauldron cares about Justus?

I glance back her way, finding her heavy-lidded gaze already on me. Though she does not yawn, she's as pale as the bust Dante damaged with his petulance. I only now realize whose face it represents: Xema Rossi. Not only did the artist manage to capture the ancient Faerie's caustic stare and razor-sharp wrinkles to absolute perfection, but they added a flawless replica of her dead pet parrot—the only animal I've ever loathed—on her shoulder.

Dante snaps, "Fine. Keep the smith alive. But begin training a new one." As Justus nods, he takes me in from tattered shirt to stained suede pants. "Give Fallon a bath and find her something to wear that does not make her resemble a prepubescent Racoccin male."

I sputter. "I'm no babe, Dante! I will gladly bathe but I will not *be* bathed." I grip my shirt and wring out the fabric, picturing Dante's neck.

He lingers in the vault's entrance, his gaze scraping over me once more. "She is not to be left alone for even a second."

"Of course, Maezza."

"One more thing, Rossi. Fetch paper. Plenty of it. I want to use the month ahead to learn every sigil known to Shabbin-kind."

"I shall have vellum and ink stocked immediately."

"No need for ink. I will be using Fallon's blood." With a cruel smile, he whirls and strides out of the vault. "Fresh from the source."

My pulse jumps, battering my skin with unadulterated anger, but then it jumps again, this time in dread. If we're married, he'll know

Meriam's spell worked because he'll be able to use my magic. I glance toward my fellow Shabbin, but her gaze is locked on Justus's. Although they do not speak, something seems to pass between them.

She must sense the weight of my gaze because she murmurs, "Worry not. I will teach him only erroneous symbols."

I side-eye Justus who seems to be fluent in sigils.

"Worried I teach him correct ones?" Justus volleys a scheming smile.

I blink.

At him.

At Meriam.

Oh. My. Gods.

Justus understands Shabbin!

And Meriam . . . she doesn't bat an eyelash.

"Come. Your grandmother needs rest." As Meriam's head finally tips toward her shoulder, Justus strides ahead of me, posture so straight that his long ponytail barely swishes as he marches.

"I will not give that man a milliliter of my blood," I hiss as Meriam's lids close in exhaustion.

Justus halts before rounding on me, stepping so near that, to keep my gaze leveled on his, I must crane my neck. He may not be as tall as Lore or Dante, but Justus Rossi is still imposing.

In a hushed voice, he says, "If you refuse, you'll be signing Antoni's demise. Is that truly what you want?"

My heart thrashes against my ribs. "Of course not."

Louder he says, "Then you will act as Dante's inkwell."

"What game are you playing, Generali?"

"The one where my granddaughter stays Queen of Luce."

"I'm not your—"

"Did you miss the part about Meriam and me tying the knot, Goccolina?"

Nonna's nickname for me sounds revolting on his lips. "Never call me that."

Justus's pupils tighten.

"If you believe that you'll rule Luce through me, then you have another thing coming." When he smiles, I add, "Sorry. Did I say thing? I meant Crow. You have a Crow coming. Come to think of it, two, because my father will want nothing more than to help Lore delimb you."

Justus's smile spreads, crinkling the corners of his crafty eyes. Does he believe his marriage to Meriam will keep my mate and father from goring his ugly heart?

My own heart seizes as the reason for his glee dawns on me. He has access to Shabbin blood and knows how to use it, and not only to draw sigils, but also, to end shifter lives.

"Whisper when speak mother tongue," he murmurs, I'm guessing in Shabbin considering his strong accent.

My lashes sweep high. I'm talking in . . . in . . .

I shake off my shock. Now's not the time to marvel over my newfound skill, but *wow*, it's fucking marvelous.

Under my breath, I murmur, "How do *you* know Shabbin? Is the great and loathsome Xema Rossi secretly part sorceress, and like me, it came to you from thin air?"

"From blood. Mother tongue thrives in blood. As for my talk, Meriam and I spend years together. Someday, I tell you *my* story." He steps toward the vault door.

Loudly, and in Lucin, I ask, "What makes you think I'm interested in the story of a man who culled his own daughter's ears?"

He halts. "Is that what Ceres—" A shadow creeps across the floor, touching the side of Justus's boot. Although it doesn't reach his face, his expression darkens as though it had. "Agrippina is a disgrace to the Rossi name and to Faekind. Just like her mother."

The shadow stills.

Backing up, Justus snaps, "Cato, since you seem to tolerate the Serpent-charmer best, escort her to the bathing chamber before she further infects our tunnels with her carrion stench."

I should probably be taken aback, but my mind is stuck on the words that came out of his mouth right before Cato made his presence known.

Was he about to deny being the one to have cleaved off the tips of Mamma's ears? If that was his intent, if he was for naught, then who hurt my birth mother?

CHAPTER 13

I expect to find Antoni's huddled form upon stepping out of the vault, but the only thing I come upon is a slick puddle of his blood. It sits on the blackened floor, viscous like oil.

My fingers ball into fists. "Where is he?"

"I had him moved." Cato studies the puddle before lowering his lids to block out the sight.

"You had him moved to where?"

He turns his face toward me before raising his lids. "To a room. With a cot."

"Above ground?"

He sighs. "No, Fallon. You know Dante would never allow that."

"Are there many rooms in these tunnels?" I stare down the hallway across from the one that leads to my 'room.'

"Please don't ask me questions. I'm forbidden from giving you information about your whereabouts."

"I already know we're in Tarespagia, under Xema Rossi's estate."

"How . . .?" His mouth widens before flattening anew. "Right. The vault." His gaze moves to the now closed wall of gold bearing the Rossi insignia. "Come. I'll show you to the bathing chamber."

Cato leads me to that tunnel I'd been eyeing. The stone is smooth, with barely a seam in sight, and Cauldron do I look for one because, until I figure out how to draw the sigil to pass through walls, a seam could make the difference between freedom and captivity.

Speaking of sigils . . . "How come Meriam hasn't propelled herself through a wall?"

"She sits near none, but even if she managed to prop her throne against one, she knows that Lorcan Ríhbiadh would kill her the second she emerged from this stronghold. And if she dies, so do you."

"Perhaps someone should inform him that our lives are entwined?" By someone, I mean him.

"Fallon, be realistic. Do you really believe that vulture would give anyone a single breath to explain?"

I bristle at my mate's poor reputation. "Lorcan is a most patient man, Cato."

"You've obviously not watched him behead an entire battalion of men in a matter of minutes."

"And you have?"

Cato's pale face mottles with a blush that's visible even in the faint torchlight. "I—I—should not speak of such things with you."

"You really should."

He drags his hand through his hair, snapping some strands.

"What battalion did my"—I swap the word *mate* for—"*king* decimate?"

"Please, Fallon."

I cross my arms over my bare midriff, just beneath the knot I tied in my ruined shirt. "You cannot tell me Lore murdered a whole bunch of soldiers then leave me hanging. When? Where? And for what reason? Did they attack him? He wouldn't hurt anyone who didn't deserve—" I suck in a breath. "It was the night I was taken, wasn't it? I saw Dante nod before he shut the cavern door."

"Fallon . . ." His gaze jerks right, then left. "Shh. You will get me in trouble."

"For giving me news of happenings up in Luce?"

"Yes. We're not to speak of the war."

"War?" I choke out.

Cato's posture stiffens.

"The war has begun?" My stomach feels as though it's filled with slush. I untangle my arms and reach out for the wall beside me.

"Yes. We tried peace. Ríhbiadh turned us down."

I hate that Cato uses the pronoun *we*. That he would associate himself with Dante's despotic regime. "I'm certain Lore could see reason if I was to be returned to him."

Cato balks. "Why in the world would you want to be returned to that monster?"

Because he's my monster, I think, but Cato wouldn't understand. He's evidently been too brainwashed by Dante, to the point where I'm starting to believe he's down here by choice.

"You're right. Whyever would I prefer to live freely under a king who respects me, when I can live in captivity under a king intent on exploiting me?"

"Dante made you his queen. It's a great honor, and unless I'm mistaken, marrying him was a dream of yours."

"*Was*. Past tense. Then I saw his true colors." I add that last part under my breath, in case another soldier lurks nearby and decides to relate my remark to his ruler. "And the only reason he wanted to marry me was to use my magical blood and piss off Lore."

"You know as well as anyone that royal unions are strategic. The Lucin King seeks an alliance with Shabbe so that when the wards come down, Luce will finally know peace."

I snort at his warped view of the world. "Shabbins already have allies: the Crows. If Dante exterminates them, all Lucins will know is a life of terror."

Cato grinds his molars. I hear the low scrape and click of enamel with the same clarity that I can hear my own heart's furious stampede. "Your grandmother will be so proud once she hears of the union."

"You think Nonna, who fought so hard to emancipate herself from her husband and his family, would feel pride at seeing me unwillingly married to a man who had his own brother murdered?"

His dark eyebrows bend. "Ríhbiadh killed Marco. Not Dante."

"You have your murderers mixed up, Cato."

"Ríhbiadh removed Marco's head and carried it back to the mountain. Thousands of sprites and Faeries witnessed the butchery."

I huff out a sigh of exasperation. My friends may have struck a bargain with Dante about keeping their mouths shut on his involvement, but I'm oath-free. "If I ordered Justus to stick a dagger through your heart and he indulged me, who would you deem the killer?"

"I understand what you're trying to say, Fallon, but Dante didn't ask the Crimson Crow to remove his brother from power. You did."

"I suppose you think Dante wasn't on that mountain? Where did he say he was? In Tarespagia, fucking the little Glacin Princess he was supposed to marry?" How I wish he'd go back to wooing her.

"He told us you may try to convince us that he wanted his brother gone," Cato murmurs.

"Did he? How perspicacious of him. Let me guess, he told you under salt oath."

Cato's gray eyes shift from silver to flint. "I understand you're discontent with your lot, but a smear campaign is beneath you, Fallon."

"Didn't you hear? Nothing is beneath the Crow wench anymore."

He wrinkles his nose. "Don't call yourself that."

"Oh, I didn't; your compatriots came up with that new nickname. As well as Crimson whore and Shabbin bitch."

"Which compatriots?"

"If only I knew, but Dante and Tavo reckoned finding and punishing them of no import, so their identity will remain a mystery a while longer." My heart beats with spite, until I recall Eponine offering Nebban funds to have my little blue Tarecuorin house restored. I hope she's safe. And I hope she's found a better ally than me to help her overthrow her father.

"Your grandfather will return soon with a dress. Unless you want him to be present while you bathe, we should hurry." Cato's voice is low and tight—with frustration or deliberation?

I pray it's the latter. Not only is Cato kind, but he's also smart. Surely, the light I've shed on the events that went down in Monteluce will penetrate his brain and make him realize he's betting on the wrong monarch.

As we start up again, I ask, "What of Eponine?"

"What do you mean?"

"Has she been made aware that her betrothed has wed another?"

"Eponine returned to Nebba with her father after . . ." Cato rubs his lips as though to block any more words from slipping past them.

"After?"

"You can bathe here." He pushes open a door, revealing another obsidian chamber, this one no bigger than the bedrooms at *Bottom of the Jug*.

A copper tub sits in the middle of the space. Beside it, a chamber pot, and beside that, a rack with two neatly folded towels.

"The towels are clean. The water, too." He tries to smile but it doesn't quite grab ahold of his lips. "You can take the soldier out of the barracks but you can't take the barracks out of the soldier."

I lift an eyebrow.

"Hygiene is ingrained in us."

I give him a slow nod. "Too bad it's contained to the barracks. Imagine how the army's sense of cleanliness could help in Rax."

Cato has the decency to sigh. "Once the war ends, you can make that your first order of business as queen."

The mention of this war that is being waged throughout the land sends chills scurrying up my spine. If only my Shabbin glibness hadn't started and stopped with the language. If only I knew the sigil to escape this giant coffin. The next time Justus draws it, I'll observe him like a hawk.

Cato gestures for me to step inside the humid space. "I'll turn my back."

"Meriam failed to awaken my magic. I'm powerless, Cato."

"Did that ever stop you from wreaking havoc on Luce?"

I smile, and for the first time since I woke up in Dante's inferno, it isn't artificial.

"Ceres should really have nicknamed you Havoc instead of Raindrop."

His comment is a punch to the heart.

As my smile wilts, Cato rubs the back of his neck. "How insensitive to bring her up again. You must miss her."

"Dearly," I croak. And I do, even though, in this instant, it isn't thoughts of Nonna that are rousing a maelstrom of emotions; it's the memory of the vision Lore gifted me the day Marco fell.

The day I laid eyes on my biological mother for the very first time.

The day I heard her speak the name Mamma had whispered at my birth and which Nonna adopted, explaining that I'd earned it for my slight stature. But that wasn't the origin of my name. Fallon means Raindrop in Crow, the equivalent of Goccolina.

I swallow around the lump swelling my throat as I recall the carefree morning I spent with my father in North Tavern. That morning feels like ages ago.

Whyever did you name me Raindrop, Dádhi?

He'd smiled, which had softened all the harsh angles of his face. *Your mother—she . . .*

She . . .?

He'd shut his eyes and balled his fingers, and I'd reached over and covered his fist to bring him back to me.

His luminous eyes, made brighter by grief, had opened and set on me. *Your mother was convinced you'd take our world by storm. And you have, haven't you, my little raindrop? She'll be so proud.*

Unlike Lore and me, my father had never lost hope to see her again.

To think he'd get her back soon.

To think Meriam saved her.

And yes, perhaps she'd done so in order to save herself, but the fact remains that my mother's alive. My impatience to meet her takes precedence over every little worry and thought. If only I knew where she was.

Meriam knows. I'm suddenly looking forward to being used as an inkwell because that means I'll be in Meriam's presence. I'm not sure how I'll go about asking if we have an audience, but I'm certain I'll find a way. I'm good at winging things.

I can just picture Phoebus and Sybille rolling their eyes at my conviction. The thought of my friends makes my heart thump with grief. As I untie my soiled shirt, I pray they haven't set a single toe outside the Sky Kingdom.

Cato starts to close the door but stops. "If I step out, do you promise not to try anything?"

I give him a nod, afraid that speaking any words may bind my promise to his skin and reveal my duplicity.

"Because if you did, Havoc, it won't only be Antoni who'll be punished."

Sadly, I've no doubt that loyal Cato would have to pay for my unruliness. "I will not try anything. And is Havoc going to be a thing now?"

A smile tugs at his mouth. "It suits you."

"I wonder what Nonna will think of this new pet name . . ."

His Adam's apple jostles at the mention of the woman he still burns for. "She'll undoubtedly find it fatuous. She finds most things I say fatuous."

"No, she doesn't. Nonna is just . . . older, Cato. She's lived through some horrible things, and it's disillusioned her, but that's just a shell she wears to protect herself." I realize I'm giving Cato dreams that Nonna may squash the minute they're reunited, but isn't it better to live with hope than despair? "You should really sail to Shabbe before she sheds that shell for a Shabbin male."

"Do you honestly think she'd give me the time of day if I left you down here without a friend?"

I'm glad to see that his character remains steadfast and kind, that he hasn't been both brainwashed and heartwashed. "I have Antoni." I have Meriam. And against all odds, I may even have Justus. Of course, I don't list those two other potential allies. "If you can get out of Luce, Cato, go."

Save yourself . . .

"I took an oath to protect the Crown, Fallon."

"A magical oath?"

"Magic isn't everything."

So he truly is here by choice . . .

"Anyway, bathe in peace but don't dawdle. And don't—"

"Try anything. I told you I wouldn't."

And I won't, not without Antoni, and not without knowing where Zendaya of Shabbe is being hidden. Yes, *is being* hidden. If my mother were hiding of her own volition, she would've emerged the second my father was revived for there is no way she could've resisted being with him.

I peel the shirt off my torso, then roll my pants down before doing away with my undergarments. The bath water is cool. If only Cato's element was fire.

As I lower myself into it, thin bar of soap in hand, I contemplate biting the tip of my finger to pry blood. Perhaps if I dripped some into the water, it would heat. What if it affected it some other way, though? What if it turned water into acid? What if I couldn't staunch the blood flow and I cast some catastrophic spell?

With a sigh, I decide against experimenting and make the best of the clean water. After scrubbing my skin and scalp raw, I sink beneath the foam to rinse off. Although the bathing chamber is quiet, there's nothing like the quiet of being underwater. Another Shabbin trait?

My lids flip up as a thought rockets through my mind. Am I immortal now? Well, as immortal as a Shabbin can be?

And then my lashes reel higher because a man stands over my bath, and he's staring down at me.

CHAPTER 14

I cross my arms over my chest and sit up, sputtering. "Couldn't wait to see me?"

Dante shifts his jaw from side to side as though grinding walnuts between his molars, husks and all. "You were not to be left alone."

"You may enjoy having spectators while you bathe, but I don't."

"Get out."

"You first."

He squats, long fingers gripping the edge of the copper tub. "Such a selfish girl. Never thinking of your little sailor. Brambilla, bring me—"

"No." Making sure the door is closed, I shoot to my feet, and although I loathe baring myself to this man almost as much as I loathe taking orders from him, I do as he asks. Since he stands in the way of the towel rack, I tip my head to it. "Will Your Majesty please hand me a towel?" My dulcet tone hardens Dante's already tetchy expression.

He grabs it from the rack, but doesn't lob it at me. He holds it at his side, fingers clenched around the faded gray terrycloth.

I reach out for it, but he pulls his arm back. "Dante, please."

"You're my wife."

I cross my arms over my puckered breasts and scowl. "Not according to Lucin law."

"Since when do you care about Lucin law?"

Since right this moment.

Dante's gaze skates down my naked body. It isn't the first time he's seen me naked, but unlike that day on Barrack Island, his stare feels like a violation. A violation that strengthens my resolve to sink his spurs into the soft tissue of his neck.

"If it's of great import, I'll have Justus find us a priest to—"

"You're right. I don't give a flying fuck about Lucin law." My tone is so clipped that it yanks his gaze back to mine. "The towel, Maezza."

"You've lost a lot of weight. Did Ríhbiadh not feed you?"

I hope my jutting bones repulse him. "May I please have the towel?"

He grows still. Only a nerve along his jaw ticks.

I don't know what game he's playing but I thoroughly dislike it. I'm about to ask for the towel—*again*—when he finally hands it over.

I snatch it from him and wrap it around my body. "Why are you here? Did you forget something?"

"I wanted to invite you to sup with me."

"I'd rather get basted in blood all over again."

Dante's eyes flare.

He raises his hand, I imagine to strangle me, but the door hinges squeak, making his arm freeze in midair.

"Ceres was much too lax in your education." Justus enters, gold taffeta and sparkly tulle draped over one arm. "You'll need to be taught manners."

"Are you volunteering to be my etiquette tutor?"

"Why, yes." He grins, and not with mirth. "It'll give us time to catch up on all those years apart."

I try to read his true intent but I'm not yet familiar with his facial expressions. Does he truly plan on disciplining me, or is his plan to educate me in all things Shabbin?

I shrug. "It'll be your sanity's funeral. But whatevs, Nonno."

"*Whatevs?*" His ruddy eyebrows bend.

"What-eh-ver. It's colloquial speak in Tarelexo."

"You attended the finest school in Luce. A school for which I paid a small fortune."

"Should've invested your money someplace else."

"I see that."

"How about Meriam gives me my etiquette classes? She was—*is*—after all, a princess."

"No," Justus says.

"Why not?"

"She cannot teach you"—he spaces out each syllable as though I were a toddler with an elocution problem—"for not only is she a disgrace to the crown, but she's out of sorts. I'm afraid even your lessons will have to wait, Maezza."

"How long?" Dante asks.

"Several days."

"Days!"

"After she bound Fallon's magic, she was dead to the world for an entire week."

My pulse quickens as our eyes meet and hold.

"A week?" Dante's pitch cleaves my eardrums.

Although relieved Dante will not swirl my blood on vellum, I cannot help but feel a jot of disappointment. If she's out of sorts for a whole week, then how am I to learn my mother's location? Could Justus know? Would he share it with me if he did?

As Justus shakes out the dress on his arm, I say, "I could stay with her. I mean, you want to lock me up anyway. May as well stuff me inside the vault. Way more secure. Plus that way, it'd free up my cage, which could come in handy if you end up with a prisoner of war."

Justus's eyes harden. "Letting you stay in the vault could be perilous. Meriam can be unpredictable when she awakens from one of her absences."

"Her ass is stuck to a throne." I tug hard on the towel, picturing myself collecting all the sticks Justus is tossing in my path and tossing them at his head. "Not to mention that if she kills me, she drops dead."

"She may wake up disoriented and forget that your lives are bound." Frown lines bracket his mouth as though he was sucking on a sour plum. "She may even forget that you're her granddaughter."

My eyebrows slant as I try to read whether he's bluffing or speaking the truth.

"Your bruise has healed," Dante remarks, attention on my hairline.

I pat the skin above my eye, marveling at how the lump I got the night of my kidnapping is, indeed, gone.

He shifts on his boots, which makes both his spurs and the gold beads woven into his hair clink. "How's that possible?"

My fingers freeze along with the air in my lungs, because the only explanation is magic.

"Quite some time has passed, Your Majesty."

"Her skin was still yellowish when I fetched her from the cellar."

"Fine. I confess that I healed her earlier. I imagined you'd appreciate not having to look upon her leprous mien. Especially considering she's the only female around."

Leprous mien? I almost snort, but Justus Rossi has just saved my ass, so I will let the leper comment slide.

"How very thoughtful of you, Generali. A shame that traitor Lazarus did away with all our Lucin remedial beads."

I blink because I clearly remember Lazarus telling me that Dante had refused to lend the Crows Shabbin crystals when I needed succoring after the poisoned arrow.

"I'm working on retrieving them, sire."

"Well, until you succeed"—Dante grips the edge of the gauze wrapped around his hand and begins to unroll it—"I've a wound in need of healing. Would you mind working your magic?"

I side-eye Justus, whose aplomb doesn't waver.

He takes a step toward me and holds out the dress. "I wouldn't want to put blood on your gown."

I take the garment and hold it against my chest, the prickly tulle aggravating my goosebumps. Even though I'd love nothing more than for Dante's wound to fester and become infected, I keep my fingers crossed that Justus actually knows a sigil for healing, otherwise . . . well, otherwise we're toast.

When the bandage drops, revealing the imprint of my teeth on the meat of his thumb, I rumple my nose. Not only does pus ooze from the puncture wounds, but the skin around the depressions is blackened as though I'd injected Dante with venom.

Granted I'd felt venomous, but now I have to wonder, am I?

Unless . . . unless the obsidian in my system caused this damage? What if the chemical Dante has been ingesting to immunize himself to iron and salt has made him allergic to the very stone from which he's built his fortress?

CHAPTER 15

Justus plucks a leather necklace out of his shirt, then uncorks the small vial strung onto the cord and moistens his finger with the viscous substance inside, which I assume is Meriam's blood.

"It may burn," he warns, proceeding to loop blood around each toothmark.

Dante doesn't flinch. He barely seems to breathe as he concentrates on Justus's spell.

"Do you feel anything, Maezza?"

"No."

With a sigh, Justus releases Dante's hand and dips his fingers into the bath before wiping it on a handkerchief embroidered with an 'R'. "I realize you may not want to hear it, but you should lower the dosage of—"

"I've not asked for your opinion now, Rossi, have I?"

Justus keeps wiping his fingers on his monogrammed kerchief, even though I suspect they're dry. "Once Meriam awakens, I'll ask her to heal you."

"No."

"She will not cast a spell, Maezza."

Dante's stern expression speaks volumes on what he thinks of Justus's assurance. I suppose that if I were in his gaudy shoes, I, too, would be distressed by Meriam. She may have gone through with the blood-bind, but what would prevent her from reversing the spell she placed on his bloodline?

Great Cauldron, can that be done? Even though I'm champing at the bit to escape this prison, I realize the preciousness of my proximity to both Meriam and the Faerie King. He may not let her touch him, but he doesn't fear my touch, for he isn't aware I've been activated.

Although my hair drips water down my spine, and the air holds a biting chill, I no longer feel cold. "You fear her touch, yet let her perform the Shabbin blood-binding rites?"

"I don't fear the witch; I distrust her. Like I distrust you." Dante begins to roll his soiled bandage back around his hand but rips it away with a frustrated growl. "Rossi, go find me fresh gauze and a bottle of liquor."

Liquor? Is he in so much pain that he's turned to day drinking?

The corner of the general's eye twitches at having been given such a base job. "May I assign the task to Brambilla so that I can help my granddaughter into her gown? There are many buttons to fasten."

"I may be injured, Rossi, but I'm no gimp."

The general stiffens. "Of course not, but you bleed."

Dante clasps the wrist of his injured hand, cradling it in front of his gold armor. "Then get me a fucking healer!"

"I thought you said no one comes in or out—"

"Well, I've changed my mind! A healer will prove a good addition." Dante's incensed tone booms through the low-ceilinged chamber. "My grandfather's stronghold has enough coops with cots to accommodate ten times the amount of men we've brought with us."

I frown. "Justus is your grandfather?"

"What?"

"You said your grandfather's stronghold . . ."

"I meant Costa."

My eyebrows swoop high. The Rossi estate belonged to Costa Regio? I suppose most Fae have secondary homes, so having a secondary palace shouldn't truly startle me. I wonder when it was paved in Crow-adverse stone? At its inception?

Dante slices the air with his injured hand. "What are you waiting for, Rossi? Get me a fucking healer, now!"

Justus's jaw clenches so hard that I hear his molars click.

"I'll help Fallon dress." Dante tries to steal the puff of gold from my taut arms.

"Perhaps I'm overvaluing my skills, but I do believe I'm capable of strapping my own self into a dress."

"Drop the towel, Fal. Let's get this over with."

Though I swallow hard, I don't manage to displace my swelling anger, merely to grind it into a compact lump that irritates the lining of my throat.

If only I'd agreed to marry Lore the second he'd proposed.

If only I hadn't desired to walk down the aisle surrounded by Nonna and my two mothers. Damn me and my silly romantic aspirations.

I don't even care if Lore wanted to expedite our marriage in order to control my magic. All right, I do care, but just a little, because I've zero doubt that he would've given me back all I brought into our marriage tenfold. After all, Lorcan Ríhbiadh is generous to a fault.

"Why are you still here, Rossi?"

Justus finally unthaws. "Apologies. I've not slept in several days, and I'm afraid that fatigue is catching up with me."

"Perhaps you should go nap alongside your little witch after you return with what I've asked for."

Although I've never considered Justus Rossi a comforting presence, I pray he won't heed Dante's suggestion. I may not particularly like the ancient Fae, but he knows my secret, and for reasons that still elude me, he's keeping it.

"I'll sleep when Fallon sleeps." Casting one last glance my way, he lets himself out. Whether or not intentional, he doesn't quite shut the door.

Dante walks over to it, and for a heartbeat, I think he'll let himself out, but he does not. Instead, he pushes on the blackened wood until it clicks shut.

"Why won't you allow me privacy to dress?"

His eyes trace over my bunched dress. "You're my prisoner. Prisoners don't get privileges."

"A Cauldron-given right isn't a privilege, Dante."

He hitches a single eyebrow.

"It's a very small ask, and frankly, the least you can do after you kidnapped me."

"Spare me the guilt trip. I brought you down here to give you magic and make you Queen of Luce. Neither is harrowing."

Is he fucking kidding me? "I had no desire to become your queen."

Although I want to stand my ground, when he begins to step toward me, I fall back. Too soon, my spine meets the stone. And Dante . . . he keeps advancing, irises aglow with undiluted rage.

When he finally reaches me, he wraps his uninjured hand around my neck, then presses his lips to my ear. "Think of Antoni." His tone is soft, unlike his expression. "Think of what I'll do to him if you keep disrespecting me, Serpent-charmer."

He doesn't press hard, yet I wheeze as though he were crushing my trachea. I hate him. I despise him. I want to draw a noose of blood around his neck, but I know nothing about Shabbin spell-casting.

His rank breath keeps coming hard and fast against my earlobe, accompanying words drowned out by my thundering heartbeats. I don't want to be here. I don't want to endure Dante. I don't want to marry him.

"Let me go," I croak, shoving against him, but his body is like stone, and mine like water.

His grip tightens on my throat, and his body erases every last millimeter of distance that remained between us, imprinting tulle onto my bare skin and disgust onto my heart.

I close my eyes and try to pitch myself out of this obsidian pit, away from this repulsive man. My mind fills with Lore, with his gentle touch, with his sultry voice, with his heady scent. I try to go to him like I've gone to him so many times in the past, but the slabs of obsidian surrounding me curtail the reach of my mind.

My wet lashes reel up, and I pour all the vitriol swirling through my heart into my stare. Dante's eyes narrow and so does the noose of his fingers. He mutters something else to me, but again I don't hear him.

But not because of my pulse this time.

I don't hear him because of the loud chatter surrounding me. I blink as the voices become clearer, then blink again when Dante's face is replaced by that of Cian's and Giana's.

What the—

This cannot be a memory because I've never sat at Adh'Thábhain with the two of them. I glance down and catch sight of hands. Hands that are somehow attached to my body but which aren't mine. I jerk my gaze off the thin brown fingers blemished with pink scars.

"It's done," Bronwen whispers on a rushed inhale. "Meriam's unleashed her. It's done."

Oh my Gods, I'm in Bronwen's mind!

Also, Bronwen's still breathing? Did Lore not find out about her hand in my abduction?

"Get Lorcan." Her rushed words halt my careening questions, and I hold my breath. I'm going to see Lorcan!

Cian and Giana both blink my way—Bronwen's way—before Cian lurches off the bench and morphs into his Crow, probably to make use of the link he shares with Lorcan in this form.

A moment later, he's back in skin. "You're certain Fallon's the one looking, *ah'khar*?"

"*Tà*, Cian." The room wobbles as Bronwen nods.

More Crows in skin crowd around their table. I recognize Colm and Fionn, the mates who protected me, and the tavern owner Connor with his son Reid. And Lazarus! The mammoth Fae healer is also in attendance, worry etched into the wrinkles bracketing his eyes and mouth.

Reid asks something in Crow I don't grasp.

It's Gia who answers, "Bronwen knows because Fallon is using her eyes."

To see her in the Sky Kingdom . . .

To know she's safe . . .

Oh, Gia.

My friend's gray eyes move back to Bronwen's, wide and shiny like silver coins. "Fallon's watching us."

Her words suddenly pitch me back to that day when I'd asked Bronwen if she could tell who'd used her sight, and the ancient seer had said no.

Why, Bronwen? Why did you lie? I ask through whatever link is currently binding us.

If she hears me, she doesn't respond. I'm about to ask more pressing questions, questions about the safety of the people I've come to love, when the huddled shifters part around a thick stream of dark smoke.

Smoke that materializes into the shape of a . . . of a . . .

My pulse becomes a mess of beats, punctuated by such longing to crawl through Bronwen's eyes and into Lorcan's arms.

"Where is she? Ask her where she is?" Lore pounds his fist against the table. A fist made of flesh and bone.

Dante lied!

Gabriele did not strike down one of Lore's crows, for the male before me is magnificent and whole.

"You know the Shabbin link does not work like a mating bond. You know that I cannot hear her, Mórrgaht," Bronwen replies calmly.

"Dante, you're choking her!" My grandfather's elevated voice rips me out of Bronwen's mind and away from Lore.

Gasping, I fight to retrieve the magic that gave me use of Bronwen's eyes, because I want nothing more than to scramble back to my mate through the many unseen layers of this world, but the delicate vision has slipped through my fingers like sand. I clasp my throat that aches more from grief than from Dante's abuse.

Over his shoulder, I catch sight of my grandfather's bulging eyes. I mean, Justus's. The general is not family. Not in the way the people I've just left behind are.

"You must handle her with care, Your Majesty. Fallon's not immortal." Justus barely separates his teeth as he delivers this lie.

It is a lie, right? I am immortal, am I not?

"I wasn't pressing on her larynx hard enough to choke her," Dante grumbles. "Besides, absence of air doesn't whiten irises. Why the Cauldron were her eyes white?"

"Because she was trying to reach out to her mate."

Shock makes everything in my body still.

"Her mate?" Dante spits out the word, making it sound blasphemous.

"Crows have one preordained mate."

"I wasn't born yesterday, Rossi. I bloody know that." Dante's nostrils flare and his irises darken, becoming as inky as Mareluce at twilight. "What I didn't know was that my future bride had one. Who?" His timbre is raucous as though he was the one with the abused airway.

"The Crimson Crow, Maezza."

My body flushes with anger. How could Justus Rossi betray me like this?

Because I told you, Fallon, he isn't your friend, the little devil on my shoulder whispers. I should be alarmed that I'm hearing voices, but since this is the voice of reason, I welcome it.

As I glower at the general, I wonder when he'll betray the other secret he knows about me. When will he inform Dante Regio that my blood holds magic?

CHAPTER 16

For an endless stretch of time, no one speaks. Neither Dante, nor the duplicitous general, nor I. All of us exist quietly, absorbing the secrets we keep from each other.

"How long have you known?" Dante's question shears the thick air.

Since I imagine he's asking Justus, I keep quiet, taking the opportunity to seethe some more.

"I've only just figured it out, Maeẓza. Her mother's eyes whitened the night we ambushed her in the Temple, right before we succeeded in immobilizing her mate."

My eyebrows begin to furrow. I snap them straight before anyone can catch my frown. Is this truly how Justus believes mates communicate with one another or is he covering for me? Why am I so adamant at finding a spark of goodness in Justus? His soul is surely as murky as the Racoccin canals and just as foul.

"I thought obsidian blocked Crow powers."

"Matehood is not a shifter power. But worry not, sire, for obsidian blocks their mind link." Justus's eyes are as cold as chips of ice. "That's how Bronwen managed to separate Fallon from Lorcan to bring her to us." He raises his chin a notch, looking down his nose at me as though to prove himself endowed with superior intelligence. "Right, Fallon?"

"I don't know why you're seeking confirmation, Generali. You're obviously plenty knowledgeable on the inner workings of supernatural powers."

"Even though the walls will mute their connection, would you like me to have some obsidian ground into her food as an added precaution, Maezza?"

Oh, the desire to eat iron is strong in that one . . . I picture myself plunging the ruby-encrusted sword into his neck.

"You chose Lorcan as a mate?" Dante's voice has dropped in volume, yet I don't miss the emotion limning his tone.

"They do not choose—" Justus begins, but I speak over him, "Yes. I chose him. And I will always choose him."

Shadows slither over Dante's already somber expression, blackening his mood. He squeezes his lips together, thinning their fullness, and his throat bobs as he swallows the news Rossi has just fed him.

After another long stretch of silence, he says, "I suppose that explains why the Bird King is said to have gone mad and is being abandoned by his own people."

Although Dante delivers his words without a bleep of hesitation, I was just there, in the Sky Kingdom, with Lorcan's people, and though my vision was contained to the tavern, my mate didn't seem like he was down any loyal shifters.

I tilt my head to the side. "Abandoned, you say?"

"Crows are flocking to Shabbe because they don't trust their leader's judgement." Dante seems only too content to share the news. The same way he was only too glad to inform me that Gabriele had injured my mate.

Since that was a lie, I fathom this avian exodus is, too. "Have any Crows joined your ranks, Dante?"

"Like I'd share this with a woman whose mind is linked to my enemy's." Dante adds a derisive snort that tells me everything I need to know, for only a male caught in a lie would need to put on such a production.

"You know something else you should really not do with a woman whose mind is linked to your enemy's?" I keep my tone sweet. "Force her to marry you." I pause for dramatic effect. "How do you think my mate will react once he learns you took what's his?"

Dante grins, and although his violent temper has scared me in the past, the fear I feel in this moment is tenfold stronger.

"Your mate will soon be reduced to nothing more than an animal, and though I've heard some women grow disconcertingly attached to their pets"—he casts a look Justus's way, surely alluding to Xema and her parrot, rest his rotten soul—"a pet cannot plant an heir inside your womb. A pet cannot offer you all that a man can."

He better not be thinking of planting anything inside my womb.

"Do you understand why I don't fear Lorcan Ríhbiadh coming after me? By the time we emerge, your feathered king will be reduced to a dumb little bird with not a speck of iron or sentience, and the rest of his revolting breed of half-humans will become the animals they already act like. Poof." Dante flicks his thumb over his middle and index fingers, making them click. "The Crows will be gone for good, and Luce will be, once again, safe."

The only thing that'll go poof and be gone is this man's head from his torso.

For the first time in forever, I don't shudder at the idea of a decapitation. Then again, I've pierced a man's heart. Yes, in the dark, but I felt those squishy organs and taut sinews. I felt that body give beneath my blade. I felt Dargento's breath leave his lungs and the beats leave his heart.

With a final sneer, Dante flips his attention toward Justus. "Have you already returned with a healer?"

Without shifting his gaze off me, Justus says, "Yes. I've brought the one who lives on our property. He usually tends to horses but he's learned in healing Faeries as well."

I'm taking this as confirmation that the Rossis built their manor atop Costa's underground castle.

Dante backs up slowly, seemingly reluctant to leave. Does he not trust his general? "See that Fallon gets dressed, and promptly at that."

"I'll have my granddaughter garbed and pliant in no time."

Pliant? Obsidian must hurt Faerie brains considering how daft they've all become.

With a sharp nod, Dante wheels around and marches through the open doorway beyond which stand two soldiers. Although the dark-haired one has his gaze averted, the white-haired one does not.

Cato's stance is erect, yet the outline of his body vibrates with a tangible desire to sprint into the room to assist. But is it Justus he cares to aid, or me?

"The only way I'll ever be pliant is if you knock me out with your little sleep spell again," I mutter.

He goes to the door and shuts it. I catch him uncorking the small vial and smearing blood in the shape of a knot across the wood.

"What did you just do?"

"I just ruined eavesdropping for your little Cato."

"He's not mine."

"Yes, yes. He's Ceres's. I'm aware." With a grunt, he adds, "The pedestal he's placed that woman on is so high that he's put her out of his own reach."

Anger swills behind my breastbone. "Do you get off on being petty and cruel, or is that part of the requirements to lead the Lucin army?"

"What I get off on is not something I care to discuss with you. Now put the damn gown on, Nipota, before I dress you myself."

My face blazes with fury. "I'm *not* your fucking granddaughter." Why is Justus Rossi so adamant about making me feel part of his family?

Since I wouldn't put it past him to dress me, I let the damp towel drop and plant my feet through the billows of scratchy tulle. I decide to wear the dress front to back in order to fasten the buttons myself.

"Where did you get this horrid frock anyway?" The buttons are covered in the same rich satin as the bodice, which makes them slippery to handle.

"In Domitina's closet," he says, still facing the door. "My daughter intended to wear it to her nuptials."

"Domitina's married?"

"No. When her sister bore a child out of wedlock, her betrothed canceled the ceremony, afraid for his good name."

No wonder Domitina is salty with Mamma . . . Granted the man doesn't sound like a winner, but still, she must hold my Faerie mother accountable for her failed engagement.

Justus's cheek dimples. I'd have said with a smile, but since he possesses neither dimple nor jolliness, I deduce that he must be biting the inside of his cheek. "When Marco kept me on as his general, I made sure to bury the idiot's good name."

His favoritism fills me with anger on Mamma's behalf. "So you defend the honor of one daughter and mutilate the other? What a father you are . . ."

The dimple vanishes from his cheek. "For Cauldron's sake, I did not mutilate Agrippina's ears. I never lifted a finger on my eldest child."

CHAPTER 17

My hands freeze on the endless row of buttons. "Are you implying the tips of her ears *broke* off?"

The bathing chamber is so quiet that when Justus rubs his hand against his pant leg, I hear the scrape of his fingertips against the dark fabric. "Ceres found Agrippina laying in a pool of her own blood, unconscious. She had a sprite come and fetch me because . . . because she didn't know what to do when she realized that Agrippina had cut off the tips of her ears. She didn't know what the consequences would be to the baby." His throat moves with slow breaths. "To you."

I envy his ability to breathe because I've lost mine.

"Apparently, she'd been acting . . . wild for some time after Ríhbiadh's fall. Ceres thought she may have had an affair with a Crow and that the child inside of her had turned into obsidian, but Crows and Faeries cannot reproduce because of the disparity of their blood." A beat of silence echoes against the noiseless, airless chamber. "Shifter blood contains iron, which poisons Faerie infants."

"I heard." Phoebus had informed me of this after I'd returned to the Sky Kingdom.

"When Agrippina finally came to, she wasn't herself. She was . . . absent. Could barely feed herself. Ceres blamed me for Agrippina's despondency. Apparently, teaching our daughter how to swordfight was not a proper pastime for a lady."

What the *what*? Justus taught Mamma to wield a sword?

His chest lifts with a ragged breath while mine remains motionless. "When I returned from a diplomatic visit to Glace, Ceres was gone, and so was your mother."

"Nonna said you repudiated them. She said . . . she said you sent them away because it was too shameful."

"I did no such thing." He glances over his shoulder. When he sees I'm decent, he turns, pressing a rust-colored lock behind his ear. "Your grandmother blamed me for allowing Agrippina to shadow me during my visits to Racocci. She blamed me for training her to become my successor."

"Excuse me? Your successor?"

"Agrippina was a most ambitious girl. Smart as a whip. Talented with a sword. She could stand her own against the best of my soldiers."

"Is. Not was. She still lives, Justus."

"Perhaps." He purses his lips as though to smoosh down his frothing emotions. "She gave that weasel Dargento a run for his coin once. Humiliated him in front of his entire battalion."

My heart swells as I picture the woman I've only ever known as apathetic giving Dargento a good thrashing.

"I'm afraid that spurred his antipathy toward you." After a beat, he adds, "I petitioned for his removal, but Marco was fond of the mongrel." His gaze becomes distant as though he were back in the throne room with Marco instead of down here with me. After a contemplative moment, he gives his head a little shake. "Gods, how I wish the serpents had snatched him after the attack and dragged him to Shabbin shores."

I study the man before me, and for some odd reason, I picture an onion. Not because his face is round—the general is all sharp angles—but because he's astonishingly layered. If all he says is the truth. If it isn't, then he's just a cruel liar. "Does salt affect you?"

His head jerks back a little. "Yes."

"So you're not ingesting that toxic chemical to make yourself immune to iron and salt?"

"Do I strike you as a man who cares to poison himself?"

"Not particularly, but Dante didn't either."

"Dante is a child playing at being king. He seeks out any miracle potion to make himself stronger. That iron-rich chemical Pierre Roy convinced him to take may be a notch less toxic than what the wildlings ingest—"

"The wildlings?" I startle, not expecting to hear about them.

"You know, the wild Fae who tried to kill you. Twice, if I'm not mistaken."

"I know who they are, Justus. What I didn't know was that they ingested iron."

"Didn't you notice the color of their teeth?"

Black . . .

"Or their inability to use Faerie magic?"

"Because they ingest iron," I whisper, and although it isn't a question, Justus nods.

"Correct."

Well that explains Dante's rank breath and failing magic.

Iron. How desperate must one be to willingly ingest something that could kill you?

"Who's in charge of his dosage?"

"He self-medicates."

"Any chance you could increase the iron composition?"

"What do you think I've been doing since I brought him down into the obsidian tunnels?"

What a devious man Justus Rossi is . . . "Any chance you could poison him quicker?"

"Unfortunately, no. It may kill him."

"Which is what we *all* want, right?"

He sighs. "Yes, but if you're not the one to kill him, then the Cauldron won't break Meriam's curse."

My eyes widen so fast that my lashes smack my brow bone. That's why *I* must be the one to kill him . . . to break Meriam's curse. But do I want to break her curse? What if she runs amok and stabs Lore again?

Something thumps outside the closed door, all but wrenching my heart out of my chest.

"Better hurry before he comes back," Justus murmurs.

As I go back to fastening the buttons, I steer the conversation away from one that may just get Justus tossed in a birdcage of his own. "How did Dargento get your sword?"

"He caught me heading into the tunnels and threatened to spread word of my survival. We struck a bargain—his silence for my prized blade." A small smile tugs at the corner of Justus's lips. "I knew I'd get it back eventually."

"Didn't he have a sword of his own?"

"I may have convinced him that Meriam magicked the blade to make the man handling it impervious to Crow and Shabbin magic."

I snort as I imagine how invincible Silvius must've felt carrying it around. "To think the blade he thought would keep him safe was the one to end his life."

"It wasn't the blade; it was the wielder." Justus sounds proud. Proud of me. Proud of what I did.

Although pride isn't the sentiment I harbor at having ended Dargento's life, I'm no less receptive to Justus's commendation. "Do you really intend to feed me obsidian?"

His mouth is soft, which is such an odd sight on the forever severe general. "Ground peppercorns. Similar color and texture. Tastier."

"Why did you tell Dante that Lore was my mate?"

"Would you prefer I'd told him that you'd tapped into Bronwen's sight because Meriam set your magic loose?"

"No. Most definitely not." I gnaw on my bottom lip. "So you won't tell him?"

"No."

"What if he makes you eat salt?"

"I've become good at evading the truth."

"What of oaths? Do you know a spell that'll prevent an oath from scoring itself into his skin?"

"The iron threshold of his blood is too high to allow his skin to absorb vows. I've tested it just this morning." A corner of Justus's mouth kinks up.

As I fasten the last of the buttons, not caring that the material is squashing my breasts since it's not meant to be worn this way, I think of how Nonna had known my blood was different even though she hadn't known why.

"Did you try to get them back?" I muse

He frowns. "Who?"

"Nonna and Mamma?"

With a sigh, he says, "No. For they were safer living away from Isolacuori. Especially once you were born." His gentle tone makes my fingers slip off the bodice of my dress.

What a perplexing male he is . . .

He starts to raise his palm to the door to rub out the sigil when I ask, "Whose side are you on?"

Palm hovering over the bloody knot, he says, "Yours, Nipota."

This time, when he calls me granddaughter, I don't remind him of our lack of kinship. I may not descend from him, but, through Meriam, Justus and I have become bound by blood.

Blood and secrets.

Speaking of . . . "Why did you let Meriam blood-bind us?"

"Because the blood-bind will thwart his magic." He hovers the heel of his hand over the glyph.

"I thought the Nebban supplement was taking care of that?"

"Not *that* magic," he murmurs.

Before I can ask him what the Cauldron he means, he draws the door handle down. Cato all but collapses atop Justus, evidently eavesdropping.

"At least pretend to be stealthy, Brambilla. It's more dignified of a sergeant."

A deep flush creeps up Cato's face, made redder by the stark contrast with his fair hair and uniform. "I-I-I was knocking. I was not—"

"Settle down. I've got more important business to tend to than to downgrade you to foot soldier."

I almost snort. Thankfully, I keep a lid on the sound. I cannot appear at all amused by Justus or we'll raise eyebrows that must absolutely remain flat.

Although my focus stays on the general's swishing ponytail during the walk back to my cell, I've crawled into my mind to sort through all the pieces of the past he's just given me.

My mother mutilated her own ears. It's atrocious and heartrending. Also, it does little to lessen the guilt of having invaded her womb.

I suddenly wish I'd taken better advantage of our veiled cocoon to ask Justus if there was any hope of restoring her mind. Perhaps

Meriam knows a spell? Or Zendaya? Perhaps she can undo the damage she caused? Where is she?

Out of all the questions I have for Justus and Meriam, this one is the most pressing. I decide then and there that I'll strike a bargain with Meriam the next time we meet. I'll ask for a meeting with my mother against breaking her throne curse.

INTERMINABLE DAYS PASS during which the only souls I see are the sprites and soldiers assigned to my cell. I will Justus to open my gated door, but he doesn't come. The same way I will Bronwen to take possession of my gaze—or however it is our eye link works—but however hard I will it, I don't travel to the Sky Kingdom.

The only entertainment I get is watching Dante's sprites sweat like Selvatins as they drill through the spiraling racks of wine to accommodate the four poles Cato and a fellow soldier float up. I find it far less entertaining when I understand the reason for the poles—raising my cage so that it no longer sits on the floor. No more twirling in my near future.

A fire-Faerie has just finished soldering heavy chains to the fitted poles when Justus finally whitens my cellar doorway. "Meriam has awakened. It's time for Dante's first lesson."

Dante's? Or mine?

I surmise only Dante's, for how could my grandmother in the same lesson teach him the wrong symbols, and me, the correct ones?

Perhaps she has no intention of teaching me how to use my magic. After all, she knows just as well as Justus that the second I understand how to wield spells, I'll pack up my magic and run for the hills, or rather, for Lore's mountain.

CHAPTER 18

I stop short when I emerge from the tunnel because a tree has been grown, one outfitted with fat branches that jut out in all directions. But that is not what arrests my attention. What stops both my feet and heart is the sight of my friend standing beneath the largest branch.

Antoni is propped atop a gnarled root, wrists and ankles cuffed with vines, neck collared with a thick chain, dark as tarnished silver. Although fabric stands between the iron and his pumping chest, the links must've grazed his skin for a rash has appeared along his neck.

Molars gnashing, I trail the chain to where it's been slung around the branch, before lowering my gaze back to Antoni's. His skin is as sallow as fishbones, his hair as ropy as seaweed, his eyes as haunted as Catriona's the night an arrow snuffed out her life.

"What is the meaning of this?" I growl.

"The halfling's merely present in case you give me trouble." Dante steps out of the vault whose doors are flung so wide, Meriam's throne is on full display.

"I won't."

"Then you've nothing to worry about, moya." Dante pulls down his white sleeve, adjusting the cuff over a bandage that must've been soaked in liniment for it's greenish and embalms the air with an eye-watering reek.

"I beg you, Dante. Threatening him is unnecessary. I will be the most well-behaved inkwell in the history of inkwells." My nails bite into my palms, etching crescents into the entwined rings that stain my skin.

Justus turns toward the tall, green-eyed healer. "You may take your leave."

I blink because I only now take notice of the man. Here I was expecting pointed ears and long tresses, but the man standing beside Dante sports shoulder-length locks and rounded shells. I suppose that tending to horses is far less prestigious a job than tending to Faeries. Still, it strikes me as odd that the great Xema Rossi, who seemed so very attached to her pets and the points of people's ears, would hire a halfling to oversee her stables.

"Lastra, help the man roll up his gauze or he'll be here all day!" Dante's obviously impatient to see him off.

Or perhaps, he doesn't appreciate the man's thorough scrutiny of me.

"No need. I'm all done." The male picks up the tray laden with pots of cream and strips of gauze, his shoulders straining the simple beige linen tunic he wears over slacks that have seen better days. They've been mended in so many spots that they remind me of the dresses of my youth that Nonna would have to stitch up once a fortnight because I was always snagging them against something.

Dante calls to one of his soldiers. "Escort Dottore Vanche to his chamber."

The healer's name gives me pause. I suppose it's a rather odd moniker.

"Come. Meriam's waiting." Justus touches my wrist, stealing my gaze off the curious healer.

"Not until Antoni is uncollared," I mutter.

Justus's eyes grow as hard as the rest of him. Gone is the almost-kindly general, and in his place emerges the one that Luce has come to fear. "Lastra, move away from the pulley!" He charges toward the tree.

Is Justus going to free— "*I* will be manning that rope."

I try to read his intent, but Dante steps between us, snipping my view of his general.

"Better behave for the only *just* part about Rossi resides in his forename." Dante holds up his arm.

I care to touch him about as much as I cared to handle animal innards back at *Bottom of the Jug*.

"My arm." His tone is clipped and low. "Take it."

I don't.

"Rossi, rattle the prisoner's chains!"

"No!" I clap Dante's arm just as Justus tugs on Antoni's rope, jostling the chain.

My friend doesn't utter more than a grunt, but his face folds in agony when the iron links roll off his soiled shirt and anger his skin.

"Please don't hurt him, Generali. Please." My croak warbles across the obsidian chamber.

"Then do as you're told from here on out or I will keep playing with my new puppet."

The ancient Faerie's mercurial behavior is giving me whiplash. One second, he's friend; the next, he's foe. I pray his tyranny is an act. I pray he isn't willing to sacrifice Antoni to prove a point.

Dante drops a murmur close to my ear. "That grandfather of yours is pitiless, isn't he? I wouldn't want him as my enemy." He grips my arm with his bandaged hand.

Although no noose rests around my neck and no vines strangle my limbs, I'm just as much a fly in these men's webs as Antoni.

As Dante drags me toward Meriam, I look back over my shoulder to toss Justus a pleading look, one that says, *Don't hurt him*. If he grasps my unspoken words, he doesn't react, merely stares at Antoni, whose ashen cheeks keep hollowing with ragged breaths that bloat my lids with heat and moisture. Gods, if only I could get him out.

I hunt his mass of light-brown hair for the healing crystal Lazarus gifted him to protect him from the toxicity of iron, but see nothing glint amidst his unwashed locks. Which means that if the metal collar breaks his skin . . .

If the iron comes in contact with his blood . . .

I banish the thought. I will behave so fucking well that no harm will befall my friend.

"Gold suits you." Dante's low tone makes its way to my ears but not to my heart.

I've worn the same horrid gown for days on end. Between the

corset's boning and the skirt's scratchiness, I am *so* done with Faerie frocks.

"Shall we begin, Maezza?" Meriam's voice skips across the jewels in the vault.

Dante shoves me into a chair, then twists my arm over a glass bowl. He removes a dagger from a pouch at his waist and incises my wrist. "Not yet." He clicks his fingers.

One of his soldiers peels himself away from the wall and approaches us, a bolt of black velvet dangling from his fingers. I fathom it's a bandage for my wound but I'm wrong. Dante cares not about hampering my blood flow, only my sight.

I stare at Meriam in anguish. Her skin is so wan that it makes the color of her irises pop. I silently beg her to intercede . . . to remind Dante that my blood holds no power so the blindfold is unnecessary.

"I'll gladly spell her eyelids." Meriam's murmur almost gets lost under the hefty thrashing of my heart.

"No need to waste your magic when I have perfectly suitable cloth at my disposal."

The soldier wraps the soft fabric over my eyes and knots it until the darkness is so complete that I begin to perspire.

"I assure you—" she continues.

"Until Fallon's been unbound, you're not to waste your magic, strega." Dante's breath skates over my clammy forehead like those foul gusts that lift off the Racoccin canals at the peak of summer.

"Perhaps my husband could—"

"He's busy weighing the sailor's fate. Now stop wasting my time and begin, Meriam."

I try to steal back my arm but Dante doesn't loosen his grip on my wrist, which is wet and warm with my gushing blood. My stomach soars and plummets, soars and—

I toss up my breakfast, as well as last night's supper. Even though I don't see Dante, I make sure to aim for the fingers he's got clamped around my arm.

"Fuck," he growls. "Get me a basin of soapy water now." He sounds utterly disgusted.

Good.

"Make a note to stop feeding Fallon before she's bled."

"Don't you intend to bleed me daily?" I croak, my throat feeling scraped raw by the acidity of the bile.

"I do, so either you learn to stifle your squeamishness, or you go back to being fed intravenously."

"Back to?"

"How do you think we kept you alive during the journey?" He lifts my arm and dips it into a sudsy bowl, then dries it. He must settle my wrist over a new bowl because he thumbs my wound to strengthen the gush.

My eyes sting from the white-hot burn of split flesh, and though my stomach spasms, it doesn't eject anything more. Probably because it's empty. "May I get some water to rinse out my mouth?"

"After we're done. I wouldn't want to risk diluting my ink."

One day, I will make you hurt and I will make you bleed, Dante Fucking Regio.

"Start with the handiest sigils, strega."

"Very well." Although only fabric separates me from the world, I feel like Meriam stands on the other end of the kingdom. "The most important one is the lock. It'll allow you to slip through walls. You must draw a square—"

"Do not speak the sigils! Chalk them up on the slab which my soldier holds."

The sound of chalk dragging over slate makes the fine hairs on my arms stand on end. If only she could pitch the rocky canvas at Dante's head. I pry my lids wide to try and peer through the velvet, but it's fully opaque.

Between the steady drone of her chalk and the steady drip of my blood, my lids turn sluggish and begin to lower. When I open my eyes next, I'm back in my cage, and my wrist aches.

Lore, I whimper through our silent bond. ***Find me.***

But more hours slip by, and he doesn't find me.

If only he'd listened to me about Eponine. I grow angry at him even though none of this is his fault. My anger lessens when Cato stalks into the cellar, two guards trailing behind him.

I think he's come to fetch me for Dante's lesson until I catch sight of pale pink silk fluttering off his sleeve. The fabric is so transparent that the white of his starched uniform shines right through.

"Dante has requested your presence at his supper table, Fallon." Cato's gray gaze skims the fabric draped over his sleeve.

"Hard pass."

Cato's fellow guard, along with the sprites sitting in various areas of the spiraling wine racks, gape, because no one turns down a direct order from the king.

Cato sighs. "Fallon—"

"I'm not hungry."

"You haven't eaten since you were sick, and it's been two days."

Two days. Here I thought time only flew when one was having fun . . . "Feed me intravenously."

"Please, Fallon. Please think of more than your appetite."

I realize he means: *think of me, think of Antoni.*

"Fucking fine," I mutter, peeling my spine off my mattress to sit.

At least I'll get to stretch my legs and get out of this harrowing gown that smells like stale vomit. Perhaps I'll even get to play with a fork and a knife. I picture planting both inside Dante's long neck. When my stomach fails to heave, I realize that I'd be plenty capable of such an atrocity.

Cato drops his gaze to the pastel cloth draped over his arm. "Antoni has been summoned to this supper, too."

"As a guest?"

"I—I don't know." His Adam's apple rolls as he holds out the pink thing on his arm. "You're to wear this"—a nerve jumps beside his eye—"gown."

"I'll take pants and a shirt, thank you."

Cato's throat moves again with a jagged swallow and an even sharper *please.*

A sprite lurches off his perch. "I'll go report the Beast-charmer's conduct immediately."

"Did I command you to relay anything to our king?" Cato barks, stopping the tiny Faerie midflight. "You answer to me, Dill. Don't forget it."

"Actually, he answers to me. And so do you, Brambilla." Justus presses away from the doorjamb he scrutinizes with much intensity. "Float the dress up to Fallon and depart." The second they're gone, he says, "You ready kill Dante, Fallon?"

CHAPTER 19

Even though Justus's tone is hushed, purelings have such exceptional hearing that I shoot my gaze to the tunnel entrance.

"Sigil there. I check." Justus steps nearer to my cage. "But speak Shabbin like me."

I'm again startled by the realization that I didn't automatically pick up on the reason for his odd diction.

"I'm very much ready to end Dante's life, Nonno," I reply quietly before hissing, "Was that Shabbin?"

He grins, which is such an odd sight. I've seen stealthy smiles curve his lips. Never large grins. It makes the middle-aged man look almost boyish. "Yes."

Incredible . . . Simply incredible.

I finger the slip fringed in pricey gold lace. "Must I do so dressed as a high-class doxy?"

"I picked dress so he distracted."

The way Justus speaks reminds me of Aoife, which makes my heart pinch. If I manage to kill Dante tonight, then she'll be free. Unless she's already free?

I'm about to ask Justus, when he drops his voice. "I swap what he ingests with"—he seems to thumb through his mind for the appropriate word—"placebo. Which mean he no immune to iron, but also magic return." With a very uncharacteristic wink, he adds, "Dottore Vanche, miracle worker."

I roll the fabric between my fingers. "Too bad Dottore Vanche couldn't slip him *extra* poison."

"Poison don't kill purebloods, Fallon."

"It would've weakened him. I'm no expert assassin, but wouldn't that have made my job easier?"

"No. He desensitize so much to iron, he would heal."

"Even if the iron was lodged inside his heart?"

"The Nebban powder harden skin. You would need saw and strength of ten Fae to take off head."

Bile billows at the back of my throat at the idea of axing through flesh. "Yet when I bit him, my teeth went through his flesh just fine."

"Because it concentrate in neck and chest since weak spot. That why breath rot."

I slide my lips together, storing the information. "Remind me . . . why can't you kill him yourself?"

"Because it must be blood-daughter of Meriam who curse-break, otherwise Cauldron not forgive."

I raise an eyebrow. I was aware the Cauldron was the source of all magic, but I wasn't aware it was sentient. "So technically, my mother could do it?"

He nods. "But mother . . . she not understand at moment."

I frown. "Why?"

"No time to explain now, Fallon . . . Get dress on quick."

With a sigh, I unfold the flimsy slip and hold it up. "It's exceedingly see-through, which begs the question of where you plan on having me stash a weapon."

"I planted dagger in headboard."

I snap my gaze off the fabric and back onto Justus's upturned face. *"Headboard?"*

He nods.

"Correct me if I'm wrong, but aren't headboards attached to beds?"

"You sup in king chamber."

"With Antoni?" What sort of dinner does Dante have in store for the three of us? "Will you be in attendance as well?"

"Yes."

I find that somewhat reassuring, even though I still don't love the idea of heading into Dante's bedchamber in a sheer nightgown. "You better not be expecting me to bed him."

"Only kill. But dress will weaken guard."

I fathom he means Dante will let down his guard.

"Can I don this thing *beneath* my dress?" Not that I have *any* love for the prickly gold tulle, but it beats parading around a bunch of soldiers half naked.

"No. You need distract king. And you move more easy in plain dress."

"I'd move more easily in pants and a shirt," I grumble. "Any chance I could get some fresh knickers?"

"Didn't Jus—just get bag the other day?"

"I've gone through all of them."

"All?"

"Yes, *all*. I don't know how often you swap yours, Nonno, and I've no desire to find out, so no need to share, but I very much appreciate clean underwear."

He mutters something beneath his breath. "Fine. Put dress while I find clean one."

"If by any chance you stumble upon a brassiere, I'm a taker!" I call out right before he exits the cellar with a huff.

The awkward interlude ferries a smile to my lips that chips off with every button I unfasten. Tonight is the night I end Dante Regio's life. It feels like I've been working toward this moment for years even though it's been mere weeks.

Nerves fritter my confidence, and I begin to doubt that I'm fit for the job.

He's a cruel man who kidnapped you, Fal. Who bled you. Who lied to you. Who killed your horse. Who removed Antoni's fingernails. Who hungers for nothing more than the Crows' extermination.

Those last three reminders inject steel into my backbone. Hurting me is one thing; hurting those I love is another.

By the time I've donned the pearlescent pink slip, Justus is back, his strides as brisk as his breaths. I take it the closet he's fished these from is not in the obsidian tunnels.

He tosses the undergarments into my cage. "Here."

When he doesn't pivot, I twirl my fingers. "A little privacy."

"Right." He tugs at his shirt collar as he finally spins.

"After my . . . *meal,* will you tell me where to find my mother?" I keep her name off my lips in case the sigil has lost its vigor. *Do* sigils lose vigor?

There's a long pause during which he shifts from foot to foot. Is it me, or are his boots uncharacteristically scuffed? Perhaps his journey to Domitina's closet was more arduous than I imagined.

"Justus?"

"You be told."

One more stimulus . . . Not only will I get my mate back, but I will also get my mother.

"I'm glad for your word, but I'd prefer an oath."

He starts to run his hand through his hair but stops when he encounters the leather cord binding it. Gods, he's even more distraught than I am, and yet he's not the one about to do all the stabbing.

"No oath." He taps his bicep. "Oath reveal magic."

Thank the Cauldron he remembered that.

After rolling on my underwear and binding my breasts, I curl my fingers around the bars of my cage and breathe in and out slowly, willing my courage to increase.

I think of Lore, picture him with so much vigor that he suddenly appears in all his dark splendor.

Lore?

He's talking with Cian about Gods only know what since it isn't Lucin they speak.

Lore!

I try to move toward him, but however hard I try, I don't manage to reach him. Glumly, I realize that I didn't export my body, only my mind.

Bronwen must finally pick up on my presence because she whispers, "Mórrgaht?" He whips his face toward my aunt just as she adds, "Fallon is watching."

He strides toward her, dark shadows webbing the unfocused outline of his skin. "Behach Éan?"

Though I know that neither he nor Bronwen can hear me, I whisper, "Yes. Yes, it's me."

The gold in his eyes churns. "Mórrígan, I hate that this is our only means of communication. Can you really not see how she's faring, Bronwen?"

"No. I cannot."

His chest lifts with tattered breaths. "But she can hear me?"

"She can."

"Mo khrà, Bronwen said that Justus is aiding you. Please tell that" —he growls a word full of consonants and jagged vowels, which I imagine conveys his impression of the general—"to send us a fucking smoke signal as to where you are. I have Crows circling the entire kingdom."

Bronwen says, "He'll reach out when—"

"Fallon's magic has been released. I want my mate back, and I want her back fucking now!"

"She still needs to kill Dante, Lorcan."

"What she needs is to come home to me." Lore's furious rasp strangles my already sore heart, making it tighten around its beats.

Although I fight to stay with Lore, I slip out of Bronwen's mind and land back in the obsidian dungeon, knuckles as tense as my jaw.

"Are you all right?" One of Justus's eyebrows is peaked.

I take it my eyes whitened. "Fine. I'm fine."

A lie. I won't be fine until I'm back with Lore.

Justus is still gazing at me oddly, brow ruffled as though it's the first time he's witnessed my eyes color-changing.

"Any spells I could use?"

Justus's eyebrows straighten. "Blood no work on he."

In other words, I'll have to rely on my physical and mental aptitudes.

Easy breezy.

Total cakewalk.

Like taking candy from a sprite.

Who am I kidding?

I wipe my clammy palms on my pink slip, wishing I felt brave, wishing Lorcan was at my side. But if he had been, he'd take justice into his own hands. Bronwen's prophetic words creep into my mind, clear as the morning she spoke them.

Lorcan still believes he will slay Dante and lose his humanity doing so, for that is what will happen if he's the one to remove your former lover from this world before the obsidian curse is lifted.

I'm too selfish to risk Lorcan's humanity, for I refuse to live in a world where he doesn't exist. For this reason, I don't tell Justus about signaling my whereabouts. "If only Meriam could collapse her wards."

"Soon."

Come to think of it . . . "Lore mentioned that Dante wiped away the sigil in the dungeon. Was that a lie?"

"Unless sigil fresh, no can be wiped, because blood goes deep in stone. To undo magic, witch must recall her blood."

"*You* can manipulate Meriam's blood, so technically, *you* could recall her magic, right?"

"Jus—"

"Jus . . .?"

His posture stiffens, but then he rolls his shoulders, making little bones pop. In Lucin, he mumbles, "Just maybe."

"So the ward stone endures?"

"Yes." Justus strides toward the entrance of the cellar.

"Even though it was broken?"

"Yes."

I tip my head to the side, my locks frolicking past my shoulder. "How many pieces was it broken into?"

"Three."

I'm glad for such a low number. "Are all three in the dungeon?"

"No. We discuss later, Fallon."

"But you know where all the pieces are?"

"Yes."

"Where?"

"Not in Luce," he murmurs before commanding the soldiers loitering in the cramped hallway to unlock my cage.

CHAPTER 20

I yearn to further discuss the ward rune with Justus, but we're surrounded by too many Dante enthusiasts to discuss such a sensitive topic. At least dwelling on their location keeps my mind off where I'm headed and what I'm to accomplish once I reach my destination.

As we emerge into the vault room, I scan the elaborate doors, wishing they were unsealed, wishing for a glimpse of my grandmother or a whispered encouragement, but Meriam's tucked out of my sight.

Justus guides us down the tunnel that leads to the washroom Cato brought me to the day of my unbinding. We plow past the bathing chamber, then past an endless row of closed doors.

"So Costa lived underground?" I ask Justus.

"Only at the end of his life, when he was no longer of sound mind and thought Ríhbiadh would rise without help from a Shabbin."

"So all these doors lead to rooms?"

"Not all of them. Some lead to various places in the kingdom. Places that have been walled off. In case you're considering trying to escape, know that you won't go far. Even vermin cannot find their way into Costa's tunnels."

"That halfling rat did," one of the soldiers behind me volunteers.

I spin around to uncover which idiot desires an iron blade in the testicles. When my gaze collides with a narrowed green one, I determine it's the soldier named Lastra.

"Halflings aren't vermin, Soldati Lastra, but I'll take note of your beliefs and revisit them when I rule Luce. Anyone else have an opinion on halflings they'd like to share with their future queen while they have my undivided attention?"

Lastra's lips thin and he averts his gaze. *Coward.*

"You already rule Luce, Fallon," Justus says under his breath. "You're married."

"Blood-bound. Not married."

I stare at the twined circles, my fingers itching to claw the tattoo out of my skin.

As we plod through the torchlit darkness, I sink into my mind, picturing my reunion with Lore, whose side I will *never* leave again. I'll graft myself to him. I'm certain he'd be all for it. Then again, how does one graft themselves to a man who can transform into shadows?

My heart skips a beat as I realize that I, too, will soon be capable of shifting into smoke.

Possibly today.

Although the air is crisp and damp, instead of numbing, it electrifies my skin. The deeper down the tunnel we march, the more my eardrums throb and my blood thrums. Perhaps it's my magic that's making itself known, or perhaps it's all nerves and anticipation.

What feels like an entire Tarecuorin island later, we finally reach a heavy door.

Justus knocks while I gaze around. Though faint, I think I detect the swoosh of water. Could we be near the beach? The Rossi property does boast its own private shore. I start to daydream that only a thin slab of obsidian rests between me and open air. That if I press my fingertips into the low ceiling and push, the stone will lift and—

The tunnel shivers.

"What the Cauldron was that?" Cato clasps his sword. Although he's yet to drag it from its scabbard, his bicep is taut with anticipatory adrenaline.

Justus snatches my wrist and drags it back along my side. "That was nothing," he grumbles, but his eyes tell a different story. "Keep your hands off the stone or your wrists will be bound. Understood?"

The only thing I understand is that someone is out there, on the other side of this wall.

Could my mate have found Dante's hidey-hole? ***Lore?***

I wait for a second tremor to shake the stone like the marsh dwellers wait for summer to dry up their land and warm their derelict cottages, but no other comes, which scrunches up my brow. Assuming it was my touch that spurred the answering bang, why would the Crows only attack once? The answer pricks a hole in the inflatable buoy that is my hope, because whatever struck the ceiling isn't a Crow.

What could it be? I suck in a breath as a thought pops into my brain: what if Meriam or Justus painted a sigil on the ceiling that my touch can activate? I'm trying to figure out the mechanics of this theory when Justus sweeps open the door, revealing an octagonal room paved in black stone with a round bed fitted with silken gold sheets.

I take in the gaudy headboard made of elaborately carved wood plated in gold and the matching frame that sits inclined on the wide mantle of the headboard. The light dripping from the suspended candelabrum is so thin that I find myself squinting at the canvas it encloses—a portrait of a pointy-eared black male in gold military regalia, wearing the crown that now sits on Dante's head.

Although Costa is centuries younger in this painting than in the ones hanging in every temple and school, he is unmistakable with his icy stare and quiet sneer. I used to think Dante and Costa had little in common besides strong jawbones, jeweled box braids, and blue eyes, but their rotted hearts have given them the air of conjoined twins.

"My grandfather sat for this painting the day after he took over Luce."

I turn my gaze toward the table at which both Dante and Antoni sit—Dante with both forearms on the table, Antoni with his arms tied behind his back and his mouth gagged with a vine. No place setting or plate or even goblet graces the glass surface. The only object on that table is a nondescript, palm-sized wooden box outlined in candlelight.

Both the Faerie King and the sea captain are staring at my revealing attire with varying degrees of surprise. Where Antoni's nostrils flare and his lips tremble around his gag, Dante seems to grow a little stiller, a little taller. As he rolls his shoulders, his long braids clink against the golden armor he forever sports.

To think that soon, he will be buried in it . . .

"What is she wearing, Rossi?" Dante sneers at my dress.

"Apologies, Maezza, but Domitina packed up most of her wardrobe before departing."

Departing? Where did his daughter go? And has his horrid mother also departed?

Since it's of little import at the moment, I file the question away for later and smooth my hands down the silk that's only a shade darker than my skin.

"It's way more dress than Beryl wore the day Tavo sailed her over to Barrack Island to tend to his needs. Wait, was it his needs? I can't quite recall what Catriona told me . . ." I tuck my tongue into the corner of my mouth and tap my lips, making a great show of dwelling on this, even though I don't give a flying fuck about Dante's tryst with Beryl. The only reason I even bring it up is to show him that the wool he pulled over my eyes has been sheared off.

Justus tenses beside me, his desire to yell at me so strong that it makes his jaw shiver like the flames atop the candelabrum.

Yes, yes, Nonno. I'm here to murder the asshole, not passive-aggressively insult him.

"Anyway . . . I'm starving. What's for supper?" I barrel ahead of Justus who's become one with the black wood at his back.

I start to pull out the last chair when Dante leans over the table and flicks open the top of the wooden box, revealing a small mound of translucent crystals. "Salt."

So this is no meal; this is an interrogation. Since I'm not affected by the condiment, I assume the salt will be for Antoni. Which does make me wonder why I was convened . . .

"Ungag the prisoner." Dante pushes away from the table as though to get up, except he doesn't.

The vine binding Antoni's mouth dematerializes into sparkling green magic. My friend gags and swallows a great many times, then swipes his tongue over his mouth.

His mouth whose corners bleed.

The sight of his blood hardens my stomach and amplifies my rage. Out of the corner of my twitching eye, I stare at the bed, calculating my odds of grabbing the dagger and plunging the blade into Dante's neck before the soldiers, who funneled into the room behind me, can intercept me with their magic.

The optimist in me tiptoes back because my odds are dismal. And then the optimist freezes because I catch Dante's tapered stare and the slow smile that curls his full lips.

I pray that it's my annoyance that causes him pleasure and not an awareness of Justus's ploy.

CHAPTER 21

"Sit, moya."

My heart has scaled up the length of my throat and batters the skin at its base with such force that every Faerie in attendance can no doubt hear its manic tempo. I yank on the chair so hard that its feet screech atop the black stone.

"Fal-lon," Dante singsongs my name. "I meant *here*."

When he pats his lap, I clasp the rungs of the chair with such vigor that I threaten to splinter my phalanxes.

I glance toward Justus, wishing he'd intervene, but he's wholly focused on the back of Antoni's head. I try to call to him with my eyes, but he either doesn't feel my attention or is trying to avoid it.

"Rossi, I believe Fallon will need some coaxing. I know we've done away with Antoni's nails, but his fingers are still attached, are they not?"

My heart lurches in time with my body. "No. I'm coming." I ball my fingers into fists as I circumvent Antoni's chair.

My friend swivels his head, wild gaze trailing me.

When I reach the Faerie King, I stare with revulsion at the crisp white fabric of his pants that stretches over his thickened thigh muscles.

"My lap, or his fingers. What'll it be, moya?"

Gods, I hate when he calls me wife, and he knows it, which is undoubtedly why he insists on exploiting the term.

I perch on his knee, keeping my weight into my feet in order to put as little contact as necessary between our bodies. Dante snags my waist and drags me farther back.

"Why make me sit on your lap when there's a perfectly nice and empty chair?" My jammed molars make my question come out no louder than a murmur.

Dante moves his mouth nearer to my ear, and although his breath is no longer rank, I still shudder. "Because I can." He flattens his palm against my stomach with such force that I can almost feel the shape of his fingers imprint on the spine I'm so desperately trying to keep straight.

"You can what? Humiliate me?"

"I made you sit on my legs, not kneel between them."

"Only because you fear my teeth." I hope he knows that if he tries to shove his cock into my face, I will sever the appendage. Sure, it would grow back, but not his pride.

His posture stiffens, but thankfully, no other part of his anatomy follows suit. Then again, I did casually mention I'd shorten his manhood, so odds are in my favor that it'll make itself tiny for the duration of the evening.

He fists my hair and hauls my head back with such enthusiasm that my neck cracks. "You're really not in a position to issue threats, Fal."

"That was not a threat, merely a reminder of my teeth's sharpness."

"Shall we fetch the food, Maezza?" Justus asks, sending me a pointed look, one which I interpret as, *Holster your tongue, Nipota.*

"Not yet." Dante's reply is low, yet my grandfather must hear him because he doesn't give the six soldiers behind him the order to scurry off to the kitchens.

I wonder if Justus actually thinks this a real meal because I certainly don't. Unless I misconstrued the salt's presence . . .

"First, I've some questions for Antoni." Dante's palm creeps up the side of my ribs.

I know Justus mentioned seducing the prick, but seduction meant the reins were in my hands. Right now, I'm not holding on to any reins.

"Fallon, take the salt."

Out of the corner of my eye, I scan the gaudy carvings of the headboard for the dagger I am to use. How I itch to hold it.

"Better do as I say, or I will do far worse than pry truths off your little sailor's tongue."

My hand jerks to the wooden bowl and pinches out the coarse flakes.

"Now feed it to him."

I shake with rage. Shake so hard that the coarse flakes flutter off my fingers and settle on the tabletop like snow.

The Faerie King slides his index along the underside of my breast, right beneath the band of linen on my brassiere. If only it was made of iron instead of fabric . . .

When he palms my breast, I whirl toward him. "Don't."

He moves his mouth toward my ear again, his hand creasing the silk, straining it over my ribs. "You cannot sit at my table dressed like a whore and expect to be treated like a queen."

"Should I remind you that I did not choose this dress; your general did. You've an issue with it, take it up with him. Or better yet, if you have extra armor lying around, I'd be more than glad to accessorize my nightgown."

"I've no issue with it." His hand crawls down my ribs like a bug and settles heavily on my thigh. When I feel the hem of my dress begin to drift up my shins, I grip a handful of fabric to glue it in place. "Think of your little sailor's fingers."

My blood burns at his threat.

"Feed him salt now or I hike this dress so far up your legs that—"

Though I keep one hand clamped over my dress, I fling the other toward the wooden dish. As I carry the salt to Antoni's mouth, I hold his shiny stare. I worry he's in pain until I catch his gaze lowering to Dante's hand. When his throat bobs, I realize he's hurting for me.

"Stick out your tongue, halfling." Dante's no longer pulling on my dress, but his grip hasn't slackened either.

I'm sorry, I mouth as I drop the salt on the flat of my friend's tongue.

A few breaths later, Dante asks, "Do you still burn for Fallon Rossi?"

"You fed him salt to learn about his feelings?" I ask, outraged.

"Answer, halfling." Dante's blue gaze doesn't shift off Antoni's sweat-slickened face.

He puffs out a breath. "I will always love Fallon."

"What do you think of Lorcan Ríhbiadh?"

"I'm no fan."

"And yet, you've helped him repeatedly over the years. Why is that?"

Antoni's lips are so tight that they form a white line on his pasty face. "Because I disliked the Faerie regime."

"So what does your ideal world look like?"

"I do not—"

"Now, now. Don't deflect."

"My ideal world isn't ruled by Faeries or by Crows."

"What is it ruled by? Surely you don't picture yourself in a crown. Or do you?"

"I believe it should be run by a group of learned people."

"You'd be amongst them?"

"Yes."

"Who else would you choose? The Amari sisters? That remaining cousin of yours? What's his name again? Madden?"

"Mattia."

Dante gives a slow bob of his head. "Would you pick Fallon?"

Antoni drops his eyes to the salt on the table, and although he whispers his answer, I don't miss the hushed word: "No."

Even though this questioning about a new regime is pointless, I cannot help but feel a little offended.

"Whyever not? Don't you find her intelligent?"

Antoni's jaw judders.

"Halfling, I've asked you a question."

He still doesn't answer.

Dante nods to Justus who pulls his sword from his scabbard and takes a step closer to Antoni.

Antoni finally growls, "My choice has nothing to do with her intellect."

"What does it have to do with?"

"Her allegiance."

"To Ríhbiadh, I presume."

Antoni narrows his eyes on the glass. "Yes."

"I know you want me dead, but what of the Crow King?"

My ribs cinch my lungs, cutting off my breaths, and a dull buzzing erupts against my eardrums.

"Do you want Lorcan Ríhbiadh gone, Greco?"

Antoni's lips are so strained that it awakens his wounds and dribbles blood from their corners, accentuating the downturn arc of his mouth.

"Let me rephrase my question: Do you want Lorcan Ríhbiadh, the almighty ruler of the sky, dead?"

Antoni shuts his lids and delivers a confession that tightens the muscle in my chest. "Yes."

"So our ambitions align. Now the question is, do you want him dead more than you want *me* dead?"

Antoni swallows, struggling against the effect of the truth-telling serum. "Yes."

Dante reclines in his seat and rubs his lips. "What do you think, Justus? Do you believe he can be an asset?"

"Perhaps evaluate his worth by sending him out with an obsidian sword?"

"NO!" *What the actual fuck, Justus?* "He'll just give away your location *and* get himself killed."

Dante claps his palm over my mouth. "Did I tell you that you could weigh in?" After a beat, he lowers his hand and flutters his fingers. "Take him away. I'm done with him for now."

Cato marches over to Antoni's chair and pulls it out. "Shall we escort Fallon back also?"

"No. I'm not done with her." When Dante's fingers fuse once again with my thigh and draw the fabric up, I stiffen.

Justus must sense I'm a heartbeat away from taking the wooden box and bashing Dante's skull with it because he claps his hands. "Everyone, out!"

I begin to tremble, not with distress, like Dante surely assumes, but with adrenaline.

This is it.

The moment I end the cruel ruler's life.

"If you defile her, Regio—" Antoni tears his arm from Cato's grip.

"You'll kill me? You've already mentioned it. I took note." Dante drags the fabric of my dress higher.

I think of Lore, of how furious he'd be, and the contemplation of my mate's ire centers me.

"Let me make something clear to you, Antoni. Should you come out of this war alive, Fallon will *never* be yours."

Antoni's entire body shakes. "You think she'll be yours if you rape her?"

"I had no need to resort to rape the first time she spread her legs for me." Dante tips his head to the side, sending his long tresses spilling over his shoulder.

My muscles are so tense that the disgust that rolls through me at the memory of my deflowering doesn't translate into a shudder.

I can feel Antoni call to me with his eyes, but I don't look up. I don't look anywhere but at the hand stroking my thigh against my fucking consent.

Antoni turns very quiet. He must assume I'll lay back and let Dante have his sordid way with me. Perhaps he thinks I still harbor affection for the Faerie King. "Fallon?" he croaks my name as though a vine were digging into his Adam's apple.

Dante inches the silk higher. "For fuck's sake, get him out of here."

Still, I don't react. I will not react until I reach his bed.

I pull my shoulders back, about to suggest heading there now, when Dante says, "Justus, stay behind. And shut the door."

I look up so fast that my vertebrae click.

Justus doesn't meet my panicked stare as he closes the door. He's the picture of serenity while my pulse pounds out of alignment. I tell myself not to jump to conclusions. Dante may simply be seeking a private conference with his general.

"Something on your mind, Your Majesty?"

"Many things, Rossi."

"Shall I step out to give you two privacy?" I hate how thready my voice sounds.

"No." He glides his hand through my hair, and I bristle at his touch but steel my spite, honing my disgust into a weapon that will better serve me than an impulsive reaction. "Feed me salt, Fal."

My blood pounds hard against my eardrums. "Aren't you immune to the condiment?"

"I should be, but miraculously, I've healed." He holds out the hand not brushing my hair and fans out his fingers. "Salt."

I pinch some from the bowl and carry it to his mouth. I grimace when he licks the flakes off my fingers.

"Ask me something personal, Rossi?"

Justus shifts, which makes the dull leather of his boots creak. "Do you have any affection for Fallon, or do you desire her solely for her blood?"

"I care greatly for your granddaughter and believe with all my heart that, in time, she'll come to care for me again."

Wow. *Not two brain cells left to rub together, that one . . .*

The Faerie King's fingers begin to move against my leg again. "I actually believe she may already be remembering how good we were together."

I grit my teeth to bite back the retort scorching my tongue. Dante and I were *never* good. We were friends. And then he used and discarded me, leaving me with nothing but insecurities and a torn hymen.

He runs his index finger down the length of my throat. "So soft tonight."

I'm guessing he's talking about my docile manner and not my skin's texture. Not that my skin is scaly or dry, but it's no different than usual. "Fighting against you hasn't served me."

"Is that why you're so biddable?" He hooks my hair. When his lips land on the apex of my cheekbone, I pivot my head and try to shift off his lap, but that merely makes him grip my thigh harder, hard enough to bruise. "Shh. You were doing so well, moya."

Gods, I hate this male. Of their own accord, my eyes stray back to his headboard.

Dante leans away from me but doesn't slacken his vise-like grip. "Ask me something else, Generali. Something you know I won't care to answer."

"Do you trust me?" Justus asks.

Why the Cauldron would he ask such a question? Is he trying to get caught?

"No. I don't trust you. But I trust that you want to keep your granddaughter on the throne and will do all you can to make sure she doesn't fall from my grace."

From his *grace*? The urge to snort is so strong that it rattles my sinuses.

Dante grips my waist and lifts me, setting me on my feet. "Get on the bed, moya."

Justus fists the doorknob. "I'll let myself out."

"Why are you in such a hurry to depart, Rossi?"

"Because there are some things a grandparent does not care to see."

A smile curls Dante's mouth as he rises from his chair. Instead of coming toward me, he grabs the bowl of salt and ambles toward Justus. "You dressed her, didn't you?"

"I told you, there weren't many outfits to pick from, Maezza."

"Are you certain that's the reason?"

"Yes."

He raises the wooden bowl toward Justus. "Swallow some salt and repeat your answer."

Justus's throat moves with a swallow. Without casting his gaze from Dante's, he takes some salt and eats it.

Dante stretches his neck, eliciting a series of little cracks and clicks. "Why did you select that outfit for Fallon?"

As Justus swallows, I creep closer to the headboard and glance at the shadows between it and the wall, attempting to catch the glint of a blade.

"Because it would distract you, Maezza."

"And why did you want me distracted, Generali?"

"Because if Fallon carries your child, odds are you won't kill her."

What the Cauldron? I balk at Justus. He better be ingesting that Nebban chemical, otherwise . . . otherwise he and I will have a whole lot of words after I find that damn dagger and detach Dante's head.

Just as I slide my fingers across the headboard, Dante asks, "Looking for this, Fal?"

My gaze whizzes back to where he stands, twirling a dagger between his fingers.

My complexion must go as white as the uniform he wears because he *tsks*.

"Seems like we have a traitor in our midst. Now, who"—before my next breath, Dante tosses the salt into Justus's stunned face and spears the dagger through his neck—"could it be?"

CHAPTER 22

I scream while Justus . . . he doesn't emit a single sound. How can he with a dagger wedged through his airway?

"Could it be *you*, Generali Rossi?" Dante twists the dagger.

"Stop, Dante! Stop! Justus didn't do anything." I launch myself toward them and clap my hand around Dante's bicep, managing to hurl his arm down.

Justus's eyes are so wide they're white. And his neck . . . his neck is corded and gushing crimson rivulets.

Please be taking the iron supplement, or whatever Dante was taking.

Please, please, please don't die on me.

I need you.

"Don't take me for a fool, Fallon. The fact that you suddenly care about Justus is all the proof I need. What other secrets are you keeping from me, moya?"

I lunge toward Justus and latch onto the dagger's hilt just as Dante grabs me around the waist. I twirl in his arms and swing, aiming for his throat, but my slippers catch on the salt and I skid, and the iron blade embeds itself inside his eye.

He roars and backhands me.

I lose my balance and fall. For a second, the world goes dark, but then it comes back into perfect focus and I crawl toward Justus. "Get us out of here, Justus. Paint a sigil and get us out."

He shakes his head from side to side very slowly.

Oh my Gods, he's still alive. He's still alive! "Paint a sigil and—"

He sputters, sending more blood spilling from his wound. I try to rip off a piece of my dress to staunch the wound, but that doesn't work. *Fuck, fuck, fuck.*

Keeping my palm on his neck, I scrabble to find the dagger to shear off the fabric, but Dante sent it skidding beneath his bed. Maybe if I poured some of Meriam's blood inside the wound, it would heal him.

I palm his shirt collar, attempting to hook the leather necklace, but cannot find it. Out of all the days not to wear it!

The chamber door flies open and smacks into Justus, rolling his body and pitching my fingers off his neck. I'm about to push the wooden door closed, but freeze when I catch sight of the man trying to squeeze himself through the narrow opening.

I blink like a startled serpent, before whipping my gaze toward the man sprawled on the floor before me.

"Maezza!" Justus gasps as he tries to shoulder the door open, smacking his bleeding doppelganger. "Fallon, move!"

But I cannot move.

I can barely breathe.

Justus—the one not oozing blood—crouches beside me, circles his writhing twin's wound with the tips of his index and middle fingers, then rips open the male's shirt and draws a cross over his heart. Below it, on his abdomen, he paints a strange 'M' that resembles two interlocked peaks.

"Are you hurt?" When I don't answer, he repeats his question, tagging on my name.

I shake my head, gawking at the sweat-slicked brow of the man lying lifeless before us.

Breathing raggedly, Justus sweeps his hand across his twin's forehead as though to feel for a fever. When he suddenly goes still, so does everything inside of me because, before my very eyes, lines of blood appear on the surface of the man's sallow flesh in the shape of that same strange 'M'. Justus slashes his finger through the sigil, transforming the dead version of himself into the dead version of another man—Dottore Vanche.

I sit back on my heels.

More soldiers pour into the room. I stare at them without really seeing them.

"My apologies, Maezza." Justus rises from his crouch. "I didn't know that my healer—"

"Kill him!" Dante points toward Justus. "Guards, kill him—"

No one moves. Or rather, their heads swivel but no one makes a move to end Justus's life.

Dante backs up a step, knocking into a chair, sending it skidding. "Why aren't you heeding my command! I'm your king! You don't answer to the general. You answer to me!"

Justus raises his palms. "Maezza, the perpetrator has been killed. *You* killed him." My grandfather speaks slowly, as though addressing a child.

"You—you—" Dante's finger bobs as the eye not shielded by his palm drops to me, then past me, to the corpse on the floor. "I don't —" Lips stretched in a frightening grimace, he swings his attention back up to Justus.

"I'm sorry, Maezza. Meriam put me under some spell and drew a sigil on the healer's forehead that not only made him mad, but that made him resemble"—he rolls his lips together, then wrinkles his nose as though the sight of himself dead were nauseating—"*me*. I've seen to her punishment."

"Punishment?" Dante sneers. "I will kill that witch. After I kill your granddaughter."

Well . . . fuck. I eye the door, wondering how far I could get before the soldiers catch up to me. I could hide, but then what? I roll my eyes toward the ceiling, suddenly remembering the low rumble from earlier. What if—What if I could get whatever's out there to crumble this place?

I push onto my feet.

"Grab her!" Dante roars.

Before I can raise my arms, Cato has my wrists pinned behind my back and vines are crawling around my body, incapacitating me. I stare at Justus, about to beg him to help me, but I stifle my plea because I no longer know whether he's on my side, or if it was the healer and Meriam aiding me all along.

Justus strides toward Dante. "Your Majesty, let me look at your eye."

Dante stares and stares at his general with the one I didn't injure. Slowly he lowers his palm. I'm so numb with shock that the sight of his scarlet-veined eyeball and blood-streaked cheek doesn't contort my insides.

Everything about this moment feels surreal.

"Get me some fresh gauze and a packet of the Nebban chemical!" Justus yells. "NOW!"

One of the soldiers leaps out of the room.

"Sit, Maezza." Justus gestures to the chair. "I will do all I can to counter the effect of the iron but I cannot guarantee I'll be able to save your eye."

Dante watches Justus, his expression guarded, skeptical. As he finally sits, his attention drifts to the inert healer. "I thought—I thought it was you, Justus."

"I understand how it looks, but please know that I would never betray you. I want Luce to belong to us. Only to us." Justus's words seem to slacken the tension in Dante's shoulders.

"I will kill Meriam."

"I told you. I punished her."

"She deserves to die." Dante says this while looking straight at me.

"If they die, we'll have no more magic, and the Shabbins will come and aid Lore."

I try to make sense of timelines. The healer arrived the same day as my unbinding, but Justus went to fetch him after Meriam released my magic, no? Unless he was there all along? My mind buzzes with confusion.

Justus prods the skin around the Faerie King's eye socket. "Can you see out of your left eye?"

Dante's jaw ticks as he keeps glowering my way. "No."

I do not cower under his scrutiny. I hold his stare, conveying in silence how lucky he is that vision is all he lost.

A moment later, the soldier bursts back into the room with a carefully wrapped packet that he places on the glass table.

Justus unwraps it, then pinches out some mint-green dust and feeds it to Dante. "I'll also put some on your eye. It may sting but it'll counter the effect of the iron instantly."

If it does burn, Dante doesn't show it.

Once Justus has wrapped the king's head in gauze, he turns back toward me, or rather toward the fallen body at my feet. "Brambilla, take Fallon back to her cage and lock her inside. I will deal with her once I dispose of the corpse."

Deal with me? For what? Trying to defend him, to shield him from Dante? Fucking ingrate.

"Apologies, Maezza. I know you were looking forward to spending time with Fallon this evening, but I believe it's safer she's put away until she stops acting like a feral creature."

Yes. I can vouch that it's a whole lot safer. Not that Dante looks interested in spending time with me. I'm rather certain getting stabbed in the eye will put him off being intimate with me for the duration of my imprisonment.

"I'll go toss the corpse in my mother's grove so it doesn't stink up our stronghold. I'll be back soon." Justus kneels beside the glassy-eyed healer, grabs him under the arms, and hauls him over his shoulder. And then he stands. "Walk ahead of me, Brambilla."

Cato turns, forcing me along down the darkened hallway that seems to echo with the gush of my pulse. The walk back to the vault room is quiet. Only our footfalls disturb the sense of doom that hangs around us.

I glance back over my shoulder, my gaze colliding with Justus's dusky blue stare. He seems thoughtful more than angry. Then again, it's so dark, and the body he carries, so broad, that I may be misinterpreting his strain for pensiveness.

Justus is still walking behind us when we reach the vault room. Does he not trust Cato to escort me to my cell? Just as we reach the tunnel entrance, Justus stops.

"Sergeant?" Justus eases his necklace from his collar and uncorks the vial before dripping some blood onto his fingertip.

Cato halts.

"Approach."

Cato peers into the vault room past Justus as though to check on the whereabouts of his fellow soldiers. When he sees none, he tugs me back the few steps we've taken down the tunnel until we stand so close that I can smell the tinny odor that wafts off the cadaver of brave Dottore Vanche. If only Meriam's ploy had worked out better.

He can no longer hear me, yet I mouth a silent, *Thank you for your courage*. Or was it madness? I'm reminded of the brave and kind Selvatin, Sewell, who perished trying to help me free the crow imprisoned in Xema Rossi's grove.

"No one touches her until I return, you hear me? No one." As he brings his bleeding fingertip to the wall, Justus drops his voice further. "Not even our king."

I'd have tried to gauge his expression were I not so fascinated by the shape he's drawing on the black stone—a circle fitted with a cross, the bottommost side of which lopes over the curved edge in a downward slash.

As he tows his finger off the wall, I spring my gaze to his. A mix of anger and anguish pool shadows into the sharp nooks and crannies of his face.

"Better yet, lock the cellar door." His mouth barely shifts around the command.

"Lock it? But—" A tremor goes through Cato. "But I don't have a key."

"Which is why you lock it, Brambilla." Justus gives his head a little shake. "I'll open it upon my return. Got it?"

"Yes, Generali."

"Good. Now go."

Cato tugs me away with a quiet, "Come."

As we beat a hasty retreat toward my cell, I peer over my shoulder and meet Justus's shiny stare a second before he stamps the wall with his hand and slips through.

My lungs begin to contract anew, pulsing out breath after breath that are slowly but surely bringing me back to life.

Does Justus realize he's just given me the keys to Dante's fortress?

What a silly question. That man does not commit errors, and an oversight of this grandeur would be the gravest error of all.

CHAPTER 23

The moment the cellar door clanks behind us, I pull my wrists from Cato's grip. Although not bruising, the sergeant is so fraught with nerves that he holds me tight.

"Any chance you could loosen these?" I nod to the tangle of vines strangling my upper body. "I know it's not your magic, but surely you've a nifty blade that can shear through magical restraints?"

"I'm sorry, Fallon, but I cannot—" The sergeant's throat bobs with a swallow that makes him tug on his shirt collar as though it were choking him. "I cannot free you."

"Why not?"

"*Why not?*" He sounds strangled. "You just assaulted the king!"

"Because he stabbed Justus!" I don't add that I would've assaulted Dante either way and that, had I not been distracted by the sight of my dying grandfather, I would've assaulted him better. "Wouldn't you have defended your general?"

Cato swings his gaze toward the tunnel unfurling like a dark throat beyond the locked bars, before assailing me with the full force of his crazed gaze. Clearly, I've bedeviled the poor man with my query, which does make me wonder what he'd have done had he been in my situation. Didn't he swear an oath to Justus Rossi?

"I sensed there was something strange about the general. I mean, the man posing as the general. *Merda*. I should've stayed in that room." He shoves a hand through his mussed curtain of white hair, ungluing the strands stuck to the perspiration glossing his forehead.

"I'm glad you didn't, for if you'd stayed, you may have gotten hurt."

"But at least *you* wouldn't have!"

"I didn't, Cato."

He stares at my dress, so I peer down. Between the coils of green vines, the pale pink is splattered with droplets of red.

"Not my blood."

Cato swallows. Once. Twice. After the third time, he says, "You stabbed the king's eye with an iron blade. It may not heal."

"Good."

"Good? What do you think he'll do to you?" Cato gapes at me as though I'm one crow short of a murder.

The metaphor stirs my pulse and brightens my lids with the glossy design Justus painted on the wall.

My way out.

My way back.

Cato rubs at his brow again. If his attempt is to smooth the furrows there, he's failing. "He may kill you for this."

I stare at the walls surrounding me, wondering if I could slip through them? Where would I end up? "I'm useless to him dead."

"What if he injures you? What if he removes one of your eyes?"

I shoot him a dark smile. "I dare him to try."

"Fallon, this is no laughing matter."

"Am I laughing?"

"You're smiling."

"Of course I'm smiling." Since I'm speaking through said curved lips, my words are slightly garbled. "I just dodged getting sexually assaulted by some limp-pricked pureling, Cato. Not to mention that Justus"—*showed me the way out*—"is not dead."

"Since when do you care about that man?"

"You're right. I don't. But had he been dead, then we'd all have been fucked, because we would've been stuck down here." I stare at the dusty swirl of glass bottles coating the wall. "Unless there's a door I'm not aware of?"

Cato's silence tows my gaze off the rows of corks.

"Is there?"

He glances sideways and says, "No."

I can taste the lie on his breath.

"I'm going to airlift you into the cage now, Fallon. Please don't fight me. It's the safest place for you at the moment."

"I'm perfectly safe down here."

"Not if the sprites come. They can slip through the bars of the cellar door, but they cannot slip through your cage bars. Justus has spelled them to keep anyone that isn't you out."

Just as he says this, footfalls and wingbeats echo through the tunnel.

"Please, Fallon. Please. I don't want you to get hurt."

"I'm not going back inside that cage."

"Sergeant Brambilla." Two sprites flit through the door, speaking in unison. They even pant in unison. "The king is requesting an audience with you."

Cato goes as white as the sun-bleached sheets Nonna would hang to dry outside in the summer months. "I—I—"

"Justus has the key to the cellar, so I'm afraid an audience will have to wait," I say since my friend cannot seem to form a sentence.

"Sergente, the key!" Lastra rattles the cellar door.

I repeat what I've just told the winged Faeries, then add, "Any chance you can remove your vines, Lastra?" They could potentially have been shaped by another Faerie—I was a tad distracted to check who bound me—but since his eyes are green, chances are it was him. "The door's locked. It isn't as though I can go anywhere."

"They stay on." Cato speaks between barely separated lips. "Unless you get into your cage."

I stare long and hard at the white-haired male. "You don't trust me?"

"Have you given me reason to?"

"I would never cause you harm, Cato."

He slants me a stare that makes my heart hold still. The truth is written inside his gaze. He doesn't believe me.

"Fine." My jaw hardens like my rib cage. "Don't take off my vines, but at least loosen them. They're digging into my flesh."

A nerve feathers Cato's jaw. "Do as she says, Lastra."

"Are you out of your fucking mind, Sergente? What if she—what if she stabs *you* in the eye?"

"She won't." Cato cocks an eyebrow my way. "Right?"

I almost swear an oath but bite it off my tongue a second before it can leap off. "No harm will come to the sergeant."

Lastra's thick brown eyebrows crouch so low they all but hug his lash line. "Swear it."

A tiny pearl of sweat beads down my nape as I chew on the inside of my cheek, considering how best to tell Lastra to fuck off. It's the sight of Cato's rounded jaw that inspires my reply. "I would, but I'd be breaking a vow I made to my beloved grandmother—and I do mean Justus's former wife, not the spanking-new one."

"Let her be, Lastra."

Flashing me a loaded stink eye, the soldier finally loosens the magical green ropes, allowing me to wiggle my arms back along my sides. I stretch my fingers, then my neck, all my bones clicking as the tension releases from my body.

Just as I think Lastra may be removing them altogether, his vines snake around my wrists and pin them together. I take comfort in the fact that not only are my shoulders no longer wedged back, but I've access to my fingers. Now to prick them and test Justus's nifty little sigil . . .

"Please inform His Majesty that if he cares for an audience, he will have to come to me." Cato approaches the cellar door behind which Lastra is still standing, fingers laced in sparkling green flickers that match the shade of his narrowed eyes. "Otherwise, I will go to him as soon as Justus returns."

He nods, then mutters a, "Be careful, Sergente."

After he leaves, I look up at the sprites buzzing about the cellar, beady eyes tapered on me as though I were a vile marsh creature. I've no doubt I look like one, what with all the gore staining my dress and collarbone. "Any chance you two could fetch me a washcloth and a change of clothes?"

"No," they answer as one.

"Are you afraid I may strangle you with them?" I ask sweetly.

"Just go get her what she needs." Cato sounds as bedraggled as he looks.

They toss pin-sized glowers his way.

"Did my command not reach your ears, sprites?"

I school the smile from my lips when they both jerk their heads in assent.

Right before they buzz off, I call out, "A soldier's uniform preferably! I like pants."

I'm not certain whether they heard me, but Cato certainly did because he balks as though I've just suggested the sprites take a swim in Mareluce to hand-feed the serpents. "Regio won't approve of a soldier's uniform."

I want to tell Cato that he can shove Regio's opinion of my clothing where the sun doesn't shine, which is basically everywhere, but I bite back my retort since it'll only get Cato in trouble, and that's the last thing I want.

As he unbinds his white hair to redo his mussed plait, my mind fills with the memory of Justus's key sigil. Although its shape was barely discernable, what with the dusky lighting in this glorified anthill, I can still picture the path his finger took, as well as the gleam of Meriam's blood on the black backdrop.

As I turn the image over in my mind's eye, my stomach growls.

The sound must reach Cato's broad ears because he peeks at my abdomen before shifting his gaze to the gate. "I'll have the sprites bring you something to eat when they return. Hopefully, they'll be able to ferret something through the door."

As he studies it, measuring the width between the bars, I lift my bound hands to my mouth and press the tip of my index finger against my pointiest tooth.

"What are you doing?" Cato's question startles my hand out of my mouth.

I make a show of picking something from my teeth. "Somfen stook."

It takes Cato a second to parse out my garbled words. When he does, one of his eyebrows slants low. "Really?"

"I don't know." I make a great show of running my tongue against my teeth. "You wouldn't happen to have a toothbrush laying around?"

"I'll ask the sprites once they return." After that, his stare doesn't return to the door. It stays on me.

Though I understand his distrust, it hurts a little. I amble around the cellar that's larger than my little house in Tarelexo, seeking out something pointy to jab my finger on. The stone shelves are so smooth they gleam like oil spills, not a jagged point in sight.

Glass shards it will have to be, then.

"Don't touch the wine, Fallon."

"I'm not planning on drinking it." When he slants me a look, I add, "Or smashing it on your head."

"I hadn't even considered the second option, but really don't touch anything. I could get in trouble if bottles go missing from the cellar."

Since he's on the other side of the room, I wriggle a dust-coated bottle from a shelf and gawp at the Lucin crown emblem stamped on the gold wax seal that was dripped over the cork. "This was Costa Regio's stash?"

The peeling, yellowed label reads a date that is so far in the past, it knocks my gaze toward the rest of the bottles. Vintages like these would sell for small fortunes—not coppers or silvers but gold. To think that when I smashed my cage, I took out at least two dozen bottles.

Not that I care, but Gods, there just may be more wealth stashed in this cellar than in the vault.

"Please put the bottle back, Fallon."

I pretend to slot it onto the shelf, but instead, drop it with a perhaps tad too dramatic, "Oops."

Cato huffs my name and starts toward me. Before he can blow me into the cage, I crouch and stab my finger on a serrated point. A muted hiss snakes past my teeth.

"Move away from the glass." As the wine gurgles and puddles around my gold satin slippers, tossing the scent of peaty cork into the air, my friend halts and reaches for his sword. "I said move away from the bottle, Fallon."

I raise my bound hands and do as he asks. "I'm backing up. You can put away your weapon."

But he doesn't. And damn if it doesn't sting more than my flesh wound.

"I would never attack you, Cato." I make my way toward the cellar door, toward the beveled black stone that frames the whorls of solid metal keeping me enclosed in this dank silo.

"Where are you going?"

"I'm putting some distance between us so you don't worry that I'll pounce on you while you pick up my mess."

He stares at the expensive debris before finally sheathing his sword and squatting to collect the seesawing pieces of umber glass.

Keeping one eye on him, I smoosh my finger on the stone and sketch a circle that turns out a tad lopsided. I add the cross. Satisfied that it resembles Justus's sigil, I shut my eyes and ram my palm against the stone.

I'm coming, Lore.

CHAPTER 24

When after three brisk breaths, my body still hasn't slipped through the doorframe, I fling my lids up and mutter a slew of curses, and not the magical kind. Wait, do I need to utter magical words?

Did Justus? I cannot recall his lips moving over any spell, but I was so concentrated on his design that I may have missed it. Sighing, I check over my shoulder.

Since Cato is still busy picking up the mess of glass, I attempt a second escape. My hand is so unsteady that my circle and cross end up resembling the symbol for the female gender, but I still press my hand against it and—

Nothing.

Ugh!

Just as I'm about to try a third time, since third times are the charm and all that, the sprites soar through the bars of the door. Heart wedged inside my throat, I spin around and sidle against the smooth stone, then shimmy to wipe away my failed attempts at escaping. I never thought I'd be relieved to wear a dress stained with so much gore, but here I am, relieved.

"We couldn't find a dress," the sprite hugging a soap dish as wide as he is announces. The second he spots me beside the door, he jerks several centimeters higher, the soap dish and accompanying hunk of soap clattering on the stone floor.

His friend also flits higher before dropping the wet cloth beside the soap and hammered bronze dish. I take it they're frightened of me, which is an odd sentiment since I've never inspired fright in anyone before. I admittedly like the new vibe I give off.

I can just imagine how proud Lore would be. The thought of my mate sends my heart into a tailspin, wringing beats that clatter against my ribs. I want to go home more than I've ever wanted anything in my life.

"Since you have wings, please dispose of our queen's mess in the highest stacks." Cato nods toward the glass he's piled up so neatly it resembles a modern vase.

"Our queen?" One of the sprites hikes up a hefty blond brow that vanishes behind bluntly-cut bangs.

"Yes. Queen. You would do well not to let her rank slip your mind, Dirk."

Where Dirk cocks his eyebrow even farther, his ponytailed friend swoops low to grab a wedge of glass. As he carries it up, he swerves under its weight. I rub my thumbnail into the pad of my index finger to keep the cut weeping. I'm not giving up.

I walk over to the washcloth and soap and pick both up, then grab the bronze dish. I move toward one of the walls and begin to scrub at my collarbone. I'm probably making more of a mess, but at least, it's watering down the scent of blood.

As I scour my skin, I study my reflection in the bronze dish. Although tinted copper, I don't miss the unhealthy pallor of my skin. Oh, to be outdoors again . . . I will climb onto the stone turrets of the Sky Kingdom and roast my carcass for days when I get home. I can already picture myself sandwiched between Sybille and Phoebus, guzzling down goblets of Sky wine, gossiping about all things Crow, Shabbin, and Fae.

I've never been the greatest fan of gossip yet suddenly crave it like a bee craves pollen. I want to have conversations about trivial things and laugh until my lungs ache. I want to gorge on *beinnfrhal* and that cheese flecked in salt and herbs that Connor serves at the Sky Tavern.

I squeeze my fingers into such tight fists that my pricked finger lances. Enough with the pity party, I chastise myself. I've magic.

Magic that can allow me to pass through walls! If Justus can do it, so can I.

Peeking over my shoulder to make sure Cato and the sprites are busy, I dig my thumbnail into the base of my cut to coax out more blood, then press the tip of my finger against the smooth surface of the soap dish and slowly recreate the lock symbol.

Glass crashes, flicking my pulse. I'm about to slap the washcloth against the copper dish to remove all traces of my treachery when my index, middle, and ring fingers slip right through the metal.

I gawk at my hand in awe, mesmerized by the show of flesh poking from a solid surface. Oh my Gods! It worked. It fucking worked!

My chest grows hot with emotion. My entire life, I dreamed of this moment. Although I would've loved nothing more than to share it with my family and friends, with Lore, a smile blooms along my lips.

The despair I was consumed by a minute ago vanishes like dew under a blazing sun.

I have an unlimited well of power at my fingertips. Power which I can wield.

From the corner of my eye, I catch movement. Cato is striding toward me. I yank my hand free from the soap dish, then wipe it down with the soiled towel.

Although it smudges my reflection, I catch the new spark that animates my violet eyes.

I will set myself free.

As soon as Justus opens that door, whether he allows me to surface or not, I will find my way back to the wall through which he vanished and I will paint my path to freedom.

"You've still got blood." Cato scratches the underside of his jaw. "Here."

I wipe at the patch of skin he indicates, then go to work on the silk. The manual labor makes the minutes pass by quicker and gives me time to ponder why the sigil didn't work earlier. Because my drawings were deficient, or because there was no air pocket to slip into?

I'm still thinking about it when Cato blows my mattress down from the cage and dims the fire burning in the sconces. But then I start thinking about something else entirely. How long does it take someone to dispose of a body?

"Cato?"

"Yes, Fallon?"

"How far is the Rossi grove from where we are?"

Silence.

Such a stubborn man . . . "What if Justus doesn't come back?" I ask him, studying the shelving units which I could possibly scale, but what if we're so deep underground, that even the ceiling won't let me through?

"He will. His wife is here. His granddaughter. His king. He'll come back." Is it me, or does Cato sound as though he's trying to convince himself?

My pulse suddenly dumps adrenaline into my veins. Adrenaline and hope. Lore mentioned he had Crows circling over every part of the Kingdom.

What if one of them has found Justus?

CHAPTER 25

A whisper-soft touch steals up the length of my body, tickles my hip bone, before dipping into the valley of my waist and rolling over the knolls of my rib cage. ***You left me . . .***

My heart holds very, *very* still. ***Lore?***

He rakes his nails back down the length of my body, then splays his fingers around my thigh. ***You should not have left me.***

I try to open my eyes but cannot seem to reel my lids up. It's as though my lashes were coated in honey. I want to raise my hands to scrub at them, but my hands, like my lashes, are immovable. ***Why can't I move? Why can't I see you?***

Promise to carry me in your heart always.

You're my mate, Lore. You were inside my heart before you were inside the rest of me. My breaths come out in brisk pants that make my lungs ache. ***How are we talking right now? Is Dante dead? Did I kill him?***

He runs the silken tips of his fingers over my cheek, then traces the frame of my face. ***No, Little Bird; I did.***

But—No. That's impossible. I try to shift onto my back but my body won't roll. ***Bronwen said you'd lose your humanity.***

Animals are capable of love, too, my Little Bird.

I know that, but— Why did you say that?

Spread your wings and meet me where the clouds roll over the

horizon and the stars are at their brightest. The sky, like my kingdom, is yours.

Mine? **What?** ***Lore, you're not making any sense. Did we marry while I was unconscious or something?***

His cold breath fans across my cheeks, before billowing away like wind-buffeted mist. ***Remember me.***

Lore?

Nothing.

Lore?! My throat burns like my eyes. I scream his name.

"Fallon, wake up."

I'm shaken so hard that this time, when I will my eyes open, my lids spool right up.

Cato clasps my shoulders, his hands as icy as the sweat coursing down my nape. I stare wildly around me, and although I loathe every millimeter of this prison, I've never been so glad for the sight of so much obsidian because so much obsidian means my conversation with Lore never happened.

Unless . . . "Is Dante alive?"

Cato's eyes are the gray of storm clouds. "Since when do you speak Shabbin?"

I blanch. "I—I don't."

"I may not understand your mother tongue, but I know what it sounds like."

I was sleep-talking in Shabbin? *Merda*. I glance around to see who else may have heard and find twin sets of beady eyes glaring at me.

"We should inform the king," hisses the sprite with the bangs that gobble up half his head.

At least that answers my earlier question about Dante's state of being. If he's alive, then my mate is as well. Thank the Cauldron it was only a nightmare . . .

"*I'll* be informing our king when he awakens. For now, no one is to disturb his rest." Metal clinks and hinges groan as Justus Rossi unlocks the cellar door.

I'm as glad as I am disappointed to see him, for if he's back, then that means Lorcan's sentries have yet to uncover Costa's stronghold. My nightmare wallops me upside the head, knocking sense into me.

Actually, scratch that.

I am *extremely* glad Justus wasn't spotted for if Lore knew of this underground fortress, he would probably find a way to raid it and murder all those involved with my disappearance, and though I'd be fine with the slaughter of most of my jailers, I cannot have him kill Cato, Justus, or Meriam.

"You three go get some sleep." Justus nods to my guards while I roll myself into sitting. "I'll take over." He runs his hands through his mussed, rust-colored hair, then thumbs the purple pockets rimming his eyes.

"Are you certain, Generali? You look—"

"Go."

The sprites don't waste a single second.

Cato, on the other hand, stops and starts, stops and starts. Before stepping over the cellar's threshold, he asks, "Does the king still desire an audience with me?"

"No. I've promised him that no one besides Meriam and the healer were involved in the attempt on his life, so you're in the clear, Brambilla." When he still doesn't leave, Justus huffs. "Are you daft or deaf?"

The white-haired Faerie lingers, his gaze fastened to me. "You're not—"

"Spit it out, Sergente."

"You're not going to harm Fallon?"

"I'm not."

My heart lightens at Cato's concern. What a good man he is. If only he could see Dante's true colors.

Once he leaves, Justus walks over to the wall and paints the sigil for privacy on the stone frame.

"When did you and Vanche pull the switcheroo?"

He hikes up an eyebrow as he turns back toward me. "Switcheroo?"

"When did he transform into you?"

"When he devised the idiotic plan with my wife."

"So you weren't in on it?"

"Do you really think I would've sent you half-naked and weaponless into the king's chamber?"

"Where were you?"

"I had to meet with the dunce Dante left in charge of Isolacuori."

"Tavo?"

"That's the one," Justus grumbles.

"Has Lorcan not murdered him yet?"

"Surprisingly not. He's still hoping Tavo will lead him to you."

"Speaking of leading him to me, my mate's losing patience."

A corner of Justus's lips curls up. "One cannot lose something one has never been imbued with."

I smirk. "Harsh."

"But not untrue. On a scale of one to ten, what are my odds of surviving your mate's wrath?"

"Ten being none?"

He nods.

"Ninety-eight. Ninety-nine." Though I say it with humor, it's the sad truth. "Unless you return me to him . . ."

"I cannot do that yet, Fallon." He drops his eyes to the toecaps of his boots that are looking as scuffed as the healer's were earlier.

"Look, I understand why you're keeping me down here."

He peers at me, a small groove etched between his brows as though he was confused, which, admittedly, is odd considering he knows all about Bronwen's prophecy.

"I know I must be the one to kill Dante, but why keep Meriam down here? Why can't you carry her somewhere else?"

The furrow turns shallower but doesn't disappear. I suppose that between his clandestine operations and his advanced age, wrinkles are inevitable. "She cannot leave."

"Why not? Does she not trust me to finish him off? I may not inspire *much* confidence, but I'm chock-full of grit."

His smile is gentle. "Hold on to that grit, for oftentimes, that's what saves us. As for why I don't carry her away . . . I misspoke. It isn't that she *cannot* leave; it's that she *will not*. You may not believe this, but that woman cares immensely about you."

Definitely difficult to imagine. It isn't as though we've had much time to bond. And yes, blood may tie us to people biologically, but if my upbringing has taught me anything, it's that biology does not dictate to whom we give our hearts.

I stand up and stick out my hand. "Hand me your blade."

"How did that work out for you last time?"

"It worked out better for me than it did for Dargento and Dante." I add a brazen smile as I recall the dagger poking from the king's face.

Justus sighs, but a faint smile creeps along the taut edges of his lips. "He full Nebban powder now." I take it Justus has reverted to speaking in Shabbin. "So attack must wait."

In other words, his body won't allow the iron blade to slip through. "How long?"

"A day. Two. When scent returns normal, Meriam will give lesson in vault, and I will lock inside."

My claustrophobia kicks in at the idea of being locked inside an armored safe with Dante. I try to reassure myself that Meriam will be there, too. *Probably*. Unless—

"All four of us, Fallon," Justus murmurs.

I rub the side of my neck, attempting to iron out the chaotic beats of my heart. "How did Dante know about the dagger?"

"Lastra catch Vance slipping from king's chamber."

"You mean . . . Dottore Vanche?"

Justus tilts his head to the side, which sends a few loose tendrils cascading over his shoulder. He seems to be waiting. For what, I've no—

Wait. Does he mean . . . Oh my Gods. "Do you mean Vance as in *the* Vance?"

Justus's eyes dance with the flickering glow of the fire burning in the sconces, clearly getting a kick out of my discomfiture. "Yes, Fallon."

"As in the notorious rebel leader?"

He smiles and adds four words that level my brain and leave me gaping harder than the day Phoebus brought me into the Acolti vault. "As in my son."

CHAPTER 26

His son? My—my uncle? Well, *sort of* uncle.

How could Nonna not have told me?

"But his ears . . .?"

Justus's eyes hold an amused glint. "His mother isn't Ceres."

I thought I'd reached the limit of my jaw's extension, but apparently, my mandibles are mighty flexible.

Cauldron, my uncle is an infamous insurgent.

My mind suddenly fills with his face, with his wounded neck, and I correct myself: *was*, not *is*. I'm glad my shock could offer Justus a reprieve from his mourning, but how he must be hurting.

"I'm so sorry for your loss, Justus. I wish I could've saved him, but—but you and Meriam refuse to teach me anything useful."

"He alive, Fallon. He long road ahead, but he alive."

My lids lift so high that the ends of my lashes jab my brow bone. My mind is officially blown. "You're just bursting with revelations."

His wary smile softens the hard lines of his face.

I frown as something dawns on me. "Antoni knows Vance. How did he not recognize him?"

"Meriam painted face."

Is he saying that he and Meriam disguised Vance? "Do I know his real face?"

"No. I made certain paths no cross."

"Why?"

"Because he like you"—he surveys the spiraling racks of bottles—"much impetuous."

I'm so stunned that the heap of questions stacking on my tongue pile up like the fishing boats in the Tarelexian wharf.

Eventually, I manage to smooth out my train of thought. "Are you hiding any more little Rossis I should know about?"

"No."

For a long moment, neither of us speak, but then the pileup of questions fluidifies, and I ask, "Earlier, when I was walking toward Dante's chamber, I touched the tunnel walls and they trembled. Why?"

"Because chamber beneath ocean. The serpents feel you. Hopefully, they not give your location to Crows in Tarespagia."

"Here I'm hoping they did. I know, I know . . . it's selfish. I need to get rid of Dante to avoid Armageddon, or whatever happens to Luce if I don't." I mull over the prophecy for the trillionth time, parsing out each word, each syllable, each consonant. "Bronwen said that Lore would lose his humanity. Why is that?"

"Because Dante's blood hold Meriam's magic, and Crows cannot harm your bloodline. It was a—how you say?" He must not find the adequate phrasing because he drops his voice and finishes his sentence in Lucin, "A *caveat* that Queen Mara of Shabbe—or Mórrígan, as she's known to the Crows—saw to when she gave humans the power to shift. A guarantee of sorts that the race she created couldn't turn against her."

A candle sparks to life inside my mind, casting light on all the scattered pieces of information Meriam gave me the night of my unbinding. "Lore didn't lose his humanity when he beheaded Marco because Marco wasn't Andrea's true son."

Justus nods even though it isn't a question. "He recognized him as his heir only to placate his wife who threatened to have Andrea's lover murdered."

My eyes round with shock.

Justus marches over to the tunnel entrance and paints a second sigil. Since blood penetrates stone, I wonder why he adds a new one? As an additional guarantee that our conversation cannot travel down the hallway?

"Only Dante is his legitimate heir. And the sole reason Andrea even had an heir was because his wife made him ingest some Fae-made potion that confused him and made him believe she was Lazarus."

I'm so shocked and appalled that I almost feel pity for Dante, but Dante doesn't deserve my pity. "Does Bronwen know why the Crows cannot kill Dante?"

"Yes."

My relief is so great that it rids me of breath.

"You asked me the other day why the blood-bind was necessary, and I promised to explain everything. I will keep speaking in Lucin, because my knowledge of the Shabbin tongue is insufficient."

I take it that this is what prompted him to draw an additional silence spell.

He retraces his steps toward me. "The enchantment Meriam cast on the Regios created a new breed of Faeries—ones with Shabbin magic in their blood. Once she understood the gravity of what she'd done, she gave Costa the thing he desired most—a blood-bind." Justus traces the interlocked circles that mar both his palm and Meriam's. "It was the only way she could think to keep him in the dark about the amount of power she'd gifted him."

"And it worked?"

"It worked. He bled Meriam for years. Toted around vials of her blood thinking it was the only way for him to spellcast. The problem was that he passed on this new power to his son Andrea, and Andrea passed it down to his son."

Holy Crow . . . "So Dante didn't need to marry me to blood-cast?"

"No. But now he cannot spellcast without using your blood. He's stuck."

"But so am I."

"I'm sorry, Fallon, but we couldn't risk him realizing he had magic."

I slide my lips together. I understand their logic, but am I still annoyed to have been forced into a magical union with a lunatic? Fuck yes.

"Plus, we couldn't risk him dying on anyone's blade but yours or the Cauldron will never forgive Meriam and remain shut."

"Shut?"

"Did I fail to mention that the Cauldron was so furious that it sealed itself off from *everyone*?"

"Um, yes."

"I heard you wished to lift the Crows' obsidian curse, Nipota. Only the Cauldron has the power to do that."

"Are there any secrets in Luce that haven't made it to your broad ears?"

He smiles.

"You should leave, Justus."

"Even if I hadn't sworn an oath to Bronwen to keep you safe, I wouldn't leave you, Fallon. You may not be my flesh and blood, but that's never stopped me from caring. From afar and in silence, I've watched you bloom, and I couldn't be prouder of the tenacious woman Ceres has raised."

My chest heats and beats. "Many would argue I'm useless."

"*Useless*? You stole through the kingdom with an army at your heels and not only made it out alive, but also victorious." His eyes twinkle like the ocean's surface at sunrise.

"You didn't look all that proud when I showed up at Marco's revel."

"I was panicked Marco was going to murder you," he hisses, twinkle gone.

Who'd have thought Justus Rossi was so in touch with his emotions? Not me, and certainly not Nonna, who painted him out to be such a callous man that I wonder if she ever saw this side of him . . . but she must have. Why would he show it to me and not to the woman with whom he founded a family?

Like the peeling bark of a sapling in the throes of spring, the years of hatred I cultivated toward General Rossi slough away. "One more question. Where is my mother hidden?"

Justus's neck suddenly straightens, and he takes a step away from me. It's only then that I sense a nearby heartbeat. I peer into the entryway of my cell, spotting a shadow lapping at the stone floor like spume.

"Since you're here, Lastra"—Justus tilts his head to the side, his face wiped clean of our conspiring—"make yourself useful and weave Fallon a ladder so she may return to her cage."

"No cage, please, Generali. Lock the cellar door."

"Back in your cage. *Now*!" His breath is so harsh that it flutters a piece of my hair, but his eyes are soft and pleading.

His volatile attitude grooves my forehead. I'm guessing he must be worried Lastra will report his odd behavior, but locking me up is next-level.

He seizes my arm and tugs me close as the soldier concentrates on growing his vine ladder. In my ear, he murmurs, "It's powerproof."

Right. Cato mentioned that.

"Carry her mattress back up, Lastra."

The man nods and heaves the flaccid excuse for a bed up his little ladder.

"See that she receives no food and no drink for she deserves to ache for what she's done."

What a brilliant actor my grandfather is. He's even got *me* convinced that he despises me. "If I die of starvation, I won't be of much use to the cyclops king."

Justus strikes me with an incendiary stare. "Do not speak of your husband in that manner!"

I try to communicate through my stare my thorough displeasure at how seriously he's taking his role as my torturer.

"Inside your cage. Now."

Huffing, I whirl and walk toward where Lastra simpers, entirely convinced by Justus's act. As I sidestep him, I cannot help but flip him off and call him a puckered sore.

Under his breath, he hisses, "Careful, strega . . ."

"Or what?" I hiss as I reach my loathed cage. "You'll slap me?"

His eyes become as hard as jade. "Someone should."

"What was that, Lastra?" Justus's voice booms over the acres of bottles.

"Nothing, Generali."

I flash the cowed soldier a glacial smile and add, "My mate will have such fun with you."

"Your mate is down three birds." Lastra's green eyes flicker like the flames burning in the sconces. "Two more to go, and Luce will be Crow-free. *Forever*."

I look toward Justus so quickly that my neck cracks. "Is that true?"

Justus's eye twitches. "Lorcan Ríhbiadh cannot help looking for you himself. You're proving the finest lure we could've dreamed of. Now shut your door."

I'm so busy scouring his expression for the truth that I cannot get my hands to curl around the bars.

A gush of water shoots out of Justus's palm and slaps my cage door closed, leaving me blinking waterlogged lashes at his retreating figure. I scrub the droplets away, yelling out his name, but he doesn't return.

He leaves me to stew in my little cage for so long that I think I will go mad. Perhaps riling me up is part of the plan. After all, when Cato arrives hours later to replace the Faerie twerp Justus left me alone with, I'm foaming at the mouth to sink a blade not only into Lastra's neck but also into Dante's.

Luce will never be his.

Never.

I will myself to flock to the Sky Kingdom through the only conduit I have—Bronwen's eyes—but however hard I try, I stay locked inside my body that is festering with rage and aching from lack of food.

I'm past mad; I'm *feral*, made even more so by the fact that my blood magic doesn't work on the cursed bars of my cage. I reassure myself that for twenty-two years, I lived without any powers and I made it out alive. No reason my streak will change. Especially now that I'm immortal.

As long as my mother and grandmother don't get themselves killed, I should be fine.

A low roll of thunder cleaves through my darkening thoughts. I jerk as lightning forks across my vision.

"You should've carried him through the Shabbin wards when we still had the chance, Cian. He's going to end up dooming us all."

Oh my Gods, *Bronwen*? I want to scream her name and ask her for news of Lore, but I'd only garner my guards' attention.

My uncle blocks out the sight of Lore's storm, his face pale beneath his black makeup. "If I'd lost you, *ah'khar*, do you really believe I would've stayed tucked between these walls?"

"I understand his—" She must finally sense me because she sucks in a breath, and then she murmurs, "Hurry, Fallon. Hurry."

There's such anguish in her tone that my heart trips over itself, forgetting to beat, and I swoon not only out of the vision but also against my cage wall, creating such a ruckus that the sprites and Faeries in the cellar all gawp at me.

Palms clammy, I try to heave myself back upright, but my fingers slip, and I slump against my mattress.

"Sugar. Need sugar," I croak.

I don't. Well, in truth, I probably do, but what I need more than anything is to return to Bronwen.

I run what she said on a loop through my mind, dissecting each word. *He's going to end up dooming us all.*

Going to . . . Which means, he hasn't.

He may have lost some crows to his obsidian curse but not a single one fell to Shabbin blood.

Not a single fucking one.

I hold on to that sliver of optimism until the cellar fades again, but this time it's full dark and there's no Bronwen.

CHAPTER 27

Although Cato leaves to rest, he's never gone for more than a handful of hours. I've yet to figure out if it's me he distrusts or his fellow soldiers.

"I'd like to bathe," I say after yet another guard rotation.

"I'm not authorized to let you out of your cage." Cato reclines against the black wall as he peels an orange with a pocket knife, the segments of which he surreptitiously ferries into my cage on a magic-made breeze.

"Why?" I know why but I want to hear him say it.

He says nothing.

"Where's Dante?" Not that I want the Faerie King to visit but I *am* curious as to what he's up to. "How's his eye?" When Cato still does not answer, I ask, "What of Justus? Where has he gone off to?"

My guard stares squarely at his fruit in order to avoid my probing stare.

"Ugh, Cato. What exactly do you think I'm going to do with the information? I'm a fucking prisoner."

His silence stretches on and on.

"Who knew you were a man of so few words?"

"You can communicate telepathically with the Sky King, Fallon, and you wonder why I cannot share sensitive information?"

"Not surrounded by—" When his eyebrows begin to peak, I say,

"All right, fine. Yes. I can." Obviously, he cannot know what really happened when I spaced out the other day. "You got me."

"So we can talk, but not about Lucin politics."

"All right." I blow a strand of grimy hair off my face. "How's Meriam?"

"Don't you think your king would've come to see you had anything happened to her?"

"*My* king is dreadfully allergic to obsidian, so unless Meriam can crumble this cozy basement, I doubt he'd be able to pay me a visit."

Cato lowers his gray eyes to the perfect swirl of his rind, jaw ticking in exasperation.

Well, I'm exasperated too. I'm tired of doing nothing but laying on my mattress, which is so scrappy each bar feels like a bone, and pacing the tiny perimeter like a wildcat. As I'm doing at this very moment.

I suddenly halt my mad loops because, what if a sigil exists that could crack stone and crumble this underground fort?

A second thought catapults over the first one: if such a sigil existed, wouldn't Meriam have used it already? After all, who, in their right mind, wants to stay locked in prison? Then again, it is possible that Meriam's no longer of sound mind. After all, she's been held captive—on and off—for over five centuries. That would fritter away at even the sturdiest brains.

But . . . *what if*? Me and my intractable optimism. But if I shed my optimism, then I'd be left with despair, and I will not become that woman who bemoans her fate.

"That creature you call a king is murdering thousands of innocents. We've had to set up curfews to protect our people, for Crows are virtually invisible at night, especially when they shift to fucking air." I do believe it may be the first time I've heard a curse word slip past Cato's lips. "Soldiers are now posted on *every* bridge and *every* street! I understand you hate it down here, but understand that you're in the safest place in the whole land."

I watch his chest rise and fall ten times before allowing myself to reply. "Cato, I love and respect you because you've always been a friend to me, but please, *please* take off your fucking blinders."

His face, which went soft at the beginning of my sentence,

pinches by the end, and the peeled orange drops to his feet, spraying droplets of sweet juice that fragrance the stale air.

"Have you ever even met a Crow? Spoken to one?" I ask.

His mouth tightens like his gaze. "Like those creatures would ever let me speak . . . They tear off necks for sport."

Though I understand the concept of brainwashing, I'm nevertheless taken aback by his closed-mindedness. I'm tempted to drop the subject entirely, but since I have his attention and no one else is around, I ask, "The night I was taken, so was the Crow who flew me down from the Sky Kingdom. Is she being kept here?"

Cato remains silent, but his jaw flexes as though mashing back words.

"It's not like I could revive her if she's stuck between obsidian walls . . ." I prod, hoping he'll toss me a crumb.

He scoops up his fallen fruit, then gusts his air-magic over the pith-marbled flesh to remove any bits of dust.

"Cato, I'm not your enemy."

"No." He studies his orange with such intensity that his eyes cross. "You're my queen."

"Don't queens deserve the honesty of their people?"

"Not indoctrinated ones," he mutters beneath his breath.

"*Indoctrinated*?" I sputter. "Here I thought you were different. Here I thought you had more brains than ears, but apparently, you're just like the rest of your kind!"

The air around me crackles, I assume with my fury, but then I catch flames skipping over a jumble of charred logs and suck in a breath, because there's no hearth in my fermented grape hut, only sconces, which means—

"I've been waiting for you to tap back into my eyes, Fallon . . ." Bronwen's voice propels my heart against my ribs. "I've something for you."

Paper rustles and then a sheet of vellum appears between Bronwen's dainty, scarred fingers. Midnight-blue whorls decorate the cream.

"I've tried to recall my long-ago lessons with Meriam."

I hold my breath, afraid that blowing it out may blow away the soothsayer in turn. I'm probably turning blue in the face, but that can only work in my favor. After all, it's preferable Cato notices my heightened complexion before my pallid eyes.

Bronwen moves her pointer finger over the first sigil, following the trail of ink as though she can see it. I imagine she's feeling the subtle grooves left behind by the tip of her pen.

"This one can block out sound."

My heart jolts. Although Justus has traced it many times, he's done so on a dark backdrop, which made it difficult to discern. Against the light background, it stands out in stark relief.

"And this one, Fallon." She taps the paper, indicating a glyph shaped like a 'V' that sits atop an inverted 'T'. "If you forget all others, memorize this one, for this one will—"

A gust of icy air slaps me in the face, flinging my head sideways, and then my thundered name drills my eardrums.

No, no, no. Come back!

When Cato's haggard face appears beneath my cage, his hands clutching the bars, shaking it, I toss myself face-first onto my mattress and will myself to tumble back into Bronwen's mind, but try as I might, I cannot slip away from my body. Perhaps it's because Cato is still shrieking my name and shaking me like a rattle.

Will what, *Bronwen?* I growl when my flimsy bed doesn't vanish, then whip my head to the side and growl at Cato to stop.

He jumps at my harsh tone, snapping his mouth shut and releasing my cage. "And you expect me to share sensitive information with you?" Cato pants as though it took everything in him to whisk me out of my vision.

I don't bother answering. Instead, I replay the precious revelation I was just given, visualizing both shapes until their lines and curves etch themselves into my skull. I roll onto my side—the one not facing Cato—and trace the patterns on my pancake of a mattress.

I've considered using the moss-filled pad as a drawing board, but I cannot exactly leave blood stains on the fabric. "Could I get some food?"

Cato is quiet. "I'm not allowed . . ."

"Fine. Starve me. Be like the rest of them."

He sucks in a breath as though I'd asked him to traverse the Southern Sea on a worm-eaten raft. I've probably hurt his feelings.

Well, damn him.

Damn the lot of my jailers.

Damn this cage, and these obsidian walls, and—

"Here."

I twist my head and find an orange segment hovering in front of my face. "I want a proper meal heaped with every type of cheese imaginable."

"I'm afraid we're poor on variety down here, but I can try to raid the Rossi larder."

I take that to mean that the larder isn't below ground. Which leads me to wonder how Cato is able to visit it? "Isn't it ill-advised to leave sigils painted on walls?"

"I'm sorry. What?"

I gesture toward the entryway of my cell. "I suppose you need magical doors in case Justus doesn't return, but . . ." I let my voice peter out, hoping he'll answer my circumspect question about exits.

"I know you think the worst of us, but we didn't bury ourselves alive, Fallon."

"So you have a door? A real door?"

His eyes round as he realizes his faux pas. "No."

I don't even require salt to know that he lies. If there's a door, Lore will find it. But for him to find it, he needs to be searching for me here, in the west. If only Bronwen could *see* my location. My heart thuds so hard that my blood swooshes and prickles.

"Stop tormenting the poor man, moya." Dante's voice jams my spine.

Slowly, I turn my head. Find him leaning against the entryway of my obsidian chamber, arms crossed. I almost miss the strip of brown leather fitted with an eyepatch that's the same shade as his skin. I wonder if his eye is deadened or healing. Does it matter?

Soon, he'll be headless.

My concave belly doesn't even flinch at the thought of sawing through skin.

Dante pushes off the wall and ambles toward me. "Especially since he's here because of you."

I cock up an eyebrow, waiting for him to elaborate.

"Justus brought him down here because he knew you and Cato were close. Who knew the general had a considerate bone in his body?"

"Yeah. Who knew? To what do I owe the pleasure of your visit?"

He scrutinizes my soiled pink slip before his blue eye scrolls back toward my face. "Time for our lesson, moya."

My heartbeats strengthen and strengthen, until my pulse is the only thing I can hear. Adrenaline floods me and I sit up.

It's time, but not for any lesson; it's time to rip that crown from his head and carry it to Lore.

CHAPTER 28

As my cage is unlocked, I picture Lore.

Lore, who I will see this day.

Although I've not had more than three segments of orange in—Cato only knows how many days—my body strums as though I've ingested a jug of coffee and a full meal. As my cage door grinds open, I stand and reach out for the wall. Hand over hand, I balance on one bar, then the next, until I reach the gaping doorway.

My cage had openings, yet it feels like I'm being released from an airtight box. The vine ladder materializes, and I turn to climb down.

"Huh."

I freeze as the low sound punctures the silence. When I hear the swish of metal against leather, I glance over my shoulder to find Dante freeing a dagger from his scabbard.

As he runs an indolent finger against the inlaid black stone, he says, "So eager for our lesson, Serpent-charmer."

"So eager to get out of this cage." But I hesitate on the ladder, heart clocking my ribs as I look from the gleaming blade to Dante's slitted eye.

"The Crow Killer. That's the name I gave our swordsmith's brand-new design." The Faerie King holds a dagger in his hand. "Delivered it just this morning." The gold blade is inlaid with matte black, which I can only imagine is obsidian. "Catchy moniker, isn't it?"

I don't hiss at him that he's a disgusting stain on his race . . . on our entire world, and not because I fear he'll plant his little dagger in my chest—he desires the magic in my blood too much—but because he's as stable as a stick of dynamite whose wick hungers for a flame. I refuse to be the flame that sets him off because Gods only know how much chaos and destruction Dante Regio will rain upon Luce.

He taps his dagger against his open palm. "How odd that the cage Meriam spelled to keep harm at bay doesn't make you feel safe."

"Faeries can open it at will, so no, it doesn't. Besides, it's a cage." I climb down one more rung. "Want to give it a whirl and see how much you enjoy it, Maezza?"

A smirk tugs at his mouth. "Meriam warded it against Faeries, so I cannot *give it a whirl.*"

I glance back up at the golden pen.

"Were you not aware?" He twists his dagger so it catches the light.

"I wasn't. No." I hook a strand of my hair and tuck it shakily behind my ear.

"How surprising that Justus failed to impart this on you considering how much he's shared."

The adrenaline that courses through my veins funnels into my stomach and hardens it. I white-knuckle the vines, debating whether or not to scrabble up them anew and burrow into the cage, but then what? They'd shut me inside. It may be warded against Faeries, but it's also warded against blood magic. Besides, I'm done being a captive. I want my freedom and I want Dante dead.

Not to mention it would scream *guilt*, and I cannot have Dante believing I'm cavorting with his general.

"Shared? More like schooled and scolded me." I hop the rest of the way down, my heart beating triple time. "Justus Rossi loves nothing more than to make himself look imbued with supreme intelligence, doesn't he?"

I sniff the air to make sure I'm not the one walking into a trap. My pulse eases when I catch a whiff of Dante. He no longer smells like rotted seaweed; he smells like a time gone past.

I glance beyond the king, at the tunnel riddled with soldiers. If all goes to shit, I will draw the key sigil where Justus did last time so that I end up *somewhere*. Here's to hoping that pressing my palm against the blood glyph will blur the path for my jailers.

And now . . . for the essential ingredient to my contingency plan.

"Do you really think I'd still be down in this dump if Justus was on my side, Maezza?" I stroll over to Dante, so close that my thorax brushes against the tip of his dagger. "He hungers to rule Luce through me."

When blood blooms on the grubby silk encasing my chest, Dante rips his arm back and studies the cut he's inflicted upon me in horror. How interesting that he worries about hurting me when he so readily cut me for his little lesson the other day . . .

He must decide he's not so disgusted by the sight of blood on his knife because he twirls the blade in front of his face, awe lighting up his cruel blue eye. "I cannot wait to thrust this blade through Lorcan's heart. Can you imagine his surprise when he realizes whose blood has snuffed out his humanity?"

His words flog me like those barbed iron whips apparently used by humans during the Magnabellum. Back in Scola Cuori, I never doubted my Faerie professors, but now I question every lesson I ever sat through.

"Lastra, pin my wife's arms behind her back, will you?"

I blanch because if my arms are pinned behind me, then I cannot blood-cast. "Won't you need access to my wrists for your lesson?" I hold them up in front of me. "May as well bind them in front of my chest and save yourself some reshackling."

Lastra steps up beside Dante, green magic glancing off his palms. "Maezza? What would you like me to do?"

"I want you to do what I asked." He whirls on his boots, his gold spurs clicking as he heads into the tunnel. "Behind her back!" Dante's bark punches the musty air.

My spine vibrates with a chill. Since I doubt Dante fears my arms' strength, his insistence for my hands to be tethered behind me can only mean one thing: he knows Meriam released my magic.

He. Fucking. Knows.

I can only pray that he doesn't know about Justus's plan of locking him inside the vault. *Please, please, Fate, give us the upper hand. Please.*

Oh, to have a soothsayer on hand. I try to propel myself inside

Bronwen's mind, but I must be too intent on the present because I remain locked in my body. I steady my staggering spirits by reminding myself that she's seen Dante dying.

It's up to me to make sure that he dies on my blade and not Lorcan's talon.

This ends now.

CHAPTER 29

"Justus!" Dante screeches once he reaches the vault room, hand still wrapped around his dagger's hilt.

Justus ambles out of the vault where Meriam sits erect in her throne, fingers wound loosely around the armrest, pink eyes steady on me. "Yes, Maezza?"

My grandfather's blue gaze drifts over my shackled arms before unhurriedly rising to Lastra. Will he order him to release me? Would Lastra abide or would he wait for his king's approval?

Cato, who's been walking alongside me since we left my cell, takes a step nearer, and although I keep my attention on Dante, out of the corner of my eye, I spy the white-haired sergeant graze the pommel of his sword.

"Is your wife ready, Rossi?"

"She is, Your Majesty." Justus gestures for Dante to pass ahead of him, but Dante stops walking and pivots, blue eye sparking. "Lastra, Cato, bring my inkwell closer."

That I refer to myself as an inanimate object is one thing; that he refers to me that way is quite another.

Cato slides his hand around my bicep just as Lastra, only too happily, shoves me forward. The sergeant growls at his fellow soldier, "I've got her."

I try to work my fingers out of the Faerie vines, but with every hand contortion, the vine bites harder into my skin. As we pass the obsidian panel upon which Justus drew his sigil, my heart screams for me to run toward it, to get out. But my fucking wrists are fucking bound!

Meriam drums her fingers against the shiny gold. "My granddaughter cannot sit for hours with her hands bound behind her back or her veins will run dry."

I stare at Justus but he doesn't stare back. His gaze is focused on the green-eyed soldier. "My wife gave you a command, Soldati."

"I take my commands from the king."

Dante tips his head a tad higher. "Her hands stay where they are, Rossi."

"Your Majesty, be reasonable." Meriam's voice sounds hoarse from disuse.

"The last time Fallon's hands were unbound, she removed my eye." Dante's reason for binding my hands should reassure me—after all, it means that he's none the wiser about what Meriam has done—nevertheless, I'm not reassured.

Until the vault doors shut and Justus hands me his sword, I will not be reassured. I will remain a mess of crackling nerves and hasty heartbeats.

Meriam's pink eyes cut a path beyond Justus and Dante toward me before closing. "Circle the vines with blood, darling, and they will fall off."

I all but choke on my next inhale. Before a rattling cough can give away Meriam's words, I press my lips shut and breathe through my nose. Although I feel Cato's stare on my cheek, I keep my eyes facing forward and resume tugging on my restraints, but this time, to break skin.

"What was that, Meriam?" Dante's fingers flex so hard around the hilt of his dagger that it swells the veins beneath his brown skin.

"I was invoking the Cauldron, Maezza. Asking it to guide me during our lesson." Her lids reel up, and she fastens her gaze to Dante's.

"Is that what she said, Justus?" Dante shifts on his boots, and although his spurs' slow twirl makes little noise, it's all I can hear, the same way the bulging blood vessels on the back of his hand are all I can see.

I rub my wrists until my skin stings and heats, and the vines become slippery with blood. I pull one wrist up then drive it down and do the same with the other, coating the restraints with my blood, praying it will shear through Lastra's magic.

"Grip your sword, husband. I do not like the look in that man's eye." Meriam's quiet murmur reaches my thudding eardrums.

It must also reach my grandfather's because his palm settles on the ruby pommel of his sword. "I'm afraid my knowledge of Shabbin is still rather rudimenta—"

Just as one loop of vine snaps, Dante rams the blade of his dagger through my grandfather's abdomen. Meriam screams, her hand crawling up her throat to her mouth. The soldiers all flock to their king, leaving me unattended.

I stare at the wall and take a step toward it, but then my eyes go to Justus. His mouth is still parted, his eyes still open, his throat still bobbing with swallows. Beyond him, Meriam is raising a shaky hand to her forehead.

"Ruh . . .!" A ragged gulp replaces the *'n'* as Dante raises his arm, hefting Justus off the ground.

I inch toward the wall just as Dante twists the blade in Justus's gut. My grandfather spasms, his arm jerking upward before his fingers fall open around his sword. The rubies gleam as the iron weapon falls to the floor and skids in my direction. When it stops mere feet away from me, I understand that it was no spasm that drove his arm up.

"Is it you this time or is it your traitorous son again?" With his free hand, Dante gushes water into my grandfather's face. He blinks at the intensity that springs from his fingers.

I take great joy in watching Dante suck in a breath as he realizes his lack of iron immunity.

"Maezza, Meriam!" Cato gasps.

My gaze jerks to the vault just as the bloodied vines drop to the ground, their collapse as silent as my footfalls.

"What about Meriam, Brambilla?" Dante yells.

"She's gone."

My fingers close around the sword just as Dante says, "That's impossible."

But apparently, it is possible since her throne has vanished.

Dante tosses away my grandfather and pivots toward the vault. "Find the witch!"

Everyone is so wholly focused on playing peekaboo with Meriam that no one catches me snagging the fallen sword, the same way no one notices me slinking toward where Justus lies, his chest barely moving.

When his eyes find mine, he murmurs, "Go. Meriam—will distract—"

Keeping one fist clamped on his sword, I press a shaky finger against his mouth to silence him. His colorless lips turn scarlet where I touch him. Scarlet but motionless.

I yank up his shirt to reveal the wound. His cut runs from his navel to the edge of his rib cage and reveals so many organs that my own organs heave, threatening to eject the few segments of orange I ate. I clamp my lips shut, wedge my index and middle fingers together, then touch their tips to my bleeding wrist, and circle the long, gushing wound with my blood several times.

"Must I do—anything else?" I murmur around deep pants.

"You must . . . get out," he croaks, just as his gaze climbs to a place over my head and his lips part around a strangled version of my name.

I whip both my gaze and my sword upward, slashing through the pantleg of a very startled Lastra.

The man's green eyes narrow on the wrists his vines bloodied. Before he trusses me up in more, I swipe the sword again, driving it so hard against his leg that I hit bone. He squeals as he collapses, his sword falling from his fingers, hitting the puddle of gore spreading beneath Justus.

As heads spin in our direction, I jolt to my feet, snatch Justus by the collar, and drag him toward the wall.

"Leave—me—Fallon." His voice is a mere whisper, yet I hear it.

"Where do you think you're going, moya?" Dante steps toward me slowly, raising his palms when I brandish my sword.

My swallows come as hard and fast as the breaths clocking my sternum. "I wouldn't turn my back on Meriam." Perhaps she fled, but my threat makes every soldier freeze, giving me time to sketch out the lock symbol.

Dante spins back, his gaze tracking my fingers' skid across the stone wall.

My heart hastens.

He springs forward, his strides longer than his soldiers.

Three.

I wait, my palm hovering over the symbol.

Two.

The Faerie monarch throws himself onto Justus.

One.

I slam my palm against the exit, praying, as our three bodies glide through matter, that another garrison of Dante's isn't waiting on the other side of this wall.

It would greatly defeat my briskly-hatched plan of fighting him without the threat of a dozen swords pointed my way.

CHAPTER 30

I flail out of my obsidian prison and smack into a wall made entirely of turquoise glass. Dante rolls and bangs into my shins, his golden armor clipping my breath and my grip on Justus's collar. My poor grandfather's head bangs against the floor, and although a pulse still strikes the base of his neck, his lids close.

As Dante pushes onto his knees, I swing Justus's sword at his head. The blade gets stuck in the sunray crown.

You've got to be fucking kidding me!

I yank my arms back up, tearing the crown and a few slender braids free in the process. As I shake the sword to dislodge it, Dante snarls and lunges for me.

I jolt sideways, cold sweat dripping down my nape and beading along my spine. ***Lore?!***

As the Faerie straightens, I take all of one second to absorb my surroundings. The instant my eyes lock on the flight of stairs, I run, the soft soles of my slippers slapping against the white marble like fish fins. When I almost trip on my dress, I snatch up the silk and hoist it high.

Dante's footfalls thud behind me, his spurs jangling. "I knew it! I knew the witch released your magic!"

I reach the landing and whirl. The tip of my sword bites into his forearm, tearing through the sleeve and nicking the skin beneath. He gives another stunned blink before his mouth twists and he lunges for me.

I back up, gripping my weapon with both hands and swing again. This time, my blade meets his armor, and the shock of the hit rattles my bones. I scramble away, putting as much distance as possible between him and me.

"I wasn't going to hurt you," Dante growls. "But the wards be damned, I will. Kill. You."

When my shoulders thwack into a wall, my heart skips a long beat. I unfasten one of my hands from the sword and flatten it against the seashell-papered wall at my back. Keeping my eyes and blade trained on Dante, I sketch the lock symbol.

The skin around Dante's jaw erupts with a throbbing tick. The Faerie King lurches forward, but not before I manage to fall through yet another wall.

Just as my tailbone thwacks into hardwood, Lorcan's voice detonates between my temples, ***Behach Éan?***

Lore!

For a long second, he doesn't speak, but I can feel him there, on the other end of our link. I can hear him breathe, deep, raspy inhales that are no match to my chaotic pants. ***Where the bloody fuck are you, mo khrà?***

Costa's old home, which is now the Rossi estate. A glance around me reveals I've landed inside a bedroom. ***Eponine wasn't lying, Lore. That's where I've been since they took me. Underground. Meriam's here, too. She's being kept in a vault. She freed my power. She's not—she's not evil.***

I hear him curse a blue streak, and then he grows so quiet that I worry our connection has been lost.

Lore? I all but sob out his name, scrambling onto my feet when I hear the creak of a floorboard.

I whip my head from side to side until I see a wall swathed in seafoam velvet drapes. Although my bleeding wrists throb, I hold on to Justus's sword with all my might and race through the giant bedroom toward the curtains.

Why do your wrists hurt, Behach Éan? Lore's words are slow and clipped, and so very, *very* low.

It's not important, I say just as the creaking stops just outside the closed door. "*Merda,*" I mutter, hunting the blue-green folds for the seam.

The second I spot it, I shoulder my body through, then squint into the darkness for the lever to open the single-pane window. When I can't find one, I start to draw the symbol on the glass, but stop because, beyond the window, stands a garrison of Lucin soldiers.

Talk to me, mo khrà. Tell me what's happening.

I'm surrounded, Lore.

"Come out, come out, wherever you are." Dante's taunting voice slips beneath the drapes, raising goosebumps along my skin.

Although the curtain has yet to move, I can feel his heart beat just beyond. I curl my bleeding hand over my injured one and squeeze the pommel as I raise the sword and brace it in front of me. If I go down, I'll do so swinging, for if I'm caught . . . if I'm caught, Dante will either bleed me dry on Xema Rossi's immaculate carpet or pitch me back under the earth.

"Wherefore art thou, moya?" Dante's voice hits my thrumming eardrums.

When two boots dent the curtain's hem, I raise my elbows, dragging the reddened tip of the sword against the heavy fabric, past where his chest must be. I'm so familiar with Dante's physique that I position the sword just above my forehead . . . just where I know his throat will be.

Pulling in a deep lungful of courage, I sink my weapon through the curtain.

I hit flesh, not metal. Not only can I feel the wet slide of my steel blade, but I can also hear Dante's startled gurgle.

Though I tremble with adrenaline, I also shake with relief. ***I did it, Lore. I did it.***

What did you do, Behach Éan?

I killed—

The curtain is ripped aside, tearing the sword from my fingers, and there, in perfect health, stands the man I thought—the man I thought—

My hands fly to my mouth as a scream vaults up my throat. When a heavy thud shakes the floorboards, my shriek rends the air.

Dante peers sideways. "Shame. Your grandmother will be much aggrieved."

Oh my Gods, I killed . . . I killed the wrong man.

CHAPTER 31

Dante cinches my bicep and hauls me out from behind the curtain. A sob tumbles from my lips as I finally see what I've done. *Who* I've killed.

"Any chance he'll make it, or did she irreparably sever his arteries, Lastra?"

The hateful earth-Fae presses two fingers into the base of Cato's neck.

"Why is he here?" I croak. "Why was he even here?"

"He was worried about you. The rest were worried about me." Dante's fingers feel like twine wrapped too snuggly, blocking my blood circulation. Or perhaps it's the pain in my chest that's blockading my veins. "The man erupted from the stronghold like a bat from the underworld."

No, no, no, no.

This is a nightmare.

My ears begin to ring. In the distance, I think I hear Lore's voice but I cannot focus on anything but the anguished beats of my heart and the pool of blood expanding around Cato's motionless form.

Cato's name scorches up my throat and emerges as a scream. "Wake up!" The tears fall so fast that they fill my mouth with salt. "Please, Cato." The cry that comes out of me next isn't human; it's a feral keening.

What have I done? My knees soften as I try to kneel and crawl toward my friend, but Dante holds my arm in a vise, preventing me from moving.

Mo khrà, answer me godsdammit!

I jump at the tenor of Lorcan's voice. ***Lore,*** I sob. ***I k-killed . . . I killed a man.***

Are you trying to one-up me, sweetheart? For if you are, you've a long way to go.

I sniffle, then heft up the arm Dante isn't clutching and brush it against my swollen eyes and runny nose. ***He was a good man, Lore. I k-killed a g-good man.***

Was he helping you escape?

No. He was—he was . . . I cannot finish the thought.

If he kept you imprisoned—

He didn't know any better, Lore. He thought—he thought he was keeping me safe.

Though I've no doubt Lore has plenty of opinions on Cato's character, he's gracious enough not to flog me with them.

"Back to the stronghold! NOW!" Dante's shrill command bounces against my eardrums, spurring his soldiers into motion. "I've got her."

As they flock out of the bedroom, I snarl, "You don't have me! You'll never have me, you limp-pricked coward." I can hear Nonna whisper how one should never poke the serpent, except the pureling deserves to see that I'm not some spineless minnow frightened of him.

If anyone should be frightened, it's him, because what the underworld's stopping me from drawing the key sigil on his chest and sinking my hand through his ribs to yank out his heart.

Huh. Would that work? Besides the fact that the thought is utterly sickening *and* his chest is currently cloaked in armor, if I had direct access to skin, could I breach his flesh with a spell, or is he fully immune to my Shabbin magic?

"Back to the tunnels. One of you go check that Justus is dead. His body was at the bottom of the stairwell." Dante strides forward, dragging me toward the gaping doorway.

I will not go back down there. I will not!

I'm almost there, Little Bird. Almost.

I want to tell Lore to beat a hasty retreat, but I sense I'd be wasting my breath. So I warn him instead. ***There are soldiers in the Rossi garden, Lore. I didn't have time to count how many, but . . . but please be careful. I cannot lose you. Not before—*** I sob. ***Just be careful.***

I look back over my shoulder at Cato's sprawled form, at the snow-pale skin and plaited hair absorbing the sticky crimson leaking from his mangled throat.

"We cannot just—just leave him there." My voice is thready with such debilitating grief and guilt that I'm not even certain Dante, who's glued to my side, hears me.

But apparently, he does. "We'll give him a proper burial once the Crows fall."

"The Crows will never fall," I hiss as Dante yanks me out of the room and rushes us down a hallway that ends in a mirror framed with gilt seashells.

"But they will. Tonight." He watches me through the silvered glass, and although my swollen eyes make his face appear like a patchwork of blots, I don't miss the haughty smile tugging at his mouth. "Now that you've called to him. We've been trying to coax his remaining crows out of that rock he calls a kingdom for a while now."

"You haven't injured a single one of his crows," I snap, tired of his lies.

"Is that what the vulture king told you through your little mind link? How sweet that he doesn't care to worry you."

Lore, have any of your crows been hit?

His answer feels as though it takes forever to reach me. ***One. But there was no blood on the obsidian arrow.***

The floor dips and I stumble. Dante tightens his grip, keeping me upright. I cannot believe he was speaking the truth.

Are you certain?

Yes.

My mind buzzes with anguish. ***You said you wouldn't leave the Sky Kingdom!***

So did you.

I only did it because Bronwen—Bronwen tricked me, Lore.

I know, mo khrà. I know all that happened.

I lower my inflamed gaze to the hem of my pink slip that is red with blood. Mine. Justus's. Cato's.

How I loathe myself.

Lore sighs. ***He was your warden.***

He was also my friend.

Dante hooks a sharp turn, bypassing the stairs that had epitomized freedom only a moment earlier. I stare down at where I emerged from the prison, at the bloodied smear left behind by Justus's body and the crown tangled with hair sitting askew in the crimson slick. "Your crown, Maezza."

"I'll fetch it later."

"Why not now? Isn't it on the way?" In a falsely sweet voice, I add, "You've access to my blood. Oh, wait, your sigils aren't working, are they?"

His hands dig so hard into my bicep that he almost shatters the bone. Wincing, I writhe to break his grip but all that wins me is a trip on his shoulder.

"Put me down!" I ball my bloodied hands into fists and bang them against his armor, but all I manage is to bruise my knuckles. When I try to roll off, putting all my weight into my side, the arm wedged around the backs of my thighs becomes steel.

I consider yanking on his hair to lever his neck uncomfortably back, but then a better idea lights up my mind. As he yells, "Lastra, move your ass," I trace the key sigil on his armor, and my hand sinks through it. And then I paint it again on the damp fabric of his shirt and my palm hits perspiring skin.

He must feel my fingers along his flesh because, before I can even shape the first part of the symbol, he rolls me off his shoulder and flips me around, ramming my spine into his breastplate and pinning my wrists with his palm.

His breaths smack the shell of my ear. "And you wonder why I locked you in a cage."

"I never wondered, Dante." I twist my head back so that he doesn't miss a word above the clamor of the night. "I know. You, Dante Regio, fear me. The same way you fear Lorcan and my people. You are a cow—" He bands his forearm around my neck and crushes my windpipe. "—ard," I bite out the last syllable before he assumes

I'm comparing him to an agreeable, four-legged animal. Especially since cows are sweet, and Dante is not.

"Shut. Your. Mouth. Fal."

"Nev—er."

"Then I guess I'll have to shut it for you," he growls, clutching my neck so tightly that the wainscoted walls begin to fleck away like ancient stucco.

But suddenly, the ground rumbles and glass shatters. Dante mutters a curse beneath his breath and widens his stance to keep his balance, and though he doesn't remove his hand from my neck, his grip slackens.

When guttural shouts score the air in time with raucous caws, my lids prickle with more tears.

Lore's here.

My mate's here.

CHAPTER 32

I make sure to drag my feet to slow Dante's pace as we near another staircase. Though Meriam told me my magic wouldn't work on Dante, instead of clawing at his arm, I attempt to circle it in blood. How handy would it be if Meriam was wrong and I succeeded in chopping it off?

I scrabble at his sleeve until I find a spot I can circle entirely—his elbow. There, I draw a line of blood, and lo and behold, it shears off the white fabric, but like I was warned, it does diddly squat to his flesh.

"What the fuck?" he growls, his grip loosening some more.

I twist around and smack the heel of my palm into his eyepatch. Startled, and hopefully in shitloads of pain, he drops his arm and bellows for his guards to restrain me. I scramble toward a wall, my hip bumping painfully into a console table, upsetting the heavy gold candelabrum that sits on top of it. Before I can draw my key sigil, a red-eyed guard streams fire in my direction.

Though his flames don't touch my skin, they lick up the front of my dress, chewing the silk. I hinge at the waist and clap the fabric just as the Faerie jets another stream of fire. The candelabrum's wicks ignite, and so does the seashell wallpaper, which crackles and blackens. I lurch away from the wall of fire but cannot run, for Dante's garrison encircles me.

Fuck.

I seize the candles in the candelabrum and toss them at the approaching men. They sizzle as they sail through air and splash wax over a few faces. Lastra growls, long and low, driving his shoulder into his eye to remove the wax clumping his eyelashes. Face streaked with fury, he assaults me with his vines. I bat each one away, wishing it was his face.

On Dante's command, one of his men lunges at me. I swing my makeshift weapon. The candelabrum meets its mark and the male totters.

I whack him again, and his head flies sideways. Something cracks. I pray it's his skull, even though I'm not far enough gone to believe a fractured skull will suffice to kill a pure-blooded Fae. After all, purelings heal from *all* wounds, save for an iron blade through the heart or throat.

My skin goes clammy at the memory of Cato's death, but then I focus on the fact that my mate is out there, fighting to reach me, and the chills stop radiating up my spine. I grip my candelabrum with all my might and will them to come near me for I will bash all their skulls.

The ground shakes so hard that I have to soften my knees not to bang into the smoldering wall.

Fallon? Lore's voice is a shot of adrenaline straight into my heart.

Lore?

"The Crows are here, Maezza. We need to fall back!" one of the soldiers bellows as Lastra crouches beside his knocked-out friend.

He starts to haul him over his shoulder when Dante growls, "Leave him. It's Fallon we need!"

Lastra's green eyes flash with hesitation because he knows what will happen to his friend if he leaves him here—no Faerie is getting out of Xema Rossi's home alive. Yet, good little devotee that he is, he totters back to his feet. His jaw clenches as the strip of fabric tied around the cut on his thigh darkens with more blood.

I'm glad I caused him pain, but I'd be even gladder if I'd cut into another part of his body. Why couldn't he have been the one standing behind that curtain? Why Cato?

Lastra assaults me anew. I blink away the heat prickling my eyes and swing. However, it isn't vines he streams my way, but a tangle of branches. And not just regular branches but ones dappled with thorns that burst from the bark and sink into my ankles before making their way up my legs.

A scream tears up my lungs, and although I don't want to give these men my tears, they begin to trip down my cheeks, liquefying the blood that beads from so many places on my body.

"Maezza, you must come NOW!" someone screams, and Dante pivots, taking the stairs two at a time.

Lastra runs, dragging me past the ashes of his friend's fire so fast that it knocks the ground away from my feet and the air from my lungs.

I will murder this man, but first I'll torture him. I will paint a ring of blood around his cock, then flog what hasn't fallen off with his own damn thorny branches. And *then* I will kill him.

And rob me of the pleasure of avenging you, Little Bird?

"Send her down!" someone shouts.

Lastra bowls my nettle cage toward the stairs, then sprints beside it.

I squeeze my eyes shut as the stairs rush toward me. ***Lore, they're*** — Water sloshes against my face.

I think it must be Dante, trying to quicken my fall, but when my lids pull up, I realize that the water is coming at me sideways, sweeping me away from the stairs and into Lastra, who flounders before slipping and skidding with me into the giant living room where Xema Rossi hosted that grand revel in honor of Marco's betrothal.

I bang into an armchair, which drives the thorns deeper into my skin. Even though my body is flooded with adrenaline, I feel the bite of each one of Lastra's barbs and whimper.

And bleed.

Gods, do I bleed.

Crimson rivulets leak from what looks like my every pore, dispersing like ink as they hit the liquid carpet beneath us that ripples from the fight Lore is waging on Tarespagia. As much as I want him to reach me, I'm covered in so much blood. Blood that's lethal to my mate.

When the great doors rumble and shake but don't open, Lastra scrambles to his feet and splashes past me.

They've warded the fucking house against us, Behach Éan!

What? Then how come Dante rushed back downstairs?

Meriam must've drawn it to keep me away from you! I swear, I will kill that woman—

You cannot, Lore. If you kill her, that'll kill me.

I heard, he grumbles. ***I will still hurt her. A lot.***

Lore . . . I sigh.

Mo khrà, she stole centuries from me, and then she stole you ***from me.***

Deciding it's no time for a debate, I say, ***I'll come out to you. As soon as I get out of—***

The Faerie I believed dead, or back in captivity, hobbles into Lastra's path. "I believe you're heading the wrong way, Soldati."

Lastra's complexion becomes as whitewashed as Xema's furniture. "Y-y-you're alive?"

"Thanks to my granddaughter and not to the garrison I handpicked to keep Meriam and me safe. Who swore an oath, inscribed on my skin"—Justus taps one finger against his bicep—"that they would heed my every command."

A furrow forms between Lastra's brows. "The king—"

"The king didn't bring you into his home. Let you in on his secret. *I* did."

Lastra's neck moves with swallow after swallow.

"Who do you work for, Soldati Lastra?"

"For the crown."

"Wrong."

He grimaces just as the house shudders. I try to peer out the picture windows that stretch in slender lines on either side of the doors, but when I crane my neck, new thorns find their way into my skin.

"You work for me, Lastra. Now release my granddaughter."

He glances at where I lie encased in his barbed cage. "She'll k-kill me with her poisonous blood."

"No. I won't."

He blows air out the corner of his mouth as though he doesn't believe me.

"My mate requested a meet and greet with my jailers." I flash the man a toothy smile. "Did I say *meet and greet*? I meant a *cut and gut*. So like I said, *I* won't be killing you."

The man blanches, then shudders at the same time as the Rossi home. He peers over his shoulder, his eyes growing so wide that his green irises float in pools of white. But then his eyebrows drop. "How come they're not—" His shoulders square beneath his white jacket. "They can't penetrate the house, can they?"

"Lastra, I will not ask again," Justus says calmly.

The green-eyed Fae drops his hand to his scabbard and pulls out his sword.

"For fuck's sake, Lastra, free my fucking granddaughter now."

His lips draw up into a half smirk. "I think not." The house trembles again, but instead of drawing a shudder from the idiot, it makes him grin. "Sergente Lastra has a nice ring to it, doesn't it? Now that the position is open for the taking."

The bloodied finger I'm attempting to wriggle around the nearest branch freezes at Lastra's callous words. Cato was the kindest, most noble man, always treating his inferiors with the utmost respect. He doesn't deserve to be flattened by Lastra's ego, just as he didn't deserve to die on my fucking sword.

The feel of his flesh giving around my blade turns both my stomach and heart. For a long moment, I feel nothing but intractable disgust for what I've done and wallow in self-loathing. Not only did I fail—*again*—but I also murdered a friend.

Lastra's voice pierces through my deafening thoughts. "Though if I end Justus Rossi and bring Fallon back, Dante may just make me Com—"

Justus fills Lastra's mouth with water. When he begins gagging and hacking, he says, "Giuseppe Lastra, I call forth the bargain owed. Hand me your sword."

Lastra blinks at my grandfather as though he's transformed into a Crow, then spits out one last mouthful of water and begins to backpedal, but the claimed bargain contorts his features. "Get—your own—sword." He grimaces anew, rubbing the skin over his heart. "Fine. Here." He steps toward Justus, but instead of slipping the sword into Justus's waiting hand, he levels it at my grandfather's heart and thrusts.

CHAPTER 33

A hoarse shout soars up my raw throat just as metal ricochets against metal.

Lastra blinks stunned eyes at his sword that didn't penetrate my grandfather's torso.

Justus smiles as he sprays what must be scalding water into Lastra's face because the soldier drops his sword and screams as welts blister his cheekbones and brow.

I don't miss the slight wince that crinkles Justus's features as he crouches to retrieve the weapon. "You know what disheartens me most about your deed, you worthless idiot?"

Steam curls off Lastra's crimson face while a mixture of squeals and moans erupt from his blistered lips.

Justus moves nearer to Lastra, who flails backward, slipping on the slick marble and falling on his ass. "That it makes me doubt my good judgment, for only an idiot would enlist another."

Before Lastra can get up, Justus steps over him, positions the blade over the man's heart and drives it clean through. Unlike the messy death I gave Dargento, Justus doesn't miss the mark. Clearly, it's not his first time ending a Faerie's life. He may not have been alive during the Magnabellum, but he was alive during Primanivi. Though a much shorter war, the latter was just as bloody as Costa's war.

My pulse is still clocking my neck when the thorny branches vanish, releasing my body in the gory puddle of Justus's magic. For a moment, I lay there, stunned and unmoving, desperately attempting to catch my breath now that my unsolicited acupuncture session is over.

"I can't believe you truly handpicked that man," I end up saying as he plucks a metal dinner plate from inside his crimson stained shirt and lays it atop the nearest couch. *Saved by dinnerware.* How clever.

He hobbles over to me and extends his hand to help me up. "Slim pickings, Nipota."

Although my arm feels tied to an anvil, I lift it to meet his. "Should've widened your pool and enlisted round-ears."

"Half-bloods wouldn't have fared well surrounded by that much obsidian."

"Antoni is a half-blood." I press my lips together at the memory of our last conversation. When I taste blood, I scrape my thumb over the wound, but my digit bleeds just as profusely as the rest of me. "Vance, too."

"Both wore protective crystals, so their exposure didn't harm them." Once Justus has set me on my feet and ensured that my knees aren't about to give out, he releases me.

"How come the men you picked followed Dante's orders?"

"The ones I picked were Cato, Lastra, and two others. But the two others weren't amongst the ones who harassed you, for I've already claimed my bargain with them." When I incline my head and hitch up an eyebrow, he adds, "They must guard Meriam with their life."

"So the others . . .?"

"Are Dante's personal guard."

I try to peer past him, to see if the fire-Faerie I knocked out is still kaput.

Justus looks over his shoulder. "What is it?"

"I think one of Dante's men didn't make it back to the stronghold," I whisper.

"You mean the one you clouted with the candelabrum Pierre of Nebba gifted my mother?" When he turns back toward me, a small smile hangs from his lips.

Oh, how positively outraged Xema Rossi would be . . . I cannot wait till the story of her prestigious candleholder reaches her tall ears.

"He's gone."

I blink away Xema. "Gone where?"

"Gone from this world."

"How? You didn't even have a sword."

"No, but he had one."

"Why didn't you take it with you then?"

"Because you were in trouble, and it didn't fit in my scabbard, and I cannot produce half as much magic with one hand as I can with two."

My lips begin to wobble because today was a lot. Justus is a lot. I suddenly wish Nonna was here so she could see the man he's become, but then realize that if she was here, she'd see the woman I've become.

She'd see Cato's dead body.

I shake my head to clear it of the gloom, then turn to go to Lore but stop and hold out my hand. "Mind if I borrow your sword?"

Justus passes it over without hesitation, a testament as to how deeply he trusts me.

I take the bloodied weapon from him, then limp over to Lastra's corpse, and although the man's clearly dead-dead, I wedge the sword into his ugly heart for good measure.

The house rattles again, and my mate's voice explodes between my temples. ***What's keeping you, Behach Éan?***

The great doors vibrate as though Crow after Crow were launching themselves at the wood.

I just had some unfinished business. It's finished now. I hand Justus back Lastra's weapon. "Lore says the house is warded against them."

"Meriam must've wanted to secure the perimeter to give you time—"

"To finish the deed I keep botching?" I supply.

"You will—*we* will get him, Fallon. It's only a matter of time."

I swallow hard. Although Justus doesn't highlight my failure, my mind does, replaying reel after reel of moments that would've been ideal for neck-severing. "Where's the sigil?"

"Downstairs in the vault."

I pale.

"I'll go."

"You cannot go back down there. Dante wants you dead."

"I'll just . . ." His voice fades when he hooks his leather cord and slips it out of his slashed shirt. The vial with Meriam's blood is shattered. He gazes down at his crimson-smeared torso. "I may have enough of Meriam's blood on me to paint a key sigil."

"There was a door."

"It cannot be opened from this end." He stares in its general direction. "If I cannot manage to blood-cast, then I'll have you blow it up with your blood."

"I can do that?" My hands prickle with the potency of the magic at my fingertips.

He nods.

Fallon?

Though wards need to be undone, mates need to be seen.

"Give me a minute." Sodden dress clinging to my body, more crimson than pink, I hobble toward the door, close my fingers around the handle, and pull it toward me.

Something sharp shines in the indigo gloom of Lore's storm. Something that arrows straight for me. I neither start nor angle my body sideways because it's a beak, not ammunition. The Crow dissolves into smoke that puffs against the wards before reforming into a bird and swooping upward, toward a tornado of black feathers and gleaming talons. The caws that have been echoing since Lore launched his attack on the house peter out.

I start to reach out when Justus says, "Unlike the wards around Shabbe, they work both ways here. But only on those with Crow blood."

When my nails scrape against what feels like glass but looks like air, my heart crumples. For the first time in my life, I wish I hadn't been born a—

I stop myself from thinking it, from even wishing it.

"You'll have to wait until I erase Meriam's sigil." Justus's words bump against my nape, jagged like his breaths. "You'll be free soon, Fallon."

Free from this house but not from this nightmare. Not as long as the Faerie King lives.

I glance over my shoulder in the direction Dante disappeared, my mind whispering, *He's right there, Fallon, right beneath your feet.*

If I returned to my prison armed with the right spells and the right blade, true freedom could be had tonight. Thunder booms and the sky crackles. I take it my mate's no fan of my mad idea. In truth, I loathe it as well.

I turn my face back toward the blustering sky and await my midnight king, and as he rages, I finally calm.

CHAPTER 34

Streaks of smoke plummet from the sky, banging into the rain-soaked earth with such velocity that a tremor shoots into the soles of my feet, almost knocking my legs out from under me. Only my grip on the door handle keeps me from buckling, but even that becomes tenuous when the smoke knits into a hazy figure with metal-toned eyes.

Lore's name falls off my lips like a breathy whimper, and tears pop from my lash line and trundle down my cheeks. The door handle slips from my fingers, and I step toward him. Although his face is painted in shadows, his temper lights up his features, giving those golden irises of his a cold sheen.

Like an angry torrent, Lore's shadows surge forward and smack into the invisible shield. This time, the ensuing quake is so potent that I lose my balance and bang into Justus, who grunts out a shallow *oomph*. The man may be alive, but he's clearly in pain.

As Lore punches the wards with his spectral fists, thunder booms across the land, a deafening peal that agitates the green fronds.

"You must truly work on your motivational skills, Ríhbiadh." Justus's voice breezes over my damp cheek.

"What did he"—I swap out the word *say* with—"show you?" After all, my mate cannot pour words into Faerie minds, only images.

"All the ways he'll torture me if I don't return you to him immediately."

I don't ask for specifics. My stay in Dante's underworld may have tamed my squeamishness, but seeing the vigor of Lore's wrath, I suspect I may swoon from a single peek into his mind.

When the image of a carcass strapped to Monteluce and surrounded by vultures shimmers behind my lids, I wonder if I've conjured it up or if Lore sent it to me. I force it from my mind as I press away from Justus's body.

"Justus isn't our enemy, Lore."

He bloody took you from me!

"So I could kill Dante before you got the itch to take matters into your own talons and damn your soul." I replay the moment I had the Faerie cornered with my sword.

Who am I kidding? I never had that noxious weasel cornered. I did have him on his knees, though, and had it not been for his damn crown, I may have landed my blow.

"He's still alive." In spite of the anger rattling my heart, my voice is entirely toneless, like a rough rock worn down to a pebble.

The imagery feels wrong, warped. I may sound like a pebble, but Dante's magical greed chiseled me into a jagged rock, one whose edges will pierce his flesh the next time we meet, and we *will* meet again. I will haunt that man until his heart lays deadened inside my palm.

Lorcan's shadows pulse, and his phantom fingers unspool, imprinting themselves against the cruel nothingness separating us. ***The sigil, Behach Éan. Tell the Faerie to erase it now, or I swear I will show that man no mercy.***

I turn toward the general. "The sigil, Justus. How do we get rid of it?"

"*We* don't do anything; *I* will go. I can dress up as Lastra and pretend like I've found my way back in."

"Did Lastra have the combination to the vault?"

Justus presses his lips together. Evidently not.

"How will you get into the vault if the door's shut? You can't exactly use water to unlock it when the Faerie you'd be impersonating has earth magic."

Justus stares at the other dead soldier.

"That one was a fire-Fae." Though neither of us mention Cato, his magic was wind. "If you tell me where it is, I could—"

Are you out of your fucking mind, my love? Lore's tone is as hot and bright as the bolt of lightning that lights up his sky.

"You'd need to coax the blood from the marble bust of my mother, and only the witch who cast the spell has the power to do so." He looks down at his fist, the one that bears his connection to Meriam. "Or me."

I shoot my gaze in the direction of the hallway I was marched through. "I can blow up the vault's ceiling and you can drop down into it. And like that, we can carry Meriam—" I suddenly recall the vault's emptiness. "Is she still down there?"

"She is. And the vault's buried too deep beneath the earth." Justus slides his lips together right before gasping, "That's it. You'll make me invisible."

"Invisible? I can do that?" Although it's really not the time to be awestruck by the power at my fingertips, how can I *not* go slack-jawed and wide-eyed?

Oh my Gods, this is what Meriam must've done earlier to distract the lot of them!

Justus turns and I follow, staggering after him, cursing Lastra for having transformed me into an enchanted pincushion. I shove away my abhorrence for the dead man and focus on the fact that I, Fallon of Shabbe, can make a person fucking invisible!

Lore's jagged voice halts my patchy gait. ***Fallon!***

I think he's about to berate me for my speech, but he looses another frustrated breath.

I don't fucking care about your swearing at the moment, mo khrà; what I care about is keeping you in my line of sight.

"I'll be gone but a minute, Lore. I just need to draw the sigil to allow Justus to pass through the wall." When he heaves more smoke, I jab my thumb in the direction of the staircase down which Lastra tried to bowl me. "Less than a minute." My muscles creak so hard that I adjust my calculations, ***Three minutes, at most.*** I take another step and sigh. ***Fine. Closer to ten.***

I don't want you gone even a heartbeat. The shadowy shape of his fingers grows and shrinks against the wards.

I glance over at Justus who's still advancing toward the stairs. I manage to catch up since he's more broken than I am. "Justus, wait."

Lore calls out to me, but I don't stop this time. My mate must realize that yelling won't make me return because he quiets, muttering low Crow words under his breath.

"They may not see you, Justus, but they'll surely see your magic. I cannot make *that* invisible . . . or can I?"

"No." He exhales a slow breath that draws a grimace to his lips. "I'll be discreet."

Had he been an air-Fae, discretion may have been attainable, but water will splash.

He starts down the steps, one hand clasped around the railing. I don't miss his jerky intakes of air, or the amount of time he holds each one in. He's in no state to head down under and use magic that will drain him of energy.

"How bad is your pain?"

"I'll live."

"Not what I asked."

"Stop worrying. I'm fine." I think he tries to add a smile but it barely registers on his lips.

When he flattens his palm against his abdomen, I realize that he's in lots more pain than he's letting on. This mission will be the death of Lore's patience, and quite possibly, the death of the brave Faerie standing before me.

However resilient and cunning, the man cannot do this alone.

"You're not going back down there, Nipota. Swear it."

How on earth did he guess? When we reach the bottom of the steps, I say, "Nonna would be furious with me if I struck a bargain with you."

He rumbles, sounding a lot like the wards around the house that Lore pummels with his unrelenting storm.

I cross my arms. "Can you press your hand onto a sigil of my making?"

He stares at the rivulets of dried blood on my arms. "No. Which is why you'll crumble this hidden door."

My eyes draw wide with excitement.

"After which, you'll return to Ríhbiadh's side for I truly do not wish to be eviscerated tonight."

"Yep." His tapered stare prompts me to add, "Cross my heart, I'll do just that."

He holds his finger over my bleeding arm. "May I?" At my nod, he dips his fingers in one of my wounds, then paints five parallel waves with four swoops each. "The more waves you draw, the stronger the tremor."

I commit this to memory. "And now the invisibility sigil."

He collects more blood and draws a 'V'. Before he even draws the rest of it, I know that it'll stand on an inverted 'T'. And I'm right.

I close my eyes for a heartbeat. If I hadn't dropped from Bronwen's vision before she had time to explain the effect of the interlocked 'V' and 'T', I could've used it. I could've turned myself into a ghost. People don't see ghosts coming.

Not even Faerie Kings.

After all, he didn't notice Meriam's invisibility earlier, so even though I cannot kill him with my blood, I can use it to my advantage.

After frustration comes resolve. "That simple?"

"That simple."

"Am I invisible?"

"I cannot cast spells with your blood, Fallon," he says gently.

Right. "How does one remove a spell?"

"Blood on skin fades on its own—sometimes in a matter of minutes; sometimes, hours. However, if you want to remove it sooner, then you must hover your hand over the sigil until the blood rises to the surface, then either slash your finger through—if you're impatient—or wait until it collects back under your skin."

"So if I make you invisible, you'll stay invisible until I recall my magic or until my spell fades?"

"Actually, spells cast on flesh can be removed by Shabbins at will. Granted, one has to know where the sigil is drawn to lift the spell. Spells cast on objects are a different story. Those can only be removed by the spellcaster."

Fascinating. I dip my finger into my wound. "Where do you want the sigil?"

"Between my brows."

I sketch the symbol, a gasp whooshing from my lips when he winks out of existence. "I can't see you!"

"Which is the point." A smile limns his tone. One that fades when he says, "Before we resort to dynamiting the door, I'll attempt to draw a portal using the blood on my torso."

As I push my hair back in order to replicate the symbol between my own eyebrows, Justus's hidden finger swirls blood on the slab of pristine white marble. He must press his palm against the familiar shape because it smudges. I wonder if he's through until I hear the distinct sound of grumbling.

A smile twitches onto my mouth. "Allow me, Nonno."

"Why are you invisible?"

"Because an explosion will make noise and attract unwanted attention."

"Fallon," he growls.

"Would you prefer I were visible when I lead you back inside?"

"The second you're through, you come right back out, understood?" I picture his nostrils flaring.

"Yes." And it's not a lie. I do understand.

Will I be coming straight out, though? No. But I will eventually come out.

After I walk up to Dante and surprise him with a blade through the neck.

After I locate Antoni.

After I crumble Costa's ancient home and drive the pointy-eared demons from his tunnels.

I want to tell Lore of my plan, but he's going to rip Luce to shreds if he catches even a whiff of it, so I mute my thoughts and make quick work of drawing the magical door sigil. When I feel the weight of Justus's hand, I flatten my palm against the stone and carry us back into the underworld.

CHAPTER 35

We emerge inside a room I've yet to visit. Granted, Dante never gave me a grand tour of his new lodgings, surely too frightened I'd escape. And I would've, considering there was a door all along.

"Go back." Justus's murmur is brisk.

As brisk as the tremor that shoots through the low-hanging ceiling, surely Lore's doing.

My grandfather reaches out. When his fingers meet my flesh, they track it to my hand, which he carries to the door handle. "*Now*."

"I'll go back through the wall so there's no slamming." My whisper's an octave sharper than his but just as quiet.

I can feel him wait. And wait. I start to creep along the wall away from where I think he must be. When I hear a breath drop from his lips, I imagine he believes me gone. I follow his footfalls to the closed door. The handle sinks, and then the door groans. He stills, clearly waiting to see if a guard will storm into the room.

When no one charges inside, he draws the black wood wider. I tiptoe after him, emerging into the dark corridor that leads from the vault room toward Dante's chamber.

I stare left and right, then creep out. Since Justus will head to the vault, I go the opposite way. Toward Dante's room, toward that low part of the ceiling that vibrated with the pulse of the ocean, the one upon which I intend to paint *many* parallel waves. If my plan works, Costa's ancient home will soon offer sea creatures a spanking-new hidey-hole.

My heart thuds so wildly that the metallic taste of its beats coats my tongue. When the walls around me shake, I think that perhaps it isn't Lore's assault on the Rossi realm that I feel, but my own adrenaline-infused exhilaration. I pass by a gaping door and jump when I spy a man moving within.

I press my palm against my mouth to catch my breaths before they can disturb the air and give me away.

The rattle of chains and ensuing growls make me take a step nearer and gasp. Antoni must hear my surprise because he looks away from the metal bracelet he's trying to yank off his wrist. He stills and grows quiet, probably worried it's one of our jailers.

Where *are* our jailers for that matter?

I turn on myself, pushing my hearing as far as it'll go, which is quite far seeing as how I can hear the distant splash of what I imagine is Justus's water.

The prison is eerily quiet . . .

Although I'd like to believe it's silent because they're gone, their scent lingers in the air. Not to mention, where would they go?

Back to Isolacuori, my mind says, but my mind is a highly optimistic fiend.

Besides, wouldn't they have taken Antoni with them? Leaving him here seems remarkably foolish. As long as he has breath in his lungs, Dante could've used him. Then again, Antoni wants to kill both kings, so perhaps his use has waned.

A nearby creak, and not of the metal chain type, makes me whirl on myself. A door is shutting farther down the corridor—or is it opening? I squint but it's so very dark and far away that I cannot see.

Could be Justus, my optimistic self tells my realistic one. When I catch the drip of water, I wrangle my heart into a steadier rhythm. *Definitely Justus.*

I take one step forward but stop when Antoni begins to pull at his chains again, his hair dripping with sweat that mixes into the blood coursing down his fingers.

One swipe of my fingers on his shackles, and he could be free. But then what? He'll either attempt to make a run for it and get caught again, or he'll come after Lore.

I suddenly hear Antoni yelling at Dante not to lay a finger on me. Even though he despises Lorcan, he still cared enough to try and protect me.

I eye Dante's chamber, knowing my minutes are sparse, but however hard I try to take a step in that direction, I cannot abandon the sea captain. That's not who I am. So I press his door wider.

He goes as still as a corpse—an upright one—and stares wildly my way, his gaze growing whiter and wider when he finds nothing but air. His chest lifts with ragged breaths as he tries to break the bones in his hand to pull his shackles off.

"Antoni?" I murmur.

He jumps.

"Don't speak. And don't move."

Although his shoulders turn sharper beneath his tattered shirt that's as grimy and gory as the rest of him, he does as I ask. It takes me six heartbeats to sever the bangles around his ankles, and twice as many to slice open the ones around his wrists. Why? Because my touch renders him invisible, so I need to let go and reassess where to slice to avoid injuring him further.

Once done, I step back. "Where is everyone?"

"Gone," he snarls.

"Gone where?"

"They didn't stop by for a chat, Fal." His tone is so cutting that it shears the heavy air.

"Don't speak to me this way."

His lips twist. "Sorry. You're right. You don't deserve my anger."

He got his nails ripped from his fingers, so I possibly do deserve it, but it's still nice to hear him calm down in regards to me. "I'm getting us out of here, so hurry to remove your shackles for you'll need your limbs to swim."

"Swim?"

I turn and smack into a wall.

And not one made of black stone, but one made of air. My heart all but rockets from my parted lips.

Fuck, fuck, fuck.

I want to croak Justus's name to check if it's him, but what if it's a soldier or Dante? What if the Faerie I hunt made Meriam cloak him so he could be ready for when I returned because he heard about her sigil and—

"You promised to head back, Nipota."

I release the breath cramping my lungs as my heart slow-rolls back down my bobbing throat. "Did you find the sigil?"

"Yes. It's done." He must regard Antoni because he growls, "Are we breaking him out?"

"Well, we can't leave him here."

Justus expels another exasperated sigh. "Fine. Let's go before your mate destroys the house."

Just as he says this, the subterranean castle shakes so hard my teeth chatter.

I whip out my hands to keep myself steady. "Not yet."

"You're not chasing—"

"No."

"Good, because I was beginning to worry about your mental state." His sarcasm smacks my grooved forehead, warming the blood caking my brow.

"But I'm not leaving here until I've crumbled this place."

"I knew it. I knew you'd do something reckless." His hands fall away from my biceps. "The stone is thick and—"

"Not beside Dante's chamber. I could hear the ocean, Nonno. I could feel the serpents." And they could feel me. "Want to float Meriam over?"

I hear him swallow. "They took her."

Of course they did. "Where?"

"Inside the tunnels." He bites out each word.

I may not be able to see his face, but I've no doubt that if I pressed my fingertips against his jaw, it would be ticking. "Even more reason to flood this place."

"The tunnels were built on an incline."

"Dante and his little regiment are weighed down by a gold throne, so they mustn't have gotten all that far." I think of when Lore flooded the mountain trench, and it had flushed away the soldiers trailing after us. Fingers crossed it'll work this time, too. "Maybe you and Antoni can already start watering the place."

Antoni frowns—because he doesn't understand my plan, or because he believes me mad?

I fold my arms. "Either you help us, Antoni, or I transform you into a crab."

He eyes the spot I stand on, his pupils shrinking and spreading as though weighing the truth of my threat.

"A crab?" His mouth moves with a small smile. "Can she really do that, Justus?"

How neat would it be if I could? I wait with bated breath for Justus's answer. Especially since we're no longer in danger.

I feel the heat of a hand on my brow and blink. Since Antoni's lids slam down and up as well, I imagine Justus has removed my sigil.

The door swings into the stone wall. "You have one minute to draw the shockwaves before I haul you upstairs. Better hurry, Nipota."

With a sigh, I mumble a chastened, "I'll be quick." How is it that I'm twenty-two, and a powerful witch no less, yet feel knee-high to a sprite?

Once out of Antoni's cell, we march toward the black wooden door looming ahead of us. The nearer we get to it, the more my blood pounds, surging and ebbing like its own tide. Is it nerves or is it the ocean I'm feeling?

I raise my hand to the ceiling that slants so low that my fingertips skim the cool stone. When a liquid thump tickles their tips, I startle then marvel. Serpents. I may not be able to see through stone, but I know that if I drew the key sigil, I'd find myself inside the ocean.

The bedchamber door groans open, and I all but jump out of my skin.

CHAPTER 36

Antoni sidles in front of me. "Stay behind."

And I do, but mostly because I'm too startled by the fact that he's trying to shield me to move. His body is torn and broken in just as many places as my own. That he can still stand upright is a miracle.

"It's only me, you fools," Justus mutters.

His footfalls ring anew in the corridor. "I was checking no one was left behind."

Thank the Cauldron. As my heart rate dwindles, I dip my fingers into one of my many wounds and begin to paint.

Antoni stares around the resounding emptiness. "How long will it take them to reach Isolacuori by foot?"

"It took us almost a fortnight to arrive here from the valley," Justus says.

My pulse flares with indignation that I was carted around, unconscious, for almost two weeks. The desire to rip this place to shreds makes me draw faster.

"You don't think they'll exit before then?" Antoni asks softly.

"Tarespagia is full of Crows. Monteluce belongs to Lore. So no, they won't risk emerging until they're back in the eastern Fae lands."

"Once we're out of here, the Crows can fly us to Monteluce, and we can—"

"Fallon, once we're out of here, Lore will keep you under lock and key." Justus sighs. "Antoni knows those tunnels well. Together—"

"I'm done, Rossi. Lore's cause is no longer my cause. Don't give me that look, Fal."

Slipping my tongue over my lip to purge the taste of my disappointment, I return my gaze to the waves I've stopped counting.

"I'll be leaving Luce."

"Where will you go?" Justus asks.

"Wherever the wind steers my ship."

I don't try to convince Antoni to fight alongside us. In truth, it may be best he leaves.

"Should we open the rest of the doors, Rossi?" Antoni asks, staring at the handles gleaming in the dull torchlight.

"Nothing inside those rooms."

As I adorn the ceiling with more undulating lines of blood, my mind catches on a thought. "Aoife? Where did you put her, Justus?"

"I dragged her into my mother's bedroom. Her sister's there, too. And so is my son." Does Justus not speak Vance's name because he doesn't want Antoni to make the connection?

In the event I'm right, I keep it from my lips. "I thought the house was warded against Crows?"

"Live ones." When my complexion turns bloodless, he adds, "I meant, not obsidian Crows."

The ceiling begins to rumble, but I cannot tell how much of the movement is brought about by Lore's assault on the Rossi home and how much derives from my spell. I swipe my upper lip, tasting salt. Even though I'd like to think it's the ocean I taste, I'm aware it's probably just sweat.

"More." Justus must sense the ocean moving against the obsidian tunnel as well because he whispers, "Add more waves."

So I do. I paint waves from wall to wall, drawing from every wound on my flesh until the ceiling above drips. I think it's blood until I spy a wet plop scurrying across the back of my hand, clear as a dewdrop. I hunt the black stone for a fissure, expelling a gasp when bits of stone begin to rain down over me.

"We need to get back to—" A block of obsidian detaches itself from the ceiling and embeds itself inside the hallway floor, blocking our path back into the Rossi house. "Inside the bedchamber!" My grandfather hooks my wrist and tows me through the gaping door.

I shudder as I step over the threshold of the bedroom where Dante put his hands on me, and then I shudder again, but not from disgust. This time, my quaking comes from the floor that rattles like Minimus when pleased. "It's working!"

Justus must've scrubbed at his forehead, probably to mop away the anguish I've glossed his brow with, because he's visible again.

The few torches that still burn inside the hallway sizzle as new cracks appear and more drips come through.

When another hard bang shakes the obsidian castle, lengthening the crack in the hallway's ceiling, Justus mumbles a prayer under his breath.

"I didn't take you for a devout man," I murmur.

"I very much believe in the Cauldron. But I'm not currently praying; I'm listing all my favorite moments on this earth in case I expire."

I roll my eyes. "You're a pureling. A water one to boot. A little swim in the ocean won't hurt you."

"It's not the ocean I fear; it's your mate since he undoubtedly assumes I lured you back inside."

"I'll set him—" The word *straight* flies right out from my mind when his gorgeous—and extraordinarily angry—voice erupts between my temples.

We cracked the ceiling, Lore!

I pray my mate's silence comes from observing the ocean churn as the prison sucks Mareluce into its black belly.

The ocean, Lore. Fly to the ocean. I'm coming.

He still doesn't reply.

A breathy gasp slips from my lips when something wet sprinkles my forehead. I frown until I notice moisture beading along a crack in the chamber ceiling.

"Draw gills across your throat with blood." Justus's voice echoes against the black walls. "It will help you breathe."

"Won't the water wash away my spell?" I call back.

"No. The blood will penetrate into your skin and keep you breathing for a while."

Repetitive thuds bang against the collapsing ceiling as though the serpents were hurtling gondolas at it.

"How long are we talking?" I ask as I baste my fingertips in blood.

"Long enough to reach the surface with oxygen to spare; not long enough to swim to Shabbe."

"That really narrows it down."

With a sigh, he says, "It depends on the witch's blood. Since you're of Meriam's line, I suspect your *while* will be quite long."

I drag my fingers down either side of my neck. When my skin prickles, a potent thrill shoots through me.

"Antoni, get in the room!" Justus beckons him into the filling bedchamber.

Antoni doesn't move, transfixed by the swelling dribble that plops onto his upturned face.

I yell his name to snap him out of his daze. He's a half-blood, and halflings cannot survive buried beneath rubble at the bottom of the ocean.

He still doesn't move. Does he have a death wish?

"Antoni, come on!"

When another groan rolls through the stone surrounding us, I catch ahold of that gilded monstrosity of a bedframe that clashes with the bare, carceral feel of Costa's home but matches the framed portrait of him to perfection.

"Get on the bed and draw the portal sigil, Fallon!" Justus is already astride the enormous mattress, one hand held out to help me up. "Quick!"

I clasp his fingers and vault onto the squishy mattress, then raise my hand to the ceiling just as a spiderweb crack appears.

"Paint faster!" Justus mutters.

My hand jerks. I shake so hard that I cannot draw a circle for my life. Justus clasps my wrist to steady my hand. It works, until a chunk of stone detaches itself from the part of the ceiling I draw on, and a hard gush of water rushes into my eyes, stinging them.

And then a fish trundles through the fist-sized gap and plops onto the bed between Justus and me. It wriggles madly, flapping to get back to its element.

I crouch and scoop it up from where it writhes, then toss it inside the rising surf. I feel its tail brush against my ankle as it swims away.

"Really not the time to be rescuing creatures, Fallon," Justus grumbles as Antoni finally wades toward us.

He's about to jump onto the mattress when a chunk of obsidian clips him in the head, drawing blood from one of the rare spots on his body that wasn't previously bleeding. His eyes roll back, and he flops face down into the rushing tide. As his body is swept toward the corridor, I dive off the bed and grab him by the ankle, hauling his big frame back toward us.

I flip him over, then hook his neck and kick my legs to return to the mattress and finish drawing our way out. I manage to hand him to Justus just as something sharp snags my ankle, and I hiss out an unladylike curse.

"We need to go before the tunnels flood and we get swept into them!" Justus grips the ceiling lamp as the water immerses the mattress.

"I know, Nonno! I'm coming." But as hard as I kick, I cannot break free from whatever my foot has caught on.

I plop my head underwater and search the salty darkness for my restraint, find my foot has somehow managed to wedge itself between the damn wooden bedframe and the sodden mattress.

I plop my head back out and spit out my mouthful of salt water, wincing as the current tugs at my body. I flail to grab ahold of something before the ocean can snap my bones.

Justus mutters something under his breath, then pats down his pant leg until he locates a dagger he must've picked up on his way to find Meriam. He holds it out to me.

"It's my—" A fish drops onto my head, slapping me with its fins. I'm trying to say ankle and not dress when the hole in the ceiling siphons down a huge coral. Right before it can clock me, I duck underwater.

When I peek back out, Justus is waving his dagger wildly at me.

"It's my ankle!"

He mustn't hear me because he screeches, "Use the fucking thing!"

"I'm not amputating my foot!" I sputter. I may be immortal, but I'm not Fae. My appendages won't grow back. And even if they could grow back, I'd rather not be footless for several weeks.

"Not your foot," he mutters, releasing Antoni. "Grab him."

I snag the sea captain just as Justus dips beneath the liquid darkness. I feel his hand circle my foot, then feel the wood splintering around my skin.

My foot slips free and I'm suddenly whisked away toward the bedroom door.

Justus breaks the surface. "Grab the doorframe and whatever you do, don't let go."

I nod, my heart too large for my ribs.

I hook the doorframe with every last shred of strength I possess and roll my body so that it's stuck to the chamber wall. Justus bangs into the opposite wall, grabs the door and flings it closed.

It quiets the surge.

"The second you can reach the ceiling, Fallon, you draw the sigil and get out, you hear me?" Justus plucks a long strand of orange hair off his wet face and nods at the matte stone over our heads.

My skin prickles with a million goosebumps. "*We* get out."

Although the world around us is a din of cracking stone and whooshing thuds, I feel as though I've just stepped inside a bubble—a quiet, peaceful place I share with Justus Rossi and a comatose Antoni.

I raise my eyes to the deeply-fissured obsidian. Although I'm no stonemason, I estimate we have mere minutes before it caves over us. I try to touch the ceiling but it's still out of my reach. Why did it have to be built so high here?

"How deep are we?" I yell.

"A dozen or so meters, depending on the tides."

"Will you need gills?"

"I should have enough air to last me until the surface, but perhaps draw some on your friend."

I adorn either side of Antoni's neck with red stripes that absorb into his skin. "You never told me why you're doing all of this?"

"Didn't I?"

"No, you were extremely vague."

"I'm doing this because keeping Shabbin civilization locked away from ours hasn't made us greater; it's made us weaker, poorer." His eyes glaze over. "But that's not my only reason."

I wait with bated breath for him to go on.

"My true reason is that I want access to the Cauldron."

Though curious as to why a full-blooded Faerie, with Shabbin magic to boot, longs to access the Cauldron, I don't ask. Hasn't he been generous enough with his secrets?

"You could've crossed through the wards," I say instead.

"And abandon my family? I suppose you don't know me yet, Fallon, but understand that family comes first."

Does he consider *me* family?

"I may not be an outstanding specimen, but I've principles."

"You're a most perplexing man, Nonno." I stare at the face I've come to know and *not* loathe.

The single candle that still burns in the ceiling lamp gilds the silver strands in the rusty mass of the general's hair.

"What will you do once we get out?"

"I'll hunt down Meriam and Dante."

Like an ocean swell, my pulse surges and dashes itself into every little corner of my body. "You don't think he'll come out of the tunnels on his own?"

"As long as the Crows soar over Luce and the tunnels exist, he won't risk showing his teeth."

So to run him out, we will have to destroy the tunnels entirely . . . "And the Crows will never fall." I watch for his reaction as the water gulps down Costa's portrait. "Right?"

"Right."

"So we're on the same side?"

"We're on the same side."

"Will you still be on my side when I end Dante's life?"

"Hopefully, I will be *at* your side." Although I don't ask him to baste his tongue in salt, he licks his salt-crusted lips. "Fallon of Shabbe and of Luce, Child of the *Rahnach bi'Adh*, I swear to serve you until my very last breath."

I suck in a breath as the skin of my bicep prickles, burns. I peer at my pockmarked arm that now glows with a bargain. My very first one. I whip my attention toward Justus who's studying it too.

His eyes shine with tender satisfaction. "Just in case you forget to call on me in times of need."

I'm so stunned by his declaration that I barely register his intent when he swims toward me and holds out his dagger.

"Prick your finger."

I blink out of my heart-eyed daze and slash the tip over the point of the blade. I start to reach up but what if— What if we get swept away at sea and separated? "Tell me where my mother is."

"She's in the ocean."

I'm honestly so shocked he's responded that I forget all about escaping this crumpling underworld. "Where?"

"Magick us out of this chamber, and I will tell you all."

"You swear it?"

"I swear it, Fallon amZendaya, daughter of the Sky Kingdom."

My bicep prickles anew. "*Two* bargains?"

"Use them well. Ready, Nipota?"

I imagine he's asking whether I'm ready for a swim—since I'm guessing that's how we're getting out of here—or is he asking me whether I'm ready for what lays ahead?

Throat stinging with emotion, I draw the portal sigil, and it's perfect this time. "I'm ready."

Lore?

He still doesn't answer. I pray it's because I'm surrounded by too much obsidian.

Justus nods to the matte stone that glimmers with the faint tracks of my blood.

As the water rises to my chin, I shout, "Grab Antoni." The second his fingers close around the captain's leg, I slam my palm against the ceiling.

Though I didn't murder Dante, I put a real dent in his Machiavellian design to turn me into his broodmare, or should I say, *bloodmare*?

Here's to hoping Meriam doesn't reveal the reason she and Justus insisted on the blood-bind for I'd enjoy nothing more than to deliver the news that he had Shabbin magic at his fingertips all along.

I'll whisper it into his peaked ear just before I erase him from our world and make Lorcan Ríhbiadh, ruler of the sky, king of the land the Fae stole from him.

CHAPTER 37

The ocean is white with froth, dark with wingbeats, and luminous with scales.

My hand tightens around Antoni's arm as the current, stirred by so much aquatic life, pins our bodies to the coral-covered rock housing Costa's former bedchamber.

Fallon?

I hunt the foaming immensity for the source of that raucous, beautiful voice, my eyes connecting with those of the Crows pushing off the sandy bottom and drifting past me, their enormous bodies carving through the churning water before bobbing like corks on a surface needled by rain.

None have golden eyes.

The serpents settle next, rainbow scales shimmering in the weak dawn that bends through the eddies of sand and air bubbles. The ocean grows calm, as though even the mollusks are holding their breath.

You brought back a friend. I can tell from Lore's timbre that he's displeased to see Antoni.

He was chained to a wall. I couldn't just abandon him. He would've died.

You left me to save him?

I sigh. ***I left you so I could destroy Costa's old underground home.***

You could've died.

Haven't you heard? I'm immortal. I add a smile, hoping to clear his terrible mood.

If someone had knifed your neck and bled you—

Everyone was gone. They fled.

After flattening us, the liquid muscle of our world plucks our bodies off the corals and floats us up. Justus blinks like a newborn babe as we rise, his knuckles whitening around Antoni's log of a body when a serpent circles the three of us.

I part my lips. Timidly at first. When my lungs expand like sea sponges, I part my mouth wider and breathe in the deep. Wonder purls through my body and ripples through my blood. My extraordinary, magical blood.

Even though Meriam was the one to take away my gift, I cannot help but feel grateful that she's given it back.

A shadow slinks through the copse of hovering *mareserpens,* and although it holds no human attribute—or Crow one—I know exactly who's drawing nearer. When that shadow breaches the distance between us and spirals up and down my body before assuming the human shape I glimpsed outside Xema Rossi's front door, the corners of my mouth rise so high that my cheeks ache almost as terribly as my heart.

When my dress puffs like fried dough, revealing my myriad of wounds, Lore curses in Crow, then grows worryingly quiet as he inspects each and every one of them.

I will murder them all. He watches the widening crevasse beneath us, as though hoping that Faeries will start funneling out.

I'm afraid no one else will be joining our reunion.

Where's Meriam?

Dante took her with him when he fled.

His gaze scrolls over the two men at my side, settling on Justus whose ponytail is being nibbled on by a large white fish. In the fish's defense, my grandfather's hair does resemble fire-hued seaweed.

Did you miss me?

With a gentle grunt, Lore murmurs, ***Did I miss you?*** He strokes the edge of my jaw, the curve of my cheek, the point of my chin, the tips of my lashes.

What? No smart quip?

No, Behach Éan. My mind and heart are too full of brutal deliberations for humor.

Attempting to ease the tempest tossing the gold in his eyes, I point to my neck. ***I can breathe underwater thanks to gills I painted in blood on my skin.***

His liquid shadows slick over my throat, raising goosebumps on the skin that absorbed my blood. ***I wish I could've been the one to make your dream of possessing magic come true.***

I thread my fingers through the smoky wisps of hair, wishing they were solid. ***I have many other dreams, Lore. Most of which no one else but you can grant.***

Good. His spectral touch dances across my collarbone before curving around my neck, and somehow clasping it. And then he presses his forehead to mine, and although he is but smoke, I can feel the strength of his bones and the silk of his skin.

My eyes slip closed when his shadows graze my parted lips, firm yet soft, eliciting a full-body shudder from me. ***Where is your fallen crow?***

Instead of answering me, he asks, ***Are we keeping the Faeries at your side alive?***

My lids slam up, my lashes carving through his darkness. ***Yes.*** My rapid intake of breath shoots bubbles into the sand-riddled water between us. ***The same way we're keeping all of their limbs attached to their trunks.***

Lore makes a low sound at the back of his throat that tells me he isn't pleased with my request, nevertheless, he doesn't slink over to Justus to instill fear in the general, who, considering the snow-white knuckles crimping Antoni's ankle, has no need for an additional source of anxiety.

You left me. Not once. He gazes at the gutted ocean floor. ***But twice.***

I thumb the velvet frame of his face. ***And I returned to you. Not once, but twice.***

His eyes rove over mine, hunting their depths, for what . . . I'm not entirely sure. A promise never to leave his side again?

I will always find you, Lore.

One would have to be blind not to find something forever in their line of sight.

I grin.

I'm not jesting, mo khrà.

I know. I keep grinning even though he does not. I fear our time apart has eroded his ability to laugh.

Let the sea captain go.

I was trying to avoid a serpent towing him out to sea.

Please.

I've no feelings for him, Lore. Actually, I do, and they're not all that positive, but Lore doesn't need to know this. Not yet. Not now. He may encourage a serpent to snag him and drag him to Shabbe.

Come to think of it, that may be the safest place for Antoni. I consider it for a heartbeat, but then decide that it would be unjust to send him there without his consent.

I'll see that he's returned safely to land. Lore regards the fingers I have curled around Antoni's forearm with such jealousy that I let go.

Justus's eyes widen when he realizes he's adrift with Antoni. He pumps his legs, swimming back toward me just as a Crow dives in beside us. Poor Justus blanches as though all the blood from his body has leaked through the hole in his abdomen.

He releases the captain's ankle just as the giant black bird hooks iron talons around Antoni's armpits and tears him out of the ocean, spooking schools of fish that take refuge behind the endless coils of their serpent sentinels.

I point to his abdomen, and Justus peers down at himself. He must understand what I'm asking because he untucks his shirt to check on the wound which he crudely stuffed with what looks like a handkerchief.

Who tried to gut him? Lore's golden eyes are affixed to the crimson fabric Justus presses more firmly into the hole beneath his rib cage.

Dante. I don't see much point in adding that he calls his blade the Crow Killer since I will see to it that he never harms any Crows with it. ***He's on our side.*** When Lore's hazy forehead grooves, I add, ***I meant*** Justus. ***Obviously not Dante.***

He may be on our side, but he stole you from me, so do not expect me to trust or forgive him.

The only thing I expect is for you not to kill— I suck in a breath when a beast of a serpent muscles his way through the throng of his suspended kin, bright-pink scales soon becoming the focal point of my attention.

The second Minimus is within reach, he slows, and his eyes, black lid-to-lid, race over my body as though to make sure I'm whole. When his gaze knocks into my legs, his nostrils flare. He dips his large head and sniffs my calves before ribboning his forked black tongue up their length, his magical saliva sealing my wounds.

I stroke the top of his head, scratching the skin around his ivory horn. Once my skin has knitted, he tips his head and nudges my hand with his equine nose.

Justus's body bumps mine as another curious beast swims toward us, sniffing at his bandage. When he flicks out his tongue, Justus's complexion becomes as white as the albino fish still nibbling on the end of his ponytail.

I seize my grandfather's wrist and give it a squeeze, then reach down and pluck out the kerchief. His abdominal muscles clench, ejecting blood in carmine spurts. The giant beast flicks his tongue again, making Justus tense so hard that his body goes as stiff as drift-wood, and sinks.

When he finally realizes that the serpent isn't about to snack on his flesh, he looses an exhale that streams out of him like a trail of starlight. For someone who knows so much, has seen so much, has accomplished so much, I'm stunned to witness his ignorance on the magical properties of serpent saliva.

As his wound knits, he blinks at the beast tending to him, then blinks at me. I smile. His face is so stiff with shock that he doesn't. Ministrations complete, the serpent points his black gaze toward the general. I laugh because I know what the creature wants, but clearly Justus doesn't. I raise his palm and flatten it on the firm scales of his healer's cheek.

Although Justus keeps his hand where I put it, his fingers judder, but then they move, they stroke, and the beast rattles in pleasure. Justus's hand moves from beneath mine, inches toward the long tusk. He spirals his fingers around it, eyes aglitter. The serpent stills, which makes Justus jerk his hand away. Beast and Fae stare at each other for a long heartbeat, and then the serpent whirls, undulating through the liquid immensity.

The hand with which I still stroke Minimus is suddenly heaved off. I think my mate must be jealous of the affection I'm lavishing on my beast and am about to tease him about it when I catch the direction of his golden eyes.

What the fucking Cauldron is that?

CHAPTER 38

Lorcan's grown so still that I can almost feel the hard contours of his body . . . can almost feel the thumb frenziedly tracing the interlocked circles.

My eyes fasten to Lore's agitated golden ones. ***That is the mark of a blood-bind.*** I wait for understanding to grab ahold of his features and smooth them, but his brow remains a field of misty knolls and valleys.

A blood-bind? he squawks, just as my head crests the turbulent surface of Mareluce. ***And I do not bloody squawk.***

I smile.

What in Mórrígan's name is a blood-bind?

You really don't know what it is?

Do I often ask questions I know the answer to, Behach Éan?

I cannot even fault him for his tetchiness. In truth, I'm so relieved, it warms all the parts of me that have felt frozen since Dante took me underground.

I was so afraid it was another secret you were keeping from me. I carve my hand through my hair to press it out of my eyes, then knuckle the seawater off my lashes—futile, seeing as a second later, a new wave slaps me in the face. ***It's a Shabbin ritual. Perhaps my father's heard of it?***

There's nothing your father knows that I don't.

Could my mother *not* have known about it?

With the intent to ask Justus about it, I turn toward him but get walloped by yet another wave. I try to glimpse where we are, but Lore's smoke coalesces into a gauzy face, and I forget all about looking anywhere but at him. I raise my hand to touch him, fearing my fingers will fall right through his ethereal shape, but they don't. Though soft like his feathers, Lore feels solid.

The rain eases, but only over our heads where a murder of Crows fly dizzyingly fast. Everywhere else, it smacks the ocean like the hooves of a thousand warhorses.

Tell Justus that your father will fly him to dry land. Filaments of his dark smoke graze the seam of my lips. ***If he tries anything, Cathal will try something back.***

I smirk because I'm rather certain "try something back" is a euphemism for a talon through soft tissue. Lore raises a vaporous smile that confirms my suspicions. ***Such a homicidal creature you are, Mórrgaht.***

Protective, Fallon; not homicidal. A deep swallow sounds through our mental bond.

I turn to Justus and relate the first part. I don't bother adding Lore's threat. I'd rather these two begin to build a rapport, and preferably one not based on fear of severed limbs and obsidian impalements.

Does he carry obsidian? Lore asks.

"Justus, Lore wants to know if you have obsidian on your person?"

"No." My grandfather's lack of hesitation seems to surprise Lore. "In case you don't trust me, my mouth is full of salt, Ríhbiadh." Lore must send him a vision because Justus says, "I've no need to cripple myself to feel an iota more invincible."

My father drifts low, his black eyes locked on me. They're filled with so much emotion that even without words, I grasp all he is thinking.

"Álo, Dádhi."

His great big body seems to shudder at the sound of my voice. He swoops low, brushing my cheek with the tip of his wing. His feathers are so much softer than his callused hands; nevertheless, I decide I love both equally.

"On second thought, I'll swim," Justus murmurs. "I am a water-Fae after all."

I laugh because there's only one reason a Faerie would prefer to brave the serpents than take to the skies.

He cocks up a single eyebrow. "Something amusing, Nipota?"

"Who knew the formidable general, who's spent centuries mastering the art of terrorizing Lucins, was scared of anything?"

Justus grunts something unintelligible just as my father clicks his enormous talons around the general's biceps. With a powerful wing-beat, they take off into Lore's storm. I don't miss how rigid Justus has gone. He doesn't even reach up to hold on to the part of my father's legs not encased in iron.

Your turn, mo khrá.

Gods, I hope I'll remain his love once he finds out what a blood-bind is. When I feel his citrine stare drink in my face from creased brow to pressed lips, I wall off my mind.

I don't want him to see anything. Not yet. ***We need to make a pit stop by Xema Rossi's old home. Aoife and Imogen are there.***

A relieved sigh trundles through our mind link. ***Thank the skies. I thought they were still in those fucking tunnels.***

Actually, you'll have to thank Justus. And Vance. Who, by the way, is Justus's son.

When Lorcan doesn't react to the news, I ask, ***You knew?***

In a voice that rolls like the peals of his thunder, he says, ***Bronwen may have mentioned it.***

Did she also happen to mention how I ended up in those tunnels?

She did.

Since she's still alive, I assume she was forgiven.

I'll never forgive her, Behach Éan, but I will also never take her away from Cian.

His shadows firm into two giant crows that lift me from the careening surf, and it's only once I'm airborne that I notice from where we emerged.

I grip his talons. ***How could you take such a risk?***

What risk, Behach Éan?

To shift into your crows so close to the Tarespagian coastline.

Even though the Faeries staring up at us are as trifling as ants, and none are brandishing obsidian spears, I cannot help the spasms crimping my stomach at the sight of a beach dark with people, some turbaned, others with hair so long it flutters around their upturned faces like wild grass.

I dare because Tarespagia is ours, mo khrà.

Since when?

Since we strong-armed Tavo into drawing up an agreement. One that Dante signed just two days ago.

My brow furrows because it seems odd that Dante would give up the land under which he was hiding. Seems odd that he would give up *any* land for that matter. Not to mention that, to my knowledge, he didn't leave his grandfather's home. Especially after I took out his eye.

What was that about Dante's eye? Lore asks as we land amidst a dozen other Crows in front of Xema Rossi's gaping front door.

I may have punctured it with an iron blade. I raise a proud smile as Lore morphs into his shadowy self. ***I was aiming for his throat, so it was a bit of a miss but not a complete fail.***

My mate's arms glide around my waist and tug me into him. ***Remind me never to get on your bad side.***

I rest my cheek against his chest and drink in his strong heartbeats, wishing that my mate was whole and his skin solid. ***Where is your fallen crow, Lore?***

He presses a featherlight kiss to my forehead. ***Let's awaken Aoife and Imogen, and then we'll deal with my fallen crow.***

Six Crows in skin march past us into the home, probably to ascertain that no enemies lurk in a dusky corner. *Could* anyone still be here? I spin around, anxiety nibbling at my insides. ***Lore, perhaps take to the sky, in case—***

What part of* 'I'm never leaving your side again' *eluded you, mo khrà?

I roll my eyes that sting from exhaustion, salt, and tears. ***Gods, I forgot how stubborn you were.***

He brackets my face between gentle palms, tipping it up and up, toward those pools of liquid gold that have devoured me alive since the very first day they alighted upon me. ***I cannot lose you again, Fallon. I will not survive it.* The world *will not survive it.***

I stare at the hazy outline of his lips and press up on my toes to reach them. Lore must gather his shadows into his face because my mouth meets something solid and cool like the surface of Mareluce at night, like the glass of my windowpane in the dead of winter.

His mouth doesn't move against mine; it just rests there, inhaling the breaths I exhale, fluttering my lips with nippy heartbeats, which I soak up and store inside every cell of my body.

"The house is secure, Mórrgaht." The deep voice pulls me from the tranquility of my mate's kiss and plunges me back into the damp and chilly here and now. Lore must ask something else of the man because he says, "Two. They've been removed."

"Two what?" I ask as I pull away from Lore to peer at the giant, russet-haired male whose head barely clears the outsized doorframe.

I faintly remember him from dinner at the Sky Tavern. I dig through my mind until his name returns: Erwin, the man who went to Nebba with my father on that fool's errand intended to keep my father distracted.

"Two bodies, milady."

My blood goes as clammy as my skin. "Where did you put them?"

Out of your sight, Lore murmurs.

"The white-haired one." When my lips begin to tremble, I lick them, and it somehow eases the cry bubbling inside my heart. "I want to—I want to give him a proper burial."

Erwin stares beyond me at Lore, waiting for his command.

I turn and crane my neck to look into my mate's face. "Please, Lore."

I'll have his body wrapped in a bedsheet and carried out of the house before we burn it to the ground.

You're going to burn the house down?

I want to wipe Costa from the face of this Earth. His smoky fingers tighten around my hip. ***I want everything he ever touched gone. Everything he ever made removed. The only place he'll exist will be in the history books we will write, so that his malevolence is never forgotten.***

"Fallon!" The gruff voice makes me jump, but it also makes me smile, because I know exactly who's speaking.

CHAPTER 39

Although crossing the threshold into the house of horrors shoots a shiver into my spine, the sight of my father striding across the foyer in all his leather and iron regalia whisks it away. Without hesitation, he opens his arms and I fall into them.

I twine my own arms around his waist, barely reaching fully around what with his cuirass, armor, and girth.

"*Ínon . . .*" The whispered word for *daughter* in Crow is a raspy murmur so full of grief that it quivers like the thick fingers sailing through the wet mass of my hair. He murmurs my name a great many times, gathering me into his large body like a mamma bear gathers her young.

Strange how an embrace, a scent, the timbre of a voice can kindle familiarity even though our interactions have been so few and far between.

"I'm sorry for disappearing again, Dádhi." His heart thuds hard against the cheek I've rested on his chest.

"Not your fault. Not your fault," he murmurs.

But isn't it a little? Yes, Bronwen told me Lore needed saving, but I could've sought a second opinion. I could've asked my father to accompany me. I assume she'd have found a way to impede me from doing so, but I didn't even try.

My father gives me one last bone-crushing squeeze before letting go.

How I wish I could've returned with my mother. Just as I'm about to tell him that Justus knows where she is, Erwin passes by us, a lumpy white form hooked over his shoulder. A whimper slips from my lips because a white braid peeks from the bedsheet.

Fallon, go wake Aoife and Imogen so we may go home.

Lore must tell my father to lead the way because he wheels around, tracking mud across Xema's white floors. "They're upstairs in the Rossi matriarch's bedroom."

Guilt drips under my skin as I realize that leading Dante into the Rossi household could've turned out deadly for Vance. I brush away my remorse and focus on the sprawling seaside manor, on the mammoth living area with its white velvet couches and turquoise throw pillows.

When we pass in front of the seashell mirror, I stiffen. Although Dante's no longer clutching me to him, I see him there, standing beside me, and it chills my blood. The mirror blackens, then shatters, and I think I just made that happen, but I don't possess that sort of power. Lore does, though.

We pass the bedroom in which I . . . in which I killed a good man.

Don't. Lore's single sharply spoken word drags my eyes away from the closed door but does little to drag my guilt from where it festers beneath my ribs.

A moment later, one of the Crows bringing up the rear says, "Immediately, Mórrgaht."

I wonder what he's asked.

That they gather oil from the kitchen and douse the house. His cool fingers stroke the faint groove between my eyebrows. ***I may not be able to obliterate your nightmares, Behach Éan, but I can eradicate their source.***

My heart swells and my eyes prick for a whole other reason than the memory of driving a sword through a friend.

But of course, the second I think of Cato, a flash of white, of red . . . of so much red brightens my lids. Though Lore's shadows blanket me, the memory of Cato's bleeding throat hits me hard and fast, scraping what little warmth Lore managed to ignite within me.

To keep the tears at bay, I focus on the glossy white marble stairs framed by golden mosaic that gives it the look of a carpet. The first-story hallway is large and airy, with a skylight cut through the ceiling. The dull dawn grays the marble but polishes the golden squares of glass that border the white up here as well. It's objectively a lovely house, the sort of oceanside home I would've dreamed of living in.

The oceanside home I will build us will be far lovelier, mo khrà.

Oceanside?

You may not have scales, but you're part Shabbin, and Shabbins need the ocean.

What of the castle on Isolacuori?

I'd prefer not to live there . . . His gold stare probes mine. ***If it's all the same to you.***

I don't want anything that's belonged to the Regios, I say as we come to a stop in front of double doors that have been flung wide.

Inside stand three Crows in skin and my grandfather. Well, Justus doesn't stand. He sits on the bedside of a man I've never seen yet know is his son. And not because of the tenderness with which he wraps a band of gauze around the sleeping male's throat, but because of the veneer of cropped sunburnt-orange hair and the spray of freckles that traipse across the bridge of his nose like a colony of red ants.

Though not Agrippina's twin, Vance could very well pass for it. I'm so stunned by their resemblance that I cannot get my bare feet to shuffle past the oversized white rug that extends around the bed like seafoam.

"Is that the last of them, Rossi?" Erwin, who blustered in behind us, asks Justus, taking a burlap sack from the female Crow who carried it out of an adjacent room.

Before stepping onto a terrace that overlooks the white-capped expanse of Mareluce, she tosses a furtive glance in my direction. Her hair's cropped close to her scalp and dark like her wide-set eyes. I still find fascinating a society in which people can grow their hair any length they fancy. I wonder when it'll stop shocking me.

As she morphs into her Crow, Justus says, "Yes. That's the last of them." He secures the gauze with a knot before finally looking away from Vance.

The missing Lucin crystals, Lore explains as Erwin extends the burlap sack upward, and the female hooks it delicately with her iron talons.

So Dante wasn't lying when he told you he had no crystals to spare . . .

He was lying. He'd stashed them inside the obsidian tunnels beneath Isolacuori. Rossi stole them from him.

I slide my lips together.

Apologies if you were searching for a spark of redemption in the louse.

I wasn't, Lore. I close my fingers around the mark of the blood-bind on my palm that feels as though it pulses with its own angry heartbeat. ***Nothing could ever redeem him.* Nothing.**

Flashes of my incarceration light up my lids—the glint of the knife with which Dante opened my veins to color his vellum, the fingers he used to hike up the dress I still wear, the vile words he—

When Lore's shadows thicken like the clouds spitting out streaks of lighting through the rapidly darkening sky, I shut down my thoughts.

No, go on, Behach Éan. Feed me your memories so they stop burdening you.

Sharing my memories will only stoke Lore's fury, and he's furious enough as it is. ***It's in the past.*** "Where are Aoife and Imogen?" I try to stalk through Lore, but with only one crow missing, he's as solid as a shrub.

"In my mother's closet." Justus's voice rises over the shield of darkness pressing against me on all sides.

When I try to sidestep my mate, he tips my chin on a curled finger. ***You will tell me everything later. And I do mean* everything.** His eyes dip to the hand clenched at my side, the one gripping the intertwined rings.

Lorcan waits until I nod before allowing me to stride past him and traverse the room toward the closet beside which my father stands, waiting.

Glittery gowns have been strewn across the marble floor, along with heeled shoes and embroidered slippers. A jeweled sandal was flung so wide that it dangles from what looks like a gold branch, probably the perch of her horrid parrot.

I don't have to ask where the sisters are. Their obsidian bodies shine black against the white marble. I crouch beside Imogen and remove the black sword speared through her thigh. Instantly, her skin pales and softens. I watch her gasp in air, and it reminds me of the babe Nonna helped birth on our scarred kitchen table. The exhausted woman had come for some herbs to lull her to sleep and had left with a beautiful, little wailing thing who would keep her from her dearly sought-out slumber.

I meet Imogen's dark stare, offering her a smile that cannot possibly right the wrongs done to her because of me.

She fell because of me, Fallon. Not because of you. Lore stands over me, over his Crow whose gaze latches on to his.

I can see the umber pool of her irises churn at the sight of her misty king.

"No Shabbin blood on the blade," I say, imagining that was the source of her worry.

Her throat bobs with a swallow, and her lips part, but no words come out.

My father reaches his hand down to help her up. "You've been immobilized for a month. I'm afraid it'll take a few hours for your voice to return."

A month . . .

As I make my way to Aoife, Lore rasps, ***Yes. One entire. Fucking. Month.*** Although his features are hazy like mist, his expression is as hard as glass. He looks about ready to shatter and rain shards all over Xema's dresses.

I crouch beside my friend whose lips were frozen around a scream. I understand why Bronwen pushed me into the devil's arms, but she had no need to steal a month of life from Aoife.

I push a lock of hair out of my eyes, then grip the arrow protruding from my friend's side and pull. I don't marvel when it slips free. I'm far too angry to marvel. I clasp her stone hand as her skin loses its onyx hue and softens. The horror trapped inside her lungs rushes past her lips, a wispy shout that clocks my heart.

I squeeze her fingers and murmur an apology. I don't realize I've started crying until a tear drops onto our twined hands and races around my knuckles. When I feel her squeeze my fingers back, more tears flow down my cheeks . . . more apologies flow from my trembling lips.

Imogen kneels beside her sister, taking her face between her palms. Aoife's lips part, but like her sister, she's mute. As Imogen leans over Aoife to press their foreheads together, I release my friend's hand and rush out of the closet, out onto the terrace. I grip the railing and tip my face up, allowing Lore's rain to wash away my sadness, his thunder to drown out the thuds of my heart, his lightning to sear my murky thoughts.

Lore envelops me from behind, his chin falling against the top of my head, his arms winding around my middle. ***Not your fault, Behach Éan. Not. Your. Fault.***

I may no longer bleed on the outside, but how I bleed on the inside. I bleed rage because everything is my fault!

Everything!

My desire to murder Dante expands along with a cry that finds its way out of me. Again and again, I scream, pouring my anger into the storm until my lungs ache and my throat feels as raw as my bruised body.

Lore waits until I'm done, stroking and caressing the wet column of my throat, gliding his mouth across my hair and his pewter nails across my waist.

Take me home, Lore.

He morphs into his Crow and crouches so that I may climb atop him. Once my arms are firmly secured around his neck, he springs away from Xema's terrace and takes us high dizzyingly fast. I suck in the rain and the cold air as we rise into an ocean of clouds and black feathers.

Crows swarm the heavens, assembling under Lore, next to Lore, but none above him, because danger will never come from the sky, only from the land. Although my father doesn't have a distinguishing feature in this form, I know exactly where he is, and not because he's carrying Justus—on his back, this time—but because there's something in his corvine expression, in the watchful, soulful gleam of his dark eyes that is unmistakably him.

Justus is just as pale now as he was when my father fished him from the ocean, but there's a hint of awe in his face as he surveys the sandstone avenues dotted with giant palms and the neat rows of estates that sprawl down the coastline of Tarespagia in various shades of blue and white. Unlike in the east where houses are rainbow-colored, here, these seem to have been constructed as an extension of the great ocean that slaps the crescent of white sand in great, foamy rolls.

I cannot believe my father allowed Justus to sit atop his back. Not that the Faerie can do much without obsidian, but still . . .

He knows where your mother is and bargained with Cathal. He promised to lead him to Daya if he gave him and his son safe passage to Monteluce.

Sure enough, a few paces away, Vance dangles from another Crow's talons, looking more Yuletide ornament than man.

Since he hasn't shared her location with you yet. Although not voiced as a question, it sounds like one.

He struck a bargain with me for a tell-all after we emerged from the tunnels. I cannot help the admiration that curls within me. What a cunning man he is . . . Keeping all his aces close to his chest. I need to learn to do that.

Cunningness is birthed by chariness. The less you trust, the more secrets you horde to use as currency. With a great sigh, he adds, ***In a few centuries, you should be just as wily as the rest of us.***

A few centuries . . . When I still believed myself a halfling, I imagined my life would span three to four hundred years. To think that now, barring any unforeseen blade to my aorta, or to my mother's, or to Meriam's, I'll live far longer than that.

Forever, Lore murmurs. ***You'll live forever.***

We *will live forever.*

The scent of smoke punches up my nose.

I glance over Lore's body to find flames gamboling over the white rooftop of Xema's house . . . Costa's home.

I owe you an apology, mo khrà.

For?

For not believing you when you told me that Meriam was in Tarespagia. For not exploring the possibility that the rodent tunnels the Fae spent centuries building under Luce could link to the refuge Costa built for himself after he stabbed me. But most of all, I'm sorry for my attempt at preserving the peace the day you made me whole. I should've eradicated the Regios from our world right there and then.

Except you would've lost your humanity.

Not if another hand than mine had accomplished the deed.

I pry my gaze off the pyre, scrolling it over the grove in which Sewell lost his life, toward the stables.

The horses have been freed. No harm will come to them.

Relief warms my rain-soaked skin and grows when I catch a herd of them racing down the streets of Tarespagia. Lore must give the order to depart for we take off over the dunes of Selvati as one.

As we fly, my mind returns to Lore and his apology. ***If you'd eliminated Dante, the Faeries would've fought your dominion, which would've resulted in a terrible amount of casualties, Lore.***

The sand is dark and wet, pockmarked by puddles through which splash gaggles of bald children, attempting to keep up with the Crows' almighty wingbeats. I cannot see their expressions, but I imagine their small faces are full of wonder since normally constituted people don't run toward their fears.

At least you wouldn't have been amongst the victims.

Perhaps—I press my lips into the soft feathers of his neck—***but I'd have hated you, mo khrà . . . I'd have fought against you.*** To defuse Lore's lingering unrest, and my own, I add, ***What if I'd won?***

Obviously, the magicless girl that I was didn't stand a chance against talon-tipped beasts who could morph into smoke, but I sense it will lighten the mood to suggest I could've offered him a fair battle.

I'm wrong, though. Lorcan's mood only sours. With a sigh, I kiss his neck again, then burrow my face against his feathers, and although it doesn't ease his pulse, it does ease his temper.

As minutes turn into hours, the rain thins and sunbeams manage to cleave through the wooly cover to glaze the pale gray peaks of the Sky Kingdom.

Home.

I'm finally home.

CHAPTER 40

When I catch my father landing on the esplanade, I ask Lore to land there as well. ***You need to rest.***

I've still got a thousand and one questions for the general. ***What I need are answers, and Justus has most of them.***

The second we reach the slick pale stone, Lore disintegrates into his shadows, which he enfolds me with to buttress my body. When he senses I'm steady on my feet, he shapes himself into the man I know and adore, and reaches for my hand.

I assume he wants to hold it until he flips it over and traces the inked circles with his eyes. ***Tell me about this thing on your hand now.***

Only if you swear to keep the growling and murdering-Justus to a minimum.

I solemnly swear to you, Fallon Báeinach, that I will keep my growling to a minimum.

I jerk as a prickling sensation seizes my right bicep and another glowing band settles beneath Justus's two. I'm now the proud owner of three oaths, from two *very* influential males to boot. I already felt powerful, but now I feel downright invincible.

I grin, mentally rubbing my palms together because a bargain from Lorcan is priceless.

I'm still waiting for you to solemnly swear not to delimb Justus, Lore.

With a dark smile, he murmurs, ***You'll have to wait an eternity to hear me swear the latter, Behach Éan.***

Good thing I've an eternity to wait. Did I mention that I was immortal? Well . . . fairly immortal.

There is no fairly about your immortality, Fallon, for I dare anyone to spill a drop of your blood and live to speak of it.

I sigh because it isn't my blood I fear spilled.

More Crows land and shift, while others circle the esplanade in feathers. Imogen is amongst the Crows in skin, and so is Aoife. Both are naturally pale, made even more so by their black hair, but at the moment, their skin tone is alabaster.

My father unhands Justus and turns, shaggy black hair flopping around his haggard face in the strong wind that batters the mountain. He grumbles something in Crow, I imagine to Lore since he tacks *Mórrgaht* to the tail end of his comment. If only Meriam had had time to awaken my Crow side . . . I'd have really loved to be magically fluent in my father tongue.

"Where's my son?" Justus's blue eyes run over every Crow soaring over us, and there are many.

My father jerks his chin toward the Sky Kingdom. "Erwin carried him to Lazarus."

"*Lazarus* . . ." Justus murmurs.

"Were you not aware the healer lived with us?"

Justus's gaze returns to me. "I thought the man sailed to Shabbe."

As though to bar me from being too near my grandfather, my mate inserts himself between us, shadows solidifying, screening me off from the water-Fae.

You do realize I was with that man for a month, Lore?

He doesn't move a muscle—or rather, a wisp, since he's currently all out of muscles—but he gives me a withering stare that makes me roll my eyes.

He will not snatch me from you. He wouldn't dare. No one would. I reach up and touch his jaw that is granite in spite of being made of gossamer matter.

With a sigh, his dark form moves to my side, his edges curling around my own.

"How much do you all know about what happened in the tunnels?"

"I've told them only what Justus and I discussed before I brought you to him."

I spin around at the sound of Bronwen's voice. The milky-eyed seer glides off the back of a feathered steed, who morphs into a man —my uncle.

"My apologies for the way we parted, Fallon. I feared that if I warned you of my intent, Lorcan would interfere with Fate." She moves toward us on Cian's arm.

My uncle stares apologetically my way even though he's got nothing to be apologetic about. Unless . . . unless he knew?

He didn't, Lore says.

"I can only imagine how deeply you loathe me," she continues.

"I doubt that, but we can discuss my displeasure with your tactics at a later date. We've more pressing topics to explore at the moment."

Her purple lips thin at my reproof.

I turn back toward the others. "Where should I start, Justus? What do they know?"

Gaze on Bronwen, he says, "If Bronwen has told them everything, then they should know that Meriam unbound your magic and why you must be the one to kill Regio. They should also know about your tether to Meriam and Zendaya, and the reason for the blood-bind."

"I've learned that some things are better left related *after* they happen." The volume of Bronwen's voice is so low I barely catch her words. Her lids suddenly flutter before closing. "Lorcan, stop." Her lids squeeze, and lines appear in the rubbery skin of her temples as my mate assails her with his thoughts. "I did not tell you everything for your own good."

With a sigh, I ask, "So what *did* you tell them, Bronwen?"

"I told them that Meriam would unbind your magic and thus make you immortal, and that Justus would see that you were returned alive and well when it was done. I also told them about the tether in case Lorcan located you before Justus and Meriam were done preparing you."

Preparing me? I was not prepared. I was given magic without instruction, and then I was told of a concealed dagger that Dante located first. "Well, that leaves a lot of ground to cover. Care to fill them in on the rest?"

"I think it best you tell them, Fallon, for I care to keep my head attached to my body."

I snort. "And yet you braved coming out here . . ."

"Because *all* I did, I did for the sake of our people. We *need* the Cauldron."

"*We* need, or *you* need?" I clearly remember her telling me about her desire to jump inside to reverse her skin's ruin.

She tips her head. "Don't you want to break your mate's obsidian curse?"

Low. Blow.

My father folds his arms so snugly that his leather vambraces squeak. "Speak, ínon, and do not leave anything out."

"Like Bronwen said, Zendaya tethered us all, which means she's alive, Dádhi."

"I heard." My father's eyes are dark, made even more so by the heavy fringe of soot-colored lashes and the shadows that pool inside at my use of her first name.

I'm aware she made me, and therefore I should think of her as my mother, but I cannot. Not yet.

"Until I look upon her with my own eyes, understand that I will contain my enthusiasm."

"If she were dead, then I would be as well."

"So says the witch who doomed our people," he grumbles.

Bronwen sighs out my father's name, which wins her a pointed glower.

"I understand your reluctance to believe Justus. I truly do, but Meriam isn't the villain we've painted her out to be. She's just as much a victim of Costa Regio as the rest of us."

One set of white eyes, one set of gold, and several sets of wary, coal-lined ones observe me. "Yes, she created the wards, but it was to keep Priya out of Luce. She feared her mother would try and separate her from her Faerie lover. Apparently, the Queen of Shabbe wasn't fond of the match."

"She was not," Bronwen murmurs. "Priya reviled the man who fathered me."

I tuck a salt-hardened strand of hair behind my ear. "Locking up Shabbe was Costa's idea."

Imogen hikes up one of her black eyebrows. "Was it also his idea to give a runestone to the Glacin and Nebban kings?" Her voice, though thin, is back.

"No. It was Marco's." Justus scrapes a hand across his brow. "He used them to fetch himself an enduring alliance."

I stare in the direction of Nebba, at the stretch of ocean that resembles molten silver in the aftermath of the storm. "We have to retrieve them."

"We already have the piece that was in Luce." Cian nods to my grandfather. "Rossi gave it to my mate. And we also have Nebba's. Eponine, or should I say"—a rare smile tugs at Cian's lips—"the Queen of Nebba, handed hers over the day of her coronation."

"Queen?" I whisper. "So Pierre is— He's dead?"

Cian's smile grows as Lorcan murmurs, ***Very much so.***

Once I recover from my shock, I ask, ***Is there a way to be just*** a little *dead?*

A smile *finally* whispers across our mind link.

One that causes my eyes to roll and my heart to skip. ***Gods, you have such morbid humor, Lorcan Ríhbiadh.***

My little aside with Lore makes me miss my father's question, but not Justus's answer. "Zendaya's in the ocean."

CHAPTER 41

A lesser man may have shriveled under the intensity and weight of my father's stare, but not Justus. Then again, Justus is not a lesser man.

"Where in the ocean?" Cathal rasps.

I squint toward the frolicking surf where smears of indigo appear amongst the steel.

Lore's form unspools, his shadows grazing the frame of my face without obstructing my sight. ***If that man were as honest and trustworthy as you believe him to be, he would've told you.***

We didn't have much time to speak.

Much time? You had a bloody month!

I was unconscious for half of it.

What do you mean,* unconscious*?

Magically knocked out.

I. Will. Kill—

No one. You will kill no one. You swore.

I did not swear to that.

Please, Lore.

His phantom touch slips over the apple of my cheek. ***Why don't you use your bargain, Behach Éan? I do owe you one . . .***

I was hoping to use it for funner things.

If your definition of fun matches my own, then nothing you have in mind will require coercion.

I give him my best side-eye but end up relenting to preserve Justus's livelihood. ***Lorcan Ríhbiadh, I call forth my bargain: do not harm Justus Rossi.*** The same way I felt the bargain prick my skin, I feel it lift like snipped thread.

"Where in the ocean, Rossi?" my father repeats, brashly this time.

"Zendaya lost a lot of blood the night she was captured," Justus says.

Guilt swarms me. I may not be the only reason for her blood loss but I've no doubt I'm the greatest cause of it.

Lore pinches my chin with his phantom hand and tips my face toward his. ***Behach Éan, none of what happened is your fault.***

If she hadn't been pregnant with me—

Don't. He presses his forehead to mine, and although mine dents his, if I close my eyes and hold very still, I can almost imagine he's made of flesh and not mere eddies of darkness.

I want the whole of you back. My eyes snap open. ***Where is your fallen crow?***

One thing at a time, Little Bird. He caresses my cheek. ***First, let us find your mother.***

Why do you keep stalling? My heart hastens with newfangled disquiet. ***Your crow is salvageable, right?***

Yes.

Swear it.

I swear.

As my heartbeats ease back into a more regular rhythm, I turn my attention away from my concerns and back onto my father's.

"The only reason Meriam did what she did," Justus is saying, "was to save Zen—"

"Where in the fucking ocean is my fucking mate, Rossi?" my father snarls. "Spit it out before I pry—" My father sucks in a harsh breath, then heaves it out with such force that it sounds like a growl and cuts his eyes to Lore's. "Did I tell you to calm the fuck down when you were looking for my daughter, Lore?"

A beat of charged silence echoes around us.

"The day Fallon was born, she felt it and went mad. She tried to saw off her wrists to escape Marco's dungeon." The abounding stone amplifies Justus's grave voice. "No matter how many healing and calming Shabbin crystals I placed on her body, she wouldn't settle, so I brought her to her mother. I was desperate to ease her heartache, Cathal."

"If you were that desperate, you would've released her! You would've let her be with Fallon." Every vein in my father's body bulges and throbs.

"I did not know about Fallon until much later! As for Meriam, strange as it may sound to the lot of you, I trusted she had Zendaya's best interests at heart. I'd known her for decades by then and realized she wasn't the evil sorceress the world painted her out to be. She was a woman who'd done the wrong thing. Who'd loved the wrong man. And Gods, Cathal, how she's paid for it! She's cursed to sit in a throne that eats at her flesh! She's been locked up underground, in a vault, for five centuries!"

My father's anger detonates. "*She* put Costa on the throne! She brought this upon herself! Upon all of us!"

Lore must sense my father is a second away from murdering Justus for he swerves away from me and reappears between the two men in the form of a smoke screen.

I'm glad for the intervention for I really want to learn where in Mareluce my mother bobs. Or lies. "Can you two have it out later?"

Justus seizes the hem of his jacket and squeezes out what little moisture clings to the navy threads after our hours-long flight, muttering something about *thankless buzzards*.

"Justus." I give him a warning look to play nice.

He releases his ruined jacket, stares obsidian daggers at Cathal, then finally says, "Meriam performed the spell that she did because she knew it was the only way Zendaya could be free."

"What. Fucking. Spell?" My father heaves smoke.

Justus slips his lower lip between his teeth, as though he's weighing the best way of delivering the information. "She painted a death sigil over Zendaya's heart that immobilized her and made her body appear exsanguinated."

My mind flashes to the cross Justus drew over his son's heart days ago. Could it be the same sigil?

"No one knew of the tether that existed between the three Shabbin witches, not even I, so when I carried her exsanguinated body to Marco, he didn't question her death. He was angry, though. Gods, he was angry. He'd had Pierre of Nebba and a recently widowed Vladimir of Glace engaged in a bidding war over her."

Color leaches from my poor father's face.

"I carried her out to the ocean and slipped her into it. Although I noticed another sigil drawn on her body, my knowledge of them was dismal, so I didn't realize what Meriam had done until . . ." He turns to look at me. "Until word reached me that Fallon had befriended a *mareserpens*. And even then, I didn't put two and two together."

I've started many a journey knowing my destination, but not the path that would get me there. In this case, I've not the slightest clue where Justus is leading us.

"It wasn't until many years later, years during which Fallon formed a bond with this giant pink serpent, that I realized what Meriam had done."

"What did she do?" Although my body's made of flesh, it suddenly feels entirely made of breath.

"She performed the same spell your mother cast to keep you safe."

My eyes spread wide, but not as wide as my father's where the blood-marbled whites seem to devour the brown irises.

I blink. "She sent her into a Faerie womb?"

"Not a Faerie's."

Cian tilts his head to the side, his thick black hair sliding over his furrowed brow. "A human womb?"

My hand crawls up to my gaping mouth because I know . . .

I know exactly into whose womb Meriam sent Zendaya.

CHAPTER 42

I press my fingertips against my palpitating lips. "Oh my Gods." The chills that spread over me are so brisk they crenellate the bare skin of my forearms. "Oh my Gods! *Minimus*?!"

When Justus nods, the goosebumps sink and spill into me.

"You're certain?" I gasp.

"Meriam has since confirmed it."

All this time . . . all this time, the woman who made me with the giant who stands frozen in shock, has been at my side, watching over me, healing me, caring for me, loving me.

Back in the vault, Phoebus had joked that Minimus was related to me. To think my friend wasn't that far off the mark. To think that Minimus *is* related to me. When he hears that his jest wasn't totally awry, that the serpent he joked was my brother is, in fact, my mother . . .

Oh.

My.

Gods.

"Meriam turned Zendaya into a fucking *mareserpens*?" My poor father sounds a second away from rupturing into feathers and smoke.

"The same way Queen Mara turned you into a bird." Justus keeps his tone extra placid, surely sensing he must tread with care.

My jaw slips wider. "So my mother is a—she's a . . . a . . ."

"Serpent shifter?" someone supplies.

I'm not even sure who speaks since I've eyes only for Justus and my father.

With a sigh, Justus says, "Not yet."

Confusion grooves my brow. "What do you mean, *not yet*?"

"Zendaya will need to be blessed by the Cauldron to complete the transition."

My mouth gapes wide, but no air penetrates my lungs. "But the Cauldron is—it's sealed." When my chest begins to burn, I gasp.

"I don't believe you need more motivation to kill Regio, Fallon, but yes, until you've ended his line, your mother cannot be brought back."

Focá. Half of Lore's shadows waft back toward me; the other half cling to my father whose eyes are wide and glazed. He's evidently elsewhere. Perhaps in the ocean. Perhaps in the past.

I touch his arm, and although hard as steel, it quivers like a banged gong. "Could Meriam not perform a spell to complete Mother's transition?"

"No," Bronwen murmurs. "Meriam may be powerful, but the sort of magic needed to give men or animals the power to shift . . . only the Cauldron and its keeper can complete such a feat."

If a transition is even possible.

I snap my gaze to Lore, hunting his darkness for the twin pinpricks of gold, but he's in too many pieces for them to shine through.

"Did you know, Bronwen?" My father's lips lay so flat against his teeth that it roughens his already abysmal timbre.

"No, Cathal. I swear I didn't."

I look over my shoulder at where she stands, clutching Cian's arm. "I know the Cauldron is livid and closed for business, but maybe it would make an exception for my mother?" I shrug. "After all, she did follow its wishes and manufactured its curse-breaker."

Justus's blue eyes take on a faraway glint. "Since the wards are of Meriam's making, anyone who shares her blood will remain locked outside Shabbe until the ward rune is erased."

The furrows on my brow only deepen because I clearly remember Bronwen suggesting— "You advised Lore and me to head to Shabbe to break his curse." I don't miss the swallow that agitates her thin throat or the miniscule step she takes nearer to Cian. "Why propose something impossible?"

"Because I was trying to protect my king, Fallon. In Shabbe, he would've been safe. He wouldn't have needed to hide. He wouldn't have lost one of his crows in a place not a single one of us can reach."

Lore must yell at her because moisture beads from her white eyes and collapses down her ruined cheeks. Are those tears? I didn't think Bronwen capable of grief.

"It was my idea, Lore." Cian curls Bronwen into his much larger body and rests his chin atop the new growths darkening his mate's scalp. "If you're angry, take it out on me."

I'm aware Bronwen meant well. After all, I also wanted to send Lore to Shabbe to keep him safe. Nevertheless, I very much want her to stop interfering—or at the very least, not do it so backhandedly.

However, there's a time and place for all discussions, and right now, her bygone meddling is of little import. Not in comparison to the latter part of what she's just said.

"What did you mean by *a place no one can reach*?" Wind buffets the mountain, and although I hadn't felt cold before, between the news of my mother's whereabouts, my flimsy dress, and now *this*, chills rock me. "Where is it that you fell, Lore?"

His shadows return to me, coalescing against my pebbled skin. ***Let's get you inside. I want Lazarus to look over your wounds.***

I'm fine.

You're not fine. You tremble harder than a sprite in the company of a Crow.

Lore—

I will tell you everything tomorrow.

Stop deflecting!

I said tomorrow! His voice cracks like thunder against my temples, effectively snipping my next plea before it's even fully formed.

I pout at his pigheadedness—or rather, *crow*headedness—and cross my arms.

He sighs, his invisible breath blustering against my thrumming mind. ***I'm sorry for snapping at you, Little Bird, but I've barely slept since you were taken from me.*** His shadows fan over my cheeks, gliding over them like fingers.

The wind rushes around us, knifing the pale rocks of Lore's castle and slapping the stream that's fat with rain. Brisk gusts shear the mist, turning it into ribbons of white that wrap around us as though Lorcan had flown me into the clouds he commands.

How long will his storm last, I wonder. Until Dante dies?

I should've preserved that bargain you owed me and forced the location off your tongue, I grumble as his cool smoke thumbs across my lips as though to ease their crush. ***What will you do with Justus?***

His vaporous head turns. He must ask Justus what his plans are because the general says, "I've sworn an oath to guard and aid Fallon to the best of my abilities, Mórrgaht. Until I've no more hands to wield a sword and no more head to voice her decrees, or until she decides to replace me, I stand as your ally in Luce."

Do you trust him, Fallon?

With all my heart. And yes, I'm aware my heart hasn't always been the best judge of character, but—

Your heart led you to trust an enigmatic bird with iron appendages and the ability to speak into minds.

Although physically impossible, it feels as though Lorcan's shadows breach my skin to swaddle my oft-misguided muscle that did, in fact, guide me to this man, albeit using a most convoluted route. But it's the destination that counts, right? Or is it the journey?

I decide that in Lore's and my case, it's the destination.

Mórrígan, I've missed your musings. He presses a phantom kiss between my eyebrows before shifting into a single giant crow and unfurling his wings.

Even though the esplanade swarms with guards in both feathers and skin, it's a testament to my judgement that he dares turn solid in front of the Faerie General.

"No, I've no vials of Meriam's blood on my person," I hear Justus say as I link my arms around Lorcan's neck. "As for weapons, I carry only my iron sword."

The sword I stole a life with . . .

The rubies on the hilt gleam as though fueled by Cato's pure blood. ***Where did you put the Faerie guard I asked to bring home?***

In one of the caverns beneath the castle. Lazarus will place an embalming crystal on his body until you've decided how to send him off into his next life.

I want to carry him to his family, but his family resides in Tarecuori, and Tarecuori doesn't belong to the Crows yet. ***Did you invite Justus into the Sky Kingdom?***

We've a realm to unite, haven't we?

Imogen circles my grandfather, talon-tipped fingers skimming the salt-crusted velour of his jacket before snaring the leather strand and pulling it out from beneath his shirt. When she notices the broken vial, she releases the necklace, allowing it to settle back against the puckered line of his serpent-healed scar. She does pinch his steel sword, though.

Your friends, as well as Lazarus and Gabriele, aren't immune to iron.

CHAPTER 43

Gabriele is still—I'm about to say *alive* but switch it out for ***—here?***

He's proven himself a worthy ally. You were right to trust him.

My heart rises in time with Lore's great body. ***Dante tried to make me believe he'd planted him in the Sky Kingdom to harm you.***

What that louse wouldn't say to save face.

I swallow, hating my gullibility. ***Will you keep Justus in a cell?***

Perhaps not a cell, but a room on a higher floor. One he cannot leave as he pleases.

Lore slips through the hatch of the Market Tavern, and my whirring mind comes to a screeching halt because, although the space is relatively empty, two people stand beside the windows overlooking the esplanade.

Sybille and Phoebus spin around. The instant my feet touch stone, my friends break into a jog and slam into me, curling their arms around my chilled body in the warmest embrace.

The honking sound of a sob spreads a grin over my lips.

Phoebus drives his shoulders into his wet eyes. "The dying-goose noise came from the other one," he murmurs, his voice shot through with emotion.

Sybille looses another brassy sob, ebony cheeks reflective with tears. I laugh at her uncharacteristic effusiveness, which earns me a smack in the boob.

"Ow." I rub at my abused chest. "What was that for?"

Phoebus tucks me against him, propping his smooth chin atop my head. "Mattia and Reid have been training her at swordfight. She's become unbearably violent."

Syb rolls her gray eyes that shine the same silvery pewter as the sky above. "Don't you dare vanish again without telling anyone, and by *anyone* I mean Pheebs and me!" After a quick glance to the right, she adds, "And Lorcan. Obviously."

I flatten my hand over my heart. "Never again, Syb. I've learned my lesson."

"Have you, Picolina?" Phoebus's square chin digs into my skull as he speaks. "Because you're rather mediocre at listening to the voice of reason." He moves his mouth to my ear. "Even when said voice shouts reason directly into your ear."

I start to roll my eyes when Syb yanks my hand off my chest and looks at the entwined rings marring my palm. "What the underworld is that?"

On a sigh, I say, "The mark of a blood-bind."

Lorcan's gossamer shape coils closer, licking across my right shoulder and the ridge of my collarbone, golden eyes fastened to the loathed mark.

"A what now?" Syb asks.

"It's an ancient Shabbin ritual. Meriam magicked the Regio bloodline a long time ago. The spell made them immune to our magic, but it also gave them our magic."

Sybille's eyes flare so wide the irises resemble pebbles tossed into foam.

"The only way she found to keep Costa from realizing the amount of power she'd given him was using a blood-bind, which is a Shabbin ritual that enables—"

"Husbandstomakeuseoftheirwifesmagic." There's no pause between Phoebus's words. "Lazarus told me about it."

Lore's shadows stiffen, which makes my body go stiff in turn. ***Husbands?***

Merda. "No. It's not—like that." I extricate myself from Phoebus's arms just as my mate streaks toward the heart of the market where dozens of Crows are shifting into skin. My heart judders. "Oh my Gods, he's going to kill Justus," I whisper to my friends.

"Which is . . . *a bad thing*?" Pheebs asks right before Syb screeches, "*Justus*? You married the general?"

"What?" I grimace.

"She married Dante, Syb. Costa's heir. Keep up."

"I didn't *marry* him," I mutter, just as my grandfather's body is hauled so high, he dangles in the dull light pouring through the hatch like a suspended dust mote. *Merda.* I take off, my friends hot on my heels.

"Picolina, a blood-bind is a magical union—"

"Between veins, Pheebs, not hearts! Our bloods are bound. *Basta.* End of story. I loathe Dante. Like, a hundred thousand million more times than before." I stub my little toe against a chair, and fuck, it hurts, but I forge on because Justus is turning purple in the face. ***LORE!*** I limp the rest of the way. ***He only did it to invalidate Dante's blood magic and make him dependent on mine. Lore, please. Listen to me.***

Lore's golden eyes slant toward me, and his feathered jaw hardens as though he's biting back words. Probably another entreaty for me not to interrupt whatever it is he's planning to do to Justus.

I know you're not a stranger to bloodshed, but I also know you care about people. About this kingdom. So does Justus.

I'm all out of fucks for your general, Fallon.

Our ***general.***

Last I checked, you were married to a Faerie not to me.

Not by choice! I shout, before realizing how that sounds—like I actually believe I'm lawfully wed. Which I don't.

I understood it wasn't your choice. It's the reason I've taken Justus aside to have words.

You call towing him into the air **taking him aside*****?***

He fucking married you off to—

I know, Lore. I know! I was there. Dante said he'd cut off Antoni's tongue if I didn't go through with the blood-bind. My throat closes and opens like the fingers balled at my sides. ***So I fucking went through with it.***

Lore's pupils narrow to pinpricks at my tone, or is it my curse word? He so loathes them. The dark sky flashes with a netting of bright white lightning that paints the marketplace gray, Justus, white, and Lore, pitch-black.

Lore, put Justus down! I beg you. He must not hear my desperation over the thunderous peals of his tempest because he doesn't land. When his steel talons clamp harder around Justus's arms, I scream, ***Do NOT kill him or else—or else—*** My chest lifts and falls with harsh breaths.

Or else* what?** His voice sounds wrong—cold, punitive. It's the tone he uses with his enemies, not with me. ***You'll run back into the arms of your new husband?

He drifts back to the ground, unhooking Justus before my grandfather can get his boots beneath him. The poor man, who's already in a world of pain, tumbles onto his knees.

I glower at Lore's pettiness, not dignifying him with an answer.

"Don't you dare manhandle me again, Ríhbiadh!" Justus is red in the face, as though the sun has beaten down on his fair skin for days on end. "I went against my people to help yours!"

"Here I was hoping we'd finally get some peace and sun," Phoebus mumbles as the rain pelts the warded ceiling. "My face is as pasty as my ass, and my ass could be used as a torchlight."

I sense Phoebus is attempting to alleviate the ambient mood, but I'm so fucking pissed off that his quip doesn't even dent the darkness swarming my head and heart.

I start toward Justus, but my father steps into my path.

"What is going on, ínon?"

I raise my marked palm and stamp the air in front of his weary eyes.

He grips my wrist and peers closer, eyebrows slanting. "This is about a tattoo?"

Lorcan must share that it isn't a simple tattoo because my father rears his head back. "You bound my daughter to a fucking imbecile, Rossi!" His complexion has grown as violet as the day he found out about Lore's and my mating bond. Before my next breath, he strides toward Justus, his nails lengthening into iron talons.

I run and tackle his enormous arm, putting every last gram of my weight into my heels to stop him from eviscerating the general. "Dádhi, stop." I will his nails to pinken and recede. "Cathal Báeinach, STOP!"

I'm not sure if it's my use of his full name or my tone, but he finally quits stomping toward Justus who stands tall in spite of being ringed by ferocious shifters. "Zendaya told me that the Cauldron forbade blood-binds!"

"The Cauldron probably does but it's temporarily out of sorts," I say.

"I'm sorry, but *what?*" Phoebus and Sybille ask at the very same time.

"When Meriam spelled Costa's bloodline, the Cauldron became so angry that it sealed itself off. According to Meriam and Justus, it will only reopen for business once a descendent of Meriam snuffs out the Regio bloodline. Which is why it must be *me*—the curse-breaker."

"Bronwen?" My father whips his face in the direction of his sister-in-law, locks of damp black hair falling into his feral eyes.

"The Cauldron communicates with me, Cathal, so it mustn't have sealed itself off entirely."

"What I still fail to understand is what the Cauldron's sullenness has to do with my daughter blood-binding herself to that pointy-eared buffoon!"

"Dante has blood magic, Dádhi."

His dark eyes jerk to my violet ones. "He's Shabbin?"

"No, but his blood is. When Meriam cast her spell on the Regio bloodline, it didn't only make them immune to Shabbin magic, it changed the nature of what ran through their veins."

For a solid minute, no one speaks, but then Lore must break the silence because Justus kneads his temple and growls, "You of all people should understand why Meriam bound Dante and Fallon, Ríhbiadh. You lived with Zendaya. You witnessed her power first-hand. The magic of the royal bloodline is tenfold more potent than any other Shabbin's magic, and that was the sort of power running through Dante's veins. If we hadn't magically cuffed him to your mate, can you imagine the damage he would've reaped?"

Bronwen tightens her grip on Cian's bicep. She must sense the weight of many a stare because she says, "At the time, Meriam didn't tell me that she'd bestowed blood magic upon my genitor. All I knew was that she'd made him invincible to Shabbins."

"So you *didn't* know?" My father's voice is as sharp as the talons still tipping his fingers.

"No, Cathal. The same way I didn't know my brother or my nephew possessed magical blood, or I would've understood the reason the Cauldron kept showing me Lore—any Crow, for that matter—losing his humanity should he snuff out Dante's life."

"Why would a Crow perish?" Sybille murmurs in the crook of my ear.

"Because they cannot kill the offspring of the woman who created them," I explain. "Mórrígan is Queen Mara, and Mara is my great-great-grandmother."

When the strain in my father's body loosens, I release my death grip on his arm but begin to regret it when he flicks his gaze toward the sticky web of shadows that is my livid mate.

You better not be asking him to harm Justus.

Lore's eyes swing toward me, black pupils so slim his gaze is full-yellow.

"Do *you* have blood magic, Bronwen?" Phoebus asks.

"I was born before Meriam spelled Costa, so no, my blood holds no more magic than an earth-Fae's."

She sounds truthful, but if I've learned anything, it's that Bronwen is a master at deception.

Fallon.

I pretend not to hear Lore call out to me.

Come here, Behach Éan.

I cross my arms. ***Apologize about the whole* 'me running into my new husband's arms' *comment, and I'll consider going to you.***

You want me to apologize for fucking caring that my mate is bound to another?

I interrupt his snarling with a calm, ***That doesn't sound like an apology.***

His pupils spread and spread until they overtake the yellow, and subsequently, the entire room. What the—

I blink. *Murgadh'Thábhain* comes back into sharp focus, but it's empty save for me and Lore, who's prowling toward me. Yes, *prowling*. On feet and legs, leather trousers whispering as he erases the distance between us.

Has my swelling anger caused me to pass out? Odd, but surely not implausible. A surplus of emotion can—

You've not lost consciousness, Fallon.

Then **. . .** Oh, fucking great. Of course my mind would deem taking a walk on the dark side *now*, while my father is about to murder an inherently good man, wise. I try to transport myself back into the real Market Tavern to no avail. ***Why can't I snap out of this trance?***

Lore's warm breath breezes across my forehead. ***Because I'm inside*** **your** ***mind, Behach Éan.***

CHAPTER 44

"Now's really not a suitable time for a one-on-one, Lorcan Ríhbiadh." Gods, this was not how I pictured our reunion.

Lore pinches my chin, gently tipping my head back to force my eyes to his. "Do you think I imagined my mate coming home to me married to another man?" His expression is a chasm of darkness, as though flooded by the storm that flogs the kingdom beyond the warded ceiling.

Even though I don't uncross my arms, I loose a sigh. "Don't you think I hate this as much as you do, Lore?"

His grip turns brutal, as though he forgets that my bones are brittle and can be snapped. I'm about to ease my chin from his punishing fingers when he says, "No, Little Bird. You're upset; I'm fucking wrecked."

The pain blistering his voice makes me slide my fingers up his throat and thumb the hard tendon that runs from the edge of his collarbone to the base of his jaw. His lashes fall, skimming the faint drips of black forever ornamenting his eyes, and his neck bends until his forehead comes to rest upon mine.

"My blood may be tied to another, but my heart belongs only to you."

Although his body is one with the stone beneath his boots, as I stroke, my mate begins to thaw.

"Once this is all over, make me your queen?"

His pulse jumps beneath the pad of my thumb. "Why do you make it sound like a question?"

I wind my fingers through his silken locks, gliding each strand across my knuckles.

Though he shivers, his voice doesn't when he rasps, "Swear that you will never fucking leave me again."

I understand his worry, for in the past, I've put myself in impossible situations believing they'd benefit us, but I will never willingly return to a place he cannot reach.

"I swear that I will never fucking leave you again, Lorcan Ríhbiadh." The bargain jabs my heart, inscribing a burning dot that Lorcan will be able to use at will should I ever consider hunting Dante down on my own.

Perish the thought.

I keep caressing the taut tendons of his neck, drinking in the slick fragrance of thunder that lifts off my mate's pale skin.

He grips my hip and nudges my nose with his before dragging it along my cheekbone. In my ear, he murmurs, "You did not have to repeat me word for word."

I frown but then smile when I realize what's gotten his feathers in a bunch. He, too, smiles as his nose backtracks across my cheek. I fill my lungs with his slow, even breaths, and although I'm aware we need to return to the real Market Tavern, I hold on to this precious interlude.

Forgive me for earlier, Little Bird. I shouldn't have taken my wounded pride and heart out on you.

You're forgiven, but please, Lore, never again allude that I may want Dante, because there's only one man for me—you.

After he nods, I roll up onto my toes and press my mouth to his, but don't coax his lips apart. I let him soften at his own speed, allowing him to realize that he and I are together and safe, and though we've a million and one tribulations to contend with, none can touch us, not when he's surrounded by his Crows and I'm tucked inside his kingdom . . . inside his arms.

Lore glides his palm to the small of my back and flattens it there, then spreads his fingers until his hand spans the full breadth of my waist. Only once his body is anchored to mine does his mouth finally move.

Slowly, so slowly, his lips part mine, granting me access to his every breath and every heartbeat. I lap both up greedily, growing lightheaded from his deliberate kisses and exacting touches. Cauldron, how I've missed him.

I gorge on his heat and flavor, willing him to enter deeper, to fill every dark crevasse of my body and soul, to rush into me like the stream that tumbles down his mountain in order to flush away the last month.

His mouth draws mine open infinitesimally wider but still, his tongue does not sweep in, his teeth do not graze. I consume the precious air he feeds me until my lungs cramp, and I'm forced to give it back to the sky and land.

Did he kiss you? he whispers into my mind.

My lips stumble off his. ***I thought we were done with this topic.***

I didn't ask whether* you *kissed* him.** The corners of his eyes crease as though this conversation causes him physical pain. ***I asked whether he dared put his lips on your body.

No, Lore. I shake my head to drive my answer deeper into my chary mate. ***All Dante wanted from me was my blood.***

His eyes sweep over my brow, nose, cheeks, chin, before settling on the pulse point at the base of my neck. Is he trying to detect whether I lie from my skin's palpitation?

I bristle. "How could you think I'd kiss that man?"

Lore's fingers drop from my hair and drift down my spine before latching onto my wrist and clasping my fingers. He carries them to the organ hammering against his black leathers. "Because I'm a brutally jealous man, and you, Little Bird, are my mate. My one true everything." He splays his hand over mine. "My fucking forever."

My irritation wanes. I fell for this man hard and fast, and perhaps the falling was prompted by magic, but the staying . . . the desire to be his until the end of time . . . that has *nothing* to do with magic. I stay because this man now lives in my heart, in my bones, in my very soul.

I flick back the lock of black hair obscuring one of his citrine eyes. ***I want this to be over.***

His fingers harden over mine, and then his face tilts infinitesimally lower. "Sorry to disappoint, mo khrà, but you and I will *never* be over."

I roll my eyes that feel gummy and hot from the overload of emotion. "I was speaking of the war, *my love*."

A slow smile curls one corner of his mouth. I press up onto my toes to capture it just as my cheek is tapped repeatedly. I frown because, not only is Lore's hand nowhere near my face, but also, patting is not his style.

"I'm afraid we're needed back," he murmurs.

I feel the squeeze of his hand, and then I feel the squeeze of another hand, a slimmer, warmer one.

"Fal?" Sybille's gray eyes are as large as the platters she and I would tote around *Bottom*.

"I think she's back." Phoebus, whose complexion rivals the cloud cover whitening the hatch, studies me from head to toe.

They're both crouched in front of where I sit on a chair, a ways away from everyone else. I wonder if I dropped onto it or if they sat me down. "Sorry, I was mind-walking."

Syb jolts. "You were *mind-walking*?" Her voice hits a particularly high note.

"I *told* you," Phoebus hisses. "The same way I told you not to shake her."

"I was worried. Her eyes went white! Like full-white, and she stopped breathing! And Cathal commanded us to sit her down without an explanation."

It's a strange thing to notice, but my friend's hair hits below her shoulder blades like mine. In the Luce of the olden days, we would've been fined for letting our tresses grow so long. To think this is a thing of the past. Well, will soon be.

I roll my stiff neck. "I stopped breathing?"

Phoebus squeezes the hand not in Sybille's possession. "Syb's exaggerating."

"Even *you* were worried."

"Well, I've never actually witnessed someone mind-walk. Not many mates around." He beholds the room, and although postures are still stiff, voices are more placid.

I notice Gabriele has arrived and is discussing something with Justus, Bronwen, and Cian. I also notice Lore has taken my father and

Imogen aside, and they, too, are discussing something. When I shift my attention back onto my friends, I don't miss the anguish scrunching up their faces.

"What?"

Phoebus snorts. "*What*, she asks."

I frown, at a bit of a loss as to what's eating at them.

"You married your mate's mortal enemy, that's what," Sybille hisses.

I sigh. "Magically bound, not married. And *again*, not by choice."

"What Syb is trying to say is that the war is about to get a whole lot bloodier."

"For Dante," I point out.

Phoebus tucks back a lock of golden hair, and although his fingers don't shake, his gesture is futile as the strand slides right out from behind the point of his ear, curtaining off his wary face. "For everyone, I fear."

"At least Gia got Mamma and Pappa out."

I glance around the quiet marketplace. "They're here?"

"No." A smile takes ahold of Sybille's full lips. "They're in Nebba."

"Nebba?"

"Eponine offered the parents of her newest counselor safe passage to her queendom." Sybille's eyes spark. "My sister is the freaking royal counselor!"

"Trust me, Syb"—a brazen grin drapes across Phoebus's mouth—"Fal did not assume Eponine pined for *your* counsel."

Sybille flicks his bicep, shooting him a scowl that drags my mind off the war. "I offer *great* counsel, thank you very much."

"I'm so glad Defne and Marcello are safe."

"Not only are they safe, Fal, but they've also"—her throat must grow tighter because her voice drops in volume—"they've also forgiven us."

My ribs loosen at the news. I imagined it was a matter of time, but still, the relief I feel is as sweet as warmed honey.

"I'm so happy for your sister." I reach out and link my hand through Syb's. "You were right to trust Eponine."

"I'm almost always right." Syb's grin develops, lifting her cheeks to great heights.

"Don't stroke her ego, Picolina. It barely fits through the hallways of the Sky Kingdom, what with Mattia's constant stroking."

I laugh. Gods, it's good to be back with these two. "Where *is* your dashing sailor?"

Smile fading, Sybille casts her gaze toward the hatch where dots of azure prick through the steely white. "Blasting through the tunnels, looking for Antoni."

The mention of Antoni constricts my stomach. "He won't find him in the tunnels."

Syb's gaze veers back toward me.

Sticking my hands between my thighs, I add, "Not anymore. We got out together."

"If you got out together"—Phoebus tilts his head, which makes his blond hair frolic around his face—"then how come he isn't here?"

"He chose to stay in Tarespagia."

"I need to tell Mattia." Sybille lurches out of her crouch and bounds toward a freckle-faced Crow, probably to ask him to carry the message down to her mate.

"You were in the tunnels together?" Phoebus murmurs.

I nod. "Dante held him prisoner."

I must start shaking because Phoebus retrieves my hands from where they sit buried in the gap between my thighs and clasps both between his large, warm palms. "That bad?"

"Worse, Pheebs," I whisper hoarsely.

He squeezes my hands. "We don't have to talk about it now."

I'm not sure I'll want to talk about it later. I may have saved Antoni, but I no longer trust him. He wants my mate dead and knows a fuck lot about Crows. "Phoebus, I heard there was a hidden staircase that leads out of the Sky Kingdom."

"Yeah. The entrance was up there." He nods toward one of the cubbyholes that peppers the ten-story rock facade. It sits on the third level of the younger Crows' housing. Oddly enough, it's only then that I notice the many sets of charcoal-darkened eyes staring down at us from the indents in the rock.

"Does it still exist?"

"No. It's been destroyed. Why?"

"Because Antoni knew about it," I reply softly.

One of his eyebrows hooks up.

"Antoni wants Lore dead, Pheebs."

Though his hands don't fall away from my own, his grip slackens. "But he fought so hard to bring him back."

Dante's salt-interrogation floats back through my mind like a cloying drift of incense.

"Are you certain?"

I swallow and nod.

"Well, *merda*. That's no good." He looks toward Syb whose steps have a literal bounce to them she's so happy. "We better warn Syb before she encourages Mattia to bring him back."

"Antoni won't dare come back. He wouldn't risk his life to end my mate's." As I say this, I feel the weight of someone's stare press against the left side of my face. I know it's Lore's without having to turn. Did he hear all I've confessed to my friends?

"Why do you two look like someone's kicked a serpent?" Sybille's gaze springs from Phoebus to me until I nod.

As Phoebus fills Sybille in, Lore's voice ribbons through my mind. ***Antoni loathing me is not news to me, Little Bird.***

Before Lore can detect that loathing is the least of my worries, I seal off my thoughts, too afraid my mate will flock from the Sky Kingdom to hunt Antoni down himself, thus risking losing a second crow.

Once I've gotten ahold of my expression, I turn toward the pocket of darkness where Lore stands, boxed in by Imogen and three other Crows.

The half-Fae pines for all I have. My kingdom . . . my **mate.**

I squeeze my lips. ***I don't think he pines for me anymore, Lore.***

Did Bronwen ever tell you what the Cauldron showed her the night we set out to free my second crow?

No. She only said that if he came along, it would alter my fate. I glance toward my soothsaying aunt. ***I assume you know how?***

I do.

I hunt the darkness for the gold stare that hasn't moved off my body. ***How?***

Instead of telling me, Lorcan shows me, and though the events did not transpire, the vision goads tears down my cheeks.

CHAPTER 45

"Fal, what is it?" Phoebus's stare is filled with such earnest worry that I paste a smile onto my lips and cup his bony cheek.

"Nothing, Pheebs. It's nothing"

"Yeah. Really looks like nothing," he says with a sigh.

Sybille's throat bobs with swallow after swallow. "It's Antoni."

Not in the way she thinks, but yes, Antoni is at the root of my heartache, so I nod. Perhaps someday I will tell them about the alternate life I could've had, but right now, I don't want to contemplate a world where Lorcan Ríhbiadh does not exist.

I stand, ready to go to him, eager to be near him, when he sweeps across the Market Tavern toward me in all of his gossamer beauty. Sybille and Phoebus back up to give him room to swell.

Lore's nearness amplifies my grief. ***Don't cry, my love.***

My eyes prickle as I stare into his sparkling ones. I'd like to think I couldn't have been so easily swayed, but back when I set out to steal the five iron crows, I was so naïve that offered the right words, given the right reasons, I'd have done the wrong thing.

My mind plunges me back into the vision, and I see myself once again driving an obsidian stake into Lorcan's wing after Antoni convinced me the crow would wreak havoc on the world.

My mate's shadows glide like velvet across my cheeks, brushing away the tears before they can trip off my chin. ***It did not come to pass, Fallon.***

After grief comes anger. I tug my hair at the roots. ***But it could have, Lore. It could have! I was stupid enough—***

You are not stupid. You were never ***stupid. You were driven by your heart.*** Lore eases my fingers off my hair with his spectral ones. ***You know what I believe, mo khrà?***

No. What? I snap, still thoroughly disenchanted with myself.

I believe that your heart would've guided you back to me.

You've too much faith in my heart, I grumble.

Not only are you my mate, but you are also my Crow. If you hadn't returned to me because of the bond, you would've returned because of your heritage.

You really think Antoni would've disclosed my heritage? Derision gives my voice a hysterical pitch.

I think that your curiosity would've led you to seek out the answers on your own. The same way I think the Cauldron would not have made us mates only to deprive us of one another.

It's what it did to my parents.

The Cauldron didn't sever their bond, Fallon; Meriam did.

My ribs spread to accommodate a resounding breath.

With any luck, the Cauldron will return Daya to your father.

You don't believe in luck.

But you do. Believe it for the two of us?

Another deep sigh rolls through my lungs and up my throat.

For the three of us.

I frown. ***Three? Have you hatched a baby in my absence?***

A smile slashes through his darkness. ***No, Behach Éan. That will be your job. The only part I play is spilling my seed inside your hatch.***

Although we're discussing a tragic topic, my body heats at the mention of Lore's seed.

By three, I meant your father.

That snuffs out my smoldering. I stare around the marketplace for the man in question but cannot spot him amongst the clusters of shifters. ***Where did he go?***

He said he needed to fly.

Although I could be wrong, I imagine he's flying over the ocean, trying to spot a bright pink serpent. Gods, my mother is a serpent.

And we are birds.

That does put things in perspective.

Someone clears their throat. I peek over Lore's shoulder to find Gabriele standing there. "Sorry to interrupt." He offers me a rapid but sweet smile. "It's good to see you again, Fallon."

"It's good to see you, too."

"Didn't think you would, huh?"

"I never lost hope that I'd get out."

"I meant—" He tightens the leather strap with which he's bound his . . . his *really* short ponytail. "You know, Bronwen's prophecy about me kicking the Cauldron before the next full moon. The moon filled out, and I'm still alive."

I blink. I hadn't forgotten about her dismal prediction, but I had forgotten the timeline. "That's—I'm so glad she was wrong."

With a sigh, he says, "She still sees me dying on Tavo's sword."

"Well, I believe we're all masters of our destiny." I stare at where she now sits beside Justus at one of the communal tables, listening to my grandfather speak as he traces the inked circles on his palm with the tip of a finger.

Though Bronwen is hard to love, though her methods are violent and oftentimes borderline cruel, she does have her people's survival at heart.

The same way I do.

Would I have thrust someone into the devil's lair without preamble?

No.

Have I forgiven her?

Also no.

I don't believe I ever will. But Bronwen doesn't strike me as someone who desires forgiveness.

"Mórrgaht, Justus is asking to see his son. May I bring him to Lazarus's rooms?" Lore must spill confusing images into Gabriele's mind because a frown pleats the Faerie's brow. "Bronwen saw the Faerie *general* knifing me."

I stare between my mate's somber form and Gabriele's pallid one. "What's going on?"

Gabriele's gray eyes turn as obscure as slate. "I'll be careful around him." After a quick bow of his head, he strides back toward Justus.

Lore, did you just tell him that Justus will kill him?

I warned him to watch his back, that is all.

Why would Justus hurt him?

Because he's a ruthless man who'll stop at nothing to get what he wants. And he's a Faerie general.

Former *general.* My hands drift to my hips. ***Besides, what reason would he have to kill Gabriele?***

I didn't say he would; I merely cautioned Gabriele, and as far as I know, caution has never hurt a man.

Gods, you make Justus sound positively nefarious.

He bound himself to a witch to manipulate her magic. He kept you away from me, under the fucking earth, for weeks! I understand you look for the best in people, Little Bird, but make sure not to lose sight of the worst, because even the holiest amongst us is no stranger to sin.

I realize he's right, nevertheless, it feels like he's pitting one man against the other. Forming a bond is hard enough in times of war, but it's a darn feat when one's convinced another is out to get them.

"Justus Rossi," I murmur. "I call forth one of my bargains: do not harm or murder Gabriele Moriati."

My grandfather must feel the prickle of my claimed bargain because both his eyebrows jolt and his blue stare bangs into me.

"There. Satisfied, Lore?"

A sigh resonates through our bond. ***Can we lay down our weapons and retire for the night, mo khrà?*** He threads his shadow-hands between my arms to rope my waist. ***I'm in dire need to strip you of this soiled dress.*** He runs his ghostly nose along my cheek, eliciting goosebumps on every other part of my body.

And I'm in dire need to make you whole.

I don't need my fifth crow to make you feel good, Fallon.

That isn't why I want to find him. I shiver as his fingers travel up my spine. ***Tell me where your fifth crow lies, and I retire with you immediately.*** The stubborn press of his lips makes me add, **And *I won't bring up salvaging your missing crow until tomorrow.***

He lies in Filiaserpens.

Filiaserpens? I grin because here I was expecting Lore to tell me his crow had been carried into the tunnels beneath Isolacuori. ***Why were you so intent on keeping his location from me?***

Because, Fallon, Filiaserpens is so deep that not even Faeries can reach its floor.

Good thing I'm Shabbin.

I'm afraid even Shabbins cannot go that deep without it harming their body.

My grin falters. ***I'm immortal, Lore.***

Immortal but not invulnerable. I will not sacrifice your hearing or sight, or Mórrígan only knows what other organ, to rescue a crow I've no need for.

"No need for?" I squeak out loud.

You promised to retire with me once I told you, Behach Éan. The same way you promised not to broach the subject until daybreak. His shadows knit into feathers. ***I expect you to keep both promises.*** He presents me with his wing.

With a sigh, I blow my friends a quick kiss and climb atop Lorcan's broad back.

I can hear you thinking, he says as he flies me through the quiet kingdom.

I promised not to speak of your crow. I never promised not to dwell on how to retrieve him.

As we travel through the shadowy hallways, a plan begins to take shape. There's no depth a serpent can't reach. Not to mention that neither iron nor obsidian can harm them. ***Can you communicate with serpents, Lore?***

No. Only Shabbins can.

How?

They can plant visions inside the sea creatures' minds.

Perfect.

He swerves a little but then readjusts his trajectory. ***What is?***

I cannot tell you until daybreak. I wouldn't want to be accused of shirking my promises.

He growls my name.

Hey, it was your idea not to discuss the rescue mission.

He slows, surfing on the cool air that fills his giant hallways. ***Reid left for Shabbe days ago to discuss the matter with Priya, yet my crow***

still lies in the exact spot it's been in since it fell. After a prolonged beat, he adds, ***I fear his voyage was for naught.***

It wasn't for naught. After all, the woman to whom he gave a love stone resides in Shabbe. Did Mamma recognize him, or is her mind still a murky place filled with fear and anxiety? ***Perhaps the visions fade when the mareserpens travel through the wards?***

They helped dredge the galleon on which I'd been caged, so no, the visions don't fade. The only explanation I can come up with is that I fell somewhere even serpents cannot reach.

Like a crevasse?

Yes.

His individual crows are on the small side, but so are my arms. Lore mustn't have tuned into my thoughts because he doesn't emit another growled objection.

I'm not objecting because you swore an oath to me. One that ensures you remain at my side. Has it already slipped your mind?

I did, didn't I? I sigh. ***In that case, you'll just have to dive with me and succor your crow at my side like we did in the good old days. You were a fantastic sidekick.***

He doesn't reply until we reach his studded bedchamber door and shifts from feathers to shadows. ***Sidekick, huh?*** There's a lilt to his voice, as though some of my positivity has finally drilled through his negativity. ***I prefer the term* guide. *Or* trailblazer.**

I'm sure you do. With a taunting grin, I say, ***You are, after all, in possession of quite the ego, Mórrgaht.***

His shadows wrap around me in a caress, eliciting goosebumps everywhere. ***Mórrígan, how my world was bleak without you, Little Bird.***

My throat and lids feel thick all of a sudden. I cannot possibly be about to weep. Not again. How is it that I even have tears left after this endless day? As I reach out to stroke my storm cloud of a king, he hoists me into his spectral arms and twists the doorknob.

I gasp. ***I cannot believe you can carry me.***

The door clangs shut. ***Wait till you see what else I can do in this form.***

CHAPTER 46

A filled tub awaits me in Lore's bathing chamber. It heaves with curls of steam that snatch an eager whimper from my lips. I haven't bathed since the day of my unbinding. The memory dampens my enthusiasm.

How I wish I could wipe the last month from my mind. Forget that I was kidnapped and bound to a monster. Omit the memory of killing a good man while failing to murder a bad one. But the mind, alas, doesn't function like that.

One cannot select to keep some memories and discard others. Good and bad remain, existing alongside one another like different castes.

I try to reason that, even though my mind is no kingdom, Luce filled with only pointy-eared Faeries would be a terribly dull place to live. It's diversity that makes our world extraordinary. There is beauty even in the darkest pockets of humanity, the same way there are precious memories in the gutter of my nightmares. It's up to me to pluck them out of the filth and carry them to the light.

As Lore shapes an iron talon that he glides down my ruined slip, as the salt-hardened silk falls away from my bruised body, I pluck out the few beams that lit up my obsidian darkness: meeting my Shabbin grandmother, coming into my powers, getting to know Justus Rossi, the citrus segments Cato slipped me in spite of being ordered to starve me, learning that my mother still exists. I give these memories, however few, space to grow, polishing them until they outshine the ones I care to forget.

Lore strips me quietly and slowly, shearing through the laces of my brassiere before rolling my underwear down my legs, his cool smoke gliding down my skin like fragranced oil.

Fully nude, the tension seeps out of my bones as though he's rid me of a suit of armor instead of a skimpy slip. I feel freer and lighter, like a sail teeming with wind, like a ship carving through placid waters.

In the bath you go, Little Ship, Lore murmurs into my mind, one shadowy hand twining through mine, tugging me toward the enormous, round, steaming tub.

I cock up an eyebrow. ***Little Ship?***

Little Serpent?

I smile. ***I've a preference for Behach Éan.*** I climb the four steps that lead into the tall stone tub, then moan as I slip one foot in. ***But I am curious, how does one say serpent in Crow?***

Sífair.

"*Sea fair.*" I sound the word out loud because speaking it helps me commit it to memory. "Want to know something extremely neat?" I ask as I sink into the bath.

Neat?

Nifty.

I want to know all the neat ***things,*** he says as his shadows disperse, becoming one with the steam.

The moment I was in Meriam's presence, before she even unbound my magic, the knowledge of Shabbin came to me.

Lore's golden eyes reappear before mine. I expect awe, but that isn't the emotion rolling off the Crow King.

What? I close my eyes and recline my head until all of me, save for my nose, mouth, and eyes, is submerged.

Before she unbound your magic?

Yes. I walked into the vault and bam, I understood her. I wasn't even aware that she was speaking Shabbin. He doesn't speak for so long that I reel my lids up and straighten my neck. ***I thought it may shock you but in a good way . . . not in***—I shrug—***in a sullen way.***

I'm thrilled for you, Fallon.

You don't sound thrilled.

He rubs a bar of creamy soap between his shadow-hands until suds appear, pearlescent against his darkness. He sets down the soap and runs his fingers through my wet hair, kneading my scalp. I'd almost forgotten how divine his touch could be.

After washing my locks, he eases my head back into the warm water and rubs my scalp, drawing more moans from my lips. ***Forgive my lack of excitement, Behach Éan, but I cannot help but wonder why you're suddenly fluent in Shabbin but not in Crow.***

That does away with the joy coursing through my veins at his scalp massage. I sit up, knees gathered against my chest, hands clasping my shins, and stare into his churning irises.

"Because my Crow side is still bound?" I say, even though I realize how silly my theory is considering Shabbin came to me before my blood magic was unbound.

Though the bath is warm, a chill envelops me. ***I am Crow, right?***

You are. You're your father's daughter, and Cathal is very much a Crow.

Then . . . why? Gone is my awe. In its place is a heap of dread.

Faeries and Crows cannot reproduce. You know this, right?

I do. But what does that have to do with my aptitude to speak Crow?

What if transferring you into a Faerie womb smothered your Crow side?

It sounds like he hasn't come up with this just now. It sounds as though he's given this much thought. If he's right, then that would mean . . . that would mean I'll never be able to shift. I'll never be able to fly.

It's just a theory, Little Bird. For all we know, I could be wrong.

Perhaps, but what if he's right? What if—

You'll have to use my wings for the rest of your life. His shadows glide down my neck, chasing the droplets of water cascading from my hair. ***I could think of many worse outcomes.***

He's right. I know this. Yet disappointment balloons behind my ribs at the idea that I will never be able to grow wings and spring into the sky.

I could be wrong, he repeats, his ethereal mouth brushing across mine before settling and pressing until my lips part for him, until his kiss drives my body backward, until my spine bumps into the rim of his giant tub.

His shadows shift into hands and grip my knees, tugging them apart, spreading me. ***Give me your eyes, Behach Éan. And don't look away.***

I do as he says, and as I stare, his shadows coalesce and color, his outline firms until he becomes a man made of flesh and ink who kneels between my spread thighs. I drink my fill of the exquisite face looking down at me, trace the sharp edge of his unflawed nose and the brutal flare of his jaw, devour the unspoiled sweep of his lashes and soft bow of his mouth.

I recall him telling me that the Glacin Princess had described him as bestial, but there's nothing brutish about this man. Every centimeter of him is magnificent, honed and sensual, the finest work of art ever crafted.

I'm glad to know you're satisfied with your lot, he murmurs as his fingers rove languidly over my collarbone toward the jagged points of my shoulders

My lot. I snort at his euphemism, but then lose my train of thought as he caresses the swells of my breasts, first with his gaze, and then with his fingertips, I lift my hands from the water and hover them over the wide brim of his shoulders, afraid he'll pop like a soap bubble if I apply any pressure.

I won't, for I'm inside your mind, Fallon. He cups one of my breasts, his long fingers caging the soft flesh, then reaches up with the other to capture my wrists, which he drags lower.

When my fingers connect with his flesh, he looses a placated sigh, as though I've somehow relieved him of some great soreness. Another deep sigh travels through his broad chest when I perch my hand on his other shoulder and clasp it.

I've ached for your touch, Behach Éan. He returns his hand to my bare breast and gently begins to knead it while his other palm roams down my rib cage, the roughened pads of his fingers scraping against my stomach. ***For your smell.*** As he runs his nose along the side of my neck, tilting it to accommodate his mouth, his fingertips dip into my belly button, and although it's not a true button, I shudder as though he's flicked something on inside of me. ***For your taste.*** His tongue sweeps across the seam of my lips, coaxing them farther apart, seeking entry.

When his mouth covers mine, a moan slips out of me and into him. Gods, how I've longed for him too. With every cell of my body, every fiber of my being, every beat of the organ thundering against my sternum.

My heart swells and swells, sidling against my ribs to get as near to the hand my mate has pressed to my breast. My nipple hardens, even though it's every millimeter of skin around it to which he caters, evidently remembering that I'm not keen on nipple play.

My breathing becomes spotty, halting entirely when he slides his fingers through my wet curls. Though he has me pressed against the smooth stone of his tub and I've no chance of tumbling, I clamp my hands down, digging each phalanx into his steam-slickened skin.

How wondrous mind-walking. If only my mind could've vaulted out of my obsidian walls whilst my body stayed imprisoned. It would've added so much color to my drab days.

Lore growls into my mouth. Because my mind returned to that place he could not penetrate or because his fingers have reached a slit they *can* penetrate? He parts my sex with two fingers, then drives his middle finger down the path he's cleared. When he skims my nub, I suck in a breath so sharp it stabs my lungs, then expel a muted whimper which he licks off my mouth.

As his finger ventures lower, grazing more slick, pulsating skin, I snap out of the spell he's put me under and grip his neck, then skim my other hand down the quilt of aggressive muscles silvered with scars. I circle his nipples until they harden into minuscule points as jagged as the craggy peaks of his mountain, then drag my knuckles down the runnel of his ribs, feeling the ardent clench of his muscles and the fierce bangs of his heart.

When my hand finally meets its mark and wraps around his silken girth, he rips his mouth from mine and claps both his hands around the edge of the tub with a snarled, "Behach Éan."

His face contorts with such exquisite pleasure that I don't regret the sudden absence of his hand. Through half-lidded eyes, he watches as I drag my hand from his root to his tip, squeezing his bulging veins that swell with more and more desire.

As I pump his length, I sit up to press a kiss to the stubbled edge of his jaw before sliding my lips down his corded neck and licking the bladed apple in his throat. He rasps my name, then rasps my nickname. The sound of his barely-contained pleasure goads me to clasp him a little tighter and quicken my movement.

He shakes and shudders, rattling like a pleased serpent. Exhilarated that I'm touching him in a way that pleases him, I give him a hard squeeze, but instead of flesh, my fingers close over nothing.

And my lips . . . my lips fall through air.

"Lore?" I murmur. "Where did you go?"

Focà. I'm here, mo khrà. He swears again. ***Here.***

What happened?

You made me lose control, that's what happened.

When I finally find his eyes through the fog of his body and the steam of his bath, I murmur, "Again. But this time, take me somewhere else."

Where do you want to go?

"Surprise me."

He smiles, a gradual curl of a lip that is so wicked and beautiful it makes me forget how to breathe. ***When I say* now, *transport yourself inside my mind.***

Lore's shadows disperse like smoke atop a bonfire and rush out of the dark stone bathing chamber. I skim my hands over the bathwater's oily surface, popping the soap bubbles that have formed on top.

Now.

I recline my head on the lip of the tub and concentrate on my mate. My mind vaults from my body as though equipped with wings and reappears in a place that's so hypnotic, my neck falls back and I pirouette on myself.

CHAPTER 47

As I fill my eyes with the inky, starlit beauty above, Lore laughs. The honeyed sound twirls around my spinning body, swathing my naked skin in one more layer of splendor. When I lower my gaze from the glittering immensity, my breath is once again taken away, but not by my surroundings this time.

What stops my breath and my spinning is the sight of my mate cloaked solely in moonlight. I may be inside his mind, but his body is as real as the one he wears when all five of his crows are one.

The light plays on the bricks of his muscles and cliffs of his bones, on the spirals of his veins and brushstrokes of his raven hair. It gilds the daunting length that rests against his thigh, corded like his forearms, bobbing like the apple in his throat, glistening like his golden irises.

Though he wears no crown, no armor, no sword, Lorcan Ríhbiadh looks every bit the monarch. The line of his spine is as straight as that of his shoulders; his wide stance as solid as the stone cliff soaring at his back; his gaze as bottomless as the starlit ocean licking my heels.

"Does this location please you, mo khrà?"

The salted breeze that buffets the cove blows against my naked body, cloaking me in warmth whilst coaxing my nipples into tender points. "This location is *everything*." I start plodding toward him but come to a standstill.

Lore's black eyebrows lower over his eyes. "What is it?"

I remember him telling me, one of the first times I mind-strolled, that his mind was in the same place as his body, which would mean he's outside the walls of his castle. But then I also recall penetrating his mind and finding myself tossed into the past—first with Bronwen and then in his chamber.

Confusion overtakes concern, or rather, parks itself right alongside it.

"In sleep, my mind is tethered to my dreams. When aware, it's tethered to reality."

"So"—I lick my lips—"are you dreaming of the cove, or are you truly putting yourself in peril for a beachside tryst?"

One corner of his mouth wings up. "I'm in smoke. I cannot be harmed in this form."

Perhaps I should be reassured but I'm not.

"I have vigils circling the perimeter, and the ocean churns with gale-force winds. No Fae in their right mind—or wrong one—would dare venture into the Southern Sea."

Over my shoulder, the ocean is as smooth and flat as a mirror.

"The same way we can fade people when we mind-walk, we can fade the accuracy of our surroundings. Even change the time of day." He nods to the stars that aren't yet shimmering in real-Luce.

"You swear you're not in any danger?"

"I swear."

When I don't start moving toward him, he comes to me, stride languid yet resolute, gaze intent on the lip I'm nibbling in unease.

Fallon, my love, we're safe. He clasps my wrists and links them around his neck, then lowers his face down to mine and steals my lip from my teeth in a devastatingly languid kiss.

It's not me I'm afraid for, Lore.

I'm not at risk of losing another crow, only of losing my mind if I don't have you right now. He grabs my thighs and hoists me up.

My legs come around his waist, and I hook my ankles to keep from slipping off. Not that I'm at risk of dropping. His grip on my ass is so firm that even if I tried to squirm away, I couldn't. But why the

Cauldron would I try? There's nowhere in the entire world I'd rather be than in Lore's arms.

He presses a kiss to the crook of my neck, then suckles the skin. Will my flesh bear the mark of his mouth when I awaken from this extravagant fantasy?

Sand or sea, Little Bird?

"Wh-what?" The word stumbles out of my mouth along with my breath.

He moves his mouth to my ear and murmurs, "Where would you like me to take you? Inside the ocean or would you prefer I lay you out on the sand?"

"Surprise me."

I feel his lips curve against my skin as he steps toward the ocean, his cock sliding back and forth against my slick heat. When he's ankle-deep in the surf, he turns and kneels, rolling me atop the damp sand. And then his mouth is on my breast, soft, soft, soft, pressing slow, open-mouthed kisses until my pale pink areola puckers and my nipple threatens to stab the flat of his tongue.

My heart hastens as he flicks his gaze to my other breast. ***Pain?***

I'm shocked he remembers that my chest has never truly been a source of pleasure.

He braces himself onto his forearms. "I forget nothing, Behach Éan. Would you like me to stop paying your perfect breasts attention?"

"No." Although I don't think I could climax like Syb apparently can, I don't dislike the tingle.

Lore studies my eyes—my mind—as though he wants to make absolutely certain I'm not encouraging him only to please him.

I thread my hand through his hair and tow his face back down to my other breast, feeding it to him. My toes and fingers curl when he sucks my nipple into his mouth, scraping it with his teeth before laving it with his tongue. It's a lot. A lot good. *Fuck.* It's actually . . . The tingle races through my veins, tightening first my stomach and then my core.

Balancing himself on one hand, he smooths the other down the length of my torso like a sculptor shaping clay and forces my thighs open with the heel of his hand, then spreads my lips with his fingers and, without pause, thrusts one long finger knuckle-deep inside of me.

A choked cry tears up my throat, and my spine arches. Lore flattens me against the sand with one big palm, then gives my nipple a powerful swirl of tongue that makes both my breasts tighten even though only one is getting mauled. He releases me with an audible pop that snaps yet another tingle through my body, one that matures into a shiver as he lazily pumps his finger in and out of me.

Eyes on mine, he raises a wicked grin that he slides down the channel between my ribs, dips into my belly button, and skims down my curls. Once he reaches my pubic bone, he picks his face off my body, removes his finger from my clenching heat, and regards, with great smugness, how his skin shines.

Shifting his gaze back to mine, he sticks the finger coated with my juices inside his mouth and sucks. ***How I've hungered for your sweet taste, mate.***

The sight of him tasting me, combined with the heady groan that rumbles from his chest, fires a blush across my cheeks, one that makes the corners of his mouth curl even higher.

Once he's sucked his finger clean, he scoots backward, submerging his lower body until his long frame is settled comfortably against the sand, then he threads his arms beneath my thighs and spreads me wide.

"I thought you wanted—" He lowers his head and gives me a long lick that slams the door shut between my mouth and mind.

You thought I wanted **what, *Behach Éan?***

I thought— Another lick. ***I thought—***

He plucks my tightened nub and I give up thinking.

He chuckles, which only enhances all the sensations churning within me. After he's raided my lungs of a few moans, he braces his weight onto his elbows and tows his mouth off my core. "What did you think I wanted?"

I blink up at the sky, then roll my head off the sand and blink at him, my thoughts as distant and out of reach as the stars above.

He circles my nub with a blunt nail, teasing my pulse into a frenzy. "So . . .?"

Oh my Gods, is he serious? Does he really think now's a good time to joggle my brain? The only thing I want joggled is that part of me he's merely skimming.

He chuckles, pulsing air that hits me dead center. My thighs tense. My core clenches. I will him to once again laugh at my tawdry wherewithal, if only so his lungs can set me off since his finger seems averse to granting me pleasure.

With a wink, he replaces his finger with his tongue, and then with his mouth, drawing me between his lips and teeth with a powerful suck that has me seeing a flare so bright it seems as though the stars above have all banged into each other to become one.

I grip his hair and scream his name as I unravel against his face, in this strange plane peopled by only the two of us. He laps at me slowly, as though to catch every last drip of my climax, then drags himself to his knees, clasps my ankles, and slides me along the sand. When my ass hits a lapping wave, he scoops my boneless body into his arms and walks us into the ocean.

It's only when his engorged tip brushes along my swollen slit that I recall the end of my sentence. *Inside of me.* That's what I thought he wanted.

He scrapes his stubbled jaw along my neck, then along my cheek. "Guide me home, Behạch Éan."

His rasped entreaty is so very sweet that it caresses my thundering heart, easing the chaos until my pulse is as smooth as the glowing ocean surrounding us. I tighten the knot of my legs and lock one hand around his nape, then reach between our bodies for the weapon gloved in silk.

Using my thumb, I angle him up, then sheath him inside my body in one fell swoop. Where I sigh in bliss, he looses a guttural groan that skips along the water and collides into the rocky cliffs. His hands squeeze my ass as I rock my hips. Instead of quickening the slip and slide of his flesh into mine, the water slows our rhythm.

Lore growls, and I cannot tell if it's in frustration or contentment. He takes my mouth in a kiss that makes *me* forget to move but evidently works wonders on his concentration because the man's hands and hips never once falter as they pilot my body to the speed he desires.

It feels so real that for a moment, I wonder if it is. But it's not real. I won't be dripping with his seed because my mate is missing one crow.

Forget about my crow, he growls. ***Focus on***—he drives himself in so deep that I feel his tip dig into my stomach; I feel the ridged underside of his cock scrape against my walls—***me.***

I frame his jaw with my palms and deepen our kiss, losing myself in the here and now, in this version of him that's whole, in the breaths that cycle out of his lungs and into mine, in the powerful thrusts of his cock.

My body tenses before his does, shuddering with a second orgasm that feels as real as all the ones he gave me before we were torn apart. He suddenly stills and paints my walls with his phantom pleasure.

Dropping his head into the crook of my neck, he rasps, ***Mo ab'waile. Mo khroí.***

While he speaks the foreign words inside my mind, I can feel them adhere to my raw flesh like sea mist. ***Tell me what* oh wahleea *and* kree *mean.***

My home. He kisses one corner of my lips, then hovers his mouth over the other and murmurs, "My heart."

CHAPTER 48

I don't remember dropping from Lorcan's mind, nor do I remember getting out of his tub and into his bed. All I remember is our lovemaking in the cove, and how he split me open first with his sex and then with his words.

Even though our tryst in the ocean was a figment of our combined imaginations, as I lie in the muted glow of a new dawn, with his sheets tangled around my legs, I swear I can taste salt on my lips and feel sand between my toes.

I bend one of my legs to check for some only to find my skin clean. And yet it had felt so real. As I stretch, my bones click and my muscles groan. I feel all at once broken and invigorated, bruised and healed. Sure enough, faint purple marks and fainter scratches still pepper my skin. My Shabbin blood will fix me before sundown, but until then, I'll wear the memory of my escape with pride.

I look for my mate, first in his bed, across which I'm sprawled, then higher, I peer at the tall timber rafters, on the lookout for feathers. When I've raked my gaze across every slab of wood, I squint into the thick pool of shadows that extends to the craggy stone ceiling before finally calling out to him through our mind link.

Lore? I try not to worry. I've no reason to worry, right?

I prop myself up in bed so suddenly that my head whirls and I flop right back down. Oh my Gods, what if he was attacked last night after our tête-à-tête on the beach?

Then who carried you from the bath to the bed? my conscience queries.

I suppose there are a number of people who could *potentially* have come to check on me had anything happened to Lore.

I carried you, Little Bird.

I jump at the sound of his voice inside my head, then jump again when his shadows sweep over me like the waves rolled over his long legs last night. Palm clapped against my runaway heart, I mumble, "You've just rid me of at least one decade of life."

He snorts as his shadows take on his humanoid shape and press into me from toe to forehead, forcing my legs to flop apart. When something cold and slick nudges my entrance, my heart begins to slam against my ribs for a whole other reason.

Did I forget to mention that I can make love to you in this form too?

Ghostly fingers begin to rake across my pebbling flesh, digging into my shoulder blades before swirling over my collarbone and caressing my heaving breasts. He must shape several more sets for I feel cool hands bracket my waist and knead the base of my spine while long fingers work the knots out of my sore legs, circling my ankles, my shins, my thighs.

Holy mother of Crows, this man's talents were wasted on shepherding.

He chuckles into the bond as he adds one more finger to the mix, this time on my clit. I don't see stars, I see meteorites; I feel them slam into my thrumming body and torch my veins.

Ready for one more— What was it you called them again? Ah, yes . . . party tricks.

Can one be ready for their soul and heart to catch fire and burn?

With all twenty sets of ethereal hands still massaging my skin, Lore funnels shadows between my thighs, so many that the air is black with him. I watch in wonder as that darkness narrows and then gasp when it swoops inside of me.

My eyes roll to the back of my skull as he penetrates and stretches me, his shadows icy against my heat. They thicken and pulse like a cock, then become ridged like . . . like that sex toy Catriona kept in her room at *Bottom of the Jug*. The one she used on some of her customers. The one I found when changing her sheets and stared at with crimson cheeks.

Every hardened nib, with which Lore has festooned his shadow-cock, begins to pulsate against my walls, making them shake and clench, and shake some more. As he plays with my body, I grip the bedsheets, tearing them clean off his mattress, and moan so loudly I think every Crow in the kingdom will know that their monarch is pleasuring me.

I suck in a breath and hold it as the legs he's still tending to begin to shake. Sweat slickens my brow and beads between my breasts as every muscle in my body begins to spasm. The orgasm is so intense that my vision whitens and my throat clenches in time with my core. I choke on my scream, only managing to shape Lore's name with my mind.

His shadows slow their assault but never cease rocking over and into me.

Oh my Gods, what the fuck was that, Lore?

Language, mo khrà.

I snort and shake my head, flinging one forearm over my eyes that are still flaring with the brightness of the supernova that just rocketed through my body.

As for what that was. After fingers, I now feel lips . . . dozens of them, licking and kissing me everywhere. ***That was me showing you that I can keep you satisfied, no matter my . . . configuration.***

My arm slips off my eyes, and my lids reel up, my pleasure draining out of me like water from the tub. ***Your configuration?*** I snap, a little incensed because I'm a pro at reading between Lorcan Ríhbiadh's obdurate lines. ***The next time you make love to me, mo khrà, it will be in flesh, and not in your or my fucking head.***

I shove his billowing darkness off my body and leap out of bed, ready to carve through the ocean to retrieve his crow and rid him of his passive acceptance of never being whole again.

Fallon, he growls.

It's morning, Lore. Time for our little swim.

I've changed my mind.

Well, I haven't, and since wherever I go, you go, I fear you're stuck.

His shadows form a wall in front of me. One that prevents me from stomping into his bathing chamber to retrieve a towel to wrap around my naked self.

I try to sidestep him, but he just fashions another wall. ***What is it about this mission that makes you so anxious, Lore? You and I, we've faced so much worse.***

Though he bristles, he doesn't disperse.

I lick my lips, trying to come up with an argument that will smooth out his ruffled feathers. I find the perfect one. ***At least, in the ocean, thanks to our serpent friends, no ill-intentioned Faerie is lying in wait for us with a nocked arrow or an obsidian blade.***

Do you know how deep the trench goes?

With a sigh, I say, ***How about you tell me?***

As steep as Monteluce, Fallon! That's how deep.

I plop my hands on my hips, a little annoyed by his tone of voice. I understand it's sparked by fear and not by anger, but still. ***And you're certain you fell to the very bottom?***

No.

How about we—by *we*, I really mean ***he—look at this dive as a reconnaissance mission. If in fact you're out of my range, we'll surface and plot another method of retrieval.***

Several beats of silence echo between us before he finally mutters, ***I will carry you out of the Sky Kingdom only if you*** swear ***that if at any moment I tell you to turn back, you turn back.***

I twist my index finger over my middle one behind my back and say, ***I swear.***

He tows my crossed fingers from behind my back. ***Want to try that again, Behach Éan?***

I sigh in annoyance. ***Fine. I swear to listen to you.***

Lorcan's head tips to the side, as though to urge me to add some more weight to my promise, perhaps even his full name.

Don't you trust me, mate? My question elicits a brisk snort from the Shadow King.

I trust that your will is as unbendable as mine. I trust that your heart is in the right place.

But not my head?

I'm just glad I've a bargain to collect in case your head and heart attempt to run away with your prudence.

Pounding interrupts our little talk. I frown because I don't think the knocking came from his bedroom door.

It didn't. Come. He twines cool, smoky fingers around mine and tugs me into a stone chamber that resembles my closet, only larger. ***The Siorkahd is waiting for us in the war room.***

Us? I expect him to fling one of his tunics atop my head, but instead, he jostles a row of hangers to palm the gray stone behind them.

Yes, us. I believe it's time my future queen has a say in state decisions.

You're giving me a say?

His eyes lock on my wide ones. ***Why do you sound so surprised?***

Because queens—**Lucin** ***queens—are usually tasked with throwing memorable revels and looking pretty on their husbands' arm.***

Would you rather I make you throw revels and parade you around in lavish frocks?

I start to roll my eyes when a deep groan echoes through the torchlit closet. I freeze because the sound pitches me back into the cavern beneath the mountain. Have the Fae found a way to crumble Lore's castle?

CHAPTER 49

S*hh, Little Bird. My castle isn't crumbling. It cannot be crumbled.* His shadows swirl around me. *You're safe.* He must realize I'm not convinced because he repeats it twice more.

Then what—what was that? My skin is still covered in goosebumps, and my muscles are primed to spring.

That was a secret passageway that leads into your room. Lore gestures to the stone opening.

My eyes are pitched so wide that I cannot even blink.

Mórrígan helped build and enchant our castle. Even though I explained Crow mates didn't keep separate quarters, she insisted on building my future wife a space to call her own. Your great-great grandmother said that the woman who ended up paired with the likes of me would greatly appreciate her foresight.

The shocked circle of my lips finally thaws into a slow smile.

Care to explain the nature of your amusement, Behach Éan?

Just thinking that Mara was a wise woman.

He harrumphs, which only makes my grin expand.

You are rather intense.

You didn't seem to mind my intensity *this morning.* He skims the edge of my smile, then traces many other edges on my body with his silken shadows. *Or last night.*

I've never been so glad to be so full of edges. ***I do love your intensity, Lore, but I also love the idea of having a space to call my own.*** I think of my tiny bedroom back in Tarelexo with its paper-thin walls and teeny closet. Not that I had many outfits to fill it with, but the idea of owning a space so large that it comes with a private bathing chamber . . . it's the stuff of fairytales.

He sighs and gathers me into his arms. ***I'm glad I could give you something you've never had.***

I press my cheek against his chest and link my hands around his narrow waist, drinking in his strong heartbeats.

But just so we're clear, we never sleep apart; not even on days my intensity makes your hands itch to throttle me.

My smile reaches higher, deeper. ***I'll stick to throttling your cock in one of our two beds. Speaking of cocks, shall we go retrieve yours, mo khrà?***

Retrieve my cock, he mutters right before popping my ass cheek.

Did you just spank me?

Well, you did just call me dickless. He spins me around, his hands kneading the skin he tapped, and then he tilts my hips, and I flail forward, my fingers locking around the edge of the chest of drawers that sits like an island in the middle of his dressing chamber. ***My cock may not be made of flesh, Fallon, but it can fill you up just the same. Allow me to demonstrate.***

When he slams home, I wheeze.

Can you feel me, my love?

I can feel nothing else.

To punish me once again for having alluded to his missing manhood, he rubs my ass, then gives it a brisk smack. A dizzying current whizzes through my body, zapping a throaty mewl from my lungs.

Oh, Gods, Lore. Oh—I choke as Lore pounds into me, stretching me with his shadows—***Gods***—my climax roars through my body, jostling both my skin and marrow—***Lore!***

He keeps rocking his shadow-hips. ***Reassured?***

I didn't mean to make you feel like less of a man.

He doesn't respond, merely recalls his shadows. When a translucent trail of wetness dribbles down my inner thighs, he rips a fresh tunic off a hanger and cleans my skin.

I hook up an eyebrow. ***Was any of that yours?***

His gaze remains locked on the fabric absorbing my pleasure. ***No.***

Because he cannot come in this form . . .

If I need to come, I'll penetrate your mind before I penetrate your body. Now get dressed and meet me in the war room.

His gruff timbre makes me glance over my shoulder at where he stands, delineated in dark wisps. ***How do I reach the war room?***

Use the door beside my fireplace. It'll lead to a sitting room, which will lead you to the war room. His tone is laced with so much frost that it ices my heart.

"Lore, I'm sorry. I . . ."

He leaves before I can finish speaking. So I tell him that I love him no matter his form through our mind link, then stare around my closet for a solid minute before going to my undergarment drawer and riffling through it. I find no swimming costume, but I do find a black bodysuit. When I look at it more closely, I realize it's part of the dress Lore shredded the first night we spent together. Someone has darned the piece of fabric between the legs. They didn't bother reattaching the gossamer skirt but they did fold it up neatly beside the one-piece.

Not only is the outfit perfect for a swim, but hopefully, it will work wonders on my mate's mood. After slipping into the one-piece, I tie the skirt around my waist and swing by my bathing chamber to brush out my snarled locks, pivoting my head to admire how they move now that they reach past my collarbone. I shouldn't care about my hair's length, but apparently, even in times of uncertainty and war, I'm vain like that.

You're neither human nor Fae, my mind whispers. *Grow your damn hair to your toes if you so wish.*

I really adore my conscience sometimes.

I wrangle the tamed lengths into a short braid. Not bothering with shoes, I plod back through the secret passageway, the smooth stone floor cool beneath my bare toes. The air is so brisk I almost unknot my sash to use it as a stole, but considering how thin the fabric is, it would be rather useless so I leave it where it is.

Though Lore can slip under doors, he's left the one beside his enormous stone hearth wide open. *My grumpy, considerate mate.*

The library is dark in spite of the three small windows spitting wan light onto the high desk that is stained the same mahogany as the floor-to-ceiling shelving. The desk, which takes up a good portion of the room, is covered in an ochre map of Luce held flat by stone paperweights.

I remember this room! I mind-walked into this room.

Though the door to the war room is also propped open, and from the high tones, arguments are being had, I linger in the doorway, running my gaze over the rows of leather-bound books, absorbing all the gilt magnificence. Deciding I'll have a lifetime to explore all of Lore's books, I march ahead.

Unlike the narrower library, this room sprawls as long and wide as the Sky Tavern. Though no windows are carved into the wall, a round skylight pours brightness into the dusky room, giving the smooth stone floor the appearance of polished silver and the graphite battle scenes adorning all four walls a depth that makes the murals come alive.

Once I've drunk my fill of the space, I focus on the enormous rectangular table around which only nine people sit, even though twenty more could easily fit.

Nine very vocal people engaged in a shouting match that has my father's fingers clenching around the arms of his massive chair and growling, "Who will protect my daughter if this is some perverse trick of yours, Rossi?"

"If I'd wanted Fallon dead, Cathal, I would've bled Meriam, or gored Zendaya ages ago."

I suck in a breath.

"*Never* fucking threaten my mate." Wisps of shadows coil off my father's vambraces, dark like the carved wood he sits on.

"It was no threat, merely a reminder of where my loyalties lie." Justus speaks with the aplomb of someone who's faced many a firing squad. "Speaking of loyalties. Your daughter's arrived."

My father pivots his head in slow motion, as though it's taking everything in him to coax his incendiary gaze away from Justus. He rises from his chair even slower, his trousers whispering over the upholstered seating that has been done up in the same black leather that swathes every Crow in attendance.

The only one not garbed in black leather is Justus Rossi. Even

Gabriele sports all black. Though his face isn't striped like the Crows and his ears are pointy, he fits right in.

"Morning, ínon." My father white-knuckles the empty chair beside his and drags it out for me. "Are you rested?"

I glance toward the head of the table where golden eyes stare out from a murky face. Evidently, Lore's still vexed.

"Yes, Dádhi." I don't bother asking if he's rested. His eyes are bloodshot and rimmed with purple smudges that even his charcoal stripes cannot hide. Did he spend his evening surfing over the ocean, ruing what became of his mate?

As I tuck myself onto the wide seat, I stare at the only two faces that aren't familiar—one is a woman with cliffs for cheekbones, cropped white hair, and skin a shade lighter than the furniture; the other is a male with muscles for days, deep-set eyes, and an imposing nose that's a dead ringer for an iron beak.

"I don't believe we've met, yet. I'm Fallon."

"Naoise." The unfamiliar male nods at me, the dull light catching on his entirely bare scalp.

I smile, then turn to the woman who sits beside him, a smile tugging at her full mouth. "Sorry to disappoint you, Cathal, but your daughter took nothing from you. She's all Daya."

As he folds himself back into his chair, my father swallows, his expression turning downright somber. "Thank Mórrígan for that."

"I'm Iona. I believe you've met my son and grandson—Connor and Reid?"

"I have. It's a pleasure to make your acquaintance."

"Pleasure is all mine, Curse-breaker."

The nickname makes my stomach roil with nerves. It isn't that I've forgotten about my task, because I haven't. How could I, when the fate of two nations rests on my shoulders?

"Now that everyone's introduced, shall we run Fallon through Rossi's plan?" Iona suggests.

I perch my attention on my grandfather, who's combed and garbed in a fresh shirt the color of the clouds tiling the sky.

Imogen reclines in her chair. Though she isn't heaps taller than I am, her shoulders are so wide that, unlike me, she doesn't look dwarfed by the giant seat. "You mean Rossi's proposal to stake our king?"

I gawp in horror at Justus, then wonder how he's even still alive after uttering such a suggestion.

"Perhaps you should give Fallon a little context, Imogen." Justus's blue gaze slides to the female Crow. "Especially since your king didn't deem my idea preposterous."

CHAPTER 50

My head rears back at the news that my mate is on board with a staking.

"Dante's waiting for the Crows to fall. The second they do, he will leave his obsidian refuge." Justus rolls his shoulders, drawing my attention to the fact that his arms are pinned behind his back.

"So you suggested *immobilizing* my mate?" My voice is shrill with nerves, and though my nails don't transform into iron tips, I feel like I could shred the table whose thick edge I clutch. "No one is staking Lore." I can feel my mate smile through our mind link, which makes me whip my glower off Justus and level it on the Sky King. ***Why are you fucking smirking?***

He *tsks*.

If he tells me to watch my tongue, I will—

I smile because you look about ready to raze the world for me.

My father's chair creaks as he shifts on his seat. "I agree with my daughter. Rossi's plan is madness. The fact that you're all even entertaining it is madness."

I stare around the table at Cian, Erwin, and the two other males whose names I've yet to learn. "Why are you all even entertaining it?"

"Not *all*. Rossi neither has my vote nor Cathal's." Imogen regards the four Siorkahd members who failed to see the folly in my grandfather's plan.

"You and I both know, Fallon"—Justus blows a breath out of the corner of his mouth to displace the silver lock that's slipped in front of his left eye—"that Dante will not emerge from those tunnels until the Crows fall."

My molars clench so hard that pain shoots into my jawbone. "So you suggested orchestrating their fall?" No wonder my father was shouting at him when I arrived.

"I suggested they all flock to the battleground. One of us—be it Bronwen, myself, or you—would then drive an obsidian blade through Lore, which would turn his people into obsidian statues. While Gabriele ensures the news reaches Dante's ears, you would free Lore. The Sky King would then wait to speak the words that awakens his Crows until Dante emerges from the tunnels."

"Once out in the open and within your reach, since, apparently, *you* must murder him or the Cauldron will not unbolt, ínon"—my father glances at his brother whose chest moves with a sigh even though he's for naught in this prediction—"Lore would wake us so we can expunge his close guard and supporters, while you concentrate solely on the *annos dòfain*."

I can only imagine that *awnos duffen* is not a laudatory term.

I'm glad Aoife has yet to fill you in on your father's favorite insults. Lore's pleasant tone is so at odds with this entire moment that I cannot even find it in me to smirk that my father has favorite insults, much less ask what this one means.

But Gabriele must ask because Naoise smiles widely his way. "It means anus dejection."

"What if *I* turn to stone when Lore is staked? I'm a Crow, after all."

"If that side of you had been unleashed, you would've suffered greatly underground," Justus says.

"She did suffer greatly, Rossi," my father bites out.

Justus rolls his lips, chastened by my father's reproach.

"Another way we could go about this"—Gabriele leans forward in his seat, sliding his forearms on the scarred wood, looking so at ease amongst the Siorkahd that I take it this isn't his first roundtable—"is staking each of you individually so Lore is unharmed."

It would take too long to free everyone. You'll either have an army I can raise instantly, or you won't set foot out of my castle.

I stare at my mate and shake my head. ***I loathe this plan, Lore.***

And I loathe your plan of going for a swim, but I'm indulging you.

I toss my hands in the air. ***So I should indulge your collective lunacy?***

Only fair. Can you share my answer to Gabriele's suggestion?

I grit my teeth. "Lore says no to the individual staking of his people." Many sets of eyes warm my scowling face. "And I say no to staking him."

"The majority has voted yes to Rossi's plan." Slowly, Iona adds, "Your mate included."

"So, what? It's set in stone?" I cross my arms and lean back, probably appearing like a sprite perched on the seat of a full-grown Faerie.

"Unless you can think of a better plan during your swim"—Cian inclines his head in the direction of Mareluce—"then yes, we will go through with this plan."

I cannot tell if he thinks me as foolish as Lore does. Not that I care. All I care about is getting into the ocean. Not only will swimming allow me to distance myself from the war room, but it'll also give me time to think of another plan.

A better one.

One that doesn't involve turning my mate to iron.

As I rise from my seat, I ask, "Did Bronwen see it happen? Is that why you're all on board with turning into statues again, Uncle?"

Cian raises his grim eyes to mine. "Yes."

CHAPTER 51

I flatten my palms against the table to steady myself. "Bronwen *foresaw* Justus staking Lore?"

"She foresaw Lore turning to iron on the battlefield, and us, to stone."

My head spins from Cian's avowal. "Did she foresee all of you turning back?"

"She foresaw Dante dying at your hand."

"Except Dante dying breaks Meriam's curse, not the Crows'. Unless he's the key to yours as well?"

"She saw *you* kill Dante after our fall, Fallon." Cian repeats as though I'm daft. "That means you don't turn to obsidian. That means you live. If you live, so do we."

"No. That means *Dante* dies. Perhaps I kill him by crushing him beneath my obsidian body." My jaw's wedged so tight, my words lack volume but not punch. "Admittedly, if he dies, the Shabbin wards come down, so you'll have your pick of saviors."

Imogen snorts. "He's a Faerie. Obsidian doesn't harm the Fae. Not even a well-placed obsidian beak."

Though Lore doesn't utter a word, smoke twists off his hazy figure as though he was on fire.

"Bronwen also foresaw Gabriele dying before the last full moon, and he's still around, so excuse me if I don't eat up her prediction." I scrape my chair back, the wood shrieking against the stone.

Iona expels a snort. "I believe I was wrong about Fallon not inheriting anything from you, Cathal. She seems to have gotten your temper in spades."

"I don't suppose you have a mate, Iona." My mood turns my tone tetchy.

Her slender eyebrows slant. "I do not, but I don't see what—"

"If you did have a mate, you wouldn't tolerate anyone so much as alluding to staking him."

She presses her lips together. "It's for the greater good, Fallon."

"Driving a blade through Dante's heart is for the greater good; driving a blade through Lore's isn't." I wait for Lore to ask me to show his Siorkahd member the respect she is due, but he doesn't seem to object to me voicing my opinion. "I'm ready for that swim."

"Perhaps, but Daya isn't." My father scrutinizes his talon-tipped fingers. "She only left Tarespagian waters last night. She won't reach Tarecuori for another day, and that is, if she doesn't sense you here and linger in the Southern Sea."

I blink at my father, surprised that he refers to Minimus as Daya, surprised that he's wrapped his mind around the fact that my mother is a serpent, while I'm still grappling with the revelation.

"You'll either dive with her, or you won't dive at all, ínon. Understood?"

"We're wasting time, Dádhi."

"We've time aplenty, Fallon."

I sigh. "Fine."

I start to sit down when my father nods to the double doors cut into the far wall. "Your friends have been waiting for you in *Adh'Thábhain* since daybreak."

Daybreak? Even though Syb is used to waking early, what with working at *Bottom*, Phoebus is not a fan, which says a lot about his desire to see me.

"And while you're there, eat copiously, since clearly, you haven't been doing much of that in the last month." He levels a resonant glower Justus's way.

The former Faerie general neither flinches nor does he justify his reason for depriving me of food.

"Give me your skirt before departing."

My eyebrows knit.

"In case I cannot guide your mother to Tarecuori with my caws, I will lead her there with your scent."

Ah. I don't waste a minute unwrapping my skirt even though I feel incredibly bare without it, which is ironic seeing as the fabric wasn't covering all that much to begin with.

"Can I go sit with my son, Mórrgaht?" Justus asks.

"The stones, Rossi." Iona nods to the center of the table upon which sit two blocks of gray stone which I assumed were the Crow version of a decorative centerpiece.

"Are those . . . ?" My heartbeats jump out of alignment. "Are those the runestones?"

Lore nods, then uses his shadows to glide them toward Justus.

My grandfather stares at the gray rocks as though they were wells filled with electric eels. "You've sent a Crow to warn Priya, Ríhbiadh?" At my mate's nod, he glides his palms over the chunks of rock.

Warn her of what?

That if the wards slackened, she should refrain from murdering her daughter.

That does nothing to calibrate my heartbeats.

I sent someone to Shabbe last night, Fallon.

"Stop!" My voice jerks Justus's palms off the gray stone.

My father lurches from his seat, sending the heavy wooden thing squealing. "What is it?"

"What if the message hasn't reached Priya's ears yet, Dádhi?"

"We've stationed Crows around the wards to intercept her ships."

I chew on the inside of my cheek. I chew so hard I draw blood. "What if they swim to our shores instead of sail?"

This gives everyone pause.

But then Naoise says, "There's no reason our messenger won't be granted an audience with the Queen."

"I want Shabbe freed as much as the rest of you, but can we wait until we recover the Glacin stone so that if Justus succeeds at lifting Meriam's blood, it will crumble the wards, and a messenger can soar through them and back to confirm?" My voice warbles like my heart. "Please?"

"I agree with Fallon," Justus says, garnering many a suspect stare.

"Of course you do." My father glares hard at his former enemy. "You're in cahoots with Meriam."

The blue in Justus's eyes darkens. "I repeat: she's not evil incarnate, Cathal."

I touch my father's wrist, wishing that this wasn't how he saw Meriam, but I sense convincing him that she's worth forgiving will take a lot more than my endorsement of her character.

She robbed him of his mate, Fallon, Lore reminds me gently.

She also saved her from decades of torture.

One sadly does not cancel out the other.

"What I *can* do, Cathal, without endangering Fallon, is attempt to coax the blood to the surface. At least we'll be set as to whether I'll have the ability to cleanse the sigil once the stones are reunited." Justus turns toward Lore, waiting for his approval before proceeding.

The decision is yours, mo khrà.

I've chewed into my cheek's lining with such vigor that the coppery taste of blood fills my mouth. How I wish the wards weren't soundproof. My teeth release my pierced skin. "Could we make large signs and hold them up to the wards?"

"Signs?" Imogen asks.

"You know, painted wooden panels written with large block letters: IF YOU KILL MERIAM, FALLON KICKS THE CAULDRON? Actually, that expression may be misconstrued. Probably best to use a more direct verb like *perishes*."

I feel a shadow skim my cheekbone.

"I'm afraid to report that the wards distort words, Fallon." Justus shoots me a gentle smile.

I'm about to say, *then let's wait*, but a glance at my father's dejected expression makes me give in.

Are you certain, Behach Éan?

I nod.

"Can it be done here?" After collecting many frowns, Justus adds, "Doesn't the Sky Kingdom block Faerie and Shabbin magic?"

"You're not spellcasting, Rossi," my father murmurs. "You're magnetizing blood."

Justus bobs his head, then squints hard at the gray rock. When he shuts his eyes, I think he's failed to make the rock bleed, but then he retracts his hands, and my trapped inhale comes out as a thready gasp.

CHAPTER 52

Justus peers around the table. "Though I don't believe anyone but Meriam or I can alter it, I do suggest no one touches the stones until the last one is collected."

No one but me meets his stare for everyone else's gaze is riveted to the pattern of blood.

"May I go visit my son now, Ríhbiadh?"

My mate nods. As Gabriele leads him toward the massive entrance cut into one of the murals, I ask Lore how Vance is faring.

Lazarus got his bleeding under control, but the male has yet to wake. He reclines in his seat, golden eyes sharpening on my bare legs. ***Change before heading to the tavern.*** After a beat, he adds a, ***Please.***

Though that was my intent, I cannot help but ask, ***Isn't everyone in the Sky Kingdom aware I'm your mate?***

They are, but that does not preclude any of them from looking.

A smile slowly blossoms on my face. ***So, you love me again?***

Though he doesn't rise from his chair, he must ferry a few of his shadows my way because I feel a finger glide from the hollow of my collarbone to the point of my shoulder. ***I never stopped, Behach Éan. Even if you'd married Dante for love, I wouldn't have stopped. I physically*** **cannot** ***stop.***

I press my lips together. ***Your declaration was touching until you***

brought up the awnos duffen. I close my fingers around the disheartening symbol inked into my skin.

Lore's shadows rush toward me—all of them—and he tows my chin up. ***Forgive me.***

I nod because I do forgive him, but boy, does the memory of the blood-bind put a damper on my mood.

I'm afraid your mate is an insufferably jealous man, mo khrà. Find it in your heart to keep loving him in spite of this flaw?

I love you all the more for it, Mórrgaht. I stare into the glimmering depths of his eyes. I must lose myself in their beauty because his shadows brighten into skin and everyone in the war room winks out of existence, save for us.

I'm not sure if I'm inside Lore's mind or if he's inside mine, but I take full advantage of him being in skin to roll up onto my toes and press a closed-mouth kiss to his lips. His strong hands grip my waist, and his lips, so plush yet so hard, part my own.

For a delicate moment, we just stand there, heart to heart, breath to breath. I can almost pretend that this isn't some mystical daydream that will fritter away when whoever carried the other out of reality lets go.

He presses his forehead to mine, robbing me of his lips. ***Perhaps I should've insisted Rossi weaken the wards. If only to have another Shabbin fetch my fallen crow.***

What if another Shabbin saving you interferes with the Cauldron's designs on my curse-breaking?

He sighs but must decide my worry is not entirely misplaced because he doesn't snap out of our bubble to call back Justus. ***I need to return to my meeting, but as soon as we finish, I will come find you. Go enjoy yourself for now, my love.***

Though I wish I could enjoy myself *with* him, he is king, and kings—true ones—cannot spend their days at taverns, reveling as though everything in the world is dandy. Especially when the world is so very *not* dandy.

It will be soon.

I grip his conviction and store it close to my heart, but more than once throughout the day, it drifts from my fingers like crumbling rock because too many lives are still at stake.

What if I don't retrieve Lore's fallen crow?

What if he goes ahead with Justus's mad plan and doesn't awaken after being staked?

What if I fail at killing Dante?

What if my mother never shifts out of her scaled form?

SYBILLE TAPS the rim of my stein. "Liquor her up, Pheebs. Fal's just crawled back into her head."

I sigh as he splashes the content of the pitcher inside my metal cup.

"*Woe is me* is not a good look on you, sweets." He nods to the brown shirt I wear over brown leggings. "Very much like that outfit." He shudders.

I roll my eyes at him. "I will have you know that these clothes were in my closet."

"Perhaps, but they're surely meant to be worn separately. Together, they make you look like a turd with spindly legs."

I wedge my index and middle fingers together and flip my blond friend off.

The male settles back in his chair with a grin. "I've decided I will become your stylist since you clearly cannot style yourself."

"I don't need a stylist." Elbow on the table, I snatch my glass up and tip it to my lips.

"All queens need a stylist," Sybille pitches in.

"Not a queen," I mutter, staring at the tangle of bare branches on the platter Lore's mother brought to the tavern an hour or so after I joined my friends there.

Arin sat with us for a while, and we conversed through Phoebus, who's become surprisingly fluent in Crow. After watching me polish off every pink berry with an amused curl of lip, she excused herself to help Connor with the Siorkahd's meal.

"*Yet,*" Sybille and Phoebus say in unison, both grinning like loons.

"Arin and I have begun . . ." Phoebus's lips clamp together.

"Begun?" I ask.

"Growing a lot more *beinnfrhal,*" Sybille finishes for him. "I mean, you *are* back, and you're like a beaver with that fruit. In whichever form it comes." She nods to my wine, which I start to lower.

And it strikes me that she hasn't reached for her cup more than once. "Speaking of drinking, why aren't you doing any of that?"

"I'm drinking." Phoebus demonstrates by picking up his cup and taking a large swig.

"I meant Syb."

My friends exchange a look, one that makes me bounce out of my slouch. Sky wine sloshes over the rim of my cup and drenches my sleeve, but I can hardly feel it over the clamor of my heart.

"Oh my Gods, are you—are you and Mattia—"

The grin that spreads over Sybille's mouth is so blinding that all her white teeth are on display. "It's early days still, but yes"—she presses her palm to her stomach—"I'm growing a little halfling."

Phoebus raises his hand to his mouth and mock-whispers to me, "Let's hope the babe gets Mattia's disposition and Syb's pilosity. The other way around would be disastrous."

Sybille snags one of the bare *beinnfrhal* branches and pitches it at Phoebus's head. It catches in his shoulder-length locks.

He plucks it out then tosses it back onto the platter. "Your maturity level is alarming, Syb."

She raises her chin and smirks, while I blink as though someone blew dust into my face.

When I finally manage to bang my stein down, I spring out of my chair and rush around the table to embrace my surreptitious friend. "When were you going to tell me?"

"Once Phoebus and I managed to make you creep out of your head. There was so much happening in there"—she taps my forehead gently—"that I didn't want to load it with more."

"Sorry for being so focused on myself." I kiss her cheek, then hug her to me once more. "I'm so happy for you." I suddenly pull away. "You're happy, right?" I cannot imagine that bringing a child into the world was planned.

"Unexpectedly so." She plumps up her breasts. "I mean, look at my rack. And my sex drive . . ." She waggles her brows. "Off. The. Charts."

"How about we stay off the subject of sex drives for those of us with blue nether regions?" Phoebus mumbles, glancing toward the bar at the dark-skinned Crow who said he was flattered but not in the right headspace for a relationship. "I still cannot believe he turned down no-strings-attached sex."

Sybille takes a branch and twirls it. "Pheebs, honey, you'd come with many strings. Even I can see them."

Though being away was no fault of mine, I hate that I've missed so much. A surprise pregnancy? Unrequited love?

I reach out and take Phoebus's hand then Sybille's and squeeze them so tight that I drag their attention back to me. "I've missed you two"—my voice grows so thick that I can hardly push out the end of my sentence—"so damn much."

My effusion puts a shimmer in my friends' eyes.

Phoebus sniffles loudly. After blotting his eyes on his sky-blue shirtsleeve, he pops out words that propel us out of our little moment.

Unsure I heard him correctly, I repeat his question slowly, "Did Meriam mention Shabbins don't menstruate?"

"Well, did she?"

I gape at my friend because one, *what*? And two . . . "This may come as a surprise, but Meriam and I did not discuss our monthlies—or lack thereof—during our imprisonment." After I've somewhat recovered from the shock of learning I will never bleed again, from there, I ask, "How do you know?"

"Books. When one isn't having much sex, one has much time to read." His tragic tone draws a smirk to Sybille's lips.

"Apparently *woe is me* is contagious." She stands. "I better get away before I'm contaminated." She grabs the empty jug of wine. "Kidding. Be right back. Just need to detour by the ladies' room because, though pea-sized, my newest tenant feels like six gold ingots have been heaped onto my bladder."

My lips finally adopt another shape than open-mouthed shock, and I laugh.

"Wow. *Finally*. We were worried Meriam forced you to give up your sense of humor to unlock your magic. You know, like a payment of sorts. I mean, we were ready to remain your friends, because *blood magic*." She winks. "But we may have invited you to hang less."

I bark out another laugh and shake my head. "I'll have you both know no trade was required. My sense of humor just needed a little dusting off after spending so much time underground. Didn't have many people to be ridiculous with."

The amused glint in Sybille's eyes dampens.

"Nope. I don't want pity." I shake my head. "Besides, I had some *not so terrible* times down there." I give those better moments room to grow and cast shadows over the *not so good* ones.

Phoebus sucks in a breath. "Were we almost replaced with Justus and Meriam?"

"Oh, definitely not. Those two have a very limited repertoire of jokes."

Phoebus shrugs, "She transformed your mother into your favorite animal, so she must have a little sense of humor, piccolo serpens."

As I roll my eyes, Sybille smacks her chest with her palm. "Thank the Cauldron. Phoebus and I were genuinely worried. It's not every day you get to be besties with a queen."

"I'm not yet *that*."

Phoebus gives my hand a squeeze before letting go to snatch his wine goblet. "Sweets, you're the fucking Princess of Shabbe and the king's mate. You do realize it's a question of seconds before Lorcan gets on one smoky knee and presents you with—" A glare from Syb makes him cough. "With his deepest love," he ends up saying.

"Okay . . . what the underworld are you two not telling me?"

"Nothing," they say in unison. Then Syb presses her hand into her abdomen and reiterates, rather loudly, that she will wet herself if she doesn't hurry.

I stare at Phoebus pointedly. "Talk."

"About?" Phoebus is studying his silver stein as though he intends on reproducing its shape during one of his stone carving sessions with Reid.

When he sees Reid again, that is, since Reid is in Shabbe with Mamma. I mean, Agrippina.

"The weather seems more clement this—oh, fuck." His wide green eyes are fixed on the doorway.

I turn in my seat because I sense we're no longer discussing Lore's aptitude for meteorology. "Did Syb not make it?"

I freeze when my gaze lands on the two men standing in the doorway of the Sky Tavern.

CHAPTER 53

I get up so quickly that I bang my knee into the table. "Connor?" I try to speak his name calmly but it comes out brashly.

He steps out from behind the bar. "*Tà*, Fallon?"

"Please escort Antoni back out of the Sky Kingdom."

Mattia gasps. "What's gotten into you? It's Antoni."

My jaw ticks from how hard I clench my molars. "Antoni's no longer welcome within these walls."

Connor regards me for a long second before closing in on Antoni whose eyes cut to mine.

My heartbeats spring against my ribs, quick like wildling arrows.

Phoebus curls his arm around my waist. "You've some nerve to show up here, Greco."

Connor nods to the hallway, but Antoni stands his ground. "I came to apologize." He tips up a chin smooth from a fresh shave.

Although I want him out of my sight, away from my mate, I'm glad to see he didn't spend his night on the street. "Has he been searched for weapons?"

The five Crows wetting their beaks in pints all glance up at Antoni. Even Mattia pivots to give his friend a once-over.

"I carry no obsidian but I do have a knife." Antoni holds one palm aloft to keep the shifters from attacking, then lowers the other to his waist and unsheathes a sharp blade that glints silver.

"You don't think he came to murder Lore here, in his own home?" Phoebus's breath smacks the shell of my ear.

Before my friend's imagination can birth a riot, I say, "No."

Mattia grips Antoni's rigid shoulder. "He needs a safe place to land and regain his strength, Fallon."

"I'll arrange for a house to be put at his disposal. Anywhere in Luce. But not here."

Mattia runs a hand through his shaggy blond mane. "Fallon, be reasonable. The streets of Luce aren't safe."

"Do *not* tell me to be reasonable, Mattia." My fingers are clenched into fists that tighten when Antoni has the audacity to shake his head in disappointment and regard me with the same iciness as the night I turned down his advances to pursue Dante.

How can he be disappointed? He wants my mate dead, and he's fucking surprised I want to pitch him outside these castle walls?

"Tarespagia belongs to the Crows," I say. "It's safe."

Mattia snorts. "There are uprisings. Homes are being looted and burned by the humans. The High Fae are setting sail in droves to Tarecuori and to Glace. Everyone is trying to get out, and you want to send him *there*?" The blond halfling's gaze settles on his friend's hands, on the bare nailbeds wrapped around his dagger's sheath. "Hasn't he suffered enough?"

"Where does your allegiance lie, Mattia?" Even though my blood feels pressurized, my stance is astoundingly steady.

"What is going on out here?" Sybille, who's returned from the loo, carves across the tavern to her sailor whose waist she encircles with a thin arm.

"Mattia?" I hold his confused blue stare. "Your allegiance . . . where does it lie?"

"With Lorcan Ríhbiadh and the Crows. What sort of question is that?"

"Then you're welcome to stay; Antoni's not."

Mattia gasps. "He let you live under *his* roof when you returned to the Fae Lands, Fal."

"Because I didn't wish to bury a knife in his throat."

Mattia pales, his eyes whipping to Antoni's stony profile, and then he's taking a step back. "You wish to bury a knife in Fallon's throat?"

"No."

The blond's thick eyebrows knit on his tall forehead. "Then I don't—"

Sybille pulls him aside to explain all I told her.

As the silence festers, I slide my teeth. "Why come here, Antoni?"

"I came to have a discussion with Lorcan. And I—"

"No."

"—will leave after he and I—"

"No."

"—talk. I wasn't aware audiences with the Sky King went through you now, Fal."

"I will let him know that you wish to speak to him. If he cares for a conversation, he'll seek you out. Can someone please fucking fly Antoni out of the castle?"

I start to turn, but Antoni's callous laughter stops me. "How unforgiving you've become."

"That's unfair."

"Is it?"

I turn my head so fast in his direction that my neck cracks. "I saved you, Antoni, but now I choose to save my mate and our people."

"I didn't come here to murder anyone. If you don't believe me, feed me salt, Fallon."

"You may have decided it was wiser to align yourself with Lore for now, but what happens once the war is over?"

"I don't know." He sheathes his dagger. "Maybe I'll buy a boat and live on a part of the ocean that's under no one's jurisdiction."

Or maybe you will plant an obsidian blade through my mate's back.

I hear I'm missing quite the showdown, Behach Éan.

I snap walls up around my thoughts before Lore can catch the scene that still haunts me. He may know Antoni loathes him, but I'd prefer he didn't find out about the sea captain's design on Luce.

You're not missing a thing. I glance around the Sky Tavern for a swirl of smoke or feathers, but the air remains clear and motionless save for the heated breaths escaping from my flaring nostrils.

Are you certain, mo khrà?

Yep. Just stay at your meeting. I've got mine handled.

"Will someone please inform Lorcan Ríhbiadh that I wish to speak with him?" Antoni huffs.

"Fallon said no," Connor replies. "Come. I will fly out."

"I wasn't aware Dante's queen held so much clout amongst Crows."

"I am *not* Dante's queen," I bite out.

"I beg to differ. After all, I *was* present at the nuptials."

The Crows in attendance shift their gazes toward me, as though Antoni has instilled doubt in their minds as to whether I can be trusted.

"By all means"—I fling my arm in a wide arc—"since you *were* there, regale everyone with the story of how I was forced to bind my blood with a fucking lunatic to keep you from losing your tongue and Gods only know what other limbs Dante would've hacked off." The anger makes my words blister the tension-filled air. "Or better yet, tell them how I unchained you from a wall and painted gills on your throat so you wouldn't fucking drown after they left you behind."

Antoni's eyes twitch.

"Even though you want to put an end to my mate's reign, I saved you. So don't come in here and accuse me of cavorting with the enemy, because I. Fucking. Despise. Dante Regio."

Shadows slink around my shoulders, my neck. They tip my head up and sweep across my trembling jaw. ***Take a breath, my love.***

I told you to stay away, I grumble.

And miss out on my mate's formidable outburst?

I give him a pointed look, which only makes his smoke curl around my body and gather me close.

What has that man done to you, Behach Éan? Lore's eyes rake over my rigid features.

Nothing. He's done nothing to me. I just want him gone.

You saved him yesterday.

I roll my lips.

What *did that male do to you?*

I close my eyes because if I tell Lore what Antoni did to me . . . or rather said to me, it's only his carcass that will be carried out of the Sky Kingdom.

Tell me.

A tear rolls down my cheek. I sweep my lashes low to clear my eyesight. Though Antoni tried to look out for me, though he lost his nails because of me, I cannot condone what he confessed, because in the end, I will always choose my mate. ***He wants you dead, Lore.***

CHAPTER 54

The second the confession flocks from my mind, I close my eyes to lock out whatever retribution Lore has in store for Antoni.

Open your eyes, mo khrà.

I prefer to keep them closed. More tears sneak down my cheeks.

Do you believe Greco capable of change?

I will not risk your life, Lore.

I repeat . . . do you believe Greco capable of change?

My lids reel up. ***Do you think I've gone deaf? Do you think Meriam made me trade both my hearing and sense of humor for magic?***

A crooked smile quirks his ghostly mouth. ***Though I am curious as to the root of that thought, no, Fallon, I don't find you lacking in any way.***

My throat is so tight it hurts to swallow. ***I don't know. All I know is that he wishes monarchies were abolished.***

A quixotic thought. Lore presses my hair behind my ears, tucking it away from my wet cheeks. ***I lived in a time when Luce was divided amongst tribes. It was a lawless place full of violence that benefited the greedy and forsook the needy. Even the Regios' dominion beat a fractured empire.***

I catch a glimpse of a mountain road littered with tiny bodies whose limbs and heads are turned at awry angles. Of a wooden house engulfed in flames. Of the shrill cries of a young man bursting from the flames like an avenging angel, the limp body of a dark-haired woman clutched in his arms.

I see him fall to his knees, black hair flopping across his brow as he presses his forehead to the woman's motionless chest. I hear him whisper, *She's dead, Lorcan.* Right as he lifts his face and fixes me with his familiar black eyes, Lore carries me out of his memory.

Who was that woman? I sound breathless, as though I'd run out of that house alongside my father.

That was your grandmother. His spectral fingers stroke up and down my spine. ***Faeries set our village on fire. By the time we saw the flames rise from the mountain pastures, the Fae had slaughtered our younger brothers and sisters, done unpardonable things to our mothers.*** The chill of his shadows sinks beneath my own flesh. ***Forgive me,*** he murmurs. ***I shouldn't have subjected you to these memories, but I wanted you to see that the world was not a better place before I sought out the first Shabbin Queen and begged her for help.*** He uncoils himself from around my body and turns the full force of his citrine stare on the sea captain.

I hug myself to counter the chill brought on by the sight of those tiny, broken bodies and my father's haunted eyes. ***What will you do to Antoni?***

I'll hear him out, then escort him outside my castle.

So you're not going to kill him?

If I killed every soul who currently wished me dead, I'd be ruling over a kingdom of corpses.

My merciful king.

I wasn't so merciful the night you were taken, Fallon. I was a monster. The winged Demon King the Fae wove into their folklore to frighten their babes.

I try to reach out and touch him but he's already drifted away.

Connor nods to the dusky hallway. "Mórrgaht says yes to meeting. Imogen bring you to him."

I catch the flash of surprise on Antoni's face, but it's soon replaced by suspicion. Does he believe he's being led to his execution?

To defuse whatever ill-intent lingers in the back of his mind, I say, "He's going to let you live, Antoni."

The brown-haired male stops mid-pivot and stares at me from

across the tavern. After a long beat, he inclines his head toward me. "Thank you."

"I've nothing to do with his clemency."

And then he's gone, and Phoebus is standing before me, eyes wide and worried. "What the underworld happened in those tunnels?"

"Didn't I say enough?"

"No, Fallon, you've said nothing about them. Well, besides what you *just* said now, but until Antoni arrived, you've clammed up every time Syb and I have tried to wheedle out the details of your imprisonment."

"I made it out alive. Everything else I prefer to put out of my mind for now." I run my hands down my face.

"Put it into *our* minds. Let us share the burden. That's what friends are for."

"By pitching it into your minds, I'll only be keeping those dark days alive. Let me forget them. For now. Once the war is over, if you and Syb still care to know all, I will tell you all, but for now, help me forget."

He slides his arms around my shoulders and tugs me into his chest. "Fine. Let's get plastered. Syb, oh favorite tavern maiden, fetch us an extra large jug of Sky wine, will you?"

"I thought I was your favorite tavern maiden," I mumble against his blue shirt.

"You, dear Fallon, are my favorite Crow wen—witch."

A smile digs into my cheeks. "Did you just call me a wench?"

"Nope. I said *witch*."

"I heard wench." Syb, expert delegator, watches Mattia head over to the bar to grab a jug. "I cannot wait for Fallon to share your newest pet name with her mate." She rubs her hands together.

Phoebus snorts. "Perhaps she should report it to Connor. You know, have *him* punish me."

I bark out a laugh.

Phoebus holds me tighter, pressing his cheek into the top of my head. I link my hands around his waist and return his hug.

"Thank you," I murmur.

"For what, Picolina?"

"For loving me unconditionally."

"It's part of the friendship manifesto I'm penning. Remember?"

My ribs tighten as though a full-grown Crow was sitting on my chest. A stone one.

"You're obviously required to love us back unconditionally"—Syb pops my ass—"wench. I mean, witch." She snickers.

"Oh, Lore?" Phoebus fake-hollers. "Did you hear what Sybille just called your mate?"

"First off, you said it before me, Pheebs. Secondly, I'm almost his favorite person."

"You're really no one's favorite person, Syb," he teases.

Another wave of laughter surges from my chest, but it crashes over me in time with a wave of tears because, though my mother healed my superficial wounds, I'm still riddled with tiny cracks that will end up sinking me if I don't find a way to plug them up, and quickly at that.

I cannot afford to sink.

I need to swim.

"YOU'LL GET in the water here. And then you'll direct your mother toward the trench." My father, whose reddened eyes speak of another sleepless night, taps an area of the ocean that borders the Racoccin woods, the last piece of land under Crow dominion. "I attached your skirt to a tree trunk. When I left, your mother was circling the waters beside the tree. Erwin has stayed behind to keep track of her."

The heart cramps brought on by too much emotion, too little sleep, and too much wine, ease at the mention that Min—my mother is waiting for me.

"I'll carry you—" My father looks up from the map to glower at Lore, who's been pacing his library at such a frenetic pace that his shadows never firm. "No. *I* will."

Lore must growl something because Cathal narrows his eyes.

"Consider yourself lucky I'm allowing you to come at all." Another beat of silence. "I know where you fell, too, Mórrgaht. I was there when you fucking flew in front of me to take that arrow. Which was fucking stupid, by the way."

I blink at the two of them.

My father tosses his large hand in the air. "It was stupid because a giant piece of obsidian would've caught on the coral barrier, not slipped right past it like your puny iron bird."

If I weren't awash with nerves, I may have cracked a smile at hearing my father describe Lore as puny but my cheeks are incapable of doing much else than pump air in and out of my mouth. I'm not even in the water and I'm already hyperventilating. I need to calm down.

We're not doing it.

Deep breath in. Deep breath out. ***We are so doing it.***

Look at you.

Look at **you.**

Fallon, he growls.

Let's go retrieve your puny bird, **Lore.**

My crack at him makes him still his pacing. ***I should've let your father be on the receiving end of that arrow. At least then his sense of humor wouldn't be rubbing off on you.***

I interrupt my breathing exercise to grin.

Cathal frowns at my smile, then shakes his head and fishes something from his trouser pocket. "Here." He dangles a leather cord fitted with a seashell. "Your mother used to wear one like this around her neck so she could prick her fingers at will."

I stare at his gift, then quickly gather my hair so he can drop it over my head. He tightens the slipknots until the shell rests in the hollow of my throat. "Thank you, Dádhi."

My father grunts. "It's no iron blade."

Apparently, my father doesn't know what to do with *thank-yous*.

"Ready?" he asks, stormy gaze locked on the seashell.

I smooth my hands down the black bodysuit I've donned for the occasion, then palm the pointy seashell and nod. "I'm ready."

But am I?

CHAPTER 55

The instant hot-pink scales carve through the agitated surface of the dawn-lit ocean, my heart thumps a little easier. The waters may teem with Faerie patrols, but with my mother at my side, as well as my father and Lore, I'll fear nothing.

Even though I don't believe in Faerie Gods, I do believe in the Cauldron. "You who made the Crows, please don't unmake them," I murmur into the gusts of wind that slap the ocean, carrying its briny scent into the still-dark air.

Between the squall Lore has fashioned that shakes the woods, and the time of day, even purebloods will not detect our little group. As my father soars closer to the ocean's surface, the delegation that flew from Monteluce with us rockets toward the cloud canopy, vanishing behind the wooly whiteness.

This is it. My head spins with elation while my stomach whirls with nerves. *And* wine. Gods, I really should've gone easier on the wine. Attempting to press back the liquid sloshing around my stomach, I prick three fingers on my seashell and drag them across my throat like Justus taught me.

Lore, who didn't speak a word during the two-hour trek, tracks my fingers' movement. ***How long will your blood-gills last?***

A long time since I'm of Meriam's line.

His mood worsens at the mention of Meriam. Oh, the reunion that'll be . . .

The second I feel my spell fading, Lore, I'll swim back to the surface and repaint my neck.

The surface will be full of bloody Faeries.

Even though he surely uses *bloody* as an invective and not a descriptor, the backs of my lids redden with a sea of blood upon which float headless bodies.

My father caws, which thankfully puts an end to my gory imaginings. The sound also makes Minimus stick his—*her* tusk out of the water.

Minimus is your mother. Your. Mother, Fallon. He *is a* she. *And she is not actually a mareserpens at all.*

Or that is all she is, that other small voice of mine whispers.

I shush that voice because pessimism has never been my style. I keep my gaze fixed on her large onyx ones.

My father lands, then tucks his wings. Though I've no need to lock air inside my lungs, instinct makes me gulp in a breath. My mother dives, then reappears a moment later right beside my father's flank.

Just like when I would unmount Furia, I toss my leg over his spine and slide off his back. The water is shockingly warm against my chilled skin.

As I splash over toward my waiting serpent, my father melts into his shadowy form and sinks. Since he cannot hold his shape very long, he's soon back in feathers and floating upward like a cork, his frustration quaking the liquid expanse that's as dark as a pot of ink.

The second you're whole, I demand sunshine for days, Lore.

His shadows wrap around me. ***Once I'm whole, I will withdraw my clouds and bake our kingdom to a crisp. Your every wish will be my command.***

I almost amend my request to ask him to roast Luce no matter the day's outcome, but that would reveal doubt, and I'm on a doubt-banishing crusade.

My mother pushes her head against my neck and sniffs. And then her forked black tongue unspools and licks across my skin.

Shoot. Had the blood absorbed? I stick my head underwater. When

I feel air sweep through the skin she's laved, the tension in my lungs and heart slacken.

My serpent dips her nose into the water and flicks her tongue along the pads of my punctured fingers. No wound gets past her.

As her magical saliva closes the tiny wounds, my mind floods with the sight of multi-hued beasts swimming around what resembles a Tarecuorin avenue hemmed in with coral shelves that glimmer as though darned with gems. My vision tunnels in on a white marble statue. Though I've seen Dante's mother only once up close—the day Dante graduated from Scola Cuori—I recognize her marble likeness immediately.

The vision fades, and I'm back in the careening surf that glimmers only with my mother's scales and my father's beak and claws.

That's where I fell. Show Daya.

Remembering what Lore told me about how Shabbins can communicate telepathically with serpents, I take her large face between my palms and stare so deep into her black eyes that my vision goes a little blurry. I replay Lore's memory, making sure to stress the marble statue.

After I blink back into the here and now, Minim—Daya doesn't magically nod, but she pivots, and then she waits. And waits.

Grab ahold of her, Behach Éan.

I paddle closer and seize her huge tusk. When she senses I'm securely connected to her, she whips her tail and pitches us into the deep. As we dart through schools of iridescent fish that scatter like the embers of fireworks, my nausea and nerves jump ship and in their place blossoms wonder.

Though the light thins the deeper we swim, the sea life somehow brightens, and not only with other serpents, but with corals that mimic our islands, rainbow-hued like the houses of Tarecuori and Tarelexo.

Gods, if I'd known what wonders lay beneath the blue, I would've spent my last ten summers exploring the ocean. I'm not sure how long we swim, but my fingers numb from my snug grip. I remove one hand and stretch it out, then clasp her tusk and repeat the stretch with my other hand.

Daya slows.

Once my ten fingers overlap, I shape the word, "Go."

She seems loathe to whip her tail. It strikes me that every time I've used that command in the past, it was to make her leave me.

I stare into her eyes and ferry a picture of myself strapped to her tusk like a piece of seaweed, gliding toward the trench. She chuffs like a horse, streaming tiny bubbles through her slitted nostrils, and then she whirls and flaps her fins. Although as thin and delicate as sea fans, they move us forward.

How much farther, Lore?

We're almost there.

I crane my neck, expecting to see gondola hulls crosshatch the surface, but either it's too early, or the storm is keeping the Fae home, because no boats, from what I can see and hear, are tearing across Filiaserpens.

I refocus on the sea floor. ***Will you be able to gauge the depth of your crow?***

Once we reach the trench, yes. The gloominess in Lorcan's tone coats my skin in goosebumps and dims my awe. ***How's your air supply?***

Perfect.

As silence settles around us again, I cannot help but wonder how I'll know when my magic stops working—will my skin simply zipper up, or will the filtration thin before vanishing?

I'm of Meriam's line, I reassure myself, *and Meriam is an almighty sorceress.* I decide that today's not the day I find out how long I can breathe underwater.

Mind made, I relax. Well, I relax as much as one about to explore the furthest reaches of our world can.

To keep my mind off my creeping nerves, I decide to broach a subject that was on my mind the better half of yesterday. ***Tell me what you and Antoni discussed.***

Lore's answer is slow to come, as though he's weighing the pros and cons of sharing it with me. ***His part in the future governing of Luce. The sea captain wants power.***

My eyebrows twist. ***He flat-out confessed this?***

Fallon, we're mates. I can see into your mind. Antoni knew that it was a question of days until I sought him out to have a little discussion of my own on the subject of his allegiance. He knew that coming to me was the only way he'd get to live out his days without forever looking

over his shoulder. With a sigh, he adds, ***I may loathe the male for coveting you, Little Bird, but as far as mortal men go, he's quick-witted and cunning.***

What did he come to you with?

A bargain.

One you accepted?

I did. The male suggested returning to the tunnels with Mattia and blasting them. The entire grid of them.

This draws my eyes wider. ***At what price?***

He wants an official seat in the Siorkahd.

So he gets the political power he so longs for . . .

Once he crumbles every last tunnel.

He knows that he cannot kill Dante, right?

He does.

I wonder how long this endeavor will take him.

Mattia and Gabriele have already blasted through all those under Monteluce. If Dante wants to reach Tarecuori, he'll have to emerge in the jungle and scale my mountain. Lore sounds like a cat playing with a mouse.

Can you please make sure to watch your back though? Like you said, Antoni's cunning.

Worry not, Behach Éan.

The desire to roll my eyes is really strong. How does he expect me *not* to worry? His back was stabbed once before.

By a friend. Antoni's no friend, nor has he ever pretended to be. After a beat, he adds, ***Contenders for my throne, my love, never get to see my back; they barely get to glimpse my front before they taste my shadows.***

I'm still not reassured, and I doubt I will be until the Cauldron allows me to curse-break. The thought yanks my mind off one foe and places it on another. I think of the plan my grandfather wants to enact once Lore is whole and desperately attempt to think of another, one that will not transform my mate to iron, but get distracted by the sight before me.

Against the pitch-blackness of a steep drop, amidst a knot of bright scaled bodies, glows the white marble likeness of Dante's mother.

We've arrived.

CHAPTER 56

My mother swims us to the statue before coming to a complete stop. We begin to sink into the trench, but a flick of her tail makes us rise back to the statue's level. A divinely warm current wraps around my bare legs and arms, smoothing away the chills that pebble my skin.

Many serpents approach, curiosity alight in their huge ebony eyes. The older ones nudge me with their long noses, the younger ones, with their ivory nubs. All collect a resounding hiss from my protective mother. I pat her long, scarred neck, and press a kiss to one of the bands of white.

The feel of the rubbery skin makes me wonder if, in human form, she'll wear the mutilations inflicted by Nonna the day I fell into the canal. I briskly shake off this deliberation. I need to focus on the reason I'm hovering over the infamous furrow that's said to be the resting place of many a dead Lucin dissident.

You won't find any corpses.

I glance toward Lore, whose golden eyes must be shut because they don't gleam amongst his shadows. ***Throughout the centuries, serpents have carried bodies that fall into Mareluce to Shabbin shores for healing. Even when there's no healing to be had.***

Though Meriam mentioned this the day of my unbinding, I'm glad for Lore's confirmation. How I hate that I fell for yet another lie propagated by the Regio regime. The Crows cannot rule this land soon enough.

Can you feel your crow?

Silence.

Lore? I press away the curious juveniles oblivious to Zendaya's hissing to peer through the dark water for the elusive shadow of my mate. ***Lore, your crow?***

When he fails to answer me—*again*—my pulse begins to slam against my ribs. Min—My mother senses my disquiet but misinterprets it because she cages me between the coils of her huge body. I stroke her before she snatches me away from the trench and my mission.

Lore, if you don't answer me right this minute, I'll—

I'm here.

Glad to hear it, but I'll be even gladder once you tell me where your missing crow fell.

We're going back.

What?

Show your mother the spot where Cathal dropped you off.

What?!

Is my voice not reaching your ears, what with your hundreds of new reptilian friends?

I give the cheek of a little serpent who managed to squeeze his head between Zendaya's makeshift fence a quick pat before pushing him away so his neck doesn't get crushed. ***What the underworld are you going on about?***

My crow cannot be retrieved at the moment. Once we free Shabbe, we'll get Priya to help.

How can my great-grandmother help but I cannot?

Because, Fallon, she knows many spells. Perhaps she'll know one to make iron rise to the surface.

How deep did you fall?

Drop it.

I will absolutely not ***drop it. I didn't come all this way—***

We came. We saw. And now we're leaving.

I leap into his head and catch the vision a second before he pitches me out.

Don't even think about it, Fallon.

But just like the day I freed his last crow from the galleon, I do more than think about it. I call to my mother with my eyes, but she's too busy fending off her brethren to take notice of me.

Even if your clever gills hold, the heat will melt your skin.

You don't know that. I kick up and seize her tusk to tip her face toward mine. The second I have her attention, I pour the image of the crevasse upon which Lore teeters—the one spurting so much steam that the waters surrounding it tremble.

Why do you think no serpents have fished me out?

Because they're no fan of warm baths. But guess what? I am. The steamier the better.

For a moment, I think I've convinced him because he says nothing, but then he inserts himself between my mother and me, a scowl carving up his shadows. ***We're not fucking talking about a trip to the Baths, mo khrà.***

I bite my lip. Lore's battering pulse calms. He must assume I'm rethinking my decision of approaching the submarine volcano, but that isn't *at all* the direction of my thoughts.

I kick up and out of my mother's scaled eddies, then grab ahold of the Queen Mother's extra large and pointy marble ear and hang there a moment. I'm still unsure how deep Lore's crow rests, but if I follow the hot stream downward, I'm bound to come upon it.

Hand over hand, I scale down Mamma Regio's face.

Fallon?

Yes? I snap up walls around my plan and focus very hard on the ledge below the one I'm dangling from.

You wouldn't be thinking of defying me now, would you?

I snort, which flings little bubbles into my eyes. ***Of course not. I'm just enjoying the view of so many jewels. Is that a pearl necklace?***

I shoot to the next ledge toward the glimmering strand of white beads wrapped around a sea fan that is, in fact, a gorgeous pearl necklace. I unwrap it from around the purple fan, careful not to injure the coral, and then I wrap it around the strap of my bodysuit for safekeeping.

I'll need to collect many more necklaces to build a fishing rod like the one I wove from long grass to hook Lore out of that ravine. Sure, the grass snapped, but I did succeed in snaring the arrow and dislodging it. Which is my goal today.

I travel down the ledge and pick up another necklace. I knot it with the pearls. Serpents approach and watch me collecting jewels. I suddenly worry they'll think I'm stealing from them. After all, these are their treasures. When a turquoise serpent swims fast toward me, head inclined, tusk aimed straight at my chest, my fingers slacken on the necklaces. Both drift to the fan.

He stops a millimeter away from me, a long chain shimmering around his tusk. He nudges my hand, and I suddenly understand that he didn't come to gore me but to gift me another necklace.

My heart warms for these extraordinary beings. I roll it off his tusk and he swims away. And then I pluck the ones I'd released and tie all three together.

Another serpent nudges my shoulder with a diamond bracelet. I take it and add it to my line.

If a trunk-load of jewels is what you desire, Fallon, I will have the most magnificent ones crafted for you out of stones that have never touched another person's skin, but please, let's go before your air supply fails.

My heart pulses out a deep beat that he remembers my silly longing to possess new things. ***My air supply is fine. Besides, there are so many pretty things down here, and they're all free for the taking.***

My mother shoulders past two other serpents who've carried riches up for me. Around her tusk is hooked an old anchor chain, minus the anchor. I grin at her offering. *Way to one-up everyone else, Mamma.*

After I've relieved her of the rusted chain, she tilts her head up almost haughtily, and a closed-lipped laugh bubbles through me.

As I bind the necklaces to the anchorless chain, I hear Lore curse. I'm guessing he's realized a desperate need to accessorize my outfits isn't at the root of my gem-picking.

Before you shriek at me, Your Highness, think back on the ravine and how my deviousness paid off. I hear him count. ***Calculating the length of my chain?*** I ask sweetly, entirely aware that the reason behind his low tally has nothing to do with measurements and everything to do with his attempt at easing his temper before he snaps my head off.

I swear, Little Bird . . .

To love and to cherish me, according to the Cauldron's holy ordi-

nance—or Mórrigan's—for better and for worse, for richer and for poorer, in iron, shadows or flesh, till the end of time?

What?

Sorry. Thought you were practicing your vows for our upcoming nuptials.

His golden eyes vanish before reappearing in a very narrowed form.

Unless you no longer care to marry me?

I may not have any mate left to marry if you toss yourself on an underwater pyre.

I snort at his dramatics. ***You do realize I'll be tossing this superb chain, not my body, down to your crow.***

He goes back to his slow counting. ***Your father's asking what's taking so long. Should I inform him of your half-baked plan?***

Half-baked? Gods, the male can be surly when things don't go *his* way. ***I suggest you tell him Daya is giving me a tour of her lair. Unless you want me fishing*** his ***immobilized crow out of the trench after I'm done gathering yours.***

Thanks to my army of obliging serpents, I'm soon equipped with the longest, sturdiest, and prettiest fishing line in the history of fishing lines. I hold it up, admiring my handiwork. ***Long enough, Lore, or should I add to it?***

He grunts.

I press my lips together at his mulishness. ***You're being very unhelpful right now.***

It'll forever be too short for my taste.

I sigh and begin to shape a reassurance but he cuts me off.

If this doesn't work, Little Bird, I'll be swimming you straight up.

It'll work. I toss the chain to the next ledge and let it drag me down, then repeat the process three more times. ***You must start manifesting what you want instead of miring yourself in negativity.*** My self-help suggestion is met with such booming silence that a smile hooks my lips. ***Are you contemplating begging the Cauldron to find you a new mate?***

I don't beg.

I roll my eyes and toss my rod to the next coral-coated ledge. ***Let me rephrase myself: will you*** appeal ***to the Cauldron for a new mate once this is over?***

No. Not even if your skin puddles off your bones.

I wrinkle my nose. ***Well, that's a foul image I did not need.***

The light thins the deeper I descend, and the water grows balmier. The ocean presses against my ears, which I must pop with greater frequency. By the fifth ledge, the serpents stop following. Except my mother. She hasn't left my side even though she's growing more and more restless, much like my mate.

I'm about to pitch my length of chain over yet another ledge when she smacks into me to keep me from going any lower. I try to capture her attention to show her the iron crow, but she keeps shaking her head and staring frenziedly around. If Lore doesn't foil my mission, she might.

How much deeper, Lore?

Once your toes begin to blister, you should be able to spot me.

Funny. I glare into the dark water around me for his familiar metallic stare, but it's either turned away from me, or my mate's slinked off somewhere.

A fight breaks out above me between two serpents. Min—My mother tips her head up. I use the distraction to lower myself and my chain. The moment she realizes I've slipped past her, she releases a keening whine and flicks her tail, but the temperature of the water must grow too harsh for her because she darts backward as though she's hit a ward.

Her round eyes grow rounder, her whining, louder. She dashes toward me and almost manages to snare my suit with her tusk, but I drop into a crouch and she misses. She looses another deep whine that seems to vibrate the entire ocean.

Are you still with me, Lore?

Where else would I fucking be, Behach Éan? he mutters as his shadows skim my skin like a cooling balm.

I climb down two more ledges before the heat becomes a little much, even for the scalding bath-lover in me. My eyeballs sting so hard from the salt and torrid temperature that I can barely keep my lids raised. Before Lore can use my discomfort to his advantage, I begin to hum a bawdy tavern song over my mother's echoing whines.

I peer over the ledge and drop my chain, then hoist my body down. Though I never stuck a limb into Marcello's soup pot, I'm guessing this must be pretty close to what it feels like.

My foot hits something that does not feel like coral, and I wince, because, yeah . . . not coral. My wince turns into a scowl when I realize what I stepped on—a fisherman's cage. I crouch beside it, my scowl deepening when I spot three fish floating inside, eyes milky like the rotten ones they would sell on the Tarelexian wharf.

I slide my lips together and lower my lids a teensy bit more, the sulfurous scent of death and volcano punching up my nose.

I smell blood.

I nicked my foot on this stupid cage. I hate cages.

Show me your foot.

My foot's fine. I grip the wiry edges of the cage entrance and pull to create a wider gap, then slide my arm through carefully and remove the dead fish. Their bodies drift up the trench like glittering lanterns.

I know I cannot save all animals, but I hate that these fish died for nothing.

How's your air?

Fine.

Like your foot?

I lower my gaze to my throbbing foot, then regard the cage again, my eyebrows tilting toward one another as an idea roots itself inside my head. I flip the cage over so that the opening faces downward, then loop my chain through the metal trellis and secure it.

And then I reel it up to display my new-and-much-improved crow-fishing contraption. Lore's eyes twinkle, and I think it's with hope. I think he's starting to believe he'll be whole today. My throat closes with emotion, and I smile at him. When my throat clenches again, this time not with emotion, my smile teeters.

Your endeavor is creative. I'll give you that much.

I force my lips to bend, and my heart to slow. My gills' efficacy may be waning, but they're still sifting oxygen.

While Lore scrutinizes my tool, I touch my bleeding toe and lift my finger to my neck to draw a line. The blood must disperse before breaching my skin because the air slinking into me remains reedy.

I must not dally.

CHAPTER 57

Before Lore can notice my distress, I seize my cage and toss it onto the next ledge. When it lands, I follow it down. I wince again, this time because of the thickening heat.

Lore's shadows harden and back me up against the trench wall, swathing me in their coolness. Gods, he feels divine. ***This is as far as I'll let you go, Little Bird.***

Is it far enough, though?

Yes.

Because you won't let me go farther?

Because my crow is right there.

I glance over his hazy shoulder, and though the water shimmers with heat, it also shimmers with the silvery glint of a crow wedged between rock and coral.

My heart thunders.

My breathing shallows.

My fingers tighten around the chain that feels hot against my skin, like those earthen pots Defne would slide out from the hearth back at *Bottom*. I glance at the chain, then at the blisters bubbling on my palms. Oddly enough, they don't hurt. I squint to make sure they're really there, but get sidetracked by a strand of faceted emeralds.

So beautiful. Like Phoebus's eyes. Phoebus would love these.

I finger the stones, then carry them up to my face before getting sidetracked by more pretties. So many pretties. And all strung together like a jump rope. Gods, Sybille would've adored to own one like this when she was younger. She'd probably still love it.

Fallon? Lore's voice sounds as though it's coming from inside the bubbling crater.

I loop it around my neck for safekeeping but then become transfixed by how gorgeously it twinkles against my skin. ***I need to make Phoebus a jump rope or he'll be jealous.***

Fuck.

Don't tell me you want one, too? I slide my finger down his ice-cold chest that feels a lot like . . . pudding.

Pudding?

A smile quirks up my mouth. ***I love pudding.***

Up we go.

What? No. I need to . . . I frown, trying to remember why I'm standing in a ravine in the middle of the night.

A vision of a crow on a ledge slams into my mind.

Of a flimsy rod made of grass.

Of two birds becoming one.

The depth is messing with your mind, Fallon.

Depth?

This is no ravine; this is Filiaserpens.

My eyes grow wide with wonder. ***I'm in Filiaserpens?*** I shake my head. ***Apparently, it glows in the winter. La-zahhhhhh . . .***

Lazarus?

Yes. Him. He said jellies come and—or was it jewels? Wait. Did I steal all the jewels?

No. You left plenty.

Stealing is bad.

You were borrowing them.

For?

For nothing. He wraps me up, and it feels as though I've fallen facefirst into a vat of churning ice-cream. ***Hold on to me.***

Is this my gelato dream? I really enjoyed that dream.

Lore's shadows morph into feathers. He flaps his great wings and carries us up. Or tries to. My cage gets stuck on a sea fan.

Pitch away your snare, mo khrà.

My . . . snare? Though my lids feel hooked to anchors, I manage to bat them up and stare around me.

The underwater world comes into sharp focus. Well, *blurry* focus. I suck in a breath except it's not a breath; it's scalding, salty water.

Lore flaps his great wings, but my chain must've gotten stuck because we don't rise. Instead, we bang into a rocky outcropping. ***Fallon, drop the damn snare.***

I give it a hard tug but it's stuck around my neck. ***I can't. Put me down. I'll unravel it.***

Though he growls and grunts, he sets me down. Lungs burning with a need for crisp air, I dig my unsteady fingers into a knot, attempting to pick the various chains apart. And I almost manage but get distracted by the sight of the cage swinging toward Lore's crow.

Merda. Lore!

What?!

The cage!

We both stare as the rusted netting skims the head of the coral that's keeping his crow from plummeting to the very bottom of the ocean. I yank on the chain, and the cage twirls, the opening aligning with Lore's crow.

My fingers freeze.

One foot. That is all that's keeping the cage from snagging Lore's crow.

One measly foot of chain.

Before Lore or my sanity can stop me, I spring off the ledge.

The cage drops, slamming down against Lore's crow.

The shock dislodges the coral head.

I jerk my body and kick my legs to stop sinking.

The cage pivots.

The coral rips, then lists and tumbles.

And so does Lore's crow.

CHAPTER 58

I sink back down. Even though the water is scalding, I pitch my lids wide and watch in trepidation and awe as the iron crow settles inside my cage.

Fallon! Lore's talons snare my arms. The second they click, he hisses and lets go.

My blood boils like when Meriam released my power.

My skin stings and my lungs tingle. Am I melting? I don't want to become a puddle.

I hate puddles.

I suddenly see myself hopping over foul-smelling ones back in Tarelexo to avoid the hem of my dresses dragging through the filth.

Fallon, get that chain off yourself. I cannot touch you as long as you're strapped to my crow.

Lore's voice springs my mind off puddles.

I blink, then gaze in awe because lodged inside my basket is his crow. ***Oh my Gods, I caught you, Lore!*** I laugh. ***I caught you!***

FALLON!!

I think he says more, but my mind begins to hum.

Like my ears.

Like my blood.

My lids begin to droop.

All of me begins to droop.

Something that feels like a giant fist wallops my chest. Hardens. Falls away.

I swear to fucking Mórrígan . . . That I will lock you up . . . In my fucking castle . . . For the rest of your bloody . . . Life.

I smile and skim my fingers against feathers which harden to metal under my fingertips. Weird.

This is the only time in my life . . . That I beg you . . . Not to touch me . . .

My lungs spasm, and I cough, except that drags wet salt down into my airway. I gag, then choke. ***Lore—I can't—breathe.***

A low, keening whine pierces my eardrums. Is Lore crying? He doesn't strike me as someone who ever weeps. The whining grows louder and brighter, like the light. The water's turning so clear that I spot bright pink.

So much pink.

My body becomes tangled in pink as though I've been gift wrapped in a ribbon.

A really large and muscular ribbon.

And scaly.

I skip my fingers over the scales, marveling at their softness, and then I marvel because the trench is growing smaller and smaller. My lungs expand so fast that they press painfully into my ribs. If my mother swims me to the surface any faster, they're going to splinter bone.

I close my eyes and concentrate on not passing out from the pain.

Lore? His name rolls through our mind link barely louder than a whisper. ***The cage?***

A beat of terrible silence echoes between us before he rasps, ***Still tied around your fucking neck.***

Though words are not made of air, especially ones spoken inside one's mind, Lore's answer feels like a deep inhale. ***And your***—everything inside of my body aches . . . everything outside, too—***crow?***

Still there, Little Bird. Still there.

Good, I whisper a second before the top of my head breaks the surface of Mareluce. I gasp, then black out from the sheer pain of oxygen biting my scorched lungs.

RAIN NEEDLES my face and salt splashes my mouth. I gag, then cough, but the coughing awakens a sharp burn that makes me hold as still as humanly possible.

I try to pry my lids open but fail. Through blistered lips, I sip in a tiny, cautious breath that burns like Fae-fire. I settle on inhaling through my nose, which hurts a smidge less. ***Lore?***

Yes. His voice sounds rife with nerves.

What's happening?

Daya is swimming you to safety.

The cage?

She's hooked it to her tusk.

Your crow?

Still inside, my love. Still inside.

He sounds like I feel—shattered.

Lore?

Rest, Behach Éan.

Has my skin puddled around my bones?

No.

Would you have kept loving me if it had?

I would love you in any form.

Even skinless?

With a quiet smile, he murmurs, ***You don't seem to mind me skinless.***

I grimace because his version of skinless is dark and smoky, whereas I'd have been bloody and bony.

Rest, Behach Éan. You need to rest.

I smile as I collapse back into oblivion.

A sweet one this time.

I'VE STOPPED MOVING, and though my bones ache, my lungs feel . . . I take a tentative breath. The air snakes down my throat like a sharp blade, then rubs against my insides like sandpaper. I guess they don't feel that much better.

I spread my fingers, which sink into something cold and grainy —sand?

Though my eyes feel full of honey, I manage to heft my lashes up a fraction. Above me sprawls a white sky, and against it, two pitch-black faces—one made of shadows, the other, of runny makeup.

I carry my hand up to my neck to feel for the chain, but my fingers encounter no beads, only dry skin and hardened, stretchy black material. "The—cage?" I croak. "Where's—the cage?" My voice is so scratchy it sounds as though it's clawing itself out of my mouth.

"*The cage*?" My father's complexion deepens, cutting a brighter contrast with the wan sky.

"Please tell me—it's here."

"Oh, it's here all right."

"And is Lore's crow—inside?"

My father's lips are wedged so tightly together that they slash up his furious face. "I have half a mind to pitch it back inside the ocean."

I prop myself up on my forearms, a myriad of aches exploding a little everywhere inside my body. "Why would you—do that?"

"Because he doesn't fucking deserve to be made whole. Not after he let you dive into a fucking submarine volcano that bubbled your fucking skin." If I hadn't realized my father was angry, his liberal use of the word *fuck* would definitely have alerted me to his mood. "Who knows what sort of damage it inflicted on your organs?"

I drop my gaze to my arms, expecting to find them covered in blisters, but my skin is as smooth as a babe's. Not even yesterday's bruises remain.

Once we were out of the Fae lands, your mother laid you out on a rock and licked the welts off your skin. And then she swam you to shore so we could tend to you.

Awe and tenderness plug my chest as I squint at the gray horizon, on the hunt for the magnificent sea dragon that happens to be related to me.

She's resting on the ocean floor. The journey and the healing took much out of her.

A heavy wash of guilt drenches my heart. "Where's the cage?"

Lore nods to the tree line behind us where four Crows in skin stand guard while several others cycle over them in feathers.

"Dádhi, you think you can help me walk to the trees?"

He purses his lips at first, as though peeved by my destination, but then he scrubs his giant hands down his face. Though he smudges his makeup some more, he also smudges his residual anger. I wouldn't call his face soft—I don't think Cathal Báeinach's face could ever be described as soft—but his expression has definitely eased.

Instead of setting me on my feet, he scoops me into his massive arms and props me against his thudding chest.

I don't complain. I'm not usually of the minimal effort mindset, but my body feels wretched. Perhaps the hot water really did braise some of my organs. I wrinkle my nose at the thought, then shake my head to clear it.

"Has the child been paid?" my father asks as we approach the swaying trees.

I frown. "Child?"

"We had to get a human child from Racocci and carry him to the beach to untangle the beads around your neck because metal is a conductor." He levels a glare Lore's way.

"Lore didn't tie it around my neck, Dádhi. I did that." I palm his bearded jaw to carry his attention to my face. "The same way I chose to retrieve his crow knowing there was a volcano."

"Well, he fucking shouldn't have let you!"

I sigh, sensing my father's in no mood to forget and forgive.

I'd understand if he never forgave me.

I pitch my gaze toward the roiling mass of shadows. ***Don't say that. You two are best friends.* Brothers. *He may not forget, but he'll forgive.***

If your skin had split open and your blood flowed . . . His shadows shudder, and his golden eyes extinguish for a long moment. ***You could've died.***

Huh. I'm rather happy I didn't contemplate this while diving into the Marelucin soup. Oblivion may not be such a terrible thing after all.

"The child was paid, Cathal. He bit into the gold piece because he couldn't believe it was real." Imogen smiles, which is such a rare occurrence that I'm momentarily transfixed by the curve of lip and white teeth.

"A gold piece to unknot beaded strands? You must've made a Crow devotee out of him."

"He was already rather fond of us," my father says. "Most humans are. The gold was for his silence. We prefer the Faeries keep believing Lore's crow lies in Filiaserpens."

"Took him close to an hour to untangle your little noose," Imogen says.

I rub my tender skin. ***Pliers or a knife would've been quicker.***

Do you really see me allowing someone to bring a sharp object near your body, mo khrà?

I suppose not.

"I hope you don't mind that I let him keep the strand of pearls, Fallon." Imogen gestures to the shimmering heap of chains and jewels. "Apparently his mother's very fond of sea beads."

"You should've given him all the necklaces, Imogen."

"*All* would've raised eyebrows; one shouldn't cause him or us any problems."

My father sets me down beside the rusted trap in which Lore's crow rests, one spread wing wedged inside, the other poking out. It's truly a wonder he didn't tip out in transit. Actually, it's not a wonder: one of his iron talons is tangled around the metal netting.

The arrow protruding from him has been reduced to a stubby piece of wood, but I manage to pinch it between my thumb and forefinger. When I attempt to drag it out, though, my fingers keep slipping off.

I flip the trap over, looking for the exit wound since it's the obsidian tip that needs to come out. The wood will just fall out of Lore once he's released from his steel mummification. With great regret, I find no exit wound. In the words of my great and mighty mate, *focà*.

I push my damp hair out of my eyes, streaking sand across my brow, then set the trap down on my crossed legs and pinch the stick poking out of the crow's belly anew. Minutes turn into a full half hour, and I'm no closer to freeing my mate. "I need fire and a metal skewer."

Planning on roasting me, mo khrà?

I tilt my head to stare up at him. His citrine eyes, for once, aren't on me. They're on that piece of him resting in my lap.

"I'm planning on burning the rotted wood and replacing it with a metal stalk to push out the obsidian tip lodged inside of you."

Sounds painful.

I don't see any other way of getting it out of you, Lore.

He must give the order to find me the tools I've asked for because two of the Crows circling us soar over the forest toward the human settlements in the swamp lands.

As I wait, I go back to trying to twist the wooden shaft, wishing I could use my magic, but since my blood combined with obsidian would turn Lore into a forever-Crow, there's absolutely no way I'm dripping any on him.

A fabric bundle drops beside me, making me jump. When I realize it's come from Lore's messengers, I unwrap it.

May this work . . .

CHAPTER 59

As I strike steel against flint, I murmur, ***I'm sorry, Lore.***

My spark leaps off the stone and onto the arrow protrusion. Though the wood is waterlogged, it still catches fire and burns down like a birthday candle. I study my mate's shadowy face as the scent of campfire fragrances the beach.

I'm so sorry.

He doesn't say a word, merely stares at the smoke curling from his iron crow.

Once the smoke stops wafting out, I tip the trap to coax the embers out, then slide the metal skewer into the hole left over by the arrow. I wince as though it's my own body I'm stabbing.

Don't cry, Behach Éan. I'm not in—he swallows—***in pain.***

How could he not be? I drive my shoulder into my wet eyes.

The tears keep coming, keep trickling down my cheeks, plopping onto the shiny iron body of my mate. I start to think I'll never get the damned arrowhead out when suddenly my skewer slides deeper into Lore, as though he weren't entirely made of metal.

I hear his breath catch as the sharpened obsidian point surfaces from the iron. I feel his pain flash white and bright through our bond. Teeth gritted, cheeks wet with compassion, I drive the skewer in hard and fast to put an end to this torture. The arrow plinks against the metal trap.

I yank out the skewer, then drop it on the sand, and glare at the weapon head with such fury, it's a wonder it doesn't burst into flames.

"Fallon." The sound of my name jolts me because it doesn't ring between my temples; it travels through the air.

I look up at the lithe body clad in black and steel, at the high cheekbones inked with a feather, at the eyes forever watching me. Watching over me. So concentrated was I on the piece of obsidian that I missed my mate dissolving into smoke and slamming into his other crows.

He extends his hand, but I don't take it. Instead, I fish the piece of obsidian from the cage, then stride to the waterline and pitch it as far as my trembling arm will allow. I know there are million more obsidian weapons stashed all over our kingdom, but I need to see this one disappear.

The second it leaves my fingers, arms band around my middle and a strong chin dips into the slope of my neck. "Thank you," my mate whispers before pressing a kiss to the skin behind my ear.

I close my eyes and lean into his body that molds around mine, all his firm muscles pressing into my bedraggled bones. The only remaining soft part of my mate in this form is his lips. No, that isn't true. I raise my hand and sink my fingers into his silken hair. *That* is the softest part on his body.

I turn my head until the corner of my mouth meets the corner of his. "I've missed you." I pull his scent of wind and storms deep into my lungs as though to fill a well gone dry.

"Four-fifths of a man wasn't enough for you?"

"Is half a kingdom enough for you?"

I feel the corner of his mouth tip. "We, Crows, are such immoderate beings."

I like that he includes me in his species.

"Even if you hadn't been born a Crow, your bravery and devotion would've earned you a spot in our midst." He catches a lock of my hair that flies into my mouth and presses it behind my ear. "At my side." He kisses the corner of my mouth. "I do believe it's time you wear our feather."

My pulse hastens as a new wave of emotion rises behind my ribs.

"Unless . . ." I can feel his attention scroll over my clumped lashes and the moisture forking down my cheeks. "Unless you aren't ready to show the world—"

"That I belong to the Crows? To you?" I turn in his arms to stare up at him. "Lorcan Ríhbiadh, I am *so* ready."

A smile touches his mouth, its radiance spilling into every pore of my being.

"But . . ."

"Of course you'd have some condition."

I snort. "I want *you* to ink it."

His arms tighten around my waist, gathering me against his chest that vibrates with a low chuckle. "Mo khrà, you do *not* want me to draw anything permanent on your body. Especially on your lovely face."

"Are your art skills that awful?"

"Abysmal."

Smiling, I press my cheek against the armor ensconcing his upper body and link my arms around his narrow waist. "I suppose that if I ended up with a turd on my cheekbone, Phoebus would renounce our friendship and Sybille would make fun of me for the rest of my life."

Laughter spills from my mate, drifting along the soft wind and rolling over the waves. As the sound fills the sky, a slender ray of sunshine burns through the clouds and drapes over us, gilding us in its honeyed light. I watch it play on my bare skin, on Lore's leathers, on the ancient grains of sand that hem this piece of our kingdom. *May the darkness be behind us.*

"Manifest the brightness, Little Bird."

With a startled laugh, I pick my face off Lore's muscle-hardened chest. "What?"

"A wise woman once told me I should manifest what I want. Just paying her advice forward."

I grin up at him, then lift my hands to his neck, roll onto my toes, and pull him down toward me. Before I press my lips to his, I whisper, "Not wise, Lore; optimistic. Confidence and wisdom may take the same shape, but there's a world of difference between them. Mark my words, though. Someday I'll be a wise old Crow like yourself, but until then, I fear you're stuck with a young dreamer."

"Oh, the hardships I must endure," he murmurs around a wink that reduces my smoldering heart to flickering embers.

Gods, who knew winks could be so panty-melting? "You must wink more often, Lore. But only at me."

His lips curve as they touch mine. ***Naturally.***

Although our lips met when we mind-walked, the sensation of this kiss is so much stronger, so much fiercer than the last we shared. Our lips are like flint and steel, creating sparks that set our souls and hearts ablaze.

At that moment, I fully grasp the impossibility of living without one's mate. As long as Lore exists, I will hunger to be with him, to touch him, to love him.

"Sorry to interrupt, but a military vessel has just veered out of the canals and is sailing this way, Mórrgaht. They must've been alerted to a disruption in Filiaserpens in spite of the heavy fog you dropped over the ocean." Imogen's already outlined with smoke, as though she's a second away from bursting into her bird form.

"Or the kid talked," another Crow suggests.

"No." Imogen shakes her head, defensive of this child that isn't even hers. "He wouldn't have."

"Shift before they see you whole, Lore." My father stands farther down the beach from us, his tired gaze affixed not to the approaching dark speck on the east, but to an area of water near the beach where, I suspect, my mother lies. "Carry my daughter away from here. They may know she's escaped Dante's prison, but I don't care for their eyes to so much as touch her."

Before he's even done speaking, Lore's in feathers, knees bent, wing extended. I don't waste a minute to climb atop his back. We're airborne before the others. Well, except for those already in the air, but they hover over the forest.

I've asked them to wait for if they fly beside me, Little Bird, the Faeries will know I'm back.

Because he's larger than the others.

As we fly west, toward the Sky Kingdom, I look over at Shabbe. To think the queendom is as vast as Luce yet appears as minuscule as a dot. I cannot wait to bring down the wards and explore the land of pink beaches and magical blood. The birthplace of our tempestuous Cauldron.

Thoughts of the Holy Cauldron steer my mind and gaze off Shabbe and onto Dante. My next and final task.

Or so I think.

CHAPTER 60

B*ehach Éan, we've arrived.*

Hmm . . . Where?

Home, my love. We're home.

I jerk upright. When my body begins to list, Lore snaps his outstretched wings higher and tilts.

Oh my Gods, I slept? And seeing as the sky is striated with pinks and purples, I assume I've been asleep for a while.

Five hours.

Five? The trip to the Racoccin beach took us two.

You needed sleep. And we were in no rush.

So did you . . . So do *you!*

I will have plenty soon.

I stare at the faint shape of the moon that's filling out in the pastel sky. *How is it that I didn't tumble off your back?*

First off, would I ever let you fall?

No, but accidents—

Happen to people with careless steeds. Besides, your father flew beneath us the entire time. You'd think he'd trust me, but apparently, seven hundred years of friendship doesn't make me worthy of his daughter.

I never imagined bliss could be painful, but between my father's fierce affection and my mate's intractable love, my heart hurts. How did I get so lucky?

I sink my hands into the feathers at Lore's neck and draw my thumbs over the hard line of his shoulders. Gods, he must be beat.

Though he doesn't quite rattle, a deep hum rolls through his bones and vibrates his muscles. ***Careful, Little Bird, or I may fly off with you.***

I smile at his threat.

Someday, I'll take you away. Just the two of us.

Though I would love nothing more than to laze around with Lore, he's king of a divided nation, one that will need to be darned and reorganized, whose laws will need to be revised and whose wide range of people will need to find a new equilibrium. Yes, he'll be able to delegate some tasks to his Siorkahd, but even his most formidable Crows cannot replace the figurehead that he represents.

He veers toward the giant hatch of the Market Tavern and floats us down. My breath catches at the sight of the candles dripping wax onto the communal tables and radiating a soft glow over the spread of food and flowers.

I'm guessing that the news of our successful mission preceded us.

Seemingly, my Crows are gossips . . .

I grin, my smile intensifying when I spot Lorcan's mother standing arm-in-arm with Phoebus, heads craned toward us, faces bright beneath their charcoal makeup. Yes, *their.* Even Phoebus wears Crow stripes tonight.

My gaze wheels over the rest of the crowd until I spot Sybille leaning against her fair-haired beau, who's deep in conversation with Gabriele, probably strategizing over their next tunnel explosion.

All three have brushed black over their eyes. Only Justus, who stands beside Bronwen, speaking in low tones, hasn't adorned his face with charcoal. I wonder whether he abstains because he doesn't feel like he's earned them, or whether his face is bare because no one's offered to paint some on him.

We're last to land. My father and Imogen, and the rest of the Crows who'd accompanied us to Filiaserpens, already stand amongst their compatriots, stein in hand. The second my feet kiss the ground, Lore morphs.

A deep whimper emerges from Arin, who springs toward her son.

When she reaches him, she brackets his face between her palms and drags his forehead down to hers. She murmurs words in Crow I don't catch, but which I can only imagine are filled with love and relief, especially when tears notch her stripes.

She tilts her son's head lower to kiss a spot between his brows, and then she comes toward me and takes my face between her hands and presses our foreheads together. My heart tightens with yet another hefty dose of bliss that she considers me someone worthy of her affection. Yes, I'm her son's mate, but that doesn't make me admirable, only companionable.

"*Tapath,* Fallon." After thanking me in Crow, she thanks me in Lucin. "*Grazi, mo ínon.*"

My bottom lip begins to quiver at being called her daughter. I never imagined that I, a girl liked by so few, could one day be loved by so many.

A hand slips around my waist and perches on my hip, not to tug me away, only to hold me. "*Mádhi,* would you do us the honor of inking my mate's cheek?"

A squeak rises over the quiet conversations that have erupted around us. Grinning, I stare over Arin's shoulder at Phoebus, who teeters on the edge of the crowd, hissing Sybille's name while shifting back and forth on his suede loafers like a child on Yuletide.

When she hears him, she bustles over, "What?"

"Fallon's getting her feather," he whisper-shouts.

She whips her gray eyes my way. They're so full of pride that I bite my lip, for I don't feel my act merits pride. It's momentous, that much is indisputable, but it's also my birthright.

"I will get mallet and ink." Arin's voice is thick with emotion.

As she departs to gather her tattooing supplies, Phoebus and Sybille shuffle to my side and, after quick hugs, frame me like proud parents as a great many shifters move toward me to express their joy and gratitude that their king is whole.

"Though the bodysuit is a vast improvement on the all-brown getup," Phoebus says out the corner of his mouth, "Syb and I brought some options over for you to change into when we heard you were on your way back."

"You brought options *here*?"

"Yes. We laid them out in Reid's room since Reid's, you know"—Phoebus shrugs—"*not* here."

Sybille plucks strands of my salt-and-sand-hardened hair and inspects them, nose rumpled. "Let's hope Reid's not too much of a one-soap-fits-all type of man."

"If he is, we'll nick a cup of cooking oil from the dip stall."

I finger the mass. "It's that bad?"

Phoebus nods. "A scarecrow with dreads, only worse."

Great.

Syb moves aside to make room for Lore. He presses his palm to the small of my back and murmurs, "Don't listen to them. You're the most exquisite woman in this room."

I doubt Lore's objective, but does it matter?

Arin fords through the loose net of shifters, clutching a leather pouch which she unrolls on the nearest table, on a space that my father has cleared of plates.

He turns his deep-brown stare toward me. "Ready, ínon?"

I roll my fingers into a fist, crushing the one and only other mark on my body. Though a feather on my cheek won't cancel Dante's brand, I cannot wait for the world to see which king I truly belong to.

CHAPTER 61

"Was it painful?" Phoebus asks, as he runs a wooden comb through my clean and heavily moisturized hair.

"Less so than your brushing." I cannot tear my gaze away from the delicate feather Arin inked beneath my left eye. The skin is still a little puffy and red, but I can already tell it's a work of art. I twist my face to the right to get a better view of it while Sybille struggles with the laces on the satin bodice of a violet gown.

"You know, Crows don't marry in gold like Faeries; they marry in dark colors—black, sapphire . . . violet." Sybille drops this in so nonchalantly that it almost sounds like a fact instead of what it is—a very obvious hint.

Phoebus rolls his eyes. "Subtle, Syb."

"I'm just saying that if Fallon wanted to go all out, I'm sure no one would raise any objection to performing a second Crow ritual. I mean, everyone's merry and *here*."

Nonna and Mamma materialize in the speckled mirror over Reid's stone sink, and then they fade and Daya appears, in both skin and scales. "I'm not getting married without Nonna and my mothers. And Gia, and your parents. I'd really like for them to be present as well. Not to mention I want this"—I spread my fingers open and stare at the interlocked rings—"*rune* gone."

Sybille peeks at Phoebus through her lashes before sliding her lips together.

The look they exchange makes my heart stutter. "What?"

Sybille yanks on the laces of my dress, driving my breath from my lungs. "Nothing."

"Come on. I may have been absent for a while, but I know the two of you, and that look clearly meant *something*."

Sybille sighs. "It's just that getting everyone together could take some time, what with Vlad making outrageous demands in order to give up his ward stone."

"He'll fold." Phoebus gives my smooth strands another thorough brush. "Lore will make him relinquish it."

Though I've no doubt my mate can bend the Glacin monarch to his will with a well-phrased threat or a well-placed iron talon, I assume Vladimir is his ally, and using force would work against this alliance. "What sort of demands?"

"Weapons, trunks of gold, a bargain from yours truly."

We all whip our attention toward the entrance to Reid's small bathing chamber that's presently dwarfed by a very large male.

Lore leans against the wooden doorway, hair damp from a shower, arms crossed over a snug black top that makes his shoulders pop. "Vlad's a king with a vested interest in remaining one. Since he knows we'd do just about anything for that stone, he's decided our old agreement requires some amending."

The sight of Lore makes my pulse hum beneath my skin, against my eardrums. For a moment, I even forget what we're discussing, but then Sybille speaks Vladimir's name, and it all rushes back to me. "Isn't it in his interest to destroy the wards?"

"The bravest Faerie fears the weakest Shabbin. Your magic both intimidates and embitters them." Lore drags his gaze down the violet silk I've been squished into, and the gold in his eyes churns approvingly. "Why do you think Pierre wanted a Shabbin wife so badly?"

"Does Vladimir want a Shabbin wife?"

Lore snaps his gaze off my dress and onto my face. "You're taken. And not by the Regio rat scurrying beneath my kingdom."

I roll my eyes. "I wasn't going to offer myself to him."

"You've done it before." Sybille shrugs off my glower.

"Don't you think bringing up Dante is a tad petty, Syb?"

"Oh, I was talking about Pierre of Nebba, Pheebs. Fallon suggested marriage against his assistance in retrieving Meriam."

The comb drops from Phoebus's hand. "You propositioned Pierre —*the Butcher*—of Nebba?"

"Not only was I bluffing, but I was also desperate to locate Meriam." I level a look Lorcan's way. Though I don't begrudge him his secrets, if he'd shared his theories on Meriam's whereabouts with me, it would've saved us all a whole lot of grief. "I imagined she'd be the solution to all our problems."

Lore unfolds his arms and pushes off the door frame, stepping deeper into the bathroom. "Could you two give Fallon and me a moment, please?"

"Of course." Sybille darts toward the door. When she realizes that Phoebus isn't following, much too busy gawping at me, she retraces her steps, snags his hand and pulls him out.

As they cross Reid's small bedroom, I hear him utter *Pierre* and *marriage* and *mate*. He's evidently disgusted by my scheme. Because I had a true mate, or because of the Nebban King's repute?

Lore steps closer to me, features so strained that I frown up at him.

"You cannot possibly still be mad at me about Pierre, Lore."

He cups my cheek, his long thumb drawing an arc over my new feather. "Though I abhor the memory of that day and of that man, I'm not angry with you, Little Bird. Only with myself for not disclosing all I knew."

"You had your reasons."

"Don't justify what I did. Not only were you my liberator, Fallon, but you were my mate." He stares at my little feather, a maelstrom of emotion stirring the gold. When I swallow, he lowers his thumb. "Forgive me. Your cheek must be tender."

I shake my head. "It doesn't hurt."

"You're certain?"

"Yes, Lore. I'm astonishingly robust; something I surely inherited from my hard-as-iron-talons father."

The shadow of a smile breaches his moodiness as he knuckles the side of my neck before sloping down my shoulder. "And yet you're so soft. So delicate."

"All an illusion."

He skims the bone in my shoulder, then traces a line down my arm before curling his fingers around my waist. I shiver when he grips the harsh indent Sybille created with her enthusiastic lace-pulling. "I'd offer to loosen them, but I cannot guarantee we'd make it to the party, and everyone is so very thrilled to celebrate you."

A blush hurtles into my cheeks at the mention of loosening my bodice. "If you didn't come to ravish me, then what is it you want?"

Using only the hand at my waist, he spins me around until my back is to his front, and we both face the mirror. "I came to paint your face, Behach Éan."

CHAPTER 62

The mention of Lore adorning my face with my Crow stripes deepens the blush splashed across my collarbone, neck, and jaw. How does this man make putting on makeup sound so seductive?

Lore reaches past my body and picks up the shrunken block of charcoal resting beside Reid's sink. "First things first"—his unctuous voice is so near my earlobe that it raises goosebumps over my scarlet flush—"you must rub the charcoal between your fingers for they will be your brushes."

He handles the charcoal with such deliberate strokes that I begin to envy the piece of charred wood. Gods, I'm pathetic.

As Lore leans over me to replace the black lump, he murmurs, "No need to be jealous of an inanimate object, mo khrà. I will be fondling your lovely body soon."

My heart jolts at his promise, shipping the heat in my face to all my other extremities.

The tip of his nose skims my earlobe and then the skin right behind it, and, Cauldron, how I shudder. "Where were we? Ah, yes . . . using one's fingers as brushes." He raises both his hands to my face, hovering his fingers in front of my lashes. "Close your eyes."

I clasp my lids and wait with bated breath to feel the glide of Lore's fingers. He must decide to draw out the sweet torture because he keeps hovering his hands over my face, filling me with the scent of scorched timbre and wild storms.

He sidles nearer. When his bulging pecs brush up against my shoulder blades and his chin scrapes against the top of my head, a shiver races up my spine. I arch my back to better fit against Lore's front and sigh when not a millimeter of space remains between us, then sigh again when his fingers finally alight on my closed lids.

I feel every ridge and callus on his skin, every bob of his Adam's apple, every pulse of his cool breath, every thrum of his strong heart. Slowly, he glides his fingers from the bridge of my nose to my temples. Though he's carried no storm inside his kingdom, he's carried one inside my body. Thunder and lightning strike my breastbone and veins.

As his fingertips flutter away from my face, he murmurs, "Open your eyes, my love."

My lashes sweep up and I stare.

And stare.

A little ink and black powder shouldn't make me feel more like what I intrinsically am, but they do. They truly do. I may not be able to break into feathers and smoke, but tonight, Lore has made me feel as though growing wings lies within the realm of my abilities.

I lean toward the mirror, turning my head this way and that. Edged by so much black, my violet eyes appear almost pink.

Lore palms my waist, reeling me back into him, then catches my chin between his stained fingers and angles my head until our lips align. "I know the mark you wear is that of my people, Behach Éan, but fuck if it doesn't feel like mine, and mine alone on you."

I swallow, attempting to ease back the emotion clogging my throat, but it stays and swells, until I think I may choke on the love I feel for this man.

After another thorough inspection of my darkened skin and tattooed cheek, he erases the space between our lips with a kiss infused by such possession and hunger that my knees go weak. I clasp the forearm pinned to my waist for balance, then reach my other arm up and sink my hand into his hair. When I tug at the silken strands, he releases a rumbling groan that echoes against my palate and tongue and courses over my skin like warm syrup.

I hinge my neck as far as it can go and lick across the seam of his mouth. My mate seizes up, and then, nostrils flaring, he growls words I don't grasp and drops the hand cradling my face to the elegant panel of violet satin sheathing my legs. He hikes it up and up, and then pushes his hand under the hem, drags aside my underwear, and sinks two fingers inside of me.

I choke on my breath, then choke again when he begins to pump them into me. "Lore—aren't we—awaited?"

"We are. Better come fast, my Little Bird."

When he begins to circle my clit with his thumb, I mewl. He sweeps away the sound with his tongue, then proceeds to swallow every little moan that spills from my throat. My toes curl in the spiky-heeled satin slippers that tie around my ankle with a pretty bow to match the one on the bodice.

Hmm . . . Later tonight, when we retire, you'll have to wear those shoes and your stripes, and nothing else.

Oh, Gods. My throat closes as every muscle in my body tightens and spasms, and heat rockets up my core.

"Good girl," he murmurs as he slow-twirls his fingers around my spasming center as though to baste them in my wet heat.

Once my body quiets and my head slumps back against his collarbone, he draws his lips and fingers from my body. My underwear settles against my still-tingling nub, eliciting another fierce shiver, and I melt against him a little more.

As my skirt unravels, settling weightily over my boneless legs, he lifts his blackened fingers and pulls them apart, emitting a satisfied hum when threads of my pleasure stretch and shine between them.

I expect him to lean over me and run water and soap over the mess I've made, but instead, he sucks them clean, streaking his mouth black, then rubs the pad of his thumb over the charcoal residue to sweep it off.

"Ready, mo khrà?"

"Um, yes. But aren't you going to wash your mouth and hands?"

"Why would I do that?"

I gape at him. "Because you're going to be interacting with people."

"Tell me, Fallon, have you ever seen me touch anyone but you with my hands or my mouth?"

"I—I . . ." I rack my brain, realizing that, *no*, Lore never touches anyone but me with his hands or mouth. *Actually* . . . "You've been known to punch my father."

A brazen smile curves his mouth. "Though I've no plan to reset his nose tonight, if I absolutely must, I'll make sure to use the hand that wasn't buried between your legs."

A new wave of heat billows up my chest at the mere mention of the place on my body his fingers quarried only minutes before.

Those same fingers now brush a smudge of charcoal off my chin. "Have I told you how exquisite you look wearing my stripes and feather?" His golden stare caresses his handiwork. "*Thu thòrt mo focèn ánach, Behach Éan.*"

Before I can ask him what *too thurt mo focken anock* means, he translates it into Lucin for me.

"You take my fucking breath away, Little Bird."

CHAPTER 63

"I still cannot believe you propositioned that pointy-eared swine in front of your mate." Phoebus shudders so hard that it vibrates the chair he's been sitting on for the last hour. "That's grounds for friendship termination."

I loose a theatrical sigh. "Thank Gods I'll still have Syb. Then again, once I'm queen, I'll probably have a whole slew of people pining to become my bestie, so replacing you should be a cinch."

He tears his gaze away from Connor to cast me a long-suffering look. "How droll you can be, Picolina."

I grin.

Sybille plops a plate topped with every offering imaginable on the table, then drags her chair back to sit. When Phoebus reaches over to pinch a roasted potato, she taps his hand. "Get your own food. Baby and I are hungry."

He sucks his oil-smeared fingers, then wipes them on his napkin. "Baby's smaller than this here fingerling potato, Syb."

"How do you expect him to grow if you steal his food?" When she drags her plate farther from him, propping her elbow on the table for good measure, I laugh.

Phoebus *tsks*. "And they call me the dramatic one . . ."

Sybille tips him a toothy grin that elicits more laughter, this time from both Pheebs and me.

How wondrous this evening is. I glance around *Murgadh'Thábhain* and sigh deeply, sated both by the delicious feast and the tangible happiness circulating around this cavern in the sky. Sitting here, in the torchlit darkness, one can almost imagine Luce is at peace and all is well with the world. But the world is far from well.

A bowl full of glistening fingerling potatoes is lowered in front of Phoebus. Both my friend and I crane our necks, tracking the large black hand that held the bowl to a certain rugged tavern owner.

Connor's Adam's apple jostles in his thick throat. "I served myself too many *bántata*."

Phoebus stares and stares, clearly at a loss for words, so I thank Connor in his stead.

As he retreats, I murmur around a smile, "Your future lover is such an attentive man."

A blush steals across Phoebus's jaw. "He runs a tavern. He's attentive to everyone's stomachs, Picolina. Besides, he's not interested."

I nudge his knee with mine. "Sweetheart, he's interested. I think you should go thank him."

"I agwee weef Fallom." Sybille's cheeks are so full of food that her words are garbled.

Phoebus bites his lip. "You really think—"

"Yes!" Syb and I say at the same time, the volume of our answer launching our friend's ass off his seat.

He runs both his hands up the sides of his face and through his hair, inhaling and exhaling in rapid successions. "What if—"

"Go," I say.

"Okay." He takes a step in the direction Connor went, but then boomerangs right back. "No." He shakes his head. "He said he wasn't in the right headspace. He's probably still not in the right headspace."

"Do you know how many times I said no to Lore?"

"Too many," someone answers softly.

I tip my head back to get a glimpse of the person who's apparently well versed in my dating history.

Have you already forgotten the sound of my voice?

It's noisy.

Lore smiles gently, fatigue crinkling the corners of his eyes. "Shall we retire? I'm shattered."

I take his extended hand and stand. "Absolutely."

Sybille's gray eyes begin to sparkle, and a smile kinks up the side of her mouth. She angles herself away from her plate and opens her arms. As I deliver her awaited hug, she murmurs, "Someone else is going to be shattered come morning. Or at least, some body parts belonging to that someone."

I laugh, then pinch her arm. "You're terrible, Syb."

In spite of my heels, I push up on my toes to drop a kiss onto Phoebus's puffing cheek and a murmur into his ear. "He brought you potatoes."

And then I twirl back toward Lore, who tucks me under his arm and says, "Do you know how one wins a war, Acolti?"

I doubt my friend can focus on much else than Connor at the moment, but he surprises me by saying, "By gathering the strongest and smartest army?"

"No. Wars are won by those who refuse to surrender, no matter how many battles are lost on the way."

When I realize his lesson in power plays is, in fact, masked relationship advice, I press my hand against his chest, over that steadfast heart of his that never quits beating. That never gives up.

Phoebus blinks, and then he nods and slingshots himself across the room toward where Connor stands beside the ale stall, filling a stein with the bubbly liquid that Crows make from barley and which tastes just as awful as the human version I drank back in Rax.

That was sweet, Lore.

You sound surprised.

Perhaps because you're not exactly a softy.

One needs not possess a soft heart to feel empathy; one needs only possess a heart.

I accompany my little headshake with a kiss. ***Come, my tough-hearted mate. Off to bed we go.***

He slides me the most devilish grin as I pull him toward the Market Tavern's southern entrance. Once outside, he releases my hand to morph into feathers, but a Crow all but barrels into him, not even bothering to land before shifting.

Lore claps Aoife's heaving shoulder, and it strikes me that I haven't crossed paths with her in the last two days.

"*Dalich,* Mórrgaht." After a deep inhale, she says, "I bring news—from Glace."

I scour her expression to work out if it will be good or bad, but even after three full circuits around her oval face, I cannot reason what news she brings.

"Justus know where Vladimir keep runestone."

"Justus?"

"Yes." She swings her head up and down in a nod, manifestly excited. "He in Glace with Cian."

I spin toward Lore. "You sent Justus to Glace?"

"Since he accompanied Marco to deliver the runestone to Vladimir two decades back, he suggested the trip."

Brilliant man.

The tightening of Lore's pupils tells me he doesn't share my conviction. He probably won't change his tune about Justus until the stone rests on the war room table. May Justus make quick work of negotiations and may he succeed in unlocking the wards.

I remind myself that he managed to draw the blood to the surface of the stone. There's no reason he won't be able to delete the rune . . . is there?

That saying Meriam shared with me, the one about the Cauldron laughing when immortals made plans, punches back my hope, but like proofing dough, it expands anew.

". . . unreasonable," Aoife is saying. "Justus asks Fallon to come." Aoife bites her lip. "To steal stone."

CHAPTER 64

"Steal?" Here I thought we were resorting to revised covenants and not larceny.

Lorcan's irises blaze like the torches speared into the walls of his kingdom.

"Justus cannot go through wall without rune," Aoife explains, "and to draw, he needs Shabbin mate's blood."

Lore's shadows tear off his flesh.

He must bark his discontentment into Aoife's mind because my poor friend sucks in a breath and drops her gaze to the floor with a soft, "*Dalich,* Mórrgaht."

I didn't **bark** ***at her.***

Then why did she apologize and is now staring at her feet?

Because I asked her—perhaps a tad too fervidly—not to employ the term **mate.** ***It's too sacred to be used for something so***—his eyes scrape across my hand, the one emblazoned with the reminder of my connection to another—***profane.***

Ah . . . I spear my fingers through his before he can fully disintegrate. ***Lore, you're my mate. Only you.***

"They found the runestone?"

I whirl toward the source of that raucous pitch. My father stands there, in the gaping entrance of *Murgadh'Thábhain,* hands balled into fists that drum his thighs.

"Yes, Cathal. In guarded room of art gallery."

The look of wonder on my father's face swells my heart. One step closer to Shabbe. One step closer to getting his mate back.

"Can't Cian slip inside?" I ask.

"His heart hardens every time he touch wall." Aoife purses her lips. "He says room must be lined with obsidian."

"*Focá,*" my father mutters.

Aoife sinks her teeth into her bottom lip. "Bronwen says Fallon can pass through walls."

"Fallon isn't going to Glace," Lore snaps.

Aoife peeks at Cathal through her lashes. "Cian arrange dinner to discuss *alliance*. He said to Vlad you and Fallon attend."

"No." Lore's shadows fall away from my fingers to bind around my waist.

"Didn't you give him the vial we retrieved?" My father strides forward, pulse striking his corded neck.

I cock an eyebrow. "What vial, Dádhi?"

"The night you were taken. We retrieved a vial of Meriam's blood from the cavern."

"It wasn't Meriam's. It was serpent blood. Apparently, none of the blood distributed to the Lucins comes from Meriam. Which isn't to say some vials aren't floating around, since Costa supposedly bled his beloved for years, and Shabbin blood never coagulates." Lore's eyes glaze over as though he were back in a time and place where the man who stabbed him in the back existed.

"*Not* supposedly; he did," I insist, though there's little point in arguing at the moment. "Let's go to Glace."

My father startles at my enthusiasm, and his eyes mist over as though he were so relieved he could weep.

"No." Lore's tone brooks no argument.

Yet my father argues. "We've time. It will take Dante another two days to reach the wildling camp."

I start. "The wildling camp?"

"This is where the tunnel now ends," my father explains. "The *only* tunnel. Rossi proved a great cartographer."

To think you all wanted to kill him.

Lore's pupils shrink. ***I still do.***

I frown.

He took you from me, Behach Éan.

I sigh, deciding to drop the subject of redemption. "And the wildlings? Are they on our side?"

"Why, yes. They were most enchanted by the trunk of gold we offered them to drill a hole into their campsite, and even more so, by the promise of a second trunk once they report that the rodents reach their destination." Lore runs the tip of his tongue over his bottom lip as though savoring delivering the news.

My pulse beats so fast that the inside of my mouth tastes like the coins the wild Fae so covet. "Are we certain they cannot be swayed to fight alongside the Faeries? After all, with all the iron they ingest, bargains don't adhere to their skin, correct?"

"Correct," Lore says slowly. "And nothing is ever certain, which is why we have some people keeping watch."

"Could Dante backtrack?"

"He could, but Mattia and Antoni have already started *quarrying*."

Perhaps instead of mining, Justus and Antoni should rally a bunch of water-Fae and fill the tunnels.

According to Rossi, that would serve little purpose since there are too many partitions and inclines.

Then we'll wait. And while we do . . . "I've always dreamed of seeing Glace. I hear the ice formations are of great beauty."

Lore shakes his head. ***The ice formations? Really?***

My father must interpret Lore's headshake as his answer to my circuitous demand to head to Glace because he says, "With the wards gone, Priya will be able to send her army. Dante won't stand a chance."

My mate's shadows feather across my skin. "He already doesn't stand a chance."

If only I could be imbued with as much confidence. I mean, I have *every* intention of ending Dante's life, but intention and skill are two very different things.

"Please, brother." My father's voice is so brittle that it wrecks my heart.

Lore's arm wraps a little more snugly around my waist. "Go get some sleep."

My father's mouth pops open, then shuts and tightens. His frustration is so potent that, if I weren't standing in the way, he'd probably punch Lore.

I stroke my mate's knuckles. ***Put him out of his misery already.***

"We've got a long flight ahead of us, Cathal, not to mention a tedious supper to sit through while Fallon raids their museum."

The corners of my father's mouth begin to wobble, and his eyes, to sparkle as though picturing my mother molting out of her pink scales and walking across the beach toward him.

Aoife's lips bend into a bright smile that I reciprocate until the weight of our imminent undertaking settles on the mantle of my shoulders. I mustn't fail for the setback will not only deprive Lore of a fellow army, but it will also shatter my father's tenuous hope.

As my companions begin to discuss logistics, I stare at the slow dance of the torch flame burning against the wall. The fire suddenly flares before snuffing out and plunging me into darkness. I blink until there's light again, but this light is muted, nature-made. It trickles through conifer needles, icing the pale hair of a girl I haven't seen since Xema's revel in Tarespagia.

"I hear you're a diviner." Alyona gathers the collar of her white fur jacket more snugly around her neck.

When I realize where I am, my stomach hardens like the ice-covered land we sleigh over. *So Bronwen is in Glace* . . . I'm not entirely sure why this comes as a surprise. After all, not only is her mate there, but she also possesses a great passion for meddling.

"I'm a conduit," she replies slowly, "not a diviner. I merely observe and carry out the visions the Cauldron decides to show me."

"Has it shown you any visions of my future, Bronwen Báeinach?" Alyona's face is so pale and delicate it looks whittled from ice.

"No."

She turns her limpid stare toward the horizon. "Probably for the best. I'd prefer not to know whether my father succeeds at forcing my hand into the talon-tipped one of your sovereign."

Even though she has no interest in my mate, I cannot help but gnash my teeth.

"I can tell you, without consulting the Cauldron, that Lorcan will never take you as his bride."

"Yes. Because he's madly in love with the girl who revived him. I've heard." Though I'm not actually sitting across from Alyona, I can taste her loathing on the brisk wind. I think she adds, "I'd rather die than marry him," but the words are muffled by both her fur collar and Bronwen's sharp intake of air.

I try to look around, to understand what rattles my aunt so, but I cannot turn Bronwen's head so I'm stuck staring at Alyona's elegant eyebrows tilting toward her porcelain nose.

"Are you all right?"

Bronwen releases a shaken breath. "Yes."

I hear my uncle's voice patter across Bronwen's skull, asking her the same question. To him, she gives a very different answer. One that tears me out of Bronwen's mind and catapults me back into the Sky Kingdom where the hum of a distant conversation tickles my eardrums.

"She does not have a second mate, Aoife," Lore's explaining gently.

"But your eyes—they not white, Mórrgaht." Aoife's charcoal-dusted face swims back into my field of vision.

"Shabbins can peer through Bronwen's eyes," my father says.

Slowly, the concern scrunching Aoife's brow lifts in time with her thick lashes.

"You all failed to mention Bronwen was in Glace." My voice is scratchy, as though I haven't used it in days.

Aoife's brow rumples anew. "Cian is mate." She says this as though it's a perfectly rational explanation as to my aunt's whereabouts. I suppose that, in my friend's mind, it is. Perhaps I would've found it reasonable had I not been so wary of her.

Lore twirls my body to face his. "What did you see?"

"I saw Bronwen and Alyona of Glace sharing a sleigh ride."

"The look on your face tells me you saw more than that, Behach Éan."

I close my eyes and repeat what Bronwen told Cian, and as I do, I picture Alyona's body outlined in crimson snow.

I see her glazed eyes staring up at a night sky tufted with stars.

I see the hilt of a dagger embellished with a diamond snowflake protruding from her breastbone.

And I see myself—for that's apparently who the Cauldron showed Bronwen—standing over Alyona's corpse.

The reason Bronwen did not see the princess's future is because I, apparently, cut it short.

"I cannot go, Lore." My cheeks burn with shame. I may not have any love for Alyona, but murdering her . . .? Gods, that'll start another war.

"You must have a good reason for murdering her, ínon."

"I don't care if I have a fucking great reason for murdering her." I don't mean to snap at my father, but I'm distraught.

How could I do such a thing? And why were her hands on her abdomen?

Could she have been . . . Could she *be* pregnant? I scrape my fingers through my hair, muttering quiet invective after quiet invective.

Fallon, look at me.

I cannot.

Lore catches my wrists and pulls my hands off the roots I tug at wildly. "My love, the snowflake is the Glacins' royal crest."

"So on top of murdering Alyona, I do so with her people's weapon? That's not going to help with your alliance, Lore." My sarcasm chisels his jaw. "You cannot let me go to Glace."

The glimmer of hope that blazed in my father's eyes extinguishes. "Just because Bronwen saw you stand over that girl's corpse doesn't mean you planted that weapon inside her chest."

"The only other person at the scene was Alyona's brother, the crown prince."

"Siblings kill each other all the time." My father's pragmatism makes me wrinkle my nose.

Lore's eyebrows are slung so low they obscure his bright irises. "Bronwen saw stars?"

I frown. "I—She said it was night. Maybe I colored-in her vision with stars. Why?"

"Because night is bright in Glace in summer," Aoife says.

I snag my lower lip with my teeth, attempting to recall her exact words. "Perhaps reach out to Cian to find out?" Though I'd prefer not murdering her at all, I *would* prefer it not be tomorrow.

While Lore calls out to my uncle through the mind link he shares with all his people, my father touches my shoulder. "If we leave at dawn, we'll reach Vladimir's continent by early afternoon."

In other words: *we can be on our way back before night even sweeps across the land.*

The apple in his throat rolls with a deep swallow as he waits for my decision.

After all he's endured, I don't have the heart to turn him down. "Fine, but please, don't let me kill any princesses."

CHAPTER 65

As we reach Lorcan's door, my nerves have become so frayed that they've begun to erode what little confidence I have. Yes, I can slip through walls, but I haven't practiced the sigil in days. What if I've forgotten how to draw it? Not to mention that I dread bleeding anywhere near my mate. Near any Crows.

What if a Glacin spots my rune and slicks his weapon in it before it can absorb into the wall? That suddenly becomes my focal point of worry, which is a pleasant change from picturing myself plunging a blade through Alyona's chest.

We'll be with you, Fallon.

My eyebrows bend because that doesn't reassure me. Not with my blood in the mix.

You worry about your runes getting discovered. We will wipe them off the walls. Lore reaches around me to open his door.

I stride ahead of him into his bedroom. "What if I fail to draw the correct rune?" *What if I murder a princess?*

"Rossi and Bronwen will be there. They'll make sure you draw the right ones."

Relief crackles some of my tension. "Won't a theft cost you your alliance with Glace?"

I try to keep Alyona's murder at bay, but it hovers on the edge of my mind.

Lore sweeps his door closed. "If it can collapse the wards, then it'll be worth it."

I whirl, finding myself nose to nose with my mate. Well, nose to chin thanks to my tall heels. The thought of them drags my mate's attention to the floor. He grips my skirt and hoists it up to reveal the satin beauties Sybille insisted would harden the limpest of cocks.

"Perspicacious woman that Sybille."

I push my foot out to give him an unobstructed view of my shoe. "Is it hardening your cock, Mórrgaht?"

He takes my hand and carries it between his legs. I smile and give the bulge in his leather pants a slow rub, which causes a deep rumble to roll through his chest. I do it again, and this time, his lids fall to half-mast and his neck begins to tip back.

I press a kiss to his throat, loving the jerk of his Adam's apple against my lips. While I keep massaging him through the leather, I grip the ties of my corset and pull. The knot slips easily. I kiss him again, stroke him again, all the while plucking at the ribbon.

As soon as I've loosened it enough, I unbind my mouth from my mate's bobbing throat and lower my hand from his pulsating cock. My sudden halt earns me a frustrated growl that quickly transforms into a delighted groan when I hook my hands into my corset to pass it over my hips and shimmy out of it.

"Fuck me," he murmurs.

Your wish is my command.

His eyes flash off my bare breasts long enough to touch my face and crinkle with a mischievous smile. And then the man is on me, his mouth dropping hungry kisses along my neck, over the swells of my breasts. He breathes hard against my nipples but doesn't touch them, instead he straightens, curls one hand around my neck, and drags my face toward his to crush our mouths together.

I must've unleashed his inner beast because he isn't gentle tonight. His grip is bruising, his kiss demanding.

I drop my hands to his pants in search of those ties that hold them up. As soon as I find them, I pull, and his trousers loosen. Sighing with contentment, I wrap my fingers around his hot, silken length.

Lore shudders at the contact, then shudders again when I give him a slow pump. And then he mutters an incoherent sequence of words that are half in Lucin, half in Crow. He morphs into shadows, unhooking my hand from that beautiful, throbbing part of him, before reappearing a heartbeat later without shoes or trousers. He still wears his top. I seize the hem and roll it off him. I don't even get a second to admire that broad chest of his before he palms my ass and lifts me off the ground.

With a little squeal, I lock my arms around his neck and my legs around his waist. He begins to walk us toward the bed, but then veers off course. I think he may carry me into his bathing chamber, but I'm wrong.

He flicks the doorknob of his library, then kicks open the door. Moonlight edges the dark wood and makes every gilt spine glitter like stars. As I gaze around in wonder, he walks me over to the enormous table covered in that yellowed map of his kingdom and lays me out on it. My shoulder bumps into a little glass pot, knocking it sideways. Ink spills, splashing both my skin and the ochre paper.

When I reach over to right it, Lore seizes my wrists and transfers them over my head, where he pins them to the paper before bending over me and scraping one of my nipples with his teeth.

I forget all about the mess of ink and arch to feed him more of me. He covers my whole nipple with his mouth and kisses it so hard that pain and pleasure collide. The dueling sensation strikes my spine and core, pooling heat between my legs.

He proceeds to inflict the same sweet torture on my other breast before popping it out of his mouth to kiss his way down to my belly button. His fingers come away from my wrists and he drags his blunt nails down the inside of my arms, coaxing goosebumps onto every corner of my being.

He scratches down my rib cage, following the line of my body to my hips. Once he reaches them, he grabs my lace underwear and rolls it off. And then he palms my skinny heels and bends my leg to kiss my ankle. Slowly, he licks a line up to my knee, and I learn that knees are most wondrous places because the pressure of his mouth *there* makes all my muscles clench hard.

He drapes my leg over his wide shoulder, then proceeds to show his devotion to my other ankle, calf, and knee before tossing that leg over his back. He draws my thighs wide, then drops into a crouch and buries his face between my legs.

I jolt when his tongue makes contact with that magical nub and sink my ink-stained fingers into his midnight hair. Not to hold him there—I don't think he needs to be held—but to hold on.

When he lashes me with the flat of his tongue, it feels as though the golden lettering springs off every leather spine and begins to twirl in the dark air over us. I gaze at Lore's bobbing head and then roll my head back and gape at the shimmering cyclone that seems to twirl faster and—

"LORE!" His name tears from my throat at the very same time as an orgasm erupts in my core, flaying me open.

Before I've even recovered, he straightens, lines up his swollen tip, and sinks into me.

I see more stars. They crackle and shine like sparklers, shoot across the stone heavens like comets.

When he's fully sheathed, a husky growl rips from his chest and unspools across my body. The tenor is so loud and deep that it shakes the wood beneath my back. He pulls his hips back, groaning as the muscles in my core grip him. Though I'm tight, he's made me so wet that he glides clean out. Before I can miss his length, he slams back in.

More ink gurgles from the toppled well, splashing my jaw. He releases one of my legs to cup my cheek. At first, I think it's to wipe the ink, but then he smooths his hand down my torso and paints me, swirling his hand over my sweat-glazed skin, darkening the dusky-pink peaks of my bouncing breasts.

Focà, mo khrà. His eyes are as glazed as his forehead, as shiny as the raven locks that crisscross his brow. ***How I've missed the softness of your skin and the heat of your body.***

Every muscle inside my body clenches, from that sex he's missed, to the heart he conquered by never giving up. "I've missed . . ."

Although I don't want to look away, my lids slam closed because he's driving the heel of his hand against my tender clit. I explode against him, around him, the tide of my pleasure sucking him in deep before rushing against him and propelling him out.

Except my mate isn't some little pebble that can be rolled away; he's a boulder against which ships crash and oceans foam. He narrows his gaze over the chaos he's reaped on my skin, his pupils tightening in time with his jaw, then slams back into my spasming depths with a feral growl and erupts, decorating those parts of me his ink failed to reach.

By the time he's spent his seed, I'm dripping, and so is he, and not just from the salt of our combined sweat and pleasure but from bliss. Bone-numbing, heartrending bliss.

Still buried deep, he leans over my body and presses a reverent kiss to the little tattoo beneath my eye before murmuring what sounds like a prayer in Crow. I decipher the names of my parents and the words *thank you* and *wind*.

I was thanking the winds for blowing your mother onto the shores of my kingdom and into your father's arms.

I twist a lock of his hair around my fingers, watching the black glide over the blue of my skin. "If only the winds hadn't torn them apart."

"The winds didn't; the Regios did."

The same way Dante ripped Lore and me apart . . . "I'll need a sword. When we get back, I mean. Don't give me one before the trip." Alyona's corpse stamps my lids. I hurl the image away. "And I'll need some training. Once we return from Glace, can you give me both?"

"Yes, but you'll need no training."

"I beg to differ, seeing as I'm completely inept at swordfighting."

"There will be no fighting."

"Are you planning on trussing up Dante and presenting him to me on a platter?"

"Something like that." He skims his thumb over the little feather on my cheekbone. "And you aren't inept with blades."

My runaway heart holds still. And not from the memory of the dagger I sunk into Dante's eye, or even the blade protruding from Alyona's rib cage, but from that of the sword I thrust through Cato's neck. Nostrils flaring with disgust and shame, I turn my head and stare at the gray floor. Though my friend isn't sprawled at my feet, I nonetheless glimpse his blood-soaked body.

I tow my hand out of Lore's hair and ball it at my side. Attempting to crumple the recollection, I shut my eyes, but the memory clings to my lids like a fresh bruise. I wish Lore hadn't brought Cato up. It isn't that I forgot about him, because I haven't—I could never—but with everything else happening, he *had* slipped from the forefront of my mind.

He was your jailer, Behach Éan.

My nails bite into my palms. ***He was also my friend.*** How many times will we have this conversation?

True friends don't keep each other trapped.

I fling my lids up and glare at Lore. ***Don't be insensitive.***

I'm not; I'm pragmatic.

And I'm not?

No. Not when it comes to that man.

I draw in a breath that's so heated it feels as though someone set my lungs on fire.

"Kiss me, Fallon."

I glower at his mouth, really not in the mood after that conversation.

With a deep sigh, he slides his arms underneath me and scoots me up until I'm sitting on the edge of the desk and he stands between my legs, stiffening cock still rooted inside of me. ***If I could've killed him instead of you, mo khrà, I would've, in a heartbeat, for I much prefer you resent me than your own self.***

Gods, he makes it impossible to stay mad.

He slides his hands underneath my thighs and hoists me off the desk. The movement steals his length from my throbbing center. ***Now off to bed we go for we need rest.***

I palm his nape, enjoying the pinch and play of tendons beneath his skin. "Perhaps detour through the bathing chamber?"

"No."

"Lore, I'm covered in ink and . . ." I gesture to the sticky wetness on the inside of my thighs, the one I'm smearing all over his trim waist. "And you."

"You'll be covered in more of me come morning. We'll shower then."

I stare at my torso with a little trepidation. "What if the ink sets into my skin?"

"Then you'll carry the imprint of my hands on your flesh for the rest of your life."

"Be serious, my nipples are blue and I'm as striped as a wildcat."

"I love your blue nipples. As for the stripes, they suit your personality."

I shoot him a droll look that draws a smirk to his mouth, but then I smile. "When my father enquires as to why I showered in ink, I will point him your way, Lore."

His eyes spark. "I'll just tell him that you were snooping around my library to glimpse the tunnels Justus drew on our map and knocked over the inkwell. I suspect your father will be a tad peeved that you've ruined Justus's work. He so loathes asking that man for assistance."

My glee ebbs, because *merda* . . . "Did I really ruin the map?"

"No, Little Bird, I ruined it. You merely ruined me."

CHAPTER 66

After a full day of flying, land appears. Unlike Luce, which glimmers gold and green, Glace is as white as the bedding Lore and I stained with our ink-soaked bodies.

Not even a shower and thorough scrubbing managed to rid me of my newest markings. To avoid raising any eyebrows, especially my father's, I donned gloves and a black turtleneck beneath the iron and leather armor Lore gifted me upon waking.

Another present he had custom-made for me. Though silly since it covers only my shoulders, chest, abdomen, and back, I feel as invincible as if I were enclosed inside a me-sized ward.

Thanks to black leather trousers and tall boots, the only visible piece of stained skin remaining is behind my ear, which prompted me to wear my hair loose. I probably shouldn't have, considering the ferocity of the polar winds.

The second I'm off my father's back, I work on combing out the snarls, all the while glancing toward the puffs of darkness that is Lore. My mate will not be shifting into skin today, primarily because no one yet knows that he's again whole, but also because he deemed it judicious to leave two of his crows in the Sky Kingdom. Also, in case there *is* a murder—hopefully, one not committed by me—we've decided it best the Glacins think he stayed behind in Luce.

I'm still tidying my hair when the snow-covered ground beside us begins to rumble.

I scramble back, colliding into Gabriele, who rode in on Colm's back. "Easy there, Fal."

Since he doesn't look alarmed, I decide that I needn't be. But still, my heartbeats do not quiet, not even when I realize that what moved isn't the ground but some glassed-in vestibule in which stands a couple draped in white furs that match their hair.

Actually *his* hair. Hers is flaxen, not full-white. King Vladimir and his wife, Milana. Even if they'd gone without their snowflake crowns, I'd have known who they were from their regal postures and the amount of soldiers that hem them in.

Though I spent much of my flight steeped in my thoughts and watching the ocean roll beneath us, I did ask Lore to polish my bare-bone knowledge of the Glacin court. I learned all about the Faerie monarch, his two children from a first marriage—Konstantin and Alyona—his much younger wife, and *their* cherished twin daughters and little son.

Konstantin, the oldest, is slated to take over Glace once his father either dies or retires. Then there's Alyona, the one that . . . that I kill. The twins are named Ksenia and Izolda and will turn sixteen before the year is out, and their little brother, Ilya, is five.

Where the twins and little Ilya take after their mother, all three golden-haired and blue-eyed, the two eldest inherited their father's silver gaze and white hair. The razor-thin shape of his face, too. Their beauty is as cold as the icicles that crown the vestibule's flat roof.

The glass walls retract into slender metal pillars that shimmer just as brightly as everything else. The sun sits low on the horizon, spilling its dimmed glow over the frosted landscape.

I cannot imagine living in a place of endless days, and after a month spent underground, I know that I wouldn't tolerate endless nights. I'm much too enamored of sunrises and sunsets.

"Did you enjoy living here?" I ask Gabriele as the king offers his queen his arm before stepping out of the vestibule and trudging across the hard-packed snow toward us.

"I did, actually. Glacins are rather friendly underneath all those furs and cool composures."

As though to prove Gabriele's point, Vladimir smiles, his teeth as blinding as the hair he wears twisted into an elaborate rope over his shoulder. Milana, though, doesn't smile as she inspects me from head to toe.

Like most purelings, she probably finds me lacking. I'd venture it's the shape of my ears that she finds off-putting; unless it's the black stripes I painted across my eyes. Or I'm wrong, and it isn't my appearance but my repute and heritage that pucker her pink-slicked mouth. After all, I'm a combination of two races Faeries fear immensely. The thought that I may actually frighten her does wonders for my self-esteem.

As the royals approach, the shifters in skin crowd me, while those in feathers circle the sky. Only Lore is missing. I call out to him through the mind link.

Just stay close to your father, Behach Éan.

I take it he's flown off somewhere, probably to scope out the gallery in which I'll commit my heist.

"General Báeinach, welcome to my humble home." Vladimir tilts his head to see past my father's hulking shoulder. "And this must be that fabled daughter of yours."

I can't decide if he uses the term fabled as a veiled insult or if he really does mean it kindly.

"A shame Ríhbiadh couldn't make it," he says, "but I understand. In times of war, a king cannot abandon his people."

Does he understand, though? "I hear you've been fortunate in Glace."

His pale brow furrows. "In what way, Lady Báeinach?"

"In the way that your kingdom has never been at war."

"Ah. Not many people desire a land hardened by ice and forever steeped in snow." He stares at his kingdom, and I can tell he loves his polar desert deeply.

I squint but a white hill obscures my view of the barren land. "Is all of it covered in snow?"

"No. We've forests and beaches of black sand." It's Konstantin who answers. Shoulder to shoulder with his father, the resemblance is uncanny. "Not tropical ones like you're used to in Tarespagia, mind you," he adds with a smile.

"Where do you grow crops?"

"In greenhouses. If you'd like a tour after supper, I'm certain

Alyona would be honored to take you around." Konstantin glances over his shoulder at his siblings who've all kept a few paces back. "I hear the two of you have met already."

"*Met* is a bit of a stretch." I tug at my seashell necklace, coaxing it out from underneath my turtleneck and settling it over the black wool. Though it doesn't resemble a weapon, it is, and I find great comfort in its shape and slight weight. "We've laid eyes on each other."

"It would be nice for her to have a friend amongst your people," he says, redirecting his stare forward. On me.

I'm rather certain Alyona does not care to be friends with the woman who ruined her chances at becoming Dante's bride.

"Yes. Very." Milana's gloved hands climb up her husband's bicep, as though to make sure I notice the man belongs to her.

I start to wrinkle my nose that she believes I may have designs on her husband but become sidetracked by her flared sleeves collapsing to her elbow, revealing stacks of carved ivory bangles inlaid with silver and diamonds. The sight of them tosses me back to the Regio trophy room where Marco so merrily boasted about the Glacins' passion for *mareserpens* tusks.

"Where's my brother?" My father's voice carries me away from Isolacuori.

"At the hunting lodge." Vladimir nods toward the top of a steep hill. "I've had supper set up there."

My stomach roils. Though Crows hunt for food, Fae hunt for sport. Yes, most end up eating their kill, but I find the thrill they take in ending the lives of wild creatures deeply unsettling. *You're wearing gloves and shoes and pants made of animal hide.* My mind's reminder of my two-facedness stifles my revulsion.

"Gabriele?" One of the twins gasps. "Gabriele Moriati?" She strides over the frozen ground, eyes as wide as a fawn's. "Ksenia said it couldn't be you, because you're—well you're—"

"A Faerie?" he supplies.

I can tell, from her spastic head bobbing, that this wasn't what she was hinting at. "I can't believe it's truly you." She gapes at him as though he's changed considerably in the few months since she's seen him. I suppose that between his shorter hairdo and his new allegiance, he's a different man, both in appearance and countenance.

King Vladimir observes Gabriele, as though only now noticing the pointed shape of his ears, but he rapidly loses interest and refocuses on my father and me. "Will you be flying or sleighing?"

Without turning away from Vlad, my father asks, "Ínon? What would you prefer?"

I eye the huge sleighs carved in tawny wood and finished with silver runners. Unlike the sleighs in the story I use to read Mamma, they aren't drawn by horses but by silver-eyed Faeries wearing pale-blue military regalia trimmed with black fur and shiny silver buttons.

"When in Glace, do as the Glacins do." I shoot the royals a smile which I hope will come off as genuine.

I don't loathe them, but I do have beef with them. Not only are they using the runestone to bribe Lore, but they also tried to pitch Alyona into my mate's bed. For my own sanity, I should let that last part go, but however hard I try to shoo it out, one look at Alyona's cold and delicate beauty carries my jealousy front and center.

If what the Cauldron showed Bronwen is true, she will not be of this world much longer. But how reliable is the Cauldron? After all, Gabriele is still alive, and he was destined to die before the last full moon. Though I don't like the princess, I hope Bronwen went heavy on the Faerie wine last night and that was the reason why her mind crafted the princess's death.

Vladimir gestures for my father and I to climb aboard the sleigh first, and then he joins us with his son while his wife, daughters, and youngest child climb into another sleigh with Gabriele. Colm, Aoife, Fionn, and the three other Crows that made the trip morph into feathers and fly.

Vlad's lips bend into a tight smile that's no smile at all. "Though flattered you've traveled over miles of sea to join my family for supper, may I ask what brings you to my icy shores? Cian was vague."

My father dips his bearded chin and fixes the northern monarch with his stare. "Your runestone."

CHAPTER 67

All right then. I guess we're not beating around the bush. Not that there seems to be many bushes in Glace. I clearly remember a conifer forest, but that must've been in some other part of this giant kingdom.

Vlad drapes his arms over the back of his seat. Clearly, he doesn't feel threatened by us or he'd keep his limbs close. "I've sent Ríhbiadh my terms."

Without missing a beat, my father says, "He requests new terms."

Vladimir drums his fingers across the back of the seat, and the sun catches on his pinkie ring—a large silver band stamped with a snowflake. "We will not budge."

"There must be something else you desire." My father sounds desperate, and I suddenly wonder if he doesn't believe I can recover the runestone.

I touch the hand with which he throttles his thigh and ease it off before he shatters the bone. When his gaze snags mine, I squeeze his fingers, attempting to communicate that I got this . . . that we don't need a treaty. All we need is access to the gallery and my blood.

Vladimir watches our exchange. "Isn't it a bit incestuous?"

My father's talons slip from his nails, and he bares his teeth. "What was that, Korol?"

Before he can rip through the Faerie's jugular and start a second war, I whisper, "Dádhi, think of Daya." The sound of my mother's name makes him take a much-needed breath.

The world around us is so quiet that I hear the creak of his thick leather and iron armor as air plows into his lungs. Once he's calmer, I dare glance around us. As though someone's suspended the passing of time, no one and nothing moves. Not the sleighs, nor their passengers, nor the sentries. Even the Crows overhead have stopped beating their wings.

"Forgive me." Vladimir tilts his head, and the small white hairs framing his face shiver in a chilly gust. "I think you misunderstood my comment. I was not remarking on *your* relationship with Fallon, Báeinach."

"Then what in Mórrígan's name were you remarking on?" my father snaps.

"The fact that you slipped your own daughter into your best friend's bed."

My eye spasms. Actually, both my eyes spasm. "Trust me, my father did not *slip me* into his best friend's bed; I slipped myself there. Which caused my father much distress. But he knew there was nothing he could do to prevent Lorcan and me from being together, what with the Sky King being my preordained mate." Perhaps I should've kept that last bit to myself, but it's not exactly a secret. Not one he can monetize, anyway. "You're aware of the importance of mates in our society, correct?"

Vlad's cold gaze scrapes across my striped face before hooking onto the feather on my cheekbone. "When one wants an ally, one must make concessions. When one wants a *charitable* ally, one must make greater concessions." He pauses as though to give his words time to register. How slow on the uptick does he believe me to be? "Besides, my demands were hardly preposterous."

What were his demands, Lore?

Silence.

Lore, what were the Glacin King's demands? I glance at the mighty birds treading the bright air. ***You better not have gotten yourself staked, mo khrà, or I will let you remain a trinket for a fucking fortnight.***

I concentrate so hard on my mate that I manage to swing myself into his mind.

He startles, almost knocking over a statue made of blue glass. "Is everything all right?"

My nostrils flare. "Just checking that you're alive and well since you're not answering me."

"Forgive me. I'm trying to find a way into the gallery to view the stone."

"Glad to see you're unharmed." I look him over but since I'm inside his mind, he appears to me in skin. "You *are* unharmed, correct?"

"Yes." He touches my cheek, but then drops his hand to his side and mutters, "*Focà.* Everything's so fucking white in this land. I'll be out in a second." Our connection crumples before I can ask why he's commenting on the royals' color scheme.

With a sigh, I refocus on the Glacin King. "So, what were those demands of yours?"

"Does your mate not trust you?"

"Excuse me?"

"I tell Milana everything."

"*Awnos duffen,*" I mutter.

Vlad's pupils shrink. "What was that?"

My father lets out a startled chuckle. Though glad that my impromptu swearing brought him a little joy, I school my features into a grim expression and puff out a dramatic sigh. "Sorry, Your Majesty. I've been taking so many lessons in Crow that certain words are coming to me faster than in my native tongue. *Awnos duffen* means *sadly not.*"

My father chokes on another laugh.

It takes everything in me to keep a straight face. "Is my accent that terrible, Dádhi?"

He shakes his head, eyes glistening with mirth. "You've a sweet accent, ínon."

"Anyway. What were we saying? Ah yes. You asked whether my mate trusted me. He does. But what with my abduction and his war, we've had little time to discuss *you.*" I slowly pluck off one glove, which I lay flat on my lap, and then I raise my ink-stained fingers to my necklace.

Confusion stirs in the monarch's eyes. "So, the Sky King sent *you*

—his mate—over to my kingdom to negotiate, and didn't think it sensible to inform you of my terms?"

"You see, I've a temper." I press the pad of my thumb against the apex of my shell until a tiny bead of blood bubbles to the surface. I make sure to angle my hand just right before slipping my pricked finger into my mouth and sucking off the ruby pearl.

Vlad seems more confused than alarmed. Doesn't he know I'm Shabbin or is it my recent unbinding that eludes him?

"A most terrible temper," my father intones.

With a roll of my eyes, I lower my finger from my mouth and pat one of his giant paws, which flips up the corners of his mouth. "I'm guessing they knew I wouldn't appreciate your terms and were trying to spare me, as loved ones often do. I'm also guessing it has to do with hawking off your eldest daughter?"

Color rises so briskly into Vlad's cheeks that I sense I hit a nerve. "*Hawking off*? You make me sound like an ignoble peddler. I love my children. They are *everything* to me. I'm merely trying to ensure their future by landing them profitable unions."

Just a prettier way of saying hawking, Vlad.

I go back to stroking my seashell. "Let me explain how Crow mating works, Your Highness." I'm hoping the use of his title will make the pill I'm about to feed him more palatable, for I'm not trying to ruin relations with Glace. "Crows have one mate, and I happen to be Lorcan's. If you're desperate to find Alyona a good match amongst my people, once we've won the war, I will gladly introduce her to eligible Crows."

He scoffs. "My daughter's a princess. She deserves a king, or at the very least, a prince."

"Well, she cannot have *my* king. As for a prince, I've yet to pop one out, but if my firstborn turns out to be a son, I'll make sure to send word. If we join forces, that is. If we don't, then—"

"Your *son*?" Is it me or do his ears seem to have enlarged? It's probably an optical illusion caused by their high color. "Alyona's almost one hundred!"

Keeping my tone placid, I say, "Thanks to her impeccable gene pool, she's bound to look just as splendid in three decades."

Unless she dies, my mind shrieks at me. I choose not to listen to it.

Vlad mutters something to his son in Glacin.

Though I don't grasp what he says, my father must because he rumbles a low, "Don't. Insult. My daughter."

Vlad's lips stop twitching.

Clutching my seashell pendant now, I say, "If you do not care for us to be your allies, then we will be your enemies."

He surveys my hand, then the giant birds gyrating overhead, and sits up, finally raking his arms toward his torso.

Now that I've got him on the defensive, I build my case for a quick and peaceful resolution that will charter my course away from Glace, away from its weapons, away from Alyona. "Erasing the wards will benefit your kingdom just as much as it will benefit ours. Not just for trade, but also because you'll have access to the Cauldron."

Vlad's pupils flare.

"If the Shabbins allow you near it, that is."

The slenderest dent appears between Konstantin's brows.

"In case you haven't heard, I'm Shabbin, and not just a common Shabbin, but Queen Priya's great-granddaughter."

The Glacin men's lack of surprise tells me that news of my ancestry *has* traveled to Glace.

"What I'm about to suggest will anger my mate, nevertheless, I'm willing to strike a bargain with you—the runestone against an audience with the Cauldron."

Vlad leans in, lust for the legendary source of all magic turning the gray in his eyes a molten silver.

Fallon, no! I forbid you from striking a bargain with the Glacins.

Relief spreads through me at the sound of my mate's voice. ***Don't you trust them?***

I trust they're happy with their lot and don't desire to see us fall, but that's as far as my trust goes.

Is the runestone easy to access?

Not easy, no. He's got a squadron of guards protecting his little museum.

Then this will save us the trouble. Besides, he probably wants to beg the Cauldron for more magic, or coin, or . . . grass.

Grass?

Well, there isn't much of that around here.

Lore is quiet for a moment. Is he contemplating the judiciousness of striking a deal? ***You will owe him, mo khrà. When he's ready to***

claim his bargain, he could ask for anything. Do not owe** any **man, save for me and your father, anything.

Fine. A heist it will be then, I sigh, just as Vladimir of Glace says, "I will take your offer, Fallon Báeinach."

Well, *focá*. How am I supposed to turn down the freely given key to the lost queendom?

CHAPTER 68

What feels like a gust of wind rushes around me, wrapping around my shoulders like a fur stole. I'm guessing it's no wind but three fluid shadows melding into one.

Ask to see the stone, Behach Éan. And have Rossi and Bronwen brought along for the visit since no Crows will be able to linger in the chamber. If it's authentic, then I will strike a bargain.

I hadn't even considered the possibility that it could be counterfeit.

After I've voiced Lore's demands, Vladimir has a sleigh sent to the hunting lodge to fetch the rest of my family, then commands his sentries to head back into the valley, toward that glass pavilion that leads beneath the earth.

My heart judders at the idea of journeying underground.

Lore must feel it clap against his shadows because he caresses my rigid spine and murmurs, ***The palace has skylights everywhere and is made up entirely of white quartz. It's nothing like where you were held.***

Still, I nibble the life out of my lip.

I'm here, Behach Éan. Your father is, too.

But you won't be able to penetrate the obsidian gallery. Even my mind-voice is shrill with nerves.

I can enter it. I just cannot remain in it for too long.

That does little to ease my qualms.

My love, I can sever necks quicker than you can blink, and I can do so just fine surrounded by the cursed stone.

I swallow, finally feeling infinitesimally calmer. Who would've known that I'd one day find comfort in the idea of beheadings?

By the time we reach the pavilion, another sleigh is gliding down the mountain with three people aboard. Though still far, I don't miss the burnt-orange hue of a long ponytail streaming behind one of the passengers.

"Shall we head inside?" Vladimir nods to his castle. "Your teeth are chattering."

Not because of the brisk temperatures . . .

"We wait." My father's eyes don't waver off the approaching sleigh.

Konstantin unhooks the fur cloak and begins to slide it off his shoulders. "Here."

When I realize he wants to give it to me, I shake my head. "I'm fine, but thank you. I appreciate your thoughtfulness."

Lore's shadows pinch one of my nipples.

What the Cauldron, Lore? I hiss.

Just trying to keep you warm, mo khrà.

By tweaking my nipples?

You stopped shivering, didn't you? No need for Konstantin's coat.

I wasn't going to take it, I grumble.

One of Vladimir's twins approaches, and as she does, I catch the sparkle of a dozen diamond snowflakes pinned into her straight, gold hair. "Why did we turn around, Atsa?"

I take it Atsa means Father in Glacin. Unless it means Your Majesty?

Father, Lore supplies. ***Majesty is Vizosh.***

Vladimir's gaze perches on my face. "We've decided to conclude our alliance before supping."

Her eyes widen. "King Ríhbiadh's accepted to marry Alyona?"

"No." My teeth have definitely stopped chattering.

"Then"—her pretty brow pleats—"then I don't understand."

He tells her of our little bargain in their tongue.

"Atsa, no. Shabbins bathe in their enemies' blood! They *drink* it! We cannot let them loose."

To think I used to believe these rumors myself. "Not only is soaking in blood positively vile, it's also surely insalubrious."

"They will sail to our shores and massacre us!"

I hitch up an eyebrow. "Why would they do that?"

"Because they're savages." She pants with such fright that even the hairs of her fur coat stand on end. "I've sailed past their island. I've seen their beaches. They're so saturated with blood that the sand has turned pink."

Although neither here nor there, I do begin to wonder what I would've been served for supper. A stein of fresh blood?

Lorcan snorts.

I slip my hand over the slow-roiling shadows of my mate, wishing he was in skin. Wishing he was standing at my side. "Have you ever traveled to Shabbe, Vizosh?"

Vladimir seems surprised by my use of the Glacin term. "No. I was born the year the wards were erected."

"Your parents then?"

"Yes."

"And do they share your daughter's conviction?"

"They said the beaches were white back then." Konstantin stares at the horizon. "That five centuries of confinement turned the matriarchal society raving mad."

"Their beaches were never white," my father says gruffly. "And they don't fucking drink blood. They use it to cast spells."

The girl gawks at my father as though he's just confirmed that they do, in fact, feast on their enemies' veins.

"Do you find me terrifying?" I ask as the sleigh we await skids to a halt a few paces away from us.

She frowns. "Why would I? Because you're the daughter of a Crow?"

"Because I'm the daughter of a Shabbin."

Her head rears back, making the diamonds twinkle in her flaxen strands. "That's impossible. No one with even an ounce of Shabbin blood can live outside those wards."

So Vladimir and his son know, but not his daughters?

"Actually, Ksenia"—Vladimir eyes the reddened apex of my seashell—"Meriam and her descendants apparently can."

Ksenia whips her head back in my direction. "But her eyes aren't pink."

I tip my head toward my father. "Mixed origins."

As Bronwen, Justus, and Cian descend from their sleigh, the Glacin Princess scrutinizes me some more. "You truly descend from Meriam?"

"Truly."

"And you don't drink blood?"

"I don't even eat meat or fish."

Her eyebrows jerk up as though my vegetarian diet is perplexing.

The other twin—Izolda—nudges her way between her father and Ksenia. "Can you blood-cast?"

Vladimir tips his head. "No. Her magic is bound, daughter."

"That's why she's able to remain on this side of the wards." Konstantin tucks a long piece of white hair behind his broad ear that's adorned with a whole line of faceted diamonds as clear as ice. "That's also why she desires the runestone. Freeing Shabbe will also free her magic. Am I right, Lady Báeinach?"

"Absolutely." I never thought I'd be so pleased about misinformation.

"My tutor said that Shabbins can behead a Faerie by circling their necks with blood." Izolda's comment not only leaches color from her sister's face, but also makes her reach into her coat and wrap her hand around the hilt of a dagger that glitters with a diamond snowflake.

My breath catches. My heart, too.

Vladimir misinterprets my surprise. "Ksenia, the Crows are our friends. Right?"

The soldiers surrounding the king begin to stir, some palming weapons, others raising hands glittering with magic.

Lore's shadows firm around my torso like armor. ***Answer him immediately. Tell him that we are his friends.***

"Right," I all but gasp. Though my reply defuses the tension surrounding me, it does nothing to ease the one roiling through me because the weapon Ksenia fingers is the weapon from Bronwen's vision.

The one that ends Alyona of Glace's life.

Justus ambles toward us, hands loose at his sides. "I thought we were to sup?"

I'm glad to see him unshackled.

"We will sup, but first"—Vlad dips his chin—"Lore's *mate* has requested a tour of my museum."

If Justus is startled by the news of my forwardness, he doesn't let it show. He merely says, "Splendid. I so enjoyed our first visit."

"I expect you'll enjoy this one even more, Rossi." Vladimir lays a hand on his daughter's head and strokes her hair. "After all, you'll get to see the infamous runestone you were so desperate to lay eyes on."

Justus doesn't even flinch at being called out. "What can I say? It's the last of its kind. Not to mention the source of considerable contention."

I so envy his unruffled composure and can only hope that someday I, too, will be able to appear calm and collected even when my insides are collapsing.

Bronwen and Cian stroll toward us, hand in hand. Though I stare at my aunt, she keeps her white eyes on the cloudless sky over our heads.

"Now that we're all here, shall we?" Vladimir sweeps his hand toward his hidden palace.

Where Izolda whirls and skips ahead, Ksenia eyes me, then eyes our delegation. Her pupils tighten, and I think she'll reach back into her coat for the dagger, but I'm wrong. "Where's Alyona?"

My heart claps my neck as I spin around and squint, the sun's harsh glare bleaching my vision.

"She went to her bedroom to fetch syrup for her stomach." Milana walks to her husband's side, their son's hand tucked into her gloved one

Vlad's high cheekbones fill with color. "How incompetent are our healers if what ails her still hasn't passed?"

I don't miss the quick look Milana shares with Konstantin, but Vladimir does.

"I'll go check on her." She pats her husband's arm and heads inside with Ilya.

Vlad turns, his thick fur boots crunching over the crisp snow. "Come. The stone awaits."

"It does not, Vizosh." Bronwen's eyes gleam like the land we stand on. "The stone does not await."

CHAPTER 69

"What do you mean, the stone does not await?" Vladimir narrows his eyes on Bronwen, which makes Cian pull her in closer.

"I mean it's no longer in its case." She levels her attention on Vladimir as though she knows exactly where he is. "What I *mean,* Vizosh, is that it's been stolen."

Konstantin gasps a muted, "What?"

My eardrums start ringing so loudly that I can barely hear anything over the harsh thrash of my pulse.

Oh, for focá's sake . . . Lore unwraps himself from around my torso, and I think he may make his presence known, which will only rile the Glacins up further.

Lore.

I need to find her. Stay with your father.

Her? I shiver as though I'm adrift in the Glacin sea. ***Who?***

My father steps in front of me, barking something at the Glacins that I cannot make out. His shoulders seem to spill outward, as though he were growing his wings, except he isn't growing wings; merely heaving smoke.

Aoife slinks against my back, murmuring, "This must be reason she dies."

I pinch myself, and then I do it again, desperate to snap out of my daze. When the world bangs back into focus, I finally make out the conversations booming around me.

Every single one is about Alyona.

About how, soon after her return from Luce, she started visiting the gallery every day, animated by a newfangled appetite for art.

"She sketched. I saw her sketch!" Izolda exclaims, cheeks reddened by how quickly she spins her head to follow conversations. "How could you accuse her of stealing, Atsa?"

"Was she ever alone in the gallery?" Konstantin asks one of the guards.

The general, perhaps? Unlike the other soldiers, his lapel is embellished by several lines of snowflake pins and his ears drip with pale-blue stones.

The blond man tosses the question out at the soldiers that have encircled us. I wait for their answers with bated breath.

"These people have motive, Atsa." She slings her gaze over my people. Over me. "What's Alyona's?"

"Her love for Dante Regio." Though quiet, my voice must reach the princess's tall ears for I become the sole recipient of her glower.

"What does my sister's crush have to do with the Shabbin wards?"

"The first Shabbin Queen, Queen Mara—or Mórrígan, as she was known by the Crows—bestowed upon Lore and his clan the power to shift into birds so they could unite Luce under one banner. You can imagine on whose side the Shabbins will be once freed." In case anyone's imagination is limited, I add, "Not the Regios."

I'm suddenly back in Costa's castle of doom, back in that vault with Meriam, hearing the history of my people recounted in detail to me for the very first time.

"I was just informed Olena took the princess to the Ice Floe Market yesterday evening, Vizosh," the man with all the pins proclaims.

Vlad's eyes darken with fury. "Fetch Olena!"

A minute ticks by, then another, and then an elderly halfling servant is dragged out of the castle, gray, shoulder-length hair swinging beside her round ears like steel blades.

"Olena!" Izolda elbows her way through the heavy throng of soldiers. "Don't hurt her!"

"Izolda, stay back." Her father's voice is as sharp as the icicles dripping from the pavilion ceiling.

The young girl skids to a halt beside her brother, her chest lifting and falling as she gawps in horror at the halfling's puffing cheeks. I hear her whisper what sounds like a plea inside her brother's broad ear.

Vlad switches to Glacin as he addresses Olena. I take it she must not speak our tongue.

"He's asking her why she took the princess to the human marketplace," Justus murmurs, sidling in nearer to me. Olena speaks again. "The nursemaid says Alyona wanted to purchase fabric to surprise her sisters with new gowns for their birthday." He listens to the next question and then to the next answer. "He reminded her that they have a royal tailor. Apparently, the princess claimed the gift wouldn't be from her if she were to use the family seamster."

One of the soldiers holding Olena says something that makes the halfling's eyes go wide and wild.

"Alyona traded one of her fur stoles for the fabric." At my frown, Justus tips his head and dips his chin. "The princess has access to a bottomless purse yet she gave the sailor a fur cloak."

"Why is that creating such a tizzy? Isn't fur a prized commodity?"

"It is. It's also hefty and heavily-lined. The perfect place to store a clunky valuable."

My jaw loosens around a muted gasp that's drowned out by a heartrending cry. Izolda throws herself on her father's sword arm just as he wrenches it across the nursemaid's face.

"Why, Atsa?" she wails. "Why did you do that?" She drops to her knees and crawls toward the silent, bleeding woman. "Why?"

"Because Olena helped your sister betray us, daughter. Be glad I used my platinum blade instead of my iron one. And be glad I only took one of her eyes and not both."

Ksenia, who's not moved from her brother's side, gasps Alyona's name, followed by a croaked flock of Glacin words.

"She asked what is to be her sister's punishment," Justus translates quietly.

My stomach knots because, if there's truth to Bronwen's vision, then she will lose far more than her sight.

"Salom, get my daughters and lock Olena up. Everyone else, find

Alyona!" Vladimir spins on his heel, droplets of halfling blood gliding off his blade and pinkening the snow.

"Atsa." Konstantin nods to the sky, to the Crow carrying a flailing white-haired girl.

The second Alyona's boots touch the ground, the bird dissolves into smoke and rushes back toward me. I wonder if anyone noticed how much smaller in stature he was to the other shifters in feathers. If anyone did, they don't seem to care. Their full attention rests on the Glacin Princess whose complexion is as pale as her hair.

Vlad advances toward her. "Who did you sell our runestone to, daughter?"

"I did not sell it to anyone." She glances over her shoulder as though to map out an escape route.

"Don't lie!"

"I'm not, Atsa. I did not sell it. I gave it," she bites out, her teeth barely separating. "I gave it to people who still care about protecting Faeries from demons." Her clear eyes vault over our striped faces.

"Why everyone think we demons?" Aoife murmurs.

"Demons are said to possess people." It seems ludicrous that Justus is taking the time to explain this to my friend. Since her brow remains ruffled, he pursues his enlightenment. "Faeries believe you're possessed by those giant birds with iron appendages."

She tilts her black eyebrows. "What means *possessed*?"

He translates the word into Crow because, of freaking course, the man's fluent in my father tongue.

"Didn't know you spoke Crow?"

"I'm an old man, Fallon. Once you reach my age, you'll be fluent in every tongue."

"To whom did you give it, Sister?" Konstantin has marched over to Alyona and now stands in front of her.

"I gave it to the General of Luce."

All heads spin toward Justus, who mutters a quiet, "*Merda*," before raising his palms in the air.

CHAPTER 70

"Shall I remind everyone that I'm not the current Lucin general. Tavo Diotto is." Still, Justus keeps his hands in the air. "Alyona, dear, please clear the matter up. You may not care if you're run through with a steel blade or an iron beak, but I care. Deeply," he adds when no Glacin soldier lowers his sword.

Alyona hunts the tight knot of Crows until her limpid stare lands on him. "Rossi? Justus Rossi?"

"Speaking."

She gasps. "Tavo said you were on our side!"

"I'm a terribly good thespian."

"What thespian mean?" Aoife murmurs.

"Actor," I whisper back.

She side-eyes Justus, then nods. "*Tà*. He really good. I thought he was bad guy."

"Thank you, Aoife."

"I don't think she meant it as a compliment, Nonno," I murmur.

"I'll take it as one anyway."

And yes, I'm aware that our aside is completely at odds with the moment, but it does wonders for my spasming nerves.

"Yesterday night," my father suddenly murmurs. "If she gave the runestone to Diotto yesterday, then his ship—"

"Hasn't yet reached Luce," I finish, my pitch as lofty as my pulse.

"Yes." His black hair flies around his face at his brutal nod.

"Lorcan!" My father scans the sky until his eyes latch on to the shadows that blunt the golden-blue hue of the polar evening.

"So your king *is* here," Vlad mutters. "You said he stayed behind in Luce."

"He did, Vizosh." Smoke begins to waft off Cian's pauldrons. "Two of his crows stayed; the other *two* came."

My father's eyes gloss with renewed hope. "We leave now!"

"What about my treaty, Ríhbiadh?" Vladimir thunders. And then his body jerks, and his eyes glaze with what I assume is a Lore-made vision. When he comes to, his jaw is tight. "All right," he mutters.

He said all right to what?

To the terms of my alliance.

What did you show him?

The fate of his kingdom should his son agree to swear an oath to us. I feel the scrape of my mate's silk on my cheek. ***I may also have shown him the fate of his kingdom should Konstantin*** **disagree.** ***I made sure to make it tremendously unappealing.***

My snort barely has time to congeal in the chilled air before Vladimir barks, "Konstantin, swear an oath to Lorcan's mate."

To me?

Yes, mo khrà. To you. I want my future queen to have influential ties to tug upon in times of trouble.

I have magical blood, Lore. And I have you.

And now you have the future King of Glace.

I thought you disliked the man.

I disliked his desire to put his cloak around your shoulders, but other than that, I like the boy just fine.

To think that boy is at least a century older than me.

Said boy's head rears back. "Atsa, no!"

"Now, Konstantin."

The prince's features sharpen until their edges are as cutting as an ice carving. "Fallon Báeinach, I—"

Alyona cackles, a sound that is as ugly as she is beautiful. "You're all doomed."

"Speak the vow, Konstantin. Let us be done with our negotiations. Let us be at peace."

"Fallon Báeinach, *ya tabim ty.*" Konstantin expels a muted gasp when the magic inscribes itself onto his chest.

I'm in such shock that I barely register the heat cinching my arm.

"Now punish your sister for her act of treason."

Konstantin's tall body seizes.

"She stole from us, son."

The look Konstantin flashes his father is filled with such melancholy that it makes my heart clench for him.

"Don't make my brother do your dirty work." Alyona squares her shoulders and lifts her chin. "You've Salom for that. Your general loves nothing more than carving up people's faces. I'm certain it'll be his pleasure to carve up mine."

The blond with all the pins narrows his eyes on the princess.

Lore, can we leave? Please? We've got a ship to locate. Not to mention, I'm itching to flee this kingdom before my hand finds itself wrapped around a Glacin's dagger.

You don't kill her, Fallon.

But Bronwen's vision . . .

He must give the order for everyone to shift because leather and iron melt into feathers and smoke. ***Climb atop Aoife. I don't trust your father not to charge headfirst into Diotto's ship.***

I'm so shocked that Bronwen was wrong that, for a full minute, all I can do is stare at Gabriele.

Fallon!

I jump at the sound of my name.

I'm swinging myself onto Aoife's back when Vladimir barks, "Iron, Konstantin. Use iron."

"But—"

"The shame your sister brought upon our family is not to be forgotten."

"Shame?" Alyona's long white hair lifts from the wind stirred by Crow wingbeats. "I tried to save our family."

"Lorcan, no!" Bronwen tightens her grip on Cian's neck. "Don't make me regret having told you."

I glance from Bronwen to my mate, who hovers over the Glacin Princess, casting her in his shadow. ***Regret having told you what, Lore?***

"The Shabbins will destroy us!" Alyona shouts as snowflakes

swirl around her. "They will command their serpents to sink our ships. They will isolate us until we fall to our knees on blood-soaked snow."

I feel a hundred sets of eyes lift toward us. The only one who doesn't look up is Vladimir of Glace.

He stares fixedly at his daughter. "You're a seer now, daughter?"

"I don't need the Cauldron to show me the future when I've eyes." Her limpid stare moves over us, her hatred lifting and scraping over my skin. "But by all means, Atsa, take them from me for I prefer not to watch our world drown in blood."

Those are the last words I hear her speak before Lorcan rockets toward the ocean, guiding us away from the land of snow and ice.

What was that, between you and Bronwen?

It takes Lorcan several heartbeats before he admits, ***She was telling me not to strike down Alyona of Glace.*** He sounds as though he's just bitten into something sour. ***Not to meddle with Fate.***

Fate?

The girl Bronwen saw standing over Alyona's body, Glacin dagger in hand, is not you, Fallon. It's our daughter.

CHAPTER 71

My clammy fingers tighten around Aoife's throat. ***Our . . . We have a daughter?***

Not yet.

I roll my eyes. ***I may have been kept in a magical coma, but it lasted two weeks; not nine months.***

Anger vibrates so loudly through our bond that I mentally kick myself for having brought up my imprisonment.

How far is the ship?

Silence.

Lore?

My mate must've flocked into his head because his silence endures.

Lore, let the past—

It will forever haunt me. As for the ship, we'll reach it in about two hours.

Will we be sinking it?

After we recover the runestone, yes.

If only we had the cover of night . . . To think that in Luce, the sky's dark with stars, but out here, on the Northern Sea, golden rays still skip across the waves.

I will conjure a storm.

I wait to hear the rest of his plan. When he doesn't elaborate, I prompt him with an, ***And . . .?***

And then I'll steal aboard the ship in shadow form. Once I detect the stone, I'll shift and carry it out of wherever they've hidden it with my talons.

I stare at him.

What?

That's a terrible plan, Lore.

Excuse me?

They'll have obsidian weapons aboard. And perhaps even pints of Meriam's blood.

All the blood that was distributed around Luce—

—is serpent blood. I know. I heard. But what if Tavo has the fucking real deal?

He mutters something under his breath.

Oh, don't you growl at me for using the word fuck. It's truly not that godsawful. No worse than your plan.

Do you have a better one?

Yes, actually, I do. I make us all invisible. We storm their ship and find the stone, toss Diotto overboard so the serpents can deal with him, and then we book it home.

Fine.

Fine what?

I like your plan.

I'm so shocked by his admission that I blink at all three of his crows.

But you're not getting on that boat.

That's a rather pivotal part of the plan.

You'll paint the invisibility sigil on all of us, but you'll stay with Aoife in the air.

Lorcan's refusal to let me take part in the action shouldn't surprise me. If it were up to him, I'd be locked in an iron bubble.

I scan the endless carpet of blue beneath us. ***Do you think they know we're coming?***

We saw their ship during the flight over, so odds are, they saw us.

They may not know that Alyona gave them up so easily . . .

One of his crows slants me a look. One that says that they'll know we broke Alyona's silence. I suppose there's little a murder of Crows cannot break.

My thoughts drift to the princess then. To the news that, someday, a child of mine will sail across this sky to Glace and spill her blood. Will it be premeditated? Will it be in self-defense? I glance over my shoulder at the white continent that gleams like a milk spill.

What will you do to my child, Alyona?

The sky growls, ripping me away from the future and hurtling me back into the present. ***Don't we still have hours of flight?***

We do, but I want them to know we're coming. I want them to taste my wrath; feel it needle their skin and turn their stomachs. I want them to rue the day they decided to become our enemy.

The clouds rush in from every direction, settling so thickly underneath us that they obscure the sea.

What if they throw the stone overboard, Lore?

There are no maritime trenches in these parts. Even a Crow will be able to dive to recover it. But they won't. It's their last defense against Shabbe. As darkness slowly drapes across the sun, weakening its reach, he adds, ***Why do you think Diotto took this mission upon himself? Why do you think he didn't entrust it to his soldiers?***

Dread begins to pool in my belly. I imagined this would be a painless recovery mission, but something so precious is bound to ignite a battle that will cost lives. May the only ones to fall be our enemies . . .

I'm still clutching that little prayer when, not even an hour later, Colm's Crow releases a gut-wrenching caw and stiffens. Color leaches from Gabriele's face and his wide, haunted eyes meet mine a second before his obsidian steed plummets through the clouds, rider still on his back.

CHAPTER 72

I scream as Colm and Gabriele fall, then scream again when Fionn plunges after his mate, surely sealing his obsidian fate.

Lore? I shout as Aoife beats her great wings to ascend higher into the sky.

My mate does not answer, and when I stare around, the only Crows I see suspended in the air are Cian and the male carrying Justus.

Fuck. Fuck. Fuck. I shout my mate's name into the bond again, and again, I get no answer.

"Aoife, I'm going to make us invisible, all right?"

She turns her head toward me, her black eyes gleaming with anxiety. I raise my shaking hand to my necklace and prick my finger, then tunnel my fingers beneath one of my sleeves and draw the sigil on my forearm.

When Aoife's wings still, I know it's worked.

"I'm still here, Aoife." Though it would be a stretch to say that the sound of my voice settles her, it does make her wings stir. "Your turn."

I plow through the feathers covering her head—as far from her heart as I can reach—and adorn her skin with the same spell.

When she becomes one with the air, I say, "Fly us to the ship. They won't see us."

I feel her head shake beneath my palm.

"Lorcan is down there, Aoife, and he's not answering me. Please." I try to gauge the ocean's distance through the covering of clouds. "Fine. I'll jump."

She must decide I'm mad enough to go through with my threat because she tucks in her wings and pitches downward. Though I cannot hear her in this form, I can just imagine her muttering to herself how Lorcan will turn her into a forever-Crow if Diotto's little army doesn't beat him to it.

The second we emerge from the clouds, my heart holds still. The galleon rocks in the churning sea, an obsidian Crow embedded inside its deck between giant wheels that smoke as they turn, launching pellets—not arrows.

Not a single Faerie, besides my fallen friend, darkens the deck. Gabriele's crumpled body is haloed in blood, his limbs bent at awry angles, one of them pinned beneath Colm's splayed obsidian wing. Though a scream claws at my throat, I wrangle it back. Gabriele is a pureling, and pure-bloods don't perish from mortal wounds.

The boat rocks, and though his upper body twists, his crushed leg keeps him from rolling into the gaping Crow-shaped hole that splinters the deck beside him.

Another spray of pellets rockets into the air. I guide Aoife's shuddering body to the right, out of their trajectory. Another burst is set free. And then a third. They're shot at intervals. I count the seconds separating each launch, and as I count, I realize that I will have mere heartbeats to board the bridge.

Unless I board the vessel from the railing . . .

The galleon lists, its masts skimming the waves. Lorcan will end up sinking the ship with his storm if he doesn't let up. I call out to him but he must've walled off his mind to avoid distractions because my voice echoes in the void.

I curl my legs tighter around Aoife's haunches as she swoops low to avoid a hail of pellets. "The second the ship rights itself, fly me down!" I scream over the creak of wood and slap of water. "Nod if you understand me."

Her nod is slow to come, but it comes.

"The moment I'm off your back, you bolt back into those clouds and you fly high, you hear me?"

The ship rights itself. She swoops low. A heartbeat before it begins to tip the other way, I jump off her back and onto the bridge. I brace myself as I smack into the rain-slicked wood and reach out to the railing.

My arm shrieks as the boat tips, my knuckles whitening as I grip the wood. I may love the ocean, but I don't want to end up in it right now. A Crow swoops nearby. Since I can see its massive dark shape, I assume it's not Aoife. Unless the rain has washed away my spell.

Lore, call off the clouds and rain, and command every Crow to fly out of the Faerie contraption's reach, all right?

Several long minutes pass.

Lore?

Ugh . . . If only I still had a bargain to call upon.

Lorcan Ríhbiadh, stop this storm immediately.

Fallon, where are you?

On the ship.

Lightning forks into the raging ocean. ***And what are you doing on the ship, mo khrà?*** He speaks so slowly that his words creak like the wooden galleon.

You weren't answering. I got worried.

Silence, then: ***Where are you exactly?***

Why?

So I can carry you the fuck away, that's why.

I flatten myself against the deck and belly-crawl toward the splintered cavity. As I press my palms into the drenched teak, little rocks embed themselves inside my palm. I start to brush them off when I catch sight of their color—black. This must be what the clay-brained Faeries are shooting at us.

Fallon?!

I don't make a peep, too afraid to drag him into the path of these pellets as I crawl over to Gabriele's side, my body airlifting and slamming down into the deck three times. ***Lore, I beg you, ease your storm before it tosses me into Mareluce.***

The ocean quiets immediately. The change is almost too quick for my liking.

I pick my head off the wooden slats and stare around me for the gleam of an iron crow. ***Lore?***

The great wheels groan, and smoke bursts against my jaw, the only place on my body not covered by fabric.

Not smoke, Behach Éan; me.

My heart slams against my ribs. ***No! Get back, Lore. Please. Get away.***

No more obsidian is being launched, mo khrà.

I blink at the wheels and find that they have, in fact, stopped spinning, then blink at my mate. ***You can see me?***

No, but I can hear your heart beat.

The world is suddenly so quiet that I can hear wet grunts and heavy thumps down below.

I tug myself nearer to the Crow-shaped crevasse and squint. Though the boat no longer lists, my stomach empties at the stench and sight below deck.

CHAPTER 73

My vomit sluices atop a head right as it rolls into the boots of a Crow in skin. Erwin.

The male peers at the noxious splash before craning his neck up to uncover its source.

Our enemies are gone, Behach Éan. You can make yourself reappear.

Gone. What a pretty way to say dead.

I flop onto my back, focusing my stinging eyes on the Crows circling the cotton balls of clouds until my stomach spasms calm. Only then do I carry my trembling palm off my abdomen and onto my forearm. I hover it over my skin like Justus had done back in the obsidian stronghold. When my skin prickles, I lower my hand and wipe.

A soft gasp sounds beside me.

I loll my head to the side to find Gabriele blinking wide eyes at me. "Hey."

He doesn't utter a single peep, just gapes.

I roll onto my side and then onto my knees. "I'm going to get Colm off you, okay?"

I stand and inspect the giant statue's overturned body for an entry wound, spotting a small depression smack in the middle of his abdomen. Unless I climb him, I won't be able to reach it. Though I'm not particularly heavy, I don't want to add to the pressure crushing my friend, so I seize Colm's wing. Gritting my teeth, I soften my knees into a squat, then push into my thighs, shoving the black wing as high as I can, which isn't high enough to break Gabriele free.

"Justus!" I grunt. "A little help."

He must hear my entreaty because his steed flies him down to the galleon's deck. "Did they find the runestone?" he asks as he makes his way toward me, casting his attention left and right as though fearing a soldier escaped the Crows' wrath.

"I don't know yet. Help me lift Colm?"

He looks down at the younger Faerie, mouth pursed with pity. "I'll lift him; you grab his body. When I say *go*, you drag him out, all right?"

I nod and drop into a crouch, grab Gabriele's arm and hook his belt. "Keep your eyes on me, Moriati." I add a smile that I hope will comfort him.

The wooden slats creak.

"Go." The word blusters out of Justus's mouth like a grunt.

I yank. Gabriele sucks in a sharp breath that transforms into a weak whimper when I skate his body out from underneath Colm's. The second his mangled leg is free, Justus releases the obsidian wing and the bird settles with a harsh thud against the deck.

Justus inspects the Faerie's leg, then roots through his jacket pocket.

When the sun catches on his ruby-encrusted snuffbox, I frown. He cannot possibly think this is a good moment for salt oaths. Besides, what confessions is he after? It isn't as though Gabriele colluded with Dante and Tavo . . . Oh my Gods, is *that* what Justus thinks?

He turns the little case over in his hand, then flicks a little latch that pops open the bottom. My eyes draw wide. The secret compartment shines with a rainbow palette of Shabbin crystals. He leans over Gabriele, then gently peels the slashed black leather off the male's mangled calf, selects three ochre crystals, and packs them into the wound.

A hiss falls from Gabriele's lips as the crystals dissolve into his blood and work their magic on his flesh.

"Stick out your tongue, Moriati." Justus roots through his little stash for another bead.

As he feeds him a purple crystal, I scale Colm's obsidian body. The pellet's embedded so deep that I'll need a tool to pinch it out. I'm about to ask for one when a scream rises from the galleon's belly. My heart vaults into my throat and expands there.

LORE?

All's well, Little Bird.

It does not sound like all's well. Who screamed?

The last of the crew. Your father was collecting information on Diotto's whereabouts.

Tavo's not on the ship?

No.

"Ínon, can you come down here and wake Fionn?"

I scramble off Colm and traipse over to the Crow-shaped crater.

My father extends his arms. He's so tall that his fingers crest the lip of the deck. I spear my hands through his and hop. The hull is dark, the air sticky with the metallic scent of blood and tangy reek of piss.

Someone must've kicked the bodiless head on which I threw up aside because it's no longer rolling around. Thank the Cauldron.

As my eyes adjust to the gloom, I pick out six Crows in skin milling about, heaping corpses. I don't bother tallying up the number of dead, but I'm admittedly stunned to find so few. "Have you tossed some of the soldiers overboard?"

"What?" My father blinks away from the hillock of white stained with so much red, the Lucin uniforms appear patterned.

I gesture to the dead.

"No." My father's lips flatten. "That was all of them."

"Lore said Diotto wasn't amongst them. Did Alyona lie about meeting with him?"

"No."

I raise my gaze to one of the portholes and gaze out at the sparkling blue beyond. "Did he board another ship?"

"No."

I swing my attention back to my father. "So he stayed in Glace?"

My father nods just as Erwin, the man whose boots I soiled earlier, tosses one more body atop the growing mound.

"Did you get their location?" Cathal asks.

I hitch up an eyebrow.

"He said the only thing he was told was to sail back to Luce with whomever was left on board and not speak of this little voyage."

Footsteps thud on the ceiling above my head, and then a door creaks and Justus appears. "Let's hope they didn't keep the stone on the floor."

I pop my lips wide to avoid breathing in through my nose. "Do you think Faerie blood will absorb into it and warp the sigil?"

"No. I'd just prefer not to get my hands dirty." As he trundles down the short flight of steps, his gaze tapers on the Shadow King. "No filthier than yours, Mórrgaht."

I sigh. "Can you two play nice? At least until the wards come down and Dante's dead?"

Though Lore has no teeth in this form, I swear I can hear them click.

"The stone's not here, Rossi." My father rolls his neck, eliciting many cracks. "The soldier we interrogated admitted that it stayed behind in Glace with Diotto, Regio, and Meriam."

CHAPTER 74

My eardrums thrum. The buzzing grows so loud that it eclipses all other sounds. Though I see Justus's lips move, I cannot hear what he says.

Dante's in Glace.

Meriam's in Glace.

"I thought they were in the tunnels," I finally say.

They fled Luce by a tunnel that led them straight into the Tarespagian harbor. Antoni and Mattia just confirmed they found tread marks on the stone that match the width of Meriam's throne.

I cannot get over the fact that Dante slipped right from under our noses and left Luce. He abandoned his people. And he calls himself a king . . .

That Faerie was never a king. He's hardly a man.

"Ínon." My father nods to Fionn. "Can you wake him so we can—so we can depart?" I'm guessing he means to Glace.

I stare at the stone Crow's bulk. "Where's the entry wound?"

"I believe he was shot in the abdomen." Erwin wipes his palms on his trousers.

"Any ideas how we can flip him over, Nonno?"

Justus comes to a stop beside me, eyes trained on Fionn's retracted wings. Had they been stretched any wider, they would've spanned the entire width of the ship.

I suppose that, worse comes to worse, Lore can sink the ship. In the water, I can swim beneath the stone bird. Not that I particularly want to test the waters of the Northern Sea, which I hear are very nippy, but if there's no other solution . . . "You wouldn't know of a rune that can pivot things?"

"I'm afraid not."

I lower my gaze to the floor glazed in blood and vomit, nose wrinkling. "I could head down to the deck beneath this one and cut open a manhole to access his abdomen."

"You could, but I've a better idea." He walks over to a wooden crate and begins to drag it over, but stops when the lid pops free. As he goes to fit the nails back into their slots, he freezes.

"What is it?" I crane my neck.

He snaps his head up and glares at the Crows. "Which one of you killed this Faerie?"

Erwin casts a cursory glance at the corpse inside the crate. "Daggers through the heart aren't our style." Erwin prods the corpse. "Besides, he's stiff as a log and smells vile. I suspect he's been dead for days."

I pad closer, but the pungency of decay is so strong that I fall back. "Was he a friend, Nonno?"

Lips pressed tight, my grandfather walks over to another crate. This time, he removes the lid and inspects the contents before dragging it my way.

"Who was that Faerie to you?"

"One of the soldiers guarding Meriam with his life." He kicks the crate between Fionn's wing and body. "We'll need a second box."

Erwin obliges.

"While I help Fallon with this spell, can you check the other crates and the other floors on this ship and let me know if you find a brown-skinned male with long black curls?"

I fathom the man he's asked the Crows to seek is the other Faerie he left in charge of Meriam's protection.

He shuts his eyes and gives his head a brief shake. "There's a spell to rapidly increase something's size."

The thrill of learning a new spell presses my concern for Meriam's slain guard aside.

"You'll want to draw an arrow facing upwards."

"That's it? An arrow?"

"Hover your finger over the symbol for it will not stop growing until you slash through the rune."

I follow his directions and draw on the wood. Before my very wide eyes, the crate begins to expand upward.

"Slash!" Justus's shout jolts my fingers across the arrow.

I perform the same spell on the other crate, this time stopping the progression before needing to be reminded.

I don't realize how silent it's become until my father murmurs, "*Dachrich*. Incredible."

I take it that's what *dockreh* translates into. It dawns on me that this is the first time my father has seen me perform magic.

I beam. "Know any sigils to create light?"

"Swirl blood into your palm." It's my father who supplies me with this answer. "I saw Daya do that once."

I start at the center of my palm and pinwheel my finger until I've reached the juncture of my thumb. For a moment, nothing happens, but then my hand absorbs every last drop of red, and my palm ignites.

I lower myself to the floor, trying to disregard the substances that soak into my hair and clothes as I slide myself beneath Fionn.

When the boat begins to list, and the crates to groan, Lore shouts, ***OUT! Get out from under him before he crushes you.***

Keep the boat steady for me, my love.

Fallon!

It takes me three heartbeats to locate the indent the pellet caused. Though I could scrape it out with my pinkie, I don't want to risk getting blood on the obsidian. "I'll need a small stick." When none appears, I say, "Or a needle-thin blade."

A second later, a fork whose tines have been crushed together scrapes across the wooden slats toward me. "Or cutlery." I grip my tool and dig it into the dint until the razor-sharp pellet plinks out, hitting my armor before rolling off.

In seconds, Fionn transforms from stone to smoke to feathers to man. His face is gray with fright; his eyes haunted. His first word is his mate's name. I nod to the bridge. He disintegrates once again into smoke and floats up.

Fork in hand, I stand just as wood groans.

"I found no other corpse, Rossi, but I did find this." Erwin uncorks a pitcher.

"This is really not the time for a tipple, brother," my father grumbles.

"Oh, it's not liquor." He holds it out to him. "Smell."

My father takes one whiff and stiffens. Whatever's inside beats down the size of his pupils.

"You think it's Meriam's, Rossi?"

Justus blinks at the black-glass pitcher. "Only one way to tell." He holds out his hand.

Erwin swings it out of his reach.

"For the last time, I don't wish harm upon any of you."

Erwin cocks a brow, then must decide he trusts Justus because he upends a little blood onto my grandfather's palm. Justus swirls his finger inside, then turns to the crate and draws an arrow that faces down. The crate shrinks and shrinks before popping into sawdust.

It's Meriam's blood, all right.

"I found it in the box with the pellets." Erwin's mouth puckers as he realizes how close his fellow Crows came to true death.

Had the pellets penetrated their hearts instead of just their bodies . . . I shudder just thinking about it.

"Can you go wake Colm, ínon?"

I nod, staring between Meriam's blood and Justus's face.

My father crouches, ropes my calves, and lifts me like a Jack in the Box. As I press my palms against the deck to hoist myself the rest of the way, I tip my face toward the sun and inhale until the bright scent of the ocean replaces the dark reek of the ship.

Colm's surgery is quicker than Fionn's since he flipped over as he fell. In under a minute, I have him back in feathers and then in skin. Like Fionn, his eyes are haunted and reddened, until he sees the man he loves striding for him. With a hoarse croak, he wraps his slighter mate into a fierce hug.

My heart swells at the sight of so much affection, but then shrivels when I spot a sallow-faced Gabriele leaning against the ship's mast while Aoife—fully visible again—binds his leg to a piece of wood with rope. I walk over to them and crouch, helping tie a snug knot.

"You lucky to have big ears, Moriati."

Gabriele winces. "They didn't help break my fall."

She stares at him in bafflement, but then a laugh trips past her curved lips, kindling a smile onto Gabriele's wan mouth and a soft chuckle from my lungs. Unfortunately, the sliver of joy that penetrated my breastbone dims fast because everyone's back on deck, gearing up to turn tail and flock back to the continent of ice and snow.

I sit back on my heels and crane my neck, willing the sun to warm my chilled blood.

I think of Bronwen's prediction, the one about Lore turning to iron, and his people, to obsidian. Either the Cauldron was wrong—like it was wrong about Gabriele—or this will not be the final showdown, for Lore cannot fall when two of his crows are safely tucked away in Luce.

Right?

CHAPTER 75

As rapid-fire Crow is spoken around me, a hand grazes my arm. "Fallon, *guhlaèr*?"

I inhale a rattling breath. "Yes, Aoife. I'm okay."

"Then why you cry?"

"Nerves. Exhaustion." I shouldn't complain considering she's been flying back and forth.

She squeezes my forearm. "We here. You not alone."

"Thank you, Aoife." I close my hand over hers and squeeze her fingers. "I'm so lucky to have a friend like you." My voice is as wooly as the turtleneck I wear beneath my armor.

Her black eyes reflect her smile. "Yes. Especially after you give me many heart stops."

I smile at her expression.

"Transparent trick was cool. When we back in Luce"—she gestures in the direction of our kingdom, which is so far away, it's not even a blip on the horizon—"you need make me air so I can spook Immy."

My smile widens as I imagine Aoife creeping up on her unflappable sister.

She holds out her palm. "Deal?"

I slap my hand into hers and echo, "Deal."

And then she tugs me to my feet.

Shadows glide around my collarbone. ***Climb onto your father's back, Behach Éan. Aoife will fly Gabriele.***

However many times my heart whispers, *Dante dies, you live,* my mind smudges my confidence and replaces it with, *The Crows fall, maybe you do as well.*

On my way to my father, my head spins, and I stagger as though Lore were tossing the ocean again. But the sea is mirror-smooth. Lore must worry I'll end up keeling over, because his shadows swirl around my body like a buoy.

My father crouches low to facilitate my climb. As I drape my leg over his back and lean forward to clasp his neck, I watch Fionn help Gabriele climb atop Aoife while his mate secures my wounded friend with coils of rope he must've clipped off the collapsed sails.

After she takes off, the two Crows take a moment to press their foreheads together. Though their lips don't form words, I've no doubt they're whispering inside each other's minds.

Lore, send everyone back to Luce. If Dante has Meriam, then he has Shabbin blood at his disposal. I won't risk any of their lives.

My father spreads his wings and springs off the galleon right as Justus appears on the deck, face mottled by fatigue and blood. Though spent, his strides are fluid as he approaches Fionn and Colm. With a hard kiss, the mates separate and shift.

My grandfather climbs atop Colm with the familiarity of someone who's flown on dragon-sized birds his entire life. Lore may not trust Justus, but my grandfather seems to have been accepted by the others.

I glance around the deck for my mate, realizing that not only has he not answered my entreaty about sending everyone away, but the coils of his shadows have also slipped off me.

Lore?

The ship shudders as though it's collided with a rock, but it isn't a rock—it's a murder of riderless Crows.

I circle my arms around my father's neck a little more snugly as I peer past his wings. Like a snapped biscuit, the ship splits into two halves that sink so fast, the Crows are still climbing into the air when the foam gobbles up the masts.

The surface settles in seconds, smoothing like a shroud over this wooden grave full of Faeries who picked the wrong camp. Though our enemies, my heart twinges for the families and friends they leave behind.

Wars are ugly things, Fallon. Full of injustice and needless loss.

I stare at the Crow who, like the ship, breaks apart. Two of Lore's birds glide on either side of me, while the other flies to the front of the winged procession, stopping beside each one of his shifters and circling the Faeries.

Though no longer a shepherd, my mate seems to be counting his sheep, making sure his flock is complete. No wonder Mara chose him to lead his people.

Send them all home, Lore. There's no need for them to risk their lives. This fight is between me and Dante.

I passed along your message before sinking the galleon, Behach Éan.

Then why is everyone flying in the direction of Glace?

Because we're a tribe, Fallon. A family. One who sticks together through thick and thin.

But Dante has Meriam and Gods only know how many soldiers.

And you've got me and fourteen of my best fighters.

Can they at least fly extra high so that no arrow or pellet can take them down?

I'll suggest it.

As the air grows chillier, I manifest our victory by picturing the giant stone hallways of the Sky Kingdom swarming with noise and life. The streets and canals of Tarecuori and Tarelexo bursting with carefree purelings and halflings. The swamp lands, the forests, and the desert overrun by jubilant humans free to grow their hair to whatever length they desire. Free to travel without papers because our world will no longer be quartered into districts dictated by the amount of magic inside one's blood. And finally, I picture women with jeweled eyes sailing up to our shores, liquid gowns snapping around their sun-kissed bodies—since Phoebus insists Shabbins wear silk to everything, even to war.

I know my vision of this future Luce is quixotic. Change may come, but it'll be gradual, and it'll be littered with rebellion, for no regime appeals to all. Still, as we ride the wind toward Luce, I glut myself on this dream of peace, willing it to buoy my spirits and inject steel into my spine.

Do you think Dante's expecting us?

Yes.

Why do you think he fled to Glace?

Because he knew it was a matter of days before we drove him out of his tunnels.

Do you think Vladimir knows he's taken refuge in Glace?

No.

As a white line appears on the horizon, I say, *Our daughter will have no more princess to slay if Alyona stashed him in her kingdom.*

I hope she did stash him, *because I'd love nothing more than to save my future child the headache of having to deal with a reckless royal.*

I smile then, because I can just imagine Lore as a father. He probably won't let our children leave the nest until their fiftieth birthday.

At the very least . . . Though a full century would be even better.

Concentrating on this elusive daughter of ours dredges my heart from the pit quarried by my nerves. But one glimpse at the looming continent of ice sends it toppling right back inside. I'm not ready for this battle. I may have armor, a seashell, and a fork—yes, I slipped the tool into the waistband of my trousers—but I don't have a steel sword.

I suppose I could cause quite a lot of damage with my fork, especially if I grow it, but I'll still need an iron weapon.

You have me, Fallon.

I may have you, Lore, but you cannot kill Dante, remember?

Yes, yes. I've not forgotten.

You better not have for I'd prefer that my daughter be yours and not some other man's.

Both his crows swerve and narrow their eyes. *Yes, indeed.*

Hopefully, that'll keep my mate from risking his humanity.

Too soon, my father angles his body downward. Lore must slip the reason for our return into the Glacin sentries' minds because the entrance to the castle rises and they scurry inside to fetch the king.

By the time we land, someone comes, but not Vladimir. We're greeted by Konstantin and the blond general, Salom, who looks as though he wrestles polar bears for fun.

"Did you forget something?" Konstantin's posture is as stiff as the icicles at his back, and his complexion, just as colorless.

I hop off my father's back, adrenaline careening through my veins.

Though I must look bedraggled, I feel as hopped-up as Syb after a glitzy revel. "We found the ship, but Tavo Diotto and the runestone weren't on board."

His dark eyebrows sweep low over his pale eyes. "Did the Lucin general fall overboard?"

"No, Korol."

I spin around at the sound of the voice that shouldn't be able to travel through air. "Lore!" I gasp. "Divide. Immediately."

But my mate doesn't fracture into smoke. He remains in iron and leather and flesh for all to behold.

For any to shoot at.

Bronwen's predictions may come true after all.

CHAPTER 76

Salom steps in front of the crown prince as though to guard him from my mate. It's rather audacious of him to believe he can protect Konstantin against a man who can dissolve into lethal smoke.

As though this was a game of chess, Lore steps in front of me.

Though I want to scream at him for taking such risks, all I say is, ***You left Luce unguarded.***

My crows were of more use here. Besides, more than half the Siorkahd is there.

I work my jaw from side to side.

"Diotto never left Glace." Lore tips his head, studying the effect of the news on the prince. "And according to my informants back in Luce and the sailors we questioned, he isn't *vacationing* alone."

Though I don't know Konstantin well, the flash of surprise that jerks his head tells me this is the first he's hearing of this.

"Any chance your sister could shed light on where she secreted our fellow Lucins?" Lore rolls and spreads his fingers a few times. The air is so quiet that the sound of his cracking knuckles echoes through the valley.

"I'm afraid my sister will not be able to share his location, *if* she's even knowledgeable about it, for she's heavily sedated at the moment."

My father parks himself beside me. "How about that nursemaid of hers? Olena?"

Without looking away from Lore, Konstantin asks his general, "Is Olena lucid?"

"I'll send someone to check."

I take in the fortress that lays beneath the snow, wondering if Dante could be hiding inside.

"Have someone check your dungeons," my father growls, as though reading my thoughts.

The Glacins stare at him a full minute before Salom dispatches three sentries to inspect the castle's prisons.

"And the gallery made of obsidian," Justus suggests. "I'd check that place out as well."

The brisk air tugs at Konstantin's roots, snapping through the white mass, which he's visibly mussed in the time we were gone. I suspect his sister's punishment ate at his aplomb. "The gallery was checked when you were last here, and it was empty."

"My wife can make herself invisible, so perhaps it's worth checking once more." Justus's blue gaze is bright and fierce as though prepared to launch into battle.

Konstantin frowns. "Your wife?"

"Did I forget to mention my recent nuptials to Meriam of Shabbe?"

I didn't think it was possible for Konstantin's face to drain of more color, but apparently, it is.

He's barely distinguishable from the landscape at his back now. "Meriam is here?"

"Yes." Lore cracks his knuckles again. "And so is Dante Regio."

"Salom, call for my father."

I close my eyes for a moment and think how I would go about trying to hide my lover. I would probably not put him up under my roof, since that would be the logical place to search for him.

Of course, Alyona may not be aware he stayed. In that case, Dante would've sought refuge on his own.

I reel my lids up so fast that the air stings my warmed eyeballs. "How far is the ice market you spoke of, Konstantin?"

"Just under an hour by sleigh. Why?"

"Because, even though my grandmother can make everyone invisible, she's stuck to a clunky throne which would've screeched had it been dragged through your castle. Dante could've had her carried, of course, but even that couldn't possibly have gone unnoticed. One of your guards would surely have caught the disturbance. Unless the sentries roaming your halls are scarce?"

"The Korol palace is besieged by guards," Justus murmurs.

Though I'm uncertain in which direction sits the market I've asked about, I raise my gaze to the hill. Alyona met with Diotto last evening, which means they've a full day of travel on us. If we were on foot, this would be a setback, but with wings, we should catch up rather easily.

"Unless Dante bargained for asylum with your father, he wouldn't have journeyed to the palace; he would've set out from the market on foot or by sleigh and traveled from there." Still staring out at the white expanse, I ask, "Do you have any obsidian caverns or Fae-made bunkers in Glace?"

"We've never been at war with Crows." Konstantin eyes the fourteen shifters. Well, fifteen, now that Lore's in the mix. "So no, Lady Báeinach, we've never had need to build bunkers."

As though chased by a pack of wild beasts, Salom rushes back out of the castle, every snowflake pin on his starched blue uniform glittering wildly. "I've made His Majesty aware—that Dante Regio is on our land," he pants. "He grants you and your Crows—freedom of flight over Glace and—free rein to dispose of your adversary as you see fit—but he asks that no Glacins—be harmed in your scuffle."

"What of a battalion?" Justus asks.

"We don't need soldiers, Rossi." Smoke wafts off Lorcan's vambraces and pauldrons. "However, my mate's in need of a steel sword, Konstantin. Would you be so gracious as to lend her one?"

Konstantin slides a hand beneath his fur cloak and extricates a dagger that makes my blood run cold. "My sister will no longer be needing this." He holds it out to me.

The diamonds set in the delicate pattern of a snowflake blind me.

"Consider it a gift from our kingdom to yours."

If Konstantin only knew what Bronwen had foreseen, he would neither give me this weapon nor would he call it a gift.

Since I find myself incapable of seizing the proffered blade, Lorcan lifts it from the crown prince's hand. "You've our gratitude, Konstantin."

The prince nods, my tangible agitation drawing his eyebrows low.

A soldier jogs out to Salom and his prince, kicking up clumps of snow. When he reaches them, he bows, then speaks in Glacin.

"Olena said that the Lucin general enquired after a sleigh maker. She says he was interested in purchasing a few to bring home to Luce."

The news whittles Konstantin's already sharp jaw until it becomes as bladed as the steel dagger Lore holds at his side. "Was a purchase made?"

"I've dispatched soldiers to the factory to find out, Vizoshtsa."

"Where is this factory?" Lore asks.

The soldier peeks at Lorcan, then blinks and falls back a step. I'm guessing he's just realized in whose presence he stands. "A little ways inland from the Ice Floe Market, Your Majesty."

"Name?" my father barks.

"Denys."

"Not yours," Salom grunts with an eyeroll.

"Oh. Volkov and Sons." Denys trembles like an autumn leaf barely clinging to the branch.

"Call back your soldiers." The wind tangles in Lore's black hair. "We'll be quicker by air."

Lore begins to break into more shadows but firms when Konstantin asks, "Why did Regio come here?"

"He came for the runestone. I believe he stayed because he knows your kingdom. Didn't he do his military training in Glace?" Lorcan's eyes glow a deep amber.

Without meaning to, I slip into his mind. His thoughts burst with such brutality and gore that I lurch out and whirl my gaze back onto Konstantin, whose mind I cannot stumble into. Thank Gods, for I've no doubt that his skull is also filled with atrocious scenes.

"Perhaps he believed he still had a chance to pocket an alliance with your kingdom," Lore continues. "Especially since Alyona is with child. *His*, I presume."

I blink at Lore. ***You know this for a fact, or are you bluffing?***

I could hear a second heartbeat when I carried her earlier. As for the father, I can only assume it's Dante's.

The Glacin Prince squares his shoulders. "There's no more baby." Though his voice is toneless, his flaring nostrils betray the effect Alyona's miscarriage had on him.

I suck in a breath. The air is so frosty that it scorches my lungs. Did she lose the babe because of the steel blade her brother ran over her face, or did her father find out and command the child be removed?

I may loathe the ice princess, but I'd never wish this sort of heartache on her. To think this is our fault. If we hadn't come—

Don't. Besides, Behach Éan, if the baby had survived, then Meriam's curse would've endured and the Cauldron would've remained locked. Would you really have preferred taking the child's life yourself?

My stomach drops because I hadn't considered that. I still feel for Alyona, but it'd be a lie to say I wasn't relieved, for I could *never* have sacrificed a child.

When Salom asks why Dante didn't just fake his death, I glance at the palm marred with his mark.

And so does Justus. "Regio cannot fake his death for we have a magical way of knowing whether his heart beats."

Salom's gaze scrolls past the heavy smog that lifts off Lore's flesh at the reminder of my tie to Dante.

"Ríhbiadh," Justus says, "I know you've wings to fly and beaks to kill, but Glacins know the lay of the land. They'll know his haunts. They'll unearth him faster than we can."

Lore eyes him.

Before my mate can reiterate that we've no need for additional forces, especially the Faerie kind, I jump on Justus's reasoning. "I think he's right, Lore. I think having people who know the land would help greatly."

"I'm afraid the king doesn't care to get involved as long as a sorceress is in the mix." A gust of wind snatches Salom's sun-hued ponytail and kicks it sideways. "And by sorceress, he means Meriam of Shabbe, not your mate, Your Majesty."

If you want soldiers, call in your bargain, and they'll have no choice but to lend us men.

Konstantin's gray eyes lock on Lorcan's as though he can tell we're discussing the oath he swore to me earlier.

What do you advise, Lore?

Hold on to it. If we cannot manage to find him on our own, then claim it.

Out loud, he says, "Do we have your blessing to begin our hunt, Konstantin?"

A slow swallow stirs Konstantin's corded throat. "Yes, Lorcan Ríhbiadh. You've Glace's blessing to find and dispose of that man." He whirls around, but not quickly enough for me to miss the curl of his lip.

Justus leans over and murmurs—in Shabbin, I suspect—"Konstantin hate Dante. Bad blood over Alyona."

Lore's eyebrows wing up. "You're full of surprises, aren't you, Rossi?"

Is he surprised by my grandfather's knowledge of Shabbin or of Glacin court gossip?

That he speaks Shabbin. As for Korol's dislike of Regio, I'd heard rumors. Why do you think I appreciate the boy in the first place? He leans over and delicately slips the dagger into the top of my boot. ***Careful when you walk.***

As he shifts, I worry my lip because Bronwen's vision brightens my lids. If Konstantin is so protective of his sister, then what will he do to my daughter after she ends Alyona of Glace's life?

CHAPTER 77

The farther north we soar, the brisker the air. If this is summer, I cannot imagine how cold it gets in this part of the world in the dead of winter. Where not a single chimney poked out of the castle, violet corkscrews of smoke inundate the human lands that rely on wood fire for warmth.

A neat strip of berthed vessels bobs on the indigo waters bordering a port made of snow and ice. Identical stalls carved from tawny timber sit side by side like orderly schoolchildren. Where the Tarelexian market is chaotic and loud, this one is tidy and quiet. Even the shoppers stream past the stalls in a disciplined fashion, a colony of ants garbed in fur.

What a culture shock. I'm aware I'm not here to sightsee or compare, but as the coastline looms closer, I cannot help but feel grateful to have been born in a kingdom full of color and noise.

As our wingbeats stir the air, fur-cloaked heads tip, mouths gape, shrill yelps resound. Evidently, the army hasn't had time to forewarn its population of our visit. I tighten my grip on my father's neck when he pitches his great body downward.

Though Lore wanted to fly me, I told him that if he didn't break into his five puffs of smoke and remain in that configuration and consistency, I would stake him with obsidian myself. Oh, how he growled, but at least he indulged me.

We swerve away from the coastline and fly parallel to a narrow white street crammed with people pulling sleds filled with goods, children, and older citizens.

All stop to stare at our delegation. I wave to them, hoping to defuse some of the tangible tension that curls off them like sooty smoke, but my affable gesticulating is cut short when my father veers abruptly to the left, forcing my arm to clap back around his neck.

Soon, we land in front of a giant building made of logs and large panels of foggy glass. A wooden sign that reads *Volkov and Sons* with a pretty sleigh painting is hammered over a double-wide door.

Though stained fingers scrape at the fog and reveal faces, no one comes out to greet us. In fact, there's the definite sound of a lock clicking into place. Either Glacins are unaware of Crows' ability to slip through walls, or they believe us too decorous to enter private property without a proper welcome.

As soon as I'm steady on the ground and bracketed by Colm, Fionn, and Justus, my father strides ahead and bangs on the wood. "Open up."

"Perhaps add, *We come in peace.*" Justus shrugs when my father shoots him a glower. "It may incite them to *open up* quicker."

Reluctantly, my father adds, "We come in peace." His tone is so gruff, it sounds more like he says, *We'll chop you into pieces*. I'm almost surprised when metal clicks and hinges groan, and the large wood door is drawn open.

A silver-eyed, silver-haired halfling regards the lot of us guardedly. "On the market for a sleigh?"

"On the market for a runaway princeling." My father is so tall that he need not extend his head to peer over the old man, who's far from short himself.

"I'm afraid I've none in stock."

My father's striped gaze drops while the corners of his mouth lift, and then he guffaws, which makes the man white-knuckle his door.

I shuffle in front of my father before he can stop the man's heart. "General Salom has informed us that some foreigners paid you a visit last night."

The male's gaze brushes over me, lingering on my purple eyes. "The general's mistaken. We've had no visitors."

Justus sidesteps me. "Here." He pulls out his ruby-encrusted snuffbox and thumbs the top lid open. "A pinch of salt does wonders for one's memory."

"My memory works fine. Now, if I may kindly ask you to leave . . ."

As he begins to shut the door in our faces, smoke distorts the lines of my father's body. I lay a quick hand on his arm to keep him from rushing inside and murdering everyone, then call out to Lore, ***No cutting off any appendages.***

A grunt sounds through the mind link, because of course my mate is contemplating bodily harm to make the man spill his secrets.

I prick my finger, then draw the arrow facing down on his door, delighting when the wood shrinks and shrinks. Right before it puffs to sawdust, I crouch and slash the sigil.

The gray-haired halfling gapes, mouth as round as his eyes. "What are you?"

"A girl looking for her Shabbin grandmother. You know, the one who created the wards around the queendom? Meriam. Name ring a bell?"

Though I painted no upward arrows on his eyeballs, they bulge like a frog's.

"Like my father mentioned, we come in peace. We *also* come with your king's blessing. Now, would you be so gracious as to tell us how many sleighs were purchased by the foreigners and in which direction they took them?"

The man's pulse strikes his throat with such gusto that I worry I may have overwhelmed him.

I paste on a smile and add a pleasant, "Please?"

The man keels over. *Merda.* Did I kill him?

A younger man rushes to his side and crouches, sinking two fingers into the crook of his neck. He must feel a pulse because he doesn't glove his hand with magic or reach for a weapon to strike us down.

He stands, orders two other men to carry his father to a cot in the back, then crosses his arms and says, "They purchased five sleighs and a tow chain."

I'm guessing the tow chain was to hook into Meriam's throne. I'm also guessing my grandmother must not have appreciated being dragged like cargo.

"As for the direction . . . They headed east but perhaps changed course. We're not in the business of tracking our customers." When his gaze sidles along my body, Lore wraps me in his shadows.

Relax, my love. The man's not seeking a flaw in my armor through which to slip a blade.

I'm aware.

Then flitter off please. I don't want you putting yourself at risk.

The only thing at risk is the half-blood's sight.

Lore . . . With a snort, I reach my fingers through the churning, vaporous body of my mate.

"How many men would you say there were?" Justus asks.

"Our sleighs fit six"—he gives my father a quick once-over—"*regular*-sized men. Four sleighs were at full occupancy, and one was packed with crates."

The fine hairs along my nape stand on end at the mention of crates, because crates mean supplies. Though I'd love nothing more than to believe the boxes were filled with food and clothes, my gut screams weapons.

Dante knew we'd come looking for him.

He knew and he prepared.

CHAPTER 78

After growing back the factory door, since the Volkovs turned out agreeable, I climb atop my father, and we take off east. The temperature over the snow-covered knolls is so brisk that, an hour into our flight, my face begins to frost over.

I tuck my seashell necklace inside the neck of my sweater, then roll up the yarn over my ears, nose, and mouth. As I lower my lids to protect my stinging eyeballs, something heavy drops onto my shoulders. I gasp when I realize it's a pelt.

I know you hate fur, but keep the cloak on.

I unhook one of my arms from around my father's neck to clasp the collar. ***Did you just skin a bear?***

No. Fionn bought it from a village of trappers. Put the hood on.

I lower the hood over my frozen ears, whispering a quick thank-you to the creature whose life was sacrificed to keep me warm. ***Bronwen wouldn't happen to have had a vision?***

No.

Aoife suddenly glides nearer to us, and I notice that Gabriele has awakened. His cheeks and lips have regained a hint of pink, and his gray eyes, a hint of sparkle. "What are we doing back in Glace?"

Right. He missed a few episodes while asleep. I make quick work of filling him in.

At the end of my account, he sucks in a breath.

"The leg?"

He surveys his splint and twists his foot. "The leg's fine. Healed, even." He touches his thigh, then moves his hand over the knots Aoife fastened and begins to tug at them.

"Gabriele?"

"Hmm?"

"Why did you inhale sharply?"

"What?"

"After I told you about the sleighs, you made a noise."

"Oh. Right. Sorry. Head's a little muddled from . . . *everything.*" He beholds the white expanse. "When we were stationed here, Alyona brought us to these giant ice caves once. I was just thinking that perhaps Dante would've headed there."

"Where?" My tone borders on hysteria. "Where are they?"

He slides his lower lip between his teeth and peers past Aoife's wing. "They were at the base of the White Fang."

"The White Fang?"

He nods to a mountain that's thin and tall, chiseled to a daunting peak.

"Fitting name." I'm about to ask if Lore heard when every Crow veers as one toward the bladed mountain.

Tell everyone to stay high, Lore.

He must, because once we reach the mountain, we linger at a great altitude.

I squint at the valley far below, on the lookout for sleighs, but my eyesight, though improved by my Shabbin blood, is not crisp enough.

My father suddenly caws, which makes me jump out of both my skin and the bear's. I whip my gaze to his wings. When I see that his feathers keep fluttering, my stationary heart begins to pound anew.

Lore, what happened?

Your father couldn't contain his excitement, Lore grumbles, one of his crows leveling off beside my face.

They're here? My pulse jumps out of alignment.

Yes. Just like Gabriele said, they've taken refuge in the ice cavern.

Gripping my father's body between my thighs, I trail the direction of Lore's gold eyes toward a turquoise smudge but then whip my gaze back to him. ***Dematerialize.***

We're too high—

Please. For my sanity, please.

With a soft sigh, he turns to smoke. After stroking my lips, he murmurs, ***I'll be right back.***

When I catch five streaks of black whizzing toward the splotch of blue, I yell, ***Lore, no! Come back immediately! LORE!*** "Dádhi, follow him."

My father doesn't heed my cry. Doesn't go after my insane mate. No one does. I growl my frustration and keep growling until the five streaks of black shoot back toward us like fireworks.

I press my lips together, so mad I cannot even ask whether he's ended every soldier's life.

I've ended no life. His tenor is as impenetrable as my mood.

I side-eye him.

Lorcan's shadows swarm toward Justus. He must drop an offensive image inside his mind because my grandfather's lip curls and he sneers, "Meriam wouldn't betray us. There must be another reason. He must've struck a bargain and used it to make her draw the sigil on all . . ."

White-hot pain sluices up my arm. I shove my sleeve up, expecting to see blood or welts or the Cauldron only knows what, but my skin is unblemished. Another hot jab of pain tears my palm from my arm. I clap my neck that burns as though someone was running a fiery poker over it.

What is this? Some sort of spell? Is Meriam casting a spell to harm me?

Fallon? I hear Lore shout, but his voice sounds as though it's coming from Luce.

My grip slackens and I list. Not even my father's great wings manage to break my fall. Caws echo all around me.

I hit a broad body that swoops upward. It takes my muddled mind a minute to realize the alarmed eyes peering back at me are yellow. ***Oh my Gods, Lore, no!***

Mo khrà, what— Before my mate can finish his sentence, his body stills, and my worst nightmare comes to pass—black feathers harden into metal.

Time seems to stop as I stare around me and meet my grandfather's stare, then Gabriele's, and finally Bronwen's. For a breath, we're all suspended in the sky, and then . . . and then we're plunging into the valley.

Two thoughts flare inside my mind—one, my Faerie companions are all purelings, so they'll survive the fall, and two, if Lore is iron, then he hasn't lost his humanity.

CHAPTER 79

"The fall broke her neck, Dee. If her magic hadn't been unleashed, she'd be dead right now, and we'd be screwed."

"I fucking know that, Tavo!"

I died?

"Don't you think I know that?" Dante's voice sounds brittle, almost as though he's truly distraught. "Fuck." He growls again, but his growl gets lost in the tremors that rattle whatever I lie on. "What the Cauldron was that?"

"Another avalanche. I'll admit that using the life tether to bring Fallon down was brilliant, but Meriam's not healing all too well. Must be affecting the Shabbin wards." Just as Tavo says this, scorching pain sluices up my neck anew.

I clench my jaw to rein in the whimper. Neither will I give these monsters the pleasure to hear me cry, nor will I reveal my alertness.

"Keep melting the snow before we're buried alive in this cavern, you idiots!" Tavo must've turned away from me because his voice isn't as brash. "And, Enrico, find a way to staunch the witch's blood!"

"I'm trying, Generali. I'm trying." Enrico sounds frantic.

"Try harder." Footfalls crunch over what I assume must be snow and ice. "Have they found Rossi and Moriati?"

"Negative, Generali. Only the seer's been retrieved."

"Wakey, wakey, Aurora." The smack of a palm echoes, just as the feel of one creeps onto my face.

I know, without cracking my lids up, that the hand belongs to Dante. His breath punches my nose, and though it no longer smells quite as foul as back in the tunnels, it turns my stomach.

Just like his touch.

How dare he lay a finger on me.

A whoosh followed by a shrill cry jostles my pulse.

"Aurora's up," Tavo singsongs. "Nothing like a little blast of fire to awaken the senses."

Did the asshole just burn her with his fire?

I. Will. Eviscerate. Tavo Diotto. If Cian doesn't beat me to it, but to beat me to it, I'd need to locate my mate so he can wake his shifters, and to locate my mate, I need to get off the floor, or wherever it is they laid me out.

"Would you like me to try blowing some fire on—"

"No." Though grateful Dante shut down Tavo's heinous idea, I'm fully aware his reply has nothing to do with mercy. He's probably worried fire will kill me if Meriam's wound doesn't. "Come on, Fal."

My whispered nickname scatters chills across my skin. Why does he even want me to wake up? What nefarious plan does he have in store for me now?

His hand finally drifts off my cheek, but sadly, not off my body. He dips two fingers into the crook of my neck, against my pulse point.

"The witch stopped bleeding," that nervous soldier—Enrico—announces, relief tangible in the man's tone.

Tavo expels a whoop that resonates against the ice. "How's Fallon's pulse?"

"Stronger," Dante murmurs.

"If I were you, I'd pucker up and try Prince Charming's method. See if her pulse jumps."

Anger surges through me so fast that I fear it injects color into my cheeks. He better fucking not—

Lips meet mine—full, warm. Not. Lore's.

Revulsion slams into me. Before I can iron out my disgust and fury, I twist my head to the side and spit.

"Look at that." Tavo all but snickers. "It worked."

My fingers ball into such tight fists that my veins strain against my skin, awakening aches and bruises everywhere. When my chest cramps with the desire to cry, I remind myself that I'm alive.

I survived. And I will keep on surviving.

To best play my hand, I need to understand the cards Fate has dealt me, so I open my eyes and take stock of my surroundings.

Blue ice shines beneath me, above me, beside me. Translucent stalactites adorn the lofty curves of the frozen ceiling, sparkling like a thousand glass swords. If it wasn't for the freezing air, I could almost believe I was anchored to the ocean floor and not on some elevated slab of frozen water inside a mountain.

I stare down at my body next, at the coils of chains that wrap around me from neck to ankle. No vines this time. Does Dante not trust his soldiers or does he believe metal will give me a harder time than magic?

I try to wriggle my arms, mainly to make sure they aren't broken like my neck apparently was, but also to test the snugness of my restraints. Although white-hot pain flares through my bones and cramps my muscles, my arms work. As do my legs.

My wonderful, miraculous body not only survived but also healed.

As I relax into my nest of fetters, the chain squeaks and clicks against my metal armor, digging into the bruises that must mottle the skin beneath my turtleneck's sleeves. How I wish I were still wrapped in that soft pelt Lore gave me, for it would've provided warmth and padding.

Oh, Lore . . .

I shudder as my mind replays the horror of feeling his body harden to iron. Of plummeting hundreds of meters through thin air. Of watching my friends and my family free-fall alongside me, faces painted with dread.

I close my eyes and breathe. Just breathe. Instead of pushing away the terror, I let it drench me . . . let it haunt and hone me, transform me from prisoner into warrior.

My pulse slows, my breathing quiets, and my blood thickens until it feels laced with the same ice that surrounds me.

"Should've listened to yours truly and kissed her sooner, Dee."

I turn my head in the direction of the idiot general I haven't seen since the night I was shot with a poisoned arrow.

Except . . .

Except the man ambling toward me isn't Tavo.

I whirl my gaze back toward the face hovering over mine, sopping up the brown skin, the full, pink mouth, the mismatched irises—one blue, one white.

How hard did I bang my head?

I blink between the simpering man and the scowling one, realizing it's no trick of the mind but a trick of blood.

That's the reason Lore rushed out of the cave without slaughtering anyone. Because every single man here shares Dante Regio's appearance.

Meriam must've cast this illusion since Dante has no knowledge of sigils and no access to my blood. I fathom it was her circuitous way of deterring the Crows from attacking and inadvertently ending Dante's life.

A realization hits me so hard and fast that I gasp. The only reason Dante would accept to enact this plot is because he knows that Crows cannot kill him.

I grow so fucking furious with Meriam for having divulged that secret that I almost decide to murder everyone in this ice cave *save* for Dante so that her manipulative ass never lifts from her godsdamn throne.

My nostrils flare.

If I wasn't so desperate to access the Cauldron to break Lore's curse and free my mother of her scales, I would've reduced Dante to a limbless stump, chained him to Meriam's lap, and sank both of them to the very bottom of Filiaserpens.

Oh, Meriam, you are . . . one . . . lucky . . . witch.

Or rather, one conniving bitch.

CHAPTER 80

Dante—the scowling one—straightens, a nerve agitating the skin at his temple. "Welcome back to the world of the living, moya."

Oh, that hateful title . . .

"Fallon?" Bronwen's raucous whisper carries my gaze away from the skeeve who stole days of my life and beats of my heart.

She sits inside one of the five wooden sleighs parked in the ice temple. If it weren't for the chains binding her wrists behind her back, she could almost pass for a passenger awaiting her air-Fae conductor.

"I'm here, Bronwen." My jaw is so tight that my teeth grind down the words to a mere whisper.

"Can you see Meriam?" Her eyes are wide and white, gleaming like my mother's tusk.

"No." I sweep my gaze left and right. When I don't catch sight of a throne, I roll my eyeballs as far back as they can reach and get rewarded with the glint of bloodied gold and auburn hair.

"Huh . . . so your aunt speaks Shabbin," the sneering version of Dante says as he flicks his gaze toward the sleigh.

I'm momentarily distracted from my rage by the glint of an amber iris. And, come to think of it, the man's inflection. Is Meriam's spell fading, or did she not alter their eye color and voices on purpose?

Though I wish to forget the night I was taken into the tunnels, I clearly remember that the soldier Justus had shaped into Nonna had called out to me in her voice.

"Meriam?" Bronwen hollers.

I banish the memory of my first kidnapping and concentrate on the latest one. "Meriam's currently *out of order*, Bronwen."

My grandmother's head hangs sideways, marbled lids closed, and long auburn lashes resting like wings against her colorless cheeks. Tracks of blood fork down her barely-moving chest and bead along the arm of her throne. Though I'm back to hating her, I cannot help but grit my jaw when I catch sight of the ruby puddle in her lap. *Heartless demons.*

"Those brutes ripped her open and bled—" Something sharp bites into my knee, and I hiss.

"How proficient you are at languages, Fal." Real-Dante holds my Glacin dagger, the diamond snowflake glittering blue in the cold sunlight that penetrates the ice. "Barely unbound yet already fluent in Shabbin." He moves the dagger up my leg, and though he doesn't carve through the leather, the steel point prods my thigh. "You'll never cease to astound me."

"And you, me. In all my wildest imaginings, I didn't envision you'd actually tuck your tail between your legs and desert the kingdom you so desire."

His fingers flex around the dagger. This time, he doesn't tease my trousers, he tears right through them, and subsequently, through my skin.

I don't wince. "I mean, I know you fear Lore—"

"I didn't run because I feared your little bird king," he all but growls. "I ran in order to lay a trap. And look . . ." His scowl morphs into a crazed grin. "You flew right into it."

"It was so fucking easy," Tavo adds. "Almost too easy. Dante, here, could hardly believe how quickly you all went down. And snagging the fully-crowed king? In all honesty, I didn't think Ríhbiadh would do something as idiotic as merging his five crows. But hey, just goes to show that he's not the smartest bird in the coop." Tavo guffaws. "You should've seen his little crows' expressions when he peeked into the cave. Admittedly, our plan of changing our appearance"—he gestures between the many versions of Dante—"was brilliant."

"*My* plan." Dante's hubris shuts Tavo's mouth for a full, pleasant minute, but then the redhead's mood lifts, and he beams.

"*Your* plan, but who learned the symbol?" He jabs both his thumbs toward himself. "I caught Meriam drawing it on herself when we were sailing across the ocean. I knocked her out and used her bleeding finger to reproduce the mark on my hand. You should've seen Dante's expression when I entered his cabin."

My eyebrows tilt with a frown. So this wasn't Meriam's scheme?

"The idiot took Rossi's face." Dante shakes his head, which makes the jewels in his long braids clink like a door chime.

"Yes, yes. But that's who I had on my mind at the time. Thank the Cauldron the sigil didn't alter my voice or eyes, or I would've been down a head."

I'm tempted to smile because, if he'd spied on Meriam a moment longer, he may have learned the complete sigil. "Though I love nothing more than to hear men boast, I have to wonder, what's the next step in your brilliant plan?" I press my fingertips against the ice, wait until they adhere before snapping them upward. I run my thumb over them. The pads are slick, but I cannot tell if it's with water or blood, and glancing at them would draw my enemies' stares, so I resort to sketching my favorite symbol—the key.

"We were waiting for you to wake before heading back to Luce." Real-Dante looks at Tavo-Dante.

"I suggested getting it over with while you were asleep, but Dante wanted you to feel it."

"Feel what?" I press my hand against the symbol and wait with bated breath for my palm to penetrate the ice, but it doesn't. *Merda*.

Real-Dante glides the knife farther up my thigh, slicing through more of my trousers and flesh. Though the seam of blood burns, I refrain from making a single sound. Even my breathing stays cadenced and easy. Where some would see torture, the silver lining enthusiast in me sees access to a limitless well of magic.

"What is it you want me to feel, Dante?"

He tows the dagger up to his face and twirls it, watching my blood ooze along the iron with an emotion akin to awe. "Your mate snuff out your life." He lowers the dagger, a spiteful smile sculpting his cheeks. "Apparently, if he kills Mara's progeny—anyone of them—he loses his humanity."

My heart stops. Starts. Stops. "How did you come across this information?" My pitch remains steady even though everything inside of me convulses.

"Soldati Lastra heard you and Justus chat."

"He understood Shabbin?"

"No. But you didn't only talk in the sorceresses' tongue, now did you?"

Fuck. We hadn't. But Justus always painted a silence sigil. Had he gotten it wrong?

"Anyway, we learned many a useful tidbit while eavesdropping. The most surprising one being that my brother was, in fact, my half-brother. I'm not even certain *Marco* was aware of this."

The green-eyed guard's hateful face drenches the backs of my lids, and I almost wish he was still alive just so I could have the pleasure of sinking my sword through his chest. As I picture the scene, I stare at Dante's plain white uniform. Did he lose his gold armor during his great escape or did he dress like the others to blend in?

I'm about to ask when I notice that he's the only one with spurs on the backs of his boots. A smile worms itself across my mouth as I understand why he's without armor—because he was incapable of reproducing it for the rest of his little brigade. This must also be the reason why he's down an eyepatch.

Oh, Dante dearest, not the sharpest icicle in the cave, are you?

"Fallon, what's going on?" Bronwen's tone crackles with nerves.

"The venereal fungi want to use Lore's body to snip my veins and bleed me dry." To the Lucins, I say, "I'll need my hands freed to wake Lore."

"Wake him?" Tavo sputters.

"Well, you *do* want him to kill me, correct?"

Dante snorts. "You seem to have misunderstood us." He taps the blood-soaked dagger against the side of my throat. "He needs not be awake to cut through your artery with his beak or talon."

CHAPTER 81

My chest prickles as though my heart has jumped ship, abandoning its task of pumping my blood. As I lay there, absorbing Dante's Machiavellian plan, the cold seeps past my skin and fills my veins with slush. "If I die, so does Meriam, Dante."

"Yes. I know." He looses a deep sigh. "And if she dies, I lose my immunity to Shabbin magic and my ability to blood-cast. A shame, especially since I've yet to enjoy the skill, what with my inkwell going rogue." He sighs. "But I'm a pure-blooded Fae, and a king to boot. Like you once so rightfully pointed out, I don't actually *need* more magic."

I scrabble to find an argument that will put an end to his madness. "Technically, you're of her bloodline as well, so you'll die too." I'm bluffing, but hopefully he doesn't catch on.

He makes a little humming noise. "If that was the case, then we'd all have perished along with my father, but here we are."

I lick my lips and try again. "You're aware the Shabbins will come for you the second the wards collapse."

"I'll be ready for them."

"They will murder you."

"Perhaps, but at least I'll have rid the world of the abomination they created."

After playing dead, my heart fires off so many beats that the inside of my mouth tastes like copper. "You're willing to die?"

"Yes, moya. I'm willing to die a martyr, for martyrs become legends and legends last forever."

"The only thing you'll become is a cautionary tale."

Tavo rolls his neck. "You weren't jesting when you said she'd turned cynical." He claps, and the sound echoes far and deep. "Shall we get this party started? I've a date with a warm bath and my favorite lady at *Frosties*."

I take it *Frosties* is a local brothel.

"Slide over the iron monarch." Dante's command dispatches six identical copies of himself toward a part of the cavern that's drenched in shadows.

Like chalk on slate, a slick scraping sound reverberates through the cave, pebbling my skin.

Skrrrr.

Skrrrr.

Skrrrr.

"Godsdamn it, Fallon, use your blood to break free!" Bronwen's harsh tone snaps my gaze off the leather ropes they've slung over my mate's deployed pewter wings. "Come on, girl!" She stands, but the bastards hooked her shackles onto the sleigh's tow hitch, and she slams back onto the wooden bench. "Come on!"

I dip my fingers in my leg wound and begin to paint blood around the links of my chain. "Bronwen, if Lore kills me without intent, would he still lose his humanity?" I know I speak in Shabbin because, not only do the syllables hiss from my lips, but also, both Dantes narrow their gazes on me before exchanging a look.

One that freezes my fingers and heart.

Tavo whirls on his heel, his hand crawling toward the pommel of his sword.

When he unsheathes it, I scream, "Bronwen, shape a vine! Tavo's coming—"

Dante slaps his palm against my mouth, muffling my warning, but I know she heard me because her eyes have grown wider and paler.

Come on, Bronwen. Come on . . . I hurry squiggling my blood on the chains. "Leever be and I stike a boggun wif you," I yelp against his palm. "With bof o' you. Jus let'er leeve."

Tavo glances over his shoulder at Dante.

Please let their greed be greater than their cruelty.

Please—

The black studs crawling up the sides of Dante's broad ears gleam like his single pupil. "I've no need for bargains. Or for her."

Before my next breath, Tavo murmurs, "*Buonotte,* Bronwen," and swings.

CHAPTER 82

I stare in horror as Tavo's steel sword penetrates Bronwen's neck and comes out the other side.

This cannot be real. This must be another trick. Another illusion.

Bronwen cannot possibly be dead.

As though he weren't enough of a fiend, Tavo wipes his blade on her frock.

Oh my Gods.

I blink and blink.

Swallow and swallow.

Cauldron, this cannot be real.

She saw us come out of this war victorious.

To think I wished this fate upon her so many times. Now I'd give anything to bring her back. But there's no bringing her back.

Oh, when Cian awakens, when he realizes that his mate is gone . . .

My stomach spasms and bile lurches up my throat, but I snap my teeth to hold it in and saw through my shackles like a mad woman.

Plink.

The chain loosens.

I sop up more blood, tuck my fingers through the slit Dante made in my leather trousers, and draw the only sigil I can think of that will buy me a chance at saving the rest of them.

As Dante watches his friend stroll back to him, wearing the smug look of a psychopath, I wink out of sight and then wheel my body off the altar of ice. I shut my lids as I smash into the hard ground, the chain making a ruckus.

Before any Faerie can circle the slab and grab me, I pitch myself sideways and roll over and over until every last length of chain has unspooled from my body.

Dante screeches at his men to find me.

They drop the reins twisted around my mate's wings and race around the butchering block they had me on. Two must step on the chain because they trip. Where one flails backward, the other smashes his forehead into the bladed ledge and drops. Both pass out, but unfortunately only one bleeds.

Not that blood or headwounds will kill these bastards. I need a sword, and preferably an iron one. Taking immense care not to step on the chain, I rise to my feet, leg muscles drumming, and tiptoe toward the fallen soldiers.

As I pluck the obsidian sword out of the bleeding Faerie's limp fingers, my touch renders him momentarily transparent. *Merda.*

"She's got a weapon!" Dante yells.

I raise my arms to strike the unconscious man in the throat when flames hit my sleeve, chewing right through the wool. I yelp and drop the weapon. The stone blade chips, becoming shorter and scragglier, but still sharp enough to cause harm.

"She's there!" Dante points at where smoke still coils off the yarn of my sweater. "Again! And for the love of the Cauldron, can someone fucking grab her!"

CHAPTER 83

I clap my arm to snuff out the flames, then scoop up my stunted weapon, and race straight for the guard coming at me, betting that everyone will assume I'm running away from my attacker.

And I'm right.

Tavo's stream of fire collides into an icicle and melts it. "Fuck."

Just before crashing into the soldier, I drop into a crouch and hold out my leg. The soldier trips. As he eats ice, Tavo wheels around and streams flames that glance harmlessly against my armor.

The other soldier running toward me teeters, skidding on the ice. Before he can whirl around and rush away, I swing my little weapon. The blade sinks into his neck, creating a deep gash that rids him of consciousness but not of life.

As the other fallen begin to groan and stir, I lurch toward each of them and plant my stubby blade into their palms so they cannot assail me with their magic. I wait for revulsion and guilt to swamp me, but neither comes. My head and heart have become as cold as the belly of this mountain.

Four soldiers bleed.

Seventeen . . . no, eighteen, to go.

Eyes widen as everyone searches for the ghost I've become.

"Maezza, what do we—"

Before the soldier can finish his sentence, I gut him with my broken sword, then lacerate his hands. And then I sneak up on two more men and give them a similar fate.

Tavo rushes toward Meriam, seizes the back of her throne, and skates her over toward Lore. What the underworld is he—

"Meriam!" I screech because I suddenly know. He's going to tip her onto Lore's beak. "Meriam, wake up!" I don't even care if my voice betrays my location. All I care about is reaching that throne and striking every soldier on the way.

Six more bodies fall; twelve more hands redden.

Not real-Dante's though.

For now, he commands the others to do his dirty work, keeping himself tucked at a safe distance from me. But he isn't safe.

"Her footsteps! You can see her footsteps," I hear him yell. "Follow the blood trail!"

One guard does as he's told. I whirl, and he skewers himself right onto my blade. He gasps, then gurgles. As my blade slurps out of him, one of the many Dantes throws himself into Tavo's path.

"I cannot let you—sacrifice her." The man's forehead is lacquered with sweat and his chest is pumping as wildly as everyone else's.

Everyone except for Meriam.

"Meriam!" I screech, sprinting now. I almost faceplant twice, but Fate must be on my side because I don't fall.

Two soldiers rush after me. I dip my finger in my bleeding thigh, then sketch an arrow on the broken black stone. Though I don't see it lengthen, I feel its weight grow. I twirl around and sweep it. When it bangs into the soldier's body, carving into his waist, I slash my finger where I hope the arrow lies.

The male running next to him stops and swings his sword, assuming I must be standing close.

With a soft grunt, I wrench the heavy length out of one body and chop into the other. The gashes I inflicted are so deep that these two won't be rising for hours.

I turn back around just as Tavo rams Meriam's throne into the soldier standing in his way, sending him flailing backward. "If you don't get out of my fucking way, Enrico, I will fucking murder you."

"I physically cannot, Generali." His palm's plastered to his chest, to his heart.

I take it he must be the guard Justus bargained with. The one supposed to keep Meriam safe at all costs. The one spared an impious crate-burial at sea.

Tavo growls, then whips out the iron sword he used on Bronwen and thrusts it through the startled soldier's chest. Pity swarms me when he crumples, but I shove it aside. For all I know, his blockade was only spurred by a bargain and not by compassion.

Something slaps my ankles and tangles around my legs. Lungs emptying of air, I skid. My arms windmill, sending my giant sword soaring from my fingers and onto the ice with a deafening clatter. I stick out my hands just as my knees slam into the ground. My bones scream, but I don't.

"Caught you," Dante singsongs, his voice originating from thin air now that we're connected by what feels like a chain.

He tugs, reeling me in like a hooked fish.

I rake my nails through the ice and kick my legs to dislodge my restraints. "Meriam!"

Her head jounces and her lids flutter.

"Meriam, Tavo wants to use Lore to cut through your veins. You have to stop him!"

She blinks her hazy pink eyes at me.

Come on. Come on. "Kill Tavo, Meriam!"

I pray to the Cauldron with every last beat of my heart that Meriam understands what I'm saying and will do something about it.

Tavo jams the butt of his sword against her temple, knocking her unconscious.

I shriek, my cry so shrill it shakes the ice cave.

A smile warps Tavo's mouth, and he laughs. He fucking laughs.

But then he stops because a fierce wind erupts from the turquoise gloom and slams against him, rooting him and Meriam to the spot.

A spot that's too close to Lore for comfort but too far for him to angle my grandmother against my mate's gleaming beak. I almost weep with relief when I see the source of the wind.

CHAPTER 84

Gabriele's here.

I'm no longer alone.

I scan the darkness for Justus, praying he, too, has found his way inside the ice cave, but then my body bumps into something. I glance over my shoulder, expecting to see Dante before remembering he's currently as invisible as I am.

I hear him mutter something about killing me himself. Though his voice is low, I can tell I still have a dozen or so seconds before I reach him.

What I bumped into reappears—one of the soldiers whose waist I sawed through. Though my arm muscles jangle, I manage to hoist him on top of me, then plaster him to the front of my body just as I stop gliding.

I push out my senses to hear Dante's breathing, but my heart is hammering too wildly to grasp much of anything over the harsh beats. Even the shouting around me barely registers.

Water sloshes over us, shaping our bodies. As I gag on a mouthful, a blade whacks into my shield of flesh with such vehemence that the impact nails the back of my skull to the ice and rattles my teeth.

I lay there, dazed, the heat of the man's life pouring from his veins and dripping around me.

The tip of Dante's sword grates against my armor, and I think he's figured out my trick, but the chain clinks, and the Faerie King reappears.

He thinks I'm bleeding out. I'm so stunned that he fell for my ruse that, for a handful of seconds, all I can do is blink.

But then Gabriele yells, "Justus, get to Fallon! She's bleeding out."

Justus is here.

A tear snakes down my cheek as I press away the dead male, keeping him anchored to my body so he doesn't reappear yet. With trembling hands, I section the links of my chain with blood, then grab a length of it and run toward Dante.

I jump onto his back and slap the chain around his neck. As we smash into the icy ground, I shout at Gabriele to blow Tavo onto Lore's beak.

"Tavo?" I hear him whisper.

"Yes! The man next to you is Tavo! I have the real Dante!" I grab a handful of the Faerie King's braids and thrust his head into the ice until blood gushes and he stops squirming.

"FALLON!" Gabriele shouts. "Behind you!"

How does he know where I am? Did the gory puddle give me away, or— *Merda*, I've reappeared!

Before I can look over my shoulder at the danger he's spotted, Tavo punches the throne into my friend's legs, making him stagger, and then, without wasting a single second, he tips Meriam.

His aim is so perfect that even from my vantage point, I can tell that her chest will meet my mate's beak.

I scream and leap off Dante, then run, but I'm too far.

I'm too far.

Gabriele jerks to his feet and pounds into the gold throne, pitching it away from my mate. Tavo roars, and with a violent stroke, he swings his iron blade.

CHAPTER 85

Another shriek burns my lungs as Gabriele's head sails away from his shoulders. Like Bronwen's, it seems to fall in slow motion.

"You monster!" I bang into Tavo with such velocity that he teeters . . . right onto my mate's beak.

Before he can unpin himself, I wrench the iron blade from his fingers and plunge it through his blackened heart. His mouth parts around a soundless gasp, and he blinks. Twice.

Then, like a doll who's lost its stuffing, his body sags, and his eyes empty of life. I'm tempted to leave him pinned to Lore for all to see, but the idea of his blood coursing into my mate's mouth revolts me, so I grip his jacket and toss him to the ground.

So many tears run down my cheeks that they blur the carnage. I wipe them with the back of my hand, but they keep coming. Though I'm aware there are more soldiers to impede and a king to murder, I crouch beside Gabriele's head and shut his lids, croaking a prayer for his soul to find peace. Words will never suffice to express my gratitude and affection, but words are all I can give this hero for now.

"Nipota?" My grandfather's gentle voice pulls my stinging eyes away from my friend.

I find him standing over Dante, one boot stamped on the Faerie's back like a hunter standing over his prized stag. All around him are scattered motionless bodies.

Lifeless, I realize as I approach on legs gone so numb, it feels as though I float.

While I avenged Gabriele, Justus Rossi planted his iron blade through every beating chest, impressing ruby blooms onto crisp white jackets. He's drenched in blood. It mattes his hair and forks down his haggard face; clouds his eyes which are filled with rage but also with heartbreak.

When I reach him, he holds out his weapon. "Will you do me the honor of ending this war with my sword?"

Without hesitation, we swap weapons. Adrenaline steadies my grip as I clasp Justus's sword and lift it, twirling the blade that's glazed in so much blood it glistens red like the rubies inset in the hilt.

"I want to look at him when I end him," I murmur.

I don't miss the grunt of pain that escapes Justus as he hinges at the waist, fists the Faerie King's white uniform, and flips him over.

Dante's spurs clink against the ice, and the chain I choked him with clatters, jolting his eyes wide.

Good.

I want him to see me win, the same way I want him lucid enough to hear my last confession.

"I've one last thing to say to you before I snuff out your miserable existence, Dante Regio." Without applying pressure, I run the tip of my blade down the seam of his rib cage, bumping against each gold button. "You never needed me to cast spells, for your veins held Shabbin magic. By binding us in matrimony, Meriam bridled your ability to blood-cast. Made you entirely dependent on my blood."

A startled breath saws through his quivering lips, and his eyes round with a mixture of horror and shock.

"Your greatest mistake, moyo, was marrying me." I finally position the sword over Dante's filthy heart and murmur, "Long live"—I lean all my weight into my arms—"the Crows."

CHAPTER 86

As the light leaves Dante's eyes and his head lolls to the side, I swallow.

I thought I'd feel triumphant, but all I feel is numb. Justus must sense that I'm about to collapse, because his arms come around me, and he crushes me into a hard embrace. "It's over."

"Bronwen's dead, Nonno."

"I know."

"And so is Gabriele."

"I know, but so is Dante, child."

"One doesn't equal out the other."

"No. No life ever replaces another." He presses a kiss to the top of my head. "But such is war. May you never live through another. Now go wake your—" He sucks in such a deep breath that I pick my head off his chest, worried he's about to keel over. Though his eyes are wide, they shimmer like the carved walls surrounding us. "Santo Caldrone."

I turn and follow his line of sight. There, beside the upturned Lucin throne, lays a body curled in on itself. Folds of glimmering silk spill over the slender form like a wave at sunset.

"It worked," Justus whispers.

The woman stirs.

Meriam.

She slides her arms beneath her. Where one gives out, the other holds. She props herself up on it, her body trembling, her long hair swishing. And then she twists her head and fastens her bright pink eyes on us.

"Fallon." My name comes out as a raucous murmur. "Justus." Her throat bobs with a swallow.

He unhooks his arm from around my waist and takes a step in her direction, but stops to make sure I'm steady on my feet.

I smile and say, "I'm all right," even though I feel all wrong.

Hopefully, waking my mate, feeling his heartbeats against my cheek and his breath in my hair will make the lie I spoke to reassure my grandfather true.

I limp toward Lore's giant steel body and study his abdomen until I spot an indent that shouldn't exist. My hands are covered in so much blood that I wipe them against the wall of ice. It judders beneath my fingertips. I think it may be because my arms are shaking, but then the ice underfoot also trembles. Another avalanche?

Once my hands are clean, I grip Lore's talon and heave myself up, then climb over to where he was hit with another one of those tiny cannonballs. "Nonno, I'm going to need something long and sharp."

He digs through his pocket. "I recovered this from where you fell." He produces the fork my father had twisted into a skewer.

He walks it over to me, then returns to Meriam who whispers something to him. I hear Lore's name but nothing else over the hectic pounding of my heart and the scrape of the fork against metal.

The very second the pellet is out of him, Lore pools into his shadows. He must sense I lay on top of him because he cushions my body, slowly tipping it until I'm back on my feet.

"Fallon," he rasps, his hands coming up to my face and clutching it as though it was the most precious thing in the world. ***It is, mo khrà. You are.***

I swallow. "Oh, Lore."

Before I can tell him of all the horror that went down in the ice cave, his arms lace around me, dragging my body against his so hard that our armor clinks, and then his lips crash into mine. My tears slide around our mouths, slicken our skin, and salt our tongues. Instead of a truth, it pries emotion from my chest. I sob from relief and grief.

I cry so hard that my lips skid off his. He tucks my head beneath his chin and just holds me. Though my eyes are closed, his are wide open.

I know the moment his gaze touches Bronwen's head, because his heart misses a beat and his lips burrow deeper into my hair around a muted, *"Focá."*

He turns us slowly, as though we were dancing instead of standing in an arena littered with corpses. He must come across Gabriele's head because his Adam's apple jostles against my temple again.

"Lorcan?"

His body goes stiff at the sound of his name. And then his leathers creak as he pivots us. I pry my lids up and watch as pink meets gold.

"I'm so sorry, Lore. I'm so sorry."

His jaw clicks and ticks.

Meriam is sagging against Justus. I suppose that five centuries sitting rids a person of the ability to stand. The ground shakes again, robbing her of her tenuous footing. When she begins to slide, my grandfather scoops her into his arms.

"Thank you," she murmurs, gazing up at him. "I owe you my life, Justus Rossi."

He sucks in a breath as a bargain inscribes itself around his bicep.

Lore watches them for a moment, and then his words move over that magical sentence that breaks his people from their obsidian spell. *"Tach ahd a'feithahm thu, mo Chréach."*

Like the first time I heard him tell his people that the sky awaited them, my skin pebbles and my stomach hardens with a slow thrill and a deep anticipation. Twin streaks of smoke burst toward him from the blue-shadows of the ice cave. As they morph into Aoife and Colm, Lore speaks it again, this time in Lucin, probably so I can understand him.

My pulse quickens, nipping at my skin like minnows at small crustaceans, and ice slides down my spine as though I was rubbing myself against the cavern walls.

Fallon?

I begin to shake, my heart thrashing like some captive bird. Lore holds me at arm's length, his metallic eyes running wildly over me.

"Fallon?!" he yells.

His voice drops into me like a spike, cracking the ice inside my veins into shards that catch in my organs and tear them open.

"What have I done?"

Though I can hear Lore, my vision goes black, then white, rubbing away the world.

"FALLON!"

I must scream because my lips are stretched as wide as my throat, and my eardrums throb with another form of pain than the one ripping through my insides like Crow talons.

My knees soften, my legs bend. I think I'm about to fall, melt right through the ice, but strong arms hold me, powerful hands wrap around my waist. And then . . . they fall right through my waist.

The next thing I know, I bang into something sharp. A giant icicle whooshes past me and collides into . . . into the ground.

The ground, which is no longer under my feet.

Oh my Gods. I'm—I'm—

Flying.

I blink away from the shards of ice, my gaze swerving toward my mate's upturned face. His eyes glimmer with a smile that curves his lips.

You're flying, Little Bird. My call must've undone the binds that were still coiled around your Crow side.

I glance sideways, finding huge black wings instead of arms. I flap them with too much verve and bang into another icicle. *Merda. Focá.* I sift through a whole bunch of other invectives that, for once, only seem to amuse Lore.

I'm flying.

I'm fucking *flying*.

The realization trickles through me like warm water on chilled skin, burning away the hoarfrost lingering from the battle. My heart swells and swells until I think it may have grown wings of its own.

Oh, Cauldron, I can fly. I can morph into smoke. I can go through walls. Well, technically I could already do that, but now I can morph into air. *Air*!

Caws resound outside the mountain that trembles again.

My mate's throat bobs with a deep swallow that steals moisture from his shimmering eyes.

Are you crying?

The corners of his mouth turn up and up.

What?

I granted you your wish, my love.

Though my beak cannot curl, I grin. *I've a beak.* I bend my leg and inspect my lethal talons. *And iron talons.* I'm as mesmerized as the day my blood guided my hand through matter.

A giant hole suddenly appears in the wall of snow that had buried the entrance to the cavern. Bright, gorgeous sunshine filters in, along with air so fresh, it whisks away the reek of death. Though two Crows swoop in, what captures my attention are the men in skin and furs standing beyond the cavern.

One in particular.

Konstantin Korol. "We thought you may need some assistance, Ríhbiadh." His gaze sweeps over the dead. "But I see you've got everything handled."

"Thank you for coming." Lore inclines his head. To me, he asks, ***Did you call in your bargain?***

No. I must tuck my wings in, because the next thing I know, I bang into the ground at Lore's feet and groan.

With another smile, Lore crouches and clasps either side of my head. ***Ouch.*** He strokes my cheeks, his thumbs sailing through my black feathers.

"Daughter." My father's hoarse voice makes my head jerk in his direction.

Easy there, my love. You've a sword for a mouth. Lore's smile only deepens, and though no other tear chases after the one that trundled down the sharp frame of his face, his eyes keep sparkling. ***Come back to me.***

I do. My transformation into flesh is as rushed as the one into feathers. I slam down, my tailbone whacking ice, and loose another groan.

With a brisk chuckle, Lore tows me upright. ***You'll get a handle on your new shape in no time.***

My father shoulders aside my mate and repeats that single, beautiful word that ties our hearts and souls together. "Daughter."

It's funny, but I don't think I've ever heard him speak the word in Lucin, and he's just said it twice.

"Your father spoke in our tongue, my love. Just like I'm doing right now."

I shouldn't be shocked. After all, Shabbin came to me even before Meriam painted me in blood, but Lore's declaration knocks me onto my figurative ass.

I can speak Crow.

I laugh, and my joy echoes against every corner of this vast temple of ice. But then another sound rings out—a deep, throaty cry.

My mouth shuts, and I burn with shame for having dared rejoice. For having dared put the deaths I brought about out of my mind for even a moment.

My father must've realized the reason for Cian's wails, because he streaks through the air toward his kneeling brother.

"Shh." Lore gathers me into his arms. "It's not your fault, my love."

I press my face into the crook of his neck, just where his armor ends, and breathe in the smell of my mate until it plugs some of the holes that riddle my heart. "Can we find the runestone and go?" My voice is thin, threaded with my uncle's pain.

"Rossi just collected it from one of the sleighs," Lore murmurs around a long breath. "He's proven himself rather helpful, hasn't he?"

"Are you finally warming up to him?"

He hums, more resonance than sound. "He did marry you off to another man."

I jerk my head off Lore's chest and raise my hand. And twirl it. My palm is bare and pink, no longer marred by that hateful mark that linked me to a man who died an imbecile instead of a legend.

Lore grips my wrist and carries my hand to his mouth, then presses a kiss to the center of my palm. ***Mine.***

I was always yours.

But now, you are* only *mine.

CHAPTER 87

The second we reach the Sky Kingdom's esplanade, my mate morphs into smoke and lingers in that form until my talons scrape against stone.

Though I practiced shifting and landing a few times before leaving Glace, and I flew most of the way back, landing on Lore's back in skin only once to rest, my mate still clearly worries about my technique. I do sport an impressive collection of bruises and cuts. Most from the fight, but a select few were acquired from pounding into packed snow and ice in this other, still foreign form of mine.

My grandfather dismounts from Colm's back, and Meriam, from Aoife's. Where the others were reluctant to offer her safe passage to Luce, Aoife squared her shoulders—well, wings—and crouched low so Justus could help the sorceress settle.

My father melts back into skin, the fur stole containing the runestone now clutched between his fingers instead of his talons, and glares at Meriam. I sense he wants to pitch her off this mountain, but Justus worried that the ward spell was too ancient and tenuous to erase on his own. *And* he worried that instead of erasing it, he'd alter it into something irrevocably worse. So before leaving Glace, Lore made Meriam swear an oath to him that she would remove the wards without ruse.

As Justus eases a still-weak Meriam down onto the bone-smooth floor, then positions himself behind her so she can use his legs as a backrest, Erwin flies up to the southernmost hatch to retrieve the two stones from the war room.

It takes him so long to return that I begin to worry something happened to them. What if Mattia, coerced by Antoni, stole those precious rocks?

I clutch my elbows, skin prickling with unease under my ruined turtleneck. The leather cord strung with my gifted seashell, that somehow survived my brutal freefall, feels as though it's choking me.

Chewing on my lip, I squint at the gently brightening sky, impatient for black to smudge the pastel expanse. When minutes tick by, and still no bird reappears, my stomach begins to bind itself into knots.

Something happened to the stones.

I'm about to ask Lore to reach out to Erwin through the mind link he shares with all his Crows when a giant bird swoops back our way, a leather rucksack darkening the space between his gleaming claws.

The breath I release is so strong, it manages to flutter my hair, a feat considering the strands are clumped with blood and sweat.

"Will you be staying in Luce?" my father asks Meriam as he sets the stone retrieved in Glace in front of my grandmother. "Or heading home?"

Though the queendom is impossible to spot from our vantage point, like a compass, her tourmaline eyes turn toward her home before scrolling back over Lore's vast kingdom. I wonder if she considers Luce a source of beauty or of pain. And then I wonder if she considers Shabbe a home.

She still hasn't answered by the time my father takes delivery of the leather sack.

"So?" He unwraps the tight bundle. "Where will you go, Meriam?"

"To Shabbe, first. I've much forgiveness to beg for."

Justus removes his gloves and pushes them into his jacket pocket before scraping his palms over his hair in an attempt to tame the blood-caked flyaways that stick out around his pale face. Like me, like Meriam, he's in dire need of a wash. *And* some more Shabbin crystals.

He used up all his healing ones on my slashed thigh and Meriam's cut neck and wrist, promising his headwound had already healed. From the way he moved, from the way his lips pinched and his wrinkles carved into his skin, I could tell he had other wounds that hadn't mended, but my grandfather's a proud man, so I accepted the crystals without insisting he keep some for himself.

Also, though I know it's the combination of my blood on obsidian that can harm Lore, and only if it finds its way into his heart, I selfishly prefer not to bleed anywhere near him.

To think that, soon, I won't have to worry about this.

My father finally lays the rock fragments in front of Meriam, fitting their jagged edges together until they form one large, unbroken brick. The crimson whorls Justus had magnetized to the surface must've sunk back into the stone, because the gray surface is unblemished.

Lore's shadows settle onto my shoulders like that fur cloak he'd given me during our flight over Glace—heavy yet soft. Though Dante's dead, and we're now in possession of a Shabbin witch who doesn't risk turning to stone—now that my Crow magic has been unleashed, I could incur that fate—Lore and I agreed that he'd keep his *unstakable* form until the wards collapse.

Cheeks stained pink with animation, eyes blazing bright with hope, my father unfurls from his squat and crosses his large arms, vambraces creaking like the rest of his leather regalia.

Lore's shadows firm at my back, spreading against my rib cage as though to hold more of me. I glance up to make sure he's still cloaked in darkness. When I catch sight of his storm cloud face, I relax into his touch, pillowing my head against his hazy shoulder, so fucking bone-weary, I want to crawl into bed and sleep for days.

Lore presses his cool lips to my forehead and holds them there as Meriam detaches her palms from the folds of her golden gown and hovers them over the stone.

Her brow slickens with perspiration and color slashes her lofty cheekbones as she recalls her sigil. Though the air between the rock and her palms is dim, I don't miss the droplets that run over the stone's surface like dew before breaking off and rising toward her quivering palms.

She dips her chin, nostrils flaring delicately yet wildly. With a breathy grunt, her fingers snap shut and her fists jounce, and then her eyes roll back into her head, and she buckles against Justus's legs. He sinks down and catches her before she can flop sideways and crack her skull against the esplanade's hard floor.

The world goes so still and quiet that when my father asks, "Did it work?" his rasp wobbles the very air.

It isn't Meriam or Justus who answers him; it's the earth we stand upon and the oxygen we breathe. Both shudder with a tremor so violent, I think it may crumble Monteluce.

As the columns shake and the mountain stream gushes, my father's riotous stare touches mine, and I can read inside his fathomless pupils the fear that bubbles there. Did Meriam bring down the wards, or did she bring down Luce?

CHAPTER 88

As suddenly as it began, the tremors halt. I stare at Justus, who blinks bloodshot eyes my way, as Aoife voices the question on everyone's mind: "Are the wards gone?"

Erwin spins toward Lore, whose shadows now envelop all of me. "Call to the rest of our people, Mórrgaht."

My mate firms at my back and then his mouth moves over the magic spell that awakened me mere hours ago.

Though I'm not locked in stone, I feel the incantation spill into my veins and galvanize my blood. I feel it crackle against my heart and prickle my skin. If the wards are down, the Crows locked in Shabbe will feel his spell as well.

A tenuous smile rises amidst the wiry hairs of my father's beard. "Ready to see Aodhan's ugly face?"

Lore snorts, curling me deeper into his body.

Why does the name Aydawn sound familiar?

Because I mentioned him the day I broke the news of our mating bond to your father.

Ah . . . I remember now. When he spoke the Crow's name, my father's complexion had purpled.

He's a terrible flirt with a penchant for disregarding direct orders. His pulse is steady against my spine. ***One of the only Crows I find more agreeable in obsidian form.***

Though my heart is heavy, Lore's dark humor snags it like a fishing hook and reels it a little higher. ***Would you like me to stake him for you?***

Hmm. Tempting. He brushes a kiss to my temple.

My father, along with several other Crows, bursts into feathers and soars over the Sky Kingdom. For a long moment, only the wind buffeting the columns of the esplanade and my mate's breaths stir the air, but then caws echo, their chorus so raucous that I spin in Lore's arms.

"It worked?"

A smile teases the edges of his mouth. "Shift."

I do.

And then his skin darkens and swells, transforming man into beast.

Together we rise into the blush of dawn where thousands upon thousands of beating wings paint the horizon black, and my mate's eyes, a smoldering shade of gold.

CHAPTER 89

As Lore greets the returnees, I retire to my bedchamber for that much-needed soak. My muscles are so riddled with exhaustion that I almost give up unhooking my armor and rolling off my clothes, but the reek of death that clings to them spurs me on.

Naked, I glance at myself in the mirror, horrified by my tattered state. Instead of a bath, I elect to take a shower and scrub so hard at my skin that I anger the puckered seam on my thigh. My scab splits anew and weeps blood.

As I lather my hair, I watch the ruby droplets fork down the side of my leg, the last mark Dante will ever leave on my body. The sight carries me back to the cave made of hard ice and chilling screams. How is it that I escaped yet still feel trapped?

I flatten my hands against the wall, shut my raw eyes, and press my forehead to the stone.

My sorrow and exhaustion are so loud and ugly, they echo over the spray and buckle my knees, driving me down to the floor where I curl in on myself like the shell around my throat.

SOMETHING SOFT PRESSES against my skin. Something softer, against the little feather on my cheek. ***I'm sorry for leaving you, Little Bird.***

I pry my aching lids wide as Lore wraps the towel around me before scooping me into his arms and carrying me out of the humid bathing chamber.

After he sets me down on the bed, he shucks off his battle leathers and boots. His armor and vambraces, I note, are already gone.

He climbs over me, taking my mouth in a hard kiss filled with such exhilaration that I can feel his heartbeats on his palate and in his tongue. He pours them into me and chases them with so much affection that my rigid spine begins to soften.

I raise my hands to his neck and my legs to his waist, and pull him flush to me. The heat of his kiss warms my skin and pools desire low in my belly. Desire that only grows as his bulge quarries my towel, trying to breach the purled cotton.

When I begin to rock my hips, he growls and grips my ass, angling it up to force the towel to fold. As it bunches around my waist, his cock springs into me and I gasp.

He groans a sigh of deep contentment that flutters the walls hugging his shaft and then he groans again as he pulls out. I feel like months have gone by since we last came together.

"The moments during which I'm not buried between your legs will always feel too long," he murmurs.

I lock my ankles around his waist, pressing his thick cock back into me. This time, I'm the one who sighs. I know we cannot spend our immortal lives making love. After all, my mate's not an idle man. He could never *be* an idle man.

I flick aside a lock of black hair gilded by the high sun outside my windows, then raise my head to kiss the little feather on his cheek. ***I love you so much, Lore.*** I know I speak in Crow because my voice crackles over the coarse syllables.

My declaration sends his mouth crashing into mine with such might that it knocks my head back against the fluffy pillow. Tongue sweeping against mine, he roots himself inside of me. The sunshine seems to brighten as he moves, turning so blinding that my mate looks haloed in its glow.

My heart vibrates as hard as the walls he stretches and strokes. I drink in a deep breath and arch my spine as the friction sparks a shudder in my very marrow.

Just as I think he will push me over the edge, he melts into shadows, leaving me cold and wanting. ***I'll be right back.***

Are you fucking serious? I glare at the perfect globes of the ass walking away from me.

With a wicked chuckle, he vanishes inside my closet. I consider getting dressed and depriving him of an orgasm like he's just deprived me. And I would've, had my muscles not felt like jelly.

He returns a minute later, cock at half-mast and glistening. I pout as he climbs back over me, collects my left hand from the bedsheets, and tows it up.

He brackets my hips between his knees and sits back on his heels, then presses a kiss to my knuckles. Molten eyes locked on mine, he says, "Fallon Báeinach of Shabbe, I know you carry the mark of my people on your skin but will you do me the immense honor of carrying my mark on your finger?"

I blink at him, then at the ring he hovers beside my nail. The stone is pale pink like the sands of Shabbe and cut into the shape of a raindrop.

Like my name.

But also like the ones that fall from the storms my mate can coax from thin air.

How perfect.

"Phoebus and Sybille spent days sifting through the trunks of uncut stones I keep in the coin tower until they agreed on this hunk of a diamond, which my mother then chiseled herself. It's never graced another finger, Little Bird. It was made for you. Just for you."

I already thought it was the most arresting jewel I'd ever seen, but now, knowing how it came to be . . . Gods, it outshines the very sun itself.

Shall I remind you, my love, that now that you're officially a Crow, you only have one god.

You're wrong. I've two gods.

He pulls his head away from mine. "Shabbins don't venerate deities, only the Cauldron."

"I meant *you*. You and Mórrígan. I'm on the fence about the Cauldron."

His flushed mouth bends. "Don't say that too loudly for we wouldn't want to offend the almighty source of all magic and risk having it seal itself off again."

My lashes sweep high. "It's open?"

"Yes."

"My father must be champing at the bit to head to Shabbe with Daya."

"He is. Just as I'm champing at the bit to hear your answer to my question." He nods to the ring.

I grin, because I thought my answer was self-evident. We're mates, after all. Not to mention that we will someday have a daughter, and though families—if I've learned anything from the patchwork of individuals that make up my own—aren't always conventionally constructed, I absolutely want to marry this wonderful man.

When he doesn't glide the ring onto my finger, apparently waiting for my consent, I say, ***Yes, yes, and*** **yes.** In case he missed my first three yeses, I shout an extra one into the golden air for all to hear.

With a quiet smile, he slides it over my knuckles. "Shall we go gather the family and share the happy news?"

The stone is so long and wide, it cloaks half my finger in its dazzling pink splendor.

"Yes, but first . . ." I reach between his legs and wrap my hand around his girth. As I slow-pump him, I watch my new ring sparkle as though filled with a million little fires.

"It looks so good"—a husky breath escapes from my mate's tipped mouth—"wrapped around me."

I laugh as he bends over and nips the sound of my bliss from my lips and makes it his.

CHAPTER 90

I'm uncertain how many Crows arrived today, but the Sky Kingdom population has, at the very least, increased tenfold. Though the crowd is considerable, the noise level is not, for the new arrivals cannot speak.

"In day or two," Aoife explains to Sybille and Phoebus, "they will find voice again. And then you will need plugs for ears because Crows screech a lot."

I smile as I take in the shifters that eddy around my mate like planets around the sun.

Aoife nudges my arm. "You really understand *everything* I say?"

"Yes. Everything." I know she's veered to Crow because her diction is perfect again. "You can have no more secrets from me."

She grins, and it presses a dimple into her cheek. "I'm going to miss our lessons."

"I've still got lots to learn, Aoife. For example, flying. I'm terrible at that." I stroke the beveled edges of my diamond, disbelieving that something so precious could belong to me and me alone. "Do you think you could teach me now that the war is over?"

Her dark eyes sparkle. "It will be my honor, Fallon."

Phoebus and Sybille, who are seated across from us, stare like spectators at the theater, their eyes huge with wonder.

"I still cannot believe you speak fluent Crow." Phoebus reclines and drapes his arm over the back of Syb's seat.

"It's totally insane," she agrees, slurping down a forkful of crustacean linguini, just as the chair next to hers groans from Mattia dropping into it.

"What a day. What. A. Day." The whites of his eyes are pinker than my grandmother's irises. "Gods, I need a drink. Or ten." He inhales a deep breath, wrinkling his nose at the smell that lifts off his black shirt as he reaches for the jug in the middle of the table. "Sorry. I should've changed after—"

I sniff the air, catching a trace of smoke.

"After?" Pheebs prompts.

Mattia lowers his eyes to his lap. "After we burned the bodies."

My heart jounces. Lore mentioned Crows buried their dead in the sky, but I didn't—I didn't realize he meant— "They incinerated Bronwen?"

"And Gabriele," Aoife murmurs. "He lived like Crow. Fought like Crow. Only right he go to next world like Crow." Her lips barely move over her murmur. "He was so kind man. I not believe—" She squeezes the bridge of her nose. "I not believe he gone. I not believe Bronwen be right. I not believe *she* gone."

Sybille snares her bottom lip and presses away the mound of pasta dotted with clams and baby shrimps, appetite, like my aunt and friend, gone.

"Was Cian there when they . . .? When they . . .?" A hiccup of grief jostles the expanding lump in my throat, making it impossible to finish my sentence.

Mattia nods. "He was so stoic. Didn't make a sound."

Probably because he was all out of sounds.

Softly, and in Crow, Aoife whispers, "Cian asked our king to make him a forever-Crow after he releases his mate's ashes into the stars."

I sensed that would be his wish, but hearing Aoife confirm it rips open my chest.

"Fallon? Is that . . . you?"

I blink out of my thoughts and up at Reid, whom I haven't seen since I was taken into the obsidian tunnels. I'm uncertain why my surprise is so great. Now that the wards are down, many will be sailing home. I suppose the romantic in me had secretly hoped he'd have reconnected with my Faerie mother. Perhaps he did?

Maybe Nonna and Agrippina are home as well. I went to find Justus when I left my bedroom earlier, but Lazarus told me he and Meriam were sleeping. Yes, the sorceress has been brought into the Sky Kingdom after she undid her wards. Lore's idea. He prefers to keep an eye on her and her magic, and since his castle prevents blood-casting, he deemed it the safest place to stow her until we fly to Shabbe in the morning and he hands her over to Priya.

I stroke the facets of my pink diamond, finding comfort in their smoothness. "How was your stay in the queendom, Reid?"

His eyebrows rise. "You speak our tongue now?"

I nod.

Sybille leans into Mattia's chest and proclaims with great sisterly pride, "She can even shift into a crow and cast spells with her blood, so you better not annoy her anymore, Reid."

The Shabbin sun has threaded the young Crow's light-brown mane with strands of gold and burnished his pale-brown skin. "I've certainly missed a great deal."

"Sit, my friend." Phoebus pats the chair next to his. "I'll fill you in."

Reid drops down as though the voyage across the Southern Sea has drained him of all his energy.

"How is my— How are the Rossi women?"

"They've settled in well. Your grandmother has taken a great liking to the matriarchal society."

Of course my strong-willed grandmother would love a land where women and round-ears aren't considered second-class citizens. I start to smile until I think of Cato. I asked Lore earlier whether I could fly him down to Tarecuori myself now that all of Luce is ours, but he told me to wait until things have settled. Hasn't Cato's family waited long enough, though? I ended up penning a letter to his parents and entrusting a fellow Crow with his homecoming.

"Has my Faerie family returned?" I ask, still caressing my ring.

"No." Reid's attention has ventured off me and is now firmly planted on the abdomen Sybille is stroking, which does seem to have grown in the last day.

"Was Agrippina happy to see you?"

The mention of my Faerie mother tears his gaze off Syb. "Why would she be?"

I frown. "I thought—I thought the two of you—Bronwen mentioned the two of you knew each other."

He crosses his arms. "Is that all Bronwen mentioned?"

I sigh, wondering why my questioning is making him so prickly. "My Faerie mother kept your love stone on a shelf in her room."

His thick eyebrows jolt, getting lost under a tousled lock.

"I pocketed it when I returned to the Fae lands. If Antoni's old home in Tarecuori hasn't been looted, it should still be there."

Reid doesn't speak.

"Once Lore allows me to venture into the Fae lands, I'll go find it and bring it back to you, so you can—"

"She doesn't fucking remember me, Fallon," he snaps, "so there's really no point in dredging up a past that will only give her more anxiety."

Perhaps Reid isn't all bad, but he has yet to win me over. "You mustn't have loved her all that much if you're giving up so easily."

His charcoal-lined gaze tapers. "Perhaps you shouldn't judge something you've no knowledge of."

"I lived with that woman for twenty-two years, Reid, and I loved her for every minute, for every second of those twenty-two years. So don't fucking tell me I'm not well-placed to judge. Mamma may not be able to love out loud, but she loves. In her own way, she loves. And if you cannot see that, then you don't deserve her."

Reid's head jerks back as though I'd slapped him. I sort of wish I could.

Everything all right, Little Bird?

Yes. Fine. I push away from the table. "I'm going to go find my uncle now. Do any of you know where he is?"

"On the esplanade with your father." Mattia runs one hand through the thick blond mop atop his head before returning his palm to Syb's shoulder and stroking her dark skin.

Before setting off, I address Reid once more. "Justus hopes the Cauldron will heal her mind." Though I think my mother deserves better than Connor's boy, whom she chooses to give her heart to is ultimately her decision, not mine.

"Justus?"

I let my friends fill in the gaps and walk over to my mate, who stands amidst a cluster of shifters, golden eyes trained on our table. *Murgadh'Thábhain* is so quiet that in spite of stepping lightly, my every footfall resonates as though I'd hooked Dante's spurs onto my boots.

The memory of the dead king makes my thigh scar itch and my fingers ball.

Before shifting and leaving the marketplace, Lore wraps an arm around my waist and tucks me against his chest. "Take a breath, my love, and put Reid and Agrippina out of your mind, for your father is going to need you greatly in the coming days."

That cleanses my mind of all the little grievances and worries that are so inconsequential when a man is about to say goodbye to his brother forever. "I wish Cian would choose to stay."

"Unlike his brother, Cian has no children to live for."

My blood runs cold as I selfishly wonder whether I'll be enough to keep my father from begging for eternal death if the Cauldron fails to return my mother to him.

Please let me be enough.

But most importantly, please bring back my mother.

CHAPTER 91

The sky is so bright with stars that it paints the gray stone of Lorcan's mountain white. The only dark spots are my father and his brother, who sit side by side on the esplanade's edge, looking out over the world like young boys on the cusp of adulthood.

Though Lore and I made no noise upon landing, they must've sensed us for they both turn.

Cian stands, dusting his hands against his leather trousers. He bends over and picks up a parcel wrapped in purple silk, and I know, without asking, what it holds. He hugs it to his chest as though it was Bronwen herself.

As he nears us, I find myself staring at his bare face. How different he looks without his stripes. His features are so much softer. I wonder if my father, too, looks soft bare of makeup.

Unlike Cian, my father doesn't come toward us. He keeps staring out at the glittering ocean that clinches our kingdom. I catch his hand lifting to his face and staying there for a few heartbeats.

I may not have any blood siblings, but if I lost Sybille or Phoebus . . . Great Cauldron, I don't think I would ever recover. When my nose begins to sting and my throat to tighten, I murmur to myself, *Strong. Be strong.*

"Have you changed your mind about leaving us, Cian?" my mate asks my uncle.

"No, Mórrgaht. My beloved awaits me in the Beyond."

My throat burns with grief.

"I know Cathal has asked you to wait until tomorrow. Will you wait?"

"I cannot, Lore."

"Cathal will need you if—"

"Don't." He closes his eyes. "Don't ask me to stay, because if Daya rises from the Cauldron, I will begrudge my brother, and I love him—" His voice breaks and tears fork down his pasty cheeks. "I love him far too much to hold his happiness against him."

"What if my mother doesn't rise?" I ask softly, hoping my voice doesn't carry to my father's ears.

"Cathal has *you*, Fallon."

Again, I wonder if I will be enough.

Though Lore doesn't touch me with his hands, wisps of his smoke curl around my fingers and stroke my knuckles. "Ready to set her free, brother?"

Cian nods to Lore.

My mate's voice suddenly echoes between my temples with words that, for once, aren't only meant for me. "Come fly, my Crows. Come accompany our sister during her final voyage."

His regal tone makes my blood dance and my skin prickle as though feathers were about to pop from my flesh. Mórrígan, can he make me shift just by using his call? Does he hold that sort of power?

I do.

Incredible.

The stars suddenly wink out and the indigo sky blackens as Crow after Crow flocks out of the Sky Kingdom.

"Once the silk falls away from my talons, Lore, set my human heart to rest." My uncle places the little pillow filled with Bronwen's ashes down at his feet with such reverence that my heart twists with shame that I couldn't save her.

Lore's grip tightens around my hand. Before he can tell me not to guilt myself, I morph and rise with the others. Another Crow swoops up beside me. My father.

He brushes the tip of his wing against my cheek. ***There's little worse than goodbyes.***

The sound of his voice and his sweet caress loosen the cage of my ribs. ***How I wish I knew a spell to take away the pain in your heart, Dádhi.***

His eyes shine like the canals of my youth, and his great chest vibrates with a caw that echoes between my ribs.

For all my desire to be strong, I feel like a sand castle tonight, one that will come crashing down with the next wave of my father's pain.

Lore is the last to take off, his wingbeats so powerful they seem to stir the very stars. ***Come to me, Fallon.***

Like a newborn foal, I teeter and dip as I join my mate at the front of the procession. My loving father rides the wind below me, clearly not trusting that I won't pinwheel toward the earth.

Silly, but it dawns on me that, though he wasn't there for my first step, he was there for my first flight; the same way my mother was there for my first swim.

Who carries Gabriele? I ask Lore, when I finally reach him.

Aoife offered to disperse his ashes. My mate nods toward my friend, who flies beside Cian.

Our procession is slow and silent with, for only noise, the wind that skips through our feathers. No Crow caws or screeches. No one swoops or flaps their wings. We all float over Cian and Aoife as they unroll the bolts of silk clutched between their talons.

We all watch the shimmering remains of the two Faeries, whose bravery and grit changed the face of our world, disperse over the gray rock of Monteluce, the wilderness of Tarespagia, and the serrated crowns of the Racoccin woods.

Aoife is the first to release the strip of silk. As soon as she's freed it, she rises higher.

My father peers up at me. Once he's ascertained I'm safe, he sinks toward his brother.

I wonder if they speak or if they simply coexist, sharing this one last moment together.

When Cian's talons open, and the silk flutters like a trail of wisteria petals, my father releases a heartrending caw that agitates my pulse and fills the hollow shafts of my feathers with frost. He tears away from his brother and streaks off toward the open sea.

I want to go after him, but Lore says, ***Stay.***

Because he worries about my flying skills, or because he thinks my father will prefer to grieve alone?

Both. He tips his head toward the two Crows ascending over the fray. ***Erwin and Naoise will follow him.***

Another caw rings out, this one hoarse and accompanied by two slow clicks. Though Cian's call doesn't translate into words, it sounds like he's wishing us all farewell.

My mate's chest expands with a desolate sigh.

How does it work?

I will speak a spell into his mind. Lore's voice is rough with sorrow. ***Like the one I use to awaken my people. Except—except, these words will lay his humanity to rest.*** Another sigh rolls from his chest and into mine. ***Fuck,*** he murmurs. ***This is one of the times where I would give anything not to be king.***

Cian's black gaze rolls toward Lore, and he nods. My mate's pupils tighten, giving more space to the gold, but it doesn't glow tonight. His irises are as murky as the forest we once galloped through after Bronwen gifted me Furia.

I hold onto that memory as glittery shadows swath the man she adores. When they disband, the gentle beast is reborn into a bird so slight it could perch on my finger.

This new version of Cian peeps upward. I wonder if he holds any memory of his past life.

No, Lore says. ***Cian is gone.***

Nevertheless, my heart twangs as he drifts away like a plucked feather.

To think my mate—to think every Crow flocking beside me almost incurred this fate.

Though the air is warm tonight, I shiver as though I was back in Glace, back in that ice cavern beneath the mountain.

I shake my head, replacing the nightmare of yesterday with the dream of tomorrow.

A tomorrow where birds can no longer be reduced to stone and steel, and where a serpent will molt from her cloak of scales and mend my father's wrecked heart.

CHAPTER 92

I beat my wings under the forever vigilant stares of my father and mate. Sybille and Phoebus also gape, but soon their eyes swivel toward the pink beaches that loom just ahead, while mine lower to the sea, to the pink shadow beyond the blue.

Lore slows as we approach the place where the invisible wall used to divide our world. He must ask Aoife, who carries Meriam, to take the lead, because she soars in front of the lot of us. As soon as she breaches the Shabbin airspace, the tension in Lore's body begins to melt.

Still, he says, ***Fly ahead of me, my love.***

Does he not trust I will be able to penetrate?

I give my wings a great pump and carve through the azure without a hitch. The second my body casts a shadow on the beach, Lore rushes to my side, while my father sinks toward the lapping waves where a massive tusk pokes out of the foam.

How do we get my mother past the ramparts?

Your father will take care of guiding her to the heart of Shabbe.

I wonder if he will need to carry her or if there's a canal that leads inland.

Sybille whoops as she soars over the pink ramparts atop Arin and then she grows so slack-jawed that not a sound escapes from her parted mouth, only air. As Phoebus passes the great sunstone walls, his fingers tunnel into Connor's feathers, and his bottom lip, like Sybille's, drops.

My father told me what to expect that one carefree afternoon we spent together, but nothing could've prepared me for the wonder that is Shabbe. Giant waterfalls roar down the ramparts that seem to stretch and stretch until they bite into the very sky. Unlike Luce, whose topography can be likened to an open book propped page-side down on a table, Shabbe resembles a cauldron with its curved walls and scooped valley.

Serpentines of water, edged with emerald vegetation, lace around the sunstone homes, carrying vessels from the foot of the ramparts to the valley and back. How is it even possible for boats to sail upstream? Are they powered by blood magic?

Yes, Lore says, forever attentive to my thoughts.

Astonishing. ***Where's the Cauldron?*** Though my eyes sting from a sleepless night, I keep them peeled to absorb the abounding splendor.

In the lowest point of the valley, at the heart of your family's castle. Lore nods to the spherical palace fashioned from the same peach sunstone as every other home in the queendom.

As we soar toward it, the sun hot on our outstretched wings, Lore regales me with tales of his first voyage to Shabbe, and how Mara sent him on a quest to prove his valor. One that included scaling the ramparts with nothing but his hands and feet.

Apparently, my father was very much against this mad quest and wanted to head back to Luce to conquer the land with swords instead of magic, but his friend refused to turn back empty-handed, so he scaled those ramparts under a sea of watchful pink eyes and glaring black ones.

I side-eye my intrepid mate. ***You never back down from a challenge, now do you?***

You know how strongly I feel about challenges, Little Bird.

I smile into our mind link because, yes, I certainly do know. I believe the day I told him he had no chance at winning me over kindled his fervor to prove me wrong. And, Great Cauldron, how he'd succeeded.

Suddenly he thunders, ***Land, my Crows.***

I retract my wings so abruptly that my body pitches forward. *Shit, shit, shit.*

With a chuckle, he swoops beneath me and straightens me out with his giant wings. ***My love, try not to land*** **inside** ***the Cauldron.***

It would certainly make for a memorable entrance.

Lore laughs. ***That, it would. But I fear the Cauldron may keep you and I'm unwilling to share you, my love.*** Lore's tone is so light it springs through my mind like the reflection of the sun on the mirror-smooth pool below. ***Perhaps avoid calling it a pool until*** **after** ***it breaks my curse.***

I suck in a breath and whisper, ***It can hear our conversation?***

Yes.

Even if I whisper?

Lore laughs. ***Yes, Little Bird, even if you whisper.***

Though I cannot bite my lip in this form, the second I land, I chew on it, almost biting through the skin when I notice that we are ringed by people. Women in liquid gowns and men in elegant linen suits stand in the trellised shade of the castle's circular patio.

I whirl on myself, and the dress Phoebus insisted I wear—after promising it wasn't fashioned from actual bird feathers but from velvet and satin replicas—puffs around my legs like one of Lore's storm clouds.

Great Mórrígan, mate . . .

What? Have I done something wrong? Oh my Gods, did the Cauldron reseal because I called it a—I drop my voice and murmur—***pool?*** —before remembering whispering is useless.

I tear my gaze away from the jewel-eyed Shabbins to stare over my shoulder at the molten surface of the source of all magic. When no iron lid slams into place, my ribs relax around my heart.

Although . . . although perhaps the Cauldron doesn't seal with an actual lid like other soup pots.

I slap both my palms over my mouth. *Oh, Great and Mighty Cauldron, forgive me for likening you to a pool and a soup pot. You are so much greater than both.*

A single bubble pops at the surface. Its version of a snort? I want to ask Lore but when I turn his way, he seems lost in the acreage of black feathers that glisten a deep sapphire like his hair.

I smooth my palms down the bustier top. ***Too much?***

You look . . . You look . . .

Well-feathered?

His hypnotic laughter eddies through the jasmine-scented air.

Like the human embodiment of a crow? I supply since he's yet to finish his earlier sentence.

Like a queen, Little Bird. He steals my hands off my waist and carries them to his mouth for a tender kiss. **My *queen.***

EPILOGUE
LORE

My mate's violet eyes haven't shut once since we soared over the ramparts of Shabbe. Nor have they stopped glittering.

Though it's been centuries since I've flown over Priya's superb queendom, I barely glanced at it as we flew, much preferring watching its splendor spool over my mate's eyes and unspool inside her vociferous mind.

"Welcome back, Lorcan Ríhbiadh." Priya's voice pares the stillness that envelops the Vale. "It has been far too long since your last visit."

I release one of Fallon's hands and tuck the other into the crook of my arm, the large diamond on her slender finger sparkling pink against the black sleeve of my jacket. Yes, jacket. For the first time in centuries, I left the Sky Kingdom without armor.

When Erwin saw me stroll into the war room this morning, his eyes almost bugged out of his ugly face. I had to remind him that we were no longer at war. Something I will indubitably have to recall myself as we repair Luce in the coming months.

Folding my fingers over Fallon's, I pivot my mate toward Priya of Shabbe, the ageless queen born a mere decade before me. Though her face, like mine, has not changed since she reached maturity, her auburn locks have gone full-white. I heard it happened when the wards closed off Shabbe.

I suspect my hair may suffer the same fate if Bronwen's vision comes to pass and I end up with a guileful daughter who takes after the woman on my arm, in both beauty and character.

Mórrígan help me . . . "Priya, I'd like to introduce you to Fallon, Zendaya and Cathal's daughter. Your great-grandchild. My mate."

A smile curves the Queen's mouth. "Oh, the news that you found a mate penetrated even my daughter's wards, Lorcan. My flesh and blood, no less. The Cauldron must hold you in high esteem."

I stroke Fallon's hand as Priya finally breaks away from her courtiers, the carmine gown she's donned for our reunion so incandescent the shade matches her irises.

Shabbins, like Faeries, have such a fondness for bright clothing. Though my mate looks magnificent in black, I suddenly worry that, by selecting only the palette of my people, I've deprived her of something she may want. I make a note of arranging a dress fitting with one of Priya's seamstresses to rectify my oversight.

The Queen studies my shifters. First, the ones circling her sky, casting moving shadows over the courtyard; then, the ones in skin standing with Fallon's friends at a short distance from us. "I heard you'd be returning with my daughter."

Ah . . . Of course that's who she seeks. "You heard correctly."

"Yet, I don't see her."

I tip my head toward Aoife. "The Crow carrying Meriam will land at my command."

Priya tilts her head, and her waist-long hair rushes over her bronzed arms. "Command her. Please."

Fallon's fingers clench around my bicep. "You cannot kill her." When Priya levels her gaze on my mate, Fallon sucks in a breath and adds a breathy, "Your Majesty."

"Call me, imTaytah. It means . . ."

"Mother of my grandmother," Fallon murmurs.

"That's right." Priya outlines my mate's face with her fingertips, the skin around her eyes creasing with the pain of seeing her beloved granddaughter's face worn by another. "As for Meriam, I've no intention of killing her. She has far too much to atone for before I will grant her passage to the next world."

When Fallon's throat clenches with a swallow, I tighten my hold on her fingers. ***Shh, my love. Your great-grandmother is a very fair woman.***

Her violet eyes jerk to mine, springing her jaw off Priya's fingers. ***She may be very fair but she was locked inside a bubble—granted, a really grand one—for the last five centuries. Not only would I have gone crowshit crazy, but I would also have grown seriously embittered.***

You could never turn bitter, Little Bird. You're far too sweet.

My sweetness is an illusion. Deep down, I'm tough as crow-nails.

I tip her a crooked smile and caress her hand. ***Tough Bird it'll be from now on.***

Gods—Goddess no. She wrinkles her nose. ***Wait, is Mara considered a goddess?***

"Fallon?" a female rasps.

My mate whirls at the sound of her name, just as the tight circle of courtiers parts around a Faerie with short raven-black hair and sparkling green eyes.

The woman palms her mouth and murmurs a raucous, "*Goccolina,*" that tears my mate away from my side.

Her identity slots into my mind—Ceres Rossi. Even if I'd forgotten who she was, the sight of Justus standing behind her, arm in arm with Agrippina, would've joggled my memory.

Gripping handfuls of her glorious gown, Fallon races across the courtyard. The woman holds her arms aloft just in time to take delivery of my sobbing mate.

"Shall we begin with your curse or with Zendaya's?" Priya asks.

"Zendaya's." Without shifting my gaze off my mate and her Faerie family, I call out to Cathal, ***How much longer before you reach the Vale?***

A handful of minutes. Has Priya asked the Cauldron how—how . . . The poor man sounds sick to his stomach.

As Fallon collects a dozen kisses on her cheeks and forehead, I ask the Shabbin Queen, "How will we go about freeing Zendaya? Must she drink a goblet of your blood before being submerged inside the Cauldron?" My tongue tingles as I recall the sweet, metallic tang of Mórrígan's blood.

"The Cauldron has asked me to drip my blood inside of *it*, and not inside of her. Like you, though, she will be submerged, and either she will be returned to us in scales, or she will rise in skin. Unfortunately, only the Cauldron knows how much—" Priya lowers her face toward the wondrous source of magic that made me into the man I am today. "How much of her is left."

Fallon steps toward Agrippina and locks her arms around her reedy shoulders. Though Agrippina stands straight as a fence post and doesn't embrace Fallon back, my mate keeps her arms curled around the redhead. It's painful seeing Justus's girl like this, for Agrippina was once so full of vigor and passion. Much like the woman who entrusted her with her most cherished possession . . . now mine.

I meet Justus's stare, and I incline my head toward the Faerie who's proven himself a man of great valor and loyalty. "Do you think the Cauldron can do something about Agrippina Rossi's mind?"

"Perhaps, but Zendaya's curse will deplete the Cauldron for a while. In all honesty, it could take weeks before we can get around to breaking your obsidian curse, Lore. Are you certain you don't wish to start with your own?"

"Yes. I'm certain."

Though he'd surely chew my ear off if he heard I picked his needs over our people's, Cathal is barely hanging on. Especially with Cian gone. I will not subject him to any more delays.

As I think of my departed brother and then of the one bursting with nerves, I watch Fallon, and the sight of her steadies my pulse. She hugs Justus, which leads Ceres to palm her chest, clearly surprised by the intractable bond Meriam has braided between Fallon and her former husband.

So? Cathal's query calls my attention away from the Rossi clan.

Priya says you'll need to drop her inside the Cauldron, I say as Fallon finally strolls back toward me, smearing her black stripes.

I hold out my hand, some more of my tension lifting when her fingers coil around mine. ***Did you hear me, Cathal?***

I heard you.

Are you ready?

No. I'm not ready.

As Fallon thumbs her cheekbones to adjust her runny stripes, I ask, ***Is Daya ready?***

I hope so.

"They're ready, Priya."

Fallon's shoulders jerk back, and her violet eyes knock into my yellow ones. ***My parents?***

I nod as Priya sidesteps us and kneels at the Cauldron's edge to drip blood onto the glassy surface. Hand still in mine, Fallon spins.

Let it work. Let it work. Let it work, I catch my mate chanting into her mind, her body trembling so hard that it flutters every satin vane on her dress. How I wish I could reassure her, but giving her false hope would be cruel.

Lore, should I fly? Cathal's voice blisters my temples.

I'm waiting for Priya's signal, brother.

An eternity trickles by before Priya stands. "The Cauldron is ready to receive her."

Now, Cathal.

A loud hiss resounds through the Vale as Cathal comes soaring over the palace, the cursed body of his mate writhing between his talons. If my heart weren't suspended like Fallon's breath, I may have gotten a kick at how Daya is attempting to gore my friend with her tusk, but I'm too fretful to so much as smile.

When he levels off over the Cauldron, Daya's obsidian gaze jolts over the crowd. Fallon hiccups a muted sob that carries the beast's stare to her. Only then does Daya calm.

I'm aware Fallon and the serpent forged a bond over the years, nevertheless, I yearn that her abrupt tranquility means that beneath her scales subsists the mother who loved her unborn child with every beat of her Shabbin heart.

When Cathal's talons unclasp, when Daya's body sinks into the Cauldron that swallows her whole, my wild-eyed brother streaks toward Fallon and morphs into skin.

My mate slips away from me to wind her arm around Cathal's hunched spine. His lips shape Daya's name along with a prayer before they press into Fallon's hair and remain there until the Cauldron's surface shivers and color reappears.

At the first glimpse of florescent pink, Cathal releases a marrow-deep wail that shakes the very stone beneath my feet. I lower my lids and curse the hope which had breached my hard-bitten heart.

But then Fallon gasps, and my eyes open.

There, on the mirror-smooth surface of the Cauldron, rests the body of a woman with a shock of pink hair.

"Daya?" Cathal croaks.

I jolt forward and grip his arm before he can trounce over the Cauldron's surface to collect the woman born from Minimus's body.

She opens her eyes, which are . . . which are . . .

"Oh, Goddess," Fallon gasps.

"Serpent eyes," Cathal murmurs.

They are, in fact, *exactly* like a serpent's—lid-to-lid black. But the rest of her features are Daya's. Save for the hue of her mane and the strange marking in the middle of her forehead that looks like a white pearl has been pressed into her skin.

The woman props herself up as the Cauldron glides her toward Priya. "Abi Djhara."

Being called Priya's *darling jewel* crimps Daya's forehead. Does she no longer speak Shabbin?

"Mádhi," Fallon murmurs in Crow, her gaze roving over the white scars that lace around Daya's torso from neck to waist, the same scars that blemished her serpent scales.

Daya swings those fathomless eyes of hers toward Fallon and lifts one arm. After frowning at it and twisting it this way and that, she extends it toward Fallon, who falls to her knees beside the Queen.

My shadows tear off my flesh when my mate clasps the returnee's fingers, then harden into skin to hold onto Fallon before she can tip herself into the Cauldron. Daya brings her daughter's fingers to her face, rubs her cheek against them, and *rattles*.

What in Mórrígan's name has the Cauldron brought back?

I have to remind myself—a great many times—that I can morph into a bird, so I've no right to be repulsed by her bestial quality.

Fallon draws Daya's hand toward her own cheek and presses a kiss to the humanoid fingers, before standing and guiding her mother to her feet. Daya unfurls slowly, shakily. Fallon steps back, still holding onto her hand, and Daya pitches forward.

Cathal catches her with a hoarse, "Mate."

The woman rolls her arresting eyes toward the male whose throat bobs with swallow after swallow. Frowning, she tips her head and pokes his beard.

Though I don't want to interrupt, I cannot help but ask Cathal, ***Can you hear her?***

Cathal releases her and takes a step back, murmuring a deadened, "No."

I splay my hands on Fallon's waist and pull her into me, irrationally terrified that the tether that binds us will snap like it snapped between Cathal and Daya.

When Cathal dissolves into smoke and soars into the sky, Fallon's breathing turns ragged. "Dádhi!"

"He'll be back, Little Bird." I press my mouth against her temple as the odd creature raises her head to watch him leave. "He'll come back."

Cathal Báeinach, you better return, because I don't want to have to break my promise to your daughter.

My brother's silence is so loud it saturates the Vale and twists around every creature that stands within it, be they Crow, Faerie, human, sorceress, or . . . or whatever Zendaya of Shabbe has become.

EPILOGUE 2

FALLON

The sunstone is warm beneath my bare feet and glitters with the light of a million stars. Though Luce will always be my favorite place on Earth, there's something otherworldly about the Queendom of Shabbe.

Perhaps the enchantment stems from it being the birthplace of the Cauldron, or perhaps it's the effect of being surrounded by so many women who share my charmed blood.

I turn away from the canopy of night and glance back over my shoulder at the doors I've just exited. The ones behind which Daya, my great-grandmother, and the Queen's advisor remain.

Though my Shabbin mother does not speak and does not grasp our spoken words—neither Lucin, nor Crow, nor Shabbin—she seems to understand the images we pour into her mind. Or at least, she reacts to them. Sometimes with trepidation; sometimes with wide-eyed wonder.

I wasn't ready to leave her side, but when imTaytah—as my great-grandmother insists I call her—arrived from her meeting with Lore, she urged me to get ready for the festivities planned in honor of Shabbe's liberation. She tasked two guards to escort me to the wing she's put at Lore's and my disposal for the duration of our visit.

A visit that will span several days, since we must wait for the depleted Cauldron to replenish in order to break my mate's obsidian curse. Leaving Luce kingless is far from ideal, but every member of the Siorkahd—save for my absentee father—has returned to the Sky Kingdom to keep the peace.

With a sigh, I start walking again, hunting the sky's inky depth for my heartbroken father. "Please come back, Dádhi." My murmur is so quiet it barely flutters my lips.

Even though Daya resembles the woman Cathal loved, she's not her. Perhaps if their connection had endured, he could've overlooked the bright hue of her hair, the black pools of her eyes, and that pearl that resides in the middle of her forehead in place of a tusk. But their mind link is gone, and with it, their shared past.

I rub the skin over my heart that aches for my parents. If only the remembrance spell imTaytah painted in blood on Mother's brow had worked. According to Behati, Priya's ancient advisor and closest friend, had Daya's memories been repressed, they would've surfaced, but the only thing that surfaced were the whorls of blood. After sinking in, they reappeared.

Zendaya is a new being—one whose life began the same day as mine. Though I feel a kinship, the obsidian-eyed woman is not my mother.

As I approach the heart of the Vale, the honeysuckle breeze tangles through my unbound locks and excites the satin vanes of the feathers coating my strapless gown. What it does not do is touch the mirror-smooth surface of the quiescent Cauldron.

I cannot believe I'm walking past the source of all magic.

I cannot believe I'm in Shabbe and that the war is over.

That I got both my Shabbin and Faerie families back.

Surreal, that's what today is. Full of joy and grief. Beauty and uncertainty.

Here I thought the day I ended Dante's life, everything would fall into place, but everything is still in shambles. I suppose that's the usual outcome of wars.

My dress swishes against the canopied flagstones that cinch the Cauldron, my footfalls noiseless since I didn't have the heart to fit my feet back into the black satin heels I donned to match my dress.

The conversation I had with imTaytah right before leaving scrolls once more through my mind.

Will she be able to shift back into a serpent? I'd asked her.

The white-haired queen had glided her knuckles down my cheek, whispering how much I resembled her beloved granddaughter. What she hadn't whispered was an answer to my question.

So I'd asked it again.

The Cauldron didn't say, my little daughter. Though she'd murmured this with perfect aplomb, her eyes had twitched.

But you believe she can, don't you?

Yes. However, it's preferable she stays in skin a few days longer. I fear that shifting will unsettle her.

Is that what she feared, or did she, like me, fear that my mother would swim up one of the salted streams that arc toward the ramparts and spill into the ocean? Before I could ask, she'd moved deeper into Daya's room, abandoning me to my escorts.

As I start down the walkway that leads to another set of tall, filigreed doors, I reach out to Lore through the mind link. ***Any news from my father?***

His response takes mere seconds to resound between my temples. ***No. He refuses to answer me.***

I run my lower lip between my teeth. ***Lore, even if he begs you to transform him into a forever-Crow, swear you won't.***

Unfortunately, I'm not the only one with the power to take away your father's humanity.

My ribs tighten until it feels as though they're splintering the pounding muscle they cage.

The guards sweep open the tall doors and bow. "We shall wait out here until you are ready, Princess."

Princess... How odd to be referred to as a princess.

"Thank you," I say in Shabbin. Though my heart still paces with worry, the feel of my mate's nearness calms me a fraction.

After the doors snick shut, I toss my shoes in the entryway, then traipse around the filigreed partition that I know will open onto a sprawling bedchamber. The same way I know one wall will be entirely made of arched windows separated by columns of sunstone.

How? Because Behati explained the palace was built like an eight-point star, and each point was identical in design, built from the same materials and tipped with the same private garden. When we flew over Shabbe earlier, I'd been so focused on the Cauldron that I hadn't paid attention to the architecture, but I would drink my fill the next time I took to the sky.

Sure enough, my wing of the castle is as grandiose as my mother's with its sunstone floors and its windowed wall of lush green that teems with colorful birds and palm-sized monkeys who swing themselves from branch to branch.

Daya and I watched their show earlier, both of us struck with the same amount of wonder. I suspected then that she had no memory of her previous life, yet I'd clung to the hope that the remembrance sigil would bring some fragments of her past rushing back. I can still taste my disappointment when, brow ruffled, Daya had palmed off Priya's blood and licked it off her fingers, tongue as pink and curved as the rest of us.

I want to tell Lore all about my afternoon but find he isn't alone. Aoife stands in front of where he sits in one of the two plush armchairs that faces a long and wide, floor sofa strewn with multi-hued pillows—the only touch of color in the otherwise subdued room. Though I don't hear what they're discussing, the tension in my friend's face reveals it's not a rejoicing subject.

I start to pad closer but stop when I catch the presence of another person—a woman with, at her feet, a bolt of beige fabric.

"Princess." She curtsies.

I frown.

"King Ríhbiadh sent for me." Her eyes blaze the same pink as every female at the palace.

"Did he?" I raise an eyebrow at my mate.

"Selma came to take your measurements. Since we'll be staying, you'll require a new wardrobe." Though he basks in the muted glow of candlelight, I don't miss the fatigue and worry etched across his brow. "See you at supper, Aoife."

I watch her leave as the seamstress crosses the room toward me.

Though I don't much feel like a dress fitting at the moment, I allow the Shabbin woman to unfasten the little satin buttons Phoebus did up for me this morning.

In under a minute the dress is gliding off my body. Though I wear drawers, my chest is bare. Reflexively my hands go to my breasts and palm them to hide them from her stare. After cocooning my lower half with the scratchy beige fabric and marking it with lines of her blood, she asks me to lower my arms.

I feel Lore's gaze sweep across my bare spine as I do as she asks. After banding me up with more fabric and drawing more seams of blood, she says that she will be back before supper with my first gown. I want to ask whether she sews with sigils, but she's already at the door. And then she's gone, and Lore and I are finally alone.

I glance around the room. ***We are alone, right?***

We are. He drinks in my almost bare body, and though it doesn't rid him of his somberness, it does make the gold in his eyes gleam a little brighter. ***Come nearer, my love.***

I approach him, the intensity of his gaze whittling my nipples into armored points. When I stand between his spread thighs, he shifts out of his regal sprawl and sits up. He lifts his elbows off the arms of the chair and slides his hands around my hips.

"Winning a war pales in comparison to having won you." His pupils dilate, pooling darkness across his irises and dampness between my thighs.

A small smile flips the corners of my mouth. "So I'm your prize?"

His eyes stroke over each one of my curves on their way to my face. "Yes, my love. You are my prize. My greatest treasure."

"The spoils of your war?"

He leans back into his seat, his fingers dancing delicately over the sides of my thighs. "Well you did, once upon a time, consider me your enemy."

My smile broadens but then freezes around a gasped breath when he sweeps one of my legs off the ground and sets my foot on the armrest.

"Now to savor my prize," he murmurs, as he hooks the black lace shielding my mound and tugs it aside.

When he leans forward and strokes up my slit with his tongue, I clap his shoulders. ***Oh my Gods, Lore.***

He rakes his nails across the inside of my raised thigh and leisurely continues feasting on my clit, alternating between licks and lashes.

My muscles thrum and my core clenches as mind-numbing pleasure begins to curl low in my belly. Just when I think I'm about to come, Lore grips my ass and tilts my hips. His tongue leaves my clit only to dive into my center. My fingers clench as hard as the walls he brutalizes with his expert tongue.

My fingernails must lengthen, because the fabric of his shirt rips, and he groans. I worry I've injured him and try to pull away, but he grinds me against his mouth until I stop fighting him.

My vision brightens . . . whitens . . . and then my orgasm explodes against his tongue.

His low rumble of satisfaction coupled with his careful ministrations titillate my core and wring a second orgasm from me. Once I've calmed, he licks back up my blazing slit and presses a kiss to my clit that makes my toes curl.

"Holy Cauldron, Lore," I murmur as he carefully sets my foot back down. The sight of his slick, swollen lips transforms my heart into putty.

"Turn, Little Bird."

But I don't turn. I kneel. Used to his trousers' fastening, I unlace them swiftly, then drag his waistband down until I've freed the engorged tip of him. As I swirl my tongue around him, my mate releases a groan of pleasure that seems to shake the very stone beneath my knees.

I palm his taut sack as I sheath more veined flesh inside my mouth. When the tip of him touches the back of my throat, I lift my head before sucking him deep again.

"Look at me." He inhales a choppy breath, then growls it out along with my name.

His eyes are hot on my face, and his fingers cool against my scalp as he plays with my hair. As I swallow the little beads of salt he feeds me, his pupils pulse and his leather-clad thighs rattle as though he's turned half-serpent, but my mate is full-Crow.

"Fuck," he groans when I take him deeper. *"Fuuuuuck."*

He draws out the word, and I think he's about to shoot his seed down my throat, but he hinges at the waist, scoops me off the floor, and whirls me. And then he snips my soaked underwear with a steel talon and slams me down onto his giant, wet cock.

And Holy . . . Great . . . Almighty . . . Cauldron . . . My eyes roll to the back of my head as he drives in and out of me. I've evidently unleashed the beast because he's lost all control.

He hooks my hair and murmurs into my ear, "I'm in complete control, Little Bird, but you're right, you *have* unleashed a beast." His hand returns to my waist which he encircles as he moves my body to the punishing rhythm of his hips.

He comes with a roar that bends my spine and scatters goosebumps everywhere. As ropes of wet heat gush against my trembling walls, his thumb plucks my clit—twice—and unbridles my own beast.

Unlike him, I don't roar; I purr.

And then I slump back against my sex god and rest my head in the scoop between his corded neck and muscled shoulder. I burrow my nose against his skin, breathing in the scent of him—thunder and pure, raw male.

"I love you," I whisper in Crow, and then I repeat it twice more—in Lucin and in Shabbin.

He runs his hands up and down my torso, blunt nails tracing the underside of my breasts, the arc of my ribs, the prominence of my hip bones. He twists his head and presses a kiss to my mouth. "Love is a pitiable word to describe the profundity of my feelings for you, my queen."

The thought of being his queen pitches a sigh from my lungs. I will not marry Lore until the man who made me returns.

My mate must grasp the direction of my thoughts because he murmurs, "I've a plan, Little Bird."

"Do tell?"

LORE'S PLAN is to sit the Crow named Aodhan beside Daya at supper. A minute in that male's presence and I understand why Lorcan prefers him in obsidian form. He's so obnoxious that his company is painful to endure. Nevertheless, Daya endures his nonstop chatter—all of it about himself—graciously and silently.

As giant platters of sun-ripened vegetables, crisp disks of bread, and colorful dips are deposited on the stone table that seems to stretch endlessly through one of the palace's public gardens, our stares meet and hold. I'm about to ask my mate to put an end to the torture that is Aodhan's company when a shadow streaks from the heavens and bangs into the ground, transforming into a man.

One with dark eyes, wild hair, and a thick beard that does nothing to hide his sneer.

Lore squeezes my knee. ***I told you my plan was good.***

My father drops one hand on Aodhan's shoulder. "You're in my seat," he growls, while Daya watches on, dark eyes stroking over her former mate's tenebrous features.

I don't know if Aodhan springs to his feet on his own or if my father hauls him up, but the loathsome Crow is vertical before my next heartbeat, and then he's gone, making his way farther down the table, toward where Phoebus sits wedged between Connor and Sybille.

Everyone stares as Cathal Báeinach sinks into the chair beside my mother.

"How was your flight, brother?" Lore asks, tone amiable.

"Restorative." The slash of Cathal's mouth softens. "Sorry I left, Daughter."

"You're forgiven, Dádhi. Well"—I shift forward in my seat, the silken fabric of my emerald gown whistling over my skin like a summer breeze—"you're forgiven, but only if you're back for good."

One corner of his mouth tips as he leans back into his seat, and his dark stare bangs into my mother's darker one. "I'm back for good."

Zendaya and Cathal's bond may be gone, yet a current crackles through the air as Crow watches Serpent, and Serpent watches right back.

Acknowledgments

Can you believe Fallore's adventures are over? I can't! When I created this world and these characters last year, I had no idea what I was in for. Which I know must sound outrageous to you since I'm the author, and authors should know *everything*.

The only thing I knew was that Fallon would end up with Lore and live happily ever after. Oh, and that Dante would perish. But that was it. I didn't envision the rest of the twists and turns, which made the adventure just as exciting for me as, I hope, it was for you.

The big reveal about Fallon's mother? That was all my alpha reader Maria. Obviously, this has earned her the honorary title of *Mother of Serpents*. Speaking of Maria . . . Lady, thank you for your enthusiasm and brilliance. This series wouldn't have been the same without you, and I truly do mean that. And now, I cannot wait to write Zendaya and Cathal's second chance romance. Hope you're ready? Especially since it's happening in Shabbe, which I know you're dying to visit again.

To my grammar police, Laetitia and Rachel, I will never stop singing—sorry, *cawing*—your praises. Not only do you put up with my crazy (schedule), but you also manage to locate all those pesky plot holes and typos that I still miss after many, *many* rereads.

To Katie, my sounding board and writing bestie, thank you for the hours spent on the phone and at taquerias discussing plots and life over margaritas. Your friendship means the world to me.

To Lore and his eel's feral following, aka my Crow Ho3s, your creature-gif messages fill my heart with love and laughter. Promise to keep them coming?

To Kat, Debbie, Shannon, Chenay, Leanne, Christina, thank you for helping me polish this big baby up at record speed.

To my Facebook street team and reader group, thank you for making me feel like a writing goddess. Especially on all those days when I feel like a complete fraud. Your encouragement and love for my harebrained tales make writing such a joy.

To my family, my tribe, my everything, thank you for being proud of me and for giving me the time and space to work. I cannot imagine how hard it must be on all of you when I shirk my mommy and wife duties to spend more time with my characters.

To you, my honorary Crows, thank you for taking a chance on a love story about a bird king. Next up: a porcupine shifter emperor with many big quills. 😉 *Kidding*.

Next up: MY DARK BEAST, a Hades & Persephone retelling with gods and mobsters, and then HOUSE OF SHIFTING TIDES!

Also by Olivia Wildenstein

FANTASY ROMANCE

***The Kingdom of Crows* series**

HOUSE OF BEATING WINGS

HOUSE OF POUNDING HEARTS

HOUSE OF STRIKING OATHS

HOUSE OF SHIFTING TIDES

House of Rising Sands (origin story)

***The Lost Clan* series**

ROSE PETAL GRAVES

ROWAN WOOD LEGENDS

RISING SILVER MIST

RAGING RIVAL HEARTS

RECKLESS CRUEL HEIRS

***The Boulder Wolves* series**

A PACK OF BLOOD AND LIES

A PACK OF VOWS AND TEARS

A PACK OF LOVE AND HATE

A PACK OF STORMS AND STARS

***Angels of Elysium* series**

FEATHER

CELESTIAL

STARLIGHT

The Quatrefoil Chronicles series

OF WICKED BLOOD

OF TAINTED HEART

CONTEMPORARY ROMANCE

GHOSTBOY, CHAMELEON & THE DUKE OF GRAFFITI

NOT ANOTHER LOVE SONG

ROMANTIC SUSPENSE

Cold Little Games series

COLD LITTLE LIES

COLD LITTLE GAMES

COLD LITTLE HEARTS

About the Author

Olivia is the byproduct of a meet-rude in a Parisian discotheque that turned into an epic love story spanning several decades. Naturally, this shaped the way she viewed romance.

After meeting her own Prince Charming—in a Parisian discotheque of all places—she decided to put fingers to keyboard and craft love stories for a living.

None of her characters have ever met in a Parisian nightclub... as of yet.

WEBSITE

HTTP://OLIVIAWILDENSTEIN.COM

FACEBOOK READER GROUP

Olivia's Darling Readers

Milton Keynes UK
Ingram Content Group UK Ltd.
UKHW040842110424
440991UK00005B/179

9 781948 463881